Anonymous

Two Years in Peru

with Exploration of Its Antiquities Thomas J. Hutchinson

Anonymous

Two Years in Peru
with Exploration of Its Antiquities Thomas J. Hutchinson

ISBN/EAN: 9783337383299

Printed in Europe, USA, Canada, Australia, Japan

Cover: Foto ©Andreas Hilbeck / pixelio.de

More available books at **www.hansebooks.com**

TWO YEARS IN PERU,

EXPLORATION OF ITS ANTIQUITIES.

BY

THOMAS J. HUTCHINSON, F.R.G.S., F.R.S.L., M.A.I.

VICE-PRESIDENT D'HONNEUR DE L'INSTITUT D'AFRIQUE, PARIS;
FOREIGN ASSOCIATE OF THE PALÆONTOLOGICAL SOCIETY OF BUENOS AYRES;
ONE OF THE ORGANIZATION MEMBERS OF THE SOCIETY OF FINE ARTS IN PERU;
AUTHOR OF "IMPRESSIONS OF WESTERN AFRICA,"
"THE PARANA AND SOUTH AMERICAN RECOLLECTIONS," &c., &c., &c.

WITH MAP BY DANIEL BARRERA, AND NUMEROUS ILLUSTRATIONS.

IN TWO VOLUMES.

VOL. II.

London:
SAMPSON LOW, MARSTON, LOW, & SEARLE,
CROWN BUILDINGS, 188, FLEET STREET,
1873.

LONDON:
GILBERT AND RIVINGTON, PRINTERS,
ST. JOHN'S SQUARE.

CONTENTS OF VOL. II.

CHAPTER XIX.

CHAPTER XX.

CHAPTER XXIII.

CHAPTER XXIV.

CHAPTER XXV.

CHAPTER XXVI.

CHAPTER XXVII.

CHAPTER XXVIII.

CHAPTER XXIX.

CHAPTER XXX.

ILLUSTRATIONS TO VOL. II.

TWO YEARS IN PERU.

CHAPTER XVII.

Dreadful revolution of July, 1872.—Sending President Balta to prison.—Aspect of Lima on first day of revolution.—Pronunciamento of Dictator Don Thomas Gutierrez.—Miss Balta's intended marriage broken off.—Congress dispersed by the military.—Protest of Congress.—Departure of Peruvian fleet from Calláo.—Noble services of Commander Kennedy, and aid of H.M.S. "Reindeer."—Cold-blooded assassination of President Balta.—Shooting of Silvestre Gutierrez.—Firing at British and American Consulates in Calláo.—Dreadful state of Calláo. —Marcellino Gutierrez shot at the fort.—Tomas Gutierrez massacred in Lima.—How he was treated by the crowd.— Burning of the three brothers in front of Lima Cathedral.— End of military despotism in Peru.—Last *coup-de-gráce* of Dictator's secretary.—Fidelity of old Peruvian soldiers.

BEFORE the plaister on the south end of the Exhibition building was dry—for some of it at that part was unfinished on the day of opening—came the dreadful four days' Reign of Terror of July, 1872; exactly three weeks and one day after the temple of peace had been inaugurated.

On the evening of the 22nd July I was returning from my Consulate in Calláo to Lima,[1] when I heard it bruited about, that Senor Don Thomas Gutierrez, the Minister of War, had deposed President Balta, and constituted himself Dictator. At first I could scarcely credit it, for I met near the station, looking as cool and as unconcerned as if everything was entirely *en régle*, Don Pedro Balta, the President's brother—at the time Prefect of Calláo.

Arriving at Lima I found the sad news to be true, with the addition that President Balta had been sent to the police-barracks at San Francisco, whence he was transferred to the prison of Santa Catalina. As I walked up to the hotel from the railway station, I met a few companies of soldiers on their way down. All the shops were shut; the doors of private houses closed; business was suspended; and every one had a look of anxiety. What must have made the revolution, in a private point of view, doubly distressing to the family of President Balta, arose from the fact, that on the very same night, one of his daughters was to be married at the palace. The invitations were not only already issued, but the proprietor of the Hotel de Maury, who was to be caterer on the occasion, had sent his

[1] During the last twelve months of my stay in Peru, I stopped at Maury's Hotel in Lima, and recommend it to every one, travelling out here. I cannot speak too highly of its cleanliness, its good fare, and the civility as well as courtesy, of its executive.

plate, and covers for 300 guests, to the palace now in possession of an usurper.

It was about two o'clock in the day when one half of the Pichincha battalion went under command of its chief—the Minister of War, Don Thomas Gutierrez, into the palace rooms, to take President Balta prisoner. This being accomplished, they remained in possession, whilst the other half with the battalion Zepita No. 3, occupied the Plaza Principal, or principal square, which they at once furnished with a number of mitrailleuses.

Congress being at the time engaged in its sittings, as soon as the news of these incidents reached the hall at about half-past two o'clock, the Deputies requested the Senators to have a meeting of consultation with their body, so that the Legislature united might decide, as to what was best to be done under the circumstances.

After due deliberation a protest was drawn up, which was immediately written out and signed. It was now near five o'clock. The greater part of the members had put their names to the document, and the others were waiting to do the same, when an armed force, sent up by Gutierrez, ordered the Legislative Body to disperse—one honourable member being obliged to retire with such precipitation, as to have the pen in his hand, when he found himself outside the door. This protest, in a very dignified manner, declares that the National

Congress, in its preparatory meeting, having in consideration,—

" 1st.—That when the Republic was in complete peace, preparing through the means of its legitimate representatives to proclaim the elected of the people, it was disturbed in its constitutional functions.

" 2nd.—That such outrage against the law, sovereignty, and power of the National Representatives, in moments so solemn, imports the consummation of the crime of *lesa patria*.

" 3rd.—That without making itself accomplice of such a grave attempt, the Congress cannot in meetings preliminary remain in silence, because it would be a treason to the high powers that it has undertaken for the Nation.

" 4th.—That it ought to pass to posterity a document which, reflecting loyally the public sentiment, may cause to be execrated the memory of the authors of such an abominable crime.

" The National Congress therefore declares :—

" 1st.—That they condemn the action taken in these moments by one part of the armed force of the National troops, and make responsible before the Nation its authors, instigators, and accomplices, considering them outside the pale of the law.

" 2nd.—That they call upon the people, and that part of the Army which remains faithful to order, to oblige those who have disturbed the public peace to return to their duty."

This was signed by the President of Congress, the Vice-Presidents, Secretaries, and as many of the Senators and Deputies as could do it, until they were ordered out by the troops.

Meanwhile the Dictator was issuing proclamations and *pronunçiamentos* of the most ridiculous style of falsehood, rant, and bombast. Unconsciously, in the second part of his first manifesto, he may have proved himself a true prophet, although not in the light intended by him when he said, " History will write in one of its cleanest pages the 22nd of July, 1872, as the date in which Peru was redeemed from servility." Every one, I should think, hopes so, as far as concerns the servility of military despotism, which Gutierrez wanted to engraft more firmly, but to which he was the unconscious means of giving a death-blow. How a man with a grain of common sense could write such bosh as to say, " I have been called, and I am at your front. The Army, the Navy, and sound society have constituted me Supreme Chief of the Republic," when no more of the Army was with him than the few under his command at the palace. To prove how little the Navy sympathized, I must add that, in an hour or two after the first piece of bunkum proclamation was issued, four of the steamers of the Peruvian Navy in Calláo harbour, namely, the " Independencia," the " Apurimac," the " Huascar," and the " Chalaco," left their moorings in the bay, and at daylight were seen off San Lorenzo Point, where the "Independencia" was at anchor. Not long after they went to sea, and for the time no one knew of their destination. That this movement was made by the consent of the loyal authorities in Calláo may be assumed from the fact, that the sailors for the forementioned ships were drafted out of the monitors in the harbour, and that these in return were supplied with troops from the shore.

During the course of the day just mentioned, and not long after the Peruvian men-of-war had steamed off, a letter was sent by Commander Kennedy, R.N., who at the time was in command of H.M.S.S. "Reindeer" in the harbour, to the editor of the *South Pacific Times*. In this Commander Kennedy offered to all British residents in Calláo, Lima, or elsewhere, not only a refuge, with their families and properties, on board the "Reindeer," but added that "any lady wishing to come afloat will be provided with a suitable escort from her house to the ship." Such a noble offer on the part of Commander Kennedy was duly appreciated at this critical moment. Some ladies availed themselves of the proffered escort, and it was a great comfort to the English residents to see their glorious Union Jack, borne by a quartermaster of the "Reindeer,"—in the midst of revolutionary bullets flying around—defending the lives and property of British subjects. The inhabitants of Calláo presented Commander Kennedy with a testimonial, to show their appreciation of his valorous protection of them, in time of difficulty and danger.

Events now succeeded each other in rapid succession, both in Lima and Calláo. As soon as it was possible to effect it, a portion of the rails, quite close to the market-place, were torn up by the people of Calláo. But finding this not sufficient to keep the troops from being sent down from Lima, they proceeded farther up, and had the track removed between Bella Vista and Lima, near a place called La Legua.

There was such a brave resistance made by the people of Calláo to the Military Dictatorship, and so many of the troops deserted from the principal fort, that Colonel Silvestre Gutierrez (brother to the usurper), and who was commanding at Calláo, repaired to Lima with the intention of bringing back a large force;—threatening that on his return to the latter place he would raze the city to the ground, and burn the ruins. At the Lima station he was fired upon and killed by the people. Whereupon Marcellino (another of the brothers Gutierrez) hurried off to the place where President Balta was a prisoner; and although the latter was in bed, on account of some slight indisposition, Marcellino ordered in a file of soldiers to shoot Balta, without even permitting him to rise from the bed. From the medical report given, of the examination of the President's body, I find he received eleven wounds, of which four were revolver-shots—one on the left jaw, another in the mouth, a third near the right ear, and the fourth in the temple. In the breast were two rifle-shots, and a couple of sabre-cuts were on the arms and body. In fact, the man was literally massacred; for the revolvers and rifles were only a few feet distant from him when fired. This brave deed done, Marcellino hastened to Calláo, to take the place of his brother Silvestre, and with a force of military marched through the streets, firing at every citizen they could get a glimpse of, either outside or inside of the houses. All communication between Lima and Calláo, except by carriages and horses, having been intercepted, I could not, of course, go to the Consulate for three days. But during the time of Marcellino's lawless marauding through the town my office was fired at, and the Vice-Consul, Mr. Braccy R. Wilson, being near the window, had a very narrow escape, as two balls passed within a few inches of his head, leaving their tracks on the wooden wainscoating of the partition. The window towards the street is of a bow shape, and Mr. Wilson assured me, that he saw a man going down on one knee, at the end of the street, to take aim with a rifle at him inside of the window. This person he afterwards recognized as Marcellino Gutierrez, when the *carte de visite* of that warrior was shown to him. Into the

American Consulate likewise several bullets were fired, and the United States Consul, Major Williamson, had a very narrow escape.

All through the town, during the day of the 25th, Calláo was in a desperate condition. As evening approached, people dreaded the coming night; for the troops in the old castle, under the command of Marcellino, had turned their guns round to shoot upon the town. A ninepounder shot had already been fired right through the house of Mr. Grace, which was nearest of the houses in Calle de Lima to the castle. This street was commanded by those who were on the castle bastions—whence it could be swept from one end to the other. Another shot was fired into the hotel where dwelt Mr. Lawton; whilst here and there, stray shots caused many lamentable accidents. Mr. Montaigne, the foreman printer of Mr. Lawton's establishment, had assisted to carry a wounded man down to the Guadaloupe Hospital—for there were no police in the streets, as the town was under martial law—and, on his returning, met his death by a rifle-ball from the castle. Another man, while on the roof of his house in the Calle Colon, received a revolver-ball through one of his ancles, though unable to ascertain the direction whence it came. Terror and distress were everywhere, till the news flew round like wild-fire that Marcellino Gutierrez had been killed by a rifle-shot whilst on the castle top.

No person could tell if this were done by one of his own soldiers, or by some one from outside. It was, however, currently reported, as well as believed, that his death resulted, as a consequence of one of his own diabolical acts, in this wise. He was about giving orders, after taking observations, to have a general bombardment of the town, when one of his captains came up and advised him to draw into a place a little more retired, as the rifle-balls, fired from the streets and houses, were falling in a shower around him. The hero of the cold-blooded assassination of President Balta gave no answer to this, except to draw out his revolver and shoot his captain on the spot, whilst stigmatizing him as a coward. In a few minutes afterwards he had arranged the largest of the cannon, so as that, when discharged, it would sweep the houses in the line of the Calle de Lima, near to which it was supposed the principal people of the town were gathered for protection, and amongst them the new Prefect, Senor Colunna, known to be a friend of Don Manuel Pardo. At this moment came the rifle-shot which struck him in the body, and laid him lifeless. Very little time sufficed for the people of Calláo to take possession of the fort, and the soldiers therein soon fraternized with them, in rejoicing at their great victory.

Unknown to the people of Callao, the fourth act of this dreadful tragedy was being enacted at Lima on the same night that Marcellino Gutierrez was killed in the fort at the former place. Of the incidents that occurred on this night, the 26th, and terminated in the terrible death of the Dictator Thomas Gutierrez, I have two accounts before me. One is the relation of a Peruvian officer, of whose rank I am ignorant, Senor Don Domingo Ayarza, to whom Thomas Gutierrez gave himself up as a prisoner, when, wandering about the streets towards midnight, he was met by Ayarza, to whom he appealed to protect him from the fury of the populace, who were hunting for him everywhere. The other is the report written on the 10th of August by the Italian apothecary, Senor Don Francisco Estevan Valverde, at whose establishment Gutierrez tried to hide himself in a bath; whence he was dragged out into the streets, and literally ripped open by the infuriated crowd, almost underneath the sacred cross overtopping the Mercedes Church.

Senor Ayarza says that on this day of the 26th the people of Lima had been fusilading against the fort of Santa Catalina,—Ayarza, joined by from twenty to twenty-five friends, amongst the number. After an attack and sally out of the forces in the barracks, and whilst Senor Ayarza was manœuvring to find out some better mode of ingress, he was walking towards Santa Catalina, and in the middle of the Calle de Yanez he met two persons. This was about ten o'clock at night. He gave the challenge, " Quien vive ? " (" Who lives ? " is the literal translation, although it means what our sentinels call out, " Who goes there ? ") The reply was, " Viva Pardo ! " (" life to Pardo.") The voice was at once recognized as that of the Dictator Gutierrez; and Senor Ayarza, advancing, caught his arm, and told him to surrender. His reply was, " I am your prisoner; it is to you only I should give myself up. Save me, my friend, from the fury of the people !" " From this moment," continues Ayarza, " all my energies became determined to save the unfortunate man, and I conferred with my companions, the principal of whom were Don Francisco Silva Santistevan, and Don N. Aquilar. It was with the greatest difficulty I prevented them from falling on him and despatching him on the spot; but, by the force of persuasion, I induced them to let him come with us as a prisoner to the house of General Canseco, the second Vice-President of the Republic, in order to place him at the disposition of that official."

But although, in the humane intention, they proceeded by several round-about ways, so as to avoid meeting the crowds of people that were everywhere in the public thoroughfares, they soon met small groups, adding to one another as they proceeded. One of these, with Sergeant-Major Cornejo at its head, took the prisoner from Ayarza, and formed a guard before and behind. They had thus reached the corners where Espaderos and Mercaderos streets join, at one side of which is the Church of the Merced, and on the other, at right angles, is Valverde's shop. Here they found a crowd of respectable people (*personas notabiles*), amongst whom were Don Lizardo Montero (Captain of the Navy), Don Ignacio Tavera (Deputy of Congress), Don Adolfo Montes, and many others. Gutierrez was now handed over to Don Lizardo Montero, on whose popularity and influence Ayarza depended to give him up to the proper authorities. Then Ayarza proceeded to the palace to report the matter to the first Vice-President, so as to have the fort of Catalina at once taken possession of, and order restored.

During the course of the walk to this point, some little conversation was held with Gutierrez, who on one ·occasion remarked to Ayarza, "I know that my brother Silvestre has been killed!"

To which the other replied, "Yes ; but the President has been also assassinated!"

"How?" he exclaimed, apparently surprised; "has he been assassinated by the soldiers ?"

"No," said Ayarza, "the man who assassinated him is your brother Marcellino."

"At once he bowed his head with a groan, and came on in silence till we separated."

From Valverde's report it appears that he, with a few others, was at the corner of his house at about twenty minutes past ten o'clock, when he saw a crowd approaching the Plazuela (small square) in front of the Merced Church. Some of the persons were very excited, and cried out that this was the proper place to shoot Gutierrez. As soon as he had discovered who were in the gathering, he asked what it was about, and they showed him Gutierrez, whom they said they were bringing to the house of General Canseco. Then the unruly ones cried out, " No, he should go no farther," and screamed, to each other, to draw back, that they might shoot him. Several rifles and revolvers were seen in their hands. At once they began to shout for the head of Montero, who they said was about to betray them. Valverde, pushing through the crowd, told Gutierrez to make a run for his shop, which was only a few yards distant, and that his assistant would help him to escape by the back door. In the middle of the cries of the clamouring multitude, he managed to slip into the shop, followed by the crowd, who were partly kept back by the strenuous efforts of Valverde. Shivering and shaking in a convulsion of terror, and with a general coldness over his body, he was helped by the assistant inside, who advised him to run for his life to the back door. But all his physical energy was gone, and he crouched himself down into a large empty bath. Then, the fury of the people getting beyond control, guns and pistols were discharged; through

the front and back doors they rushed like the
torrent of a mighty river—some crying out for the
head of Valverde, if he would stand in their way.
They broke down the counter,—smashed several
bottles,—tore through a screen,—and, finding
Gutierrez in the bath, fired off several shots of a
revolver at him, killing him on the spot.   From
some of these shots two bystanders were wounded
—one in the face, and another in the arm.   Then
they dragged their victim into the street, batter-
ing his face with several of the medicine bottles
in the shop whilst he was in progress; fired
more revolvers at him for five minutes after he
was dead; ripped open his body with daggers;
danced on that same lifeless carcase as it lay outside; and slapped it in the face with their hands.

The corpse was dragged through the street of
Mercaderas up to the plaza, where it was sus-
pended to a lamp-post, and watched all night.
Next morning it was hoisted up in front of one of
the cathedral towers, whilst that of his brother
Silvestre was pulled up at the other.[2]   Here they

---

[2] One of not the least remarkable incidents connected with
this revolution was the publication at Paris, in little more than a
month after they had occurred, of the circumstances just recorded
under the title of "Revolucion de Lima," por Hector F. Varela.
At p. 81 the brothers Gutierrez are represented as hanging together from the same tower of the cathedral, and the archi-
tectural accompaniments of that incident, as well as of the
burning on the opposite page, are very incorrect.   Others of the
illustrations in this book are decided exaggerations.

remained suspended for several hours, viewed by the whole population of Lima,—by a crowd the best conducted before such a spectacle that I ever saw in my life. At about three o'clock, by the first train that came from Calláo after the trackway was repaired, several hundred persons brought up the body of Marcellino Gutierrez. It had been buried in the native cemetery there, out of which it was disinterred from beneath six persons who had been buried atop. Arrived at the station, it was hauled by a rope along the streets to the plaza, where the two other brothers were cut down from their hanging places in front of the cathedral. Then a fire was kindled opposite the principal entrance of the holy building, and the three brothers put in; nothing remained of them a few hours after but ashes. So every friend of Peru may hope has been consumed the last remnant of military despotism in this liberated Republic.

The provisional Secretary of the Dictatorship, Senor Don Ferando Casos, was said to be the composer of these blatant, bombastic proclamations of Gutierrez. At all events he made himself famous in one way; for in two or three days after quiet was restored, and whilst the Executive power was in the hands of the first Vice-President under Balta, Colonel Don Mariano H. Zeballos, the following document appeared in the *Official Gazette*, under the rubric of Senor Don J. de la

Riva Aguerro, the Minister for Foreign Affairs, addressed to the Minister for the Home Department :—

"July 30th, 1872.

"To the Minister of the State in the Government, &c.

"Sir,—From data that have been furnished by the Government Treasury-box of this department, it appears that Don Fernando Casos has taken from the fiscal funds the quantity of 181,451 soles, and 86 centavos, from the 23rd to the 26th of the present month.'

"In consequence, I have to request that your Excellency will issue the necessary orders, and as speedily as possible, to have the said Casos arrested, as well as placed at the disposition of the competent judge.   God guard you.

"I am, &c.,

"J. DE LA RIVA AGUERRO."

At the period of the soldiers being sent to the Congress to dissolve it on the first day of the revolution (and of which I have already written), the Plaza de Bolivar, or of Independence, where my readers know the Legislative bodies have their sittings, presented a most exciting spectacle.'   A battalion of soldiers was drawn up in line in front of the House of Congress, and masses of the people

---

' This sum, not far from 16,000*l.*, was a pretty good haul for three days.

* Graphically described in the *South Pacific Times* of July 30.

thronged in every quarter, anxious to see what new act of tyranny would be attempted against the representatives of the people. With the dispersion of the members, the crowd gradually disappeared, although not without giving some shouts of *Viva Pardo!* Shortly before this took place, Silvestre Gutierrez passed the square, accompanied by a few officers of police, and some cavalry soldiers with their carbines, taking the road to the city jail.

Dr. D. E. Sanchez, the President of the Supreme Court of Justice, had already gone to see the Governor of the prison last mentioned, and give him instructions to resist every attempt to free prisoners, as far as his means allowed him. The Doctor was on the point of departing, when Gutierrez arriving, desired him to order the release of a criminal named Palacios, with several others. This was answered as to its being impossible, for the last named was under sentence of the law. Dr. Sanchez then proceeded on his way, when Gutierrez entered the jail, and, with his own hands, liberated several of the prisoners.

The Dictator, after securing the person of President Balta, went to Fort Santa Catalina, and tried to induce Colonel Don Federico La Fuente, Commandant of the Artillery, Senor Vidal Garcia, one of the Chiefs of the Artillery Corps, and some other officers, to recognize him as head of the Executive. A proposal of this kind to such a man as Colonel

La Fuente — one of the bravest of Peruvian soldiers, and who has never swerved from his duty to the existing Constitutional Government — was treated, as became him, with an indignant refusal.

As soon as it was possible to do so, before the Lima and Callao Railway had been repaired, Senor Don Ernesto Malinowski, the Engineer in Chief of Peruvian Railways, went down to Callao by the Oroya line in a hand-truck, to ask Mr. Petrie about the charter of a steamer for the purpose of bringing back Don Manuel Pardo. At eleven o'clock of the same night, the "Limena" steamed out on the commission, and next morning returned with news of all the Peruvian Navy having been found at Cerro Azul, — of its intended immediate return, — and of Don Manuel Pardo being on board the "Huascar." At two o'clock of the same day, the chosen President of the people landed on the molo at Callao, and by the first train proceeded to Lima.

Very rarely does the City of the Kings witness such an imposing spectacle as was seen on the day (30th July) when the late President Balta's body was borne in state from the Merced Church to the cathedral. He who only a week ago was Supreme Head of the Republic, and was preparing with *empressement* for the festivities of his daughter's marriage, was here felled by the hand of one, who can be stigmatized as no less

than an assassin.   Gone to his last account in the
prime of life, with all his sins and imperfections on
his head, and yet, strange to say, outside the sphere
of his own family, and one or two private friends,
with few to mourn his loss.

CHAPTER XVIII.

THE unanimous voice of the Peruvian nation had
already proclaimed Don Manuel Pardo to be the
President of their choice.   But it was necessary to
complete the formula of election, in which Congress was engaged at the time of its violation by
Gutierrez. The public, therefore, saw it announced
with very much pleasure, that Don Manuel Pardo
had been elected, and would be received by
Congress to take the oath of allegiance, as well as
go through his instalment, on the 2nd of August.

Don Manuel Pardo did not come to the position
of Chief Magistrate of the Republic as an untried
citizen, or one of unknown antecedents. His father,
Don Felipe Pardo, was a man recognized and

appreciated, not only in America, but in Europe.
An essay upon the life of his father, in the
different characters of poet, littérateur, orator,
dramatist, magistrate, and diplomatist, is published
at the end of Don Hector Varela's work just referred to, including a short biography by Senor
Don Jose Antonio Barrenechea.   Like his father,
Don Manuel Pardo completed his education in
Europe.   He speaks English well, and French
fluently.   During his early education he manifested
a taste for commercial life, and a very marked
proclivity for financial studies. On his return from
Europe he resisted all the temptations that were
offered to him to adopt a military career, and
devoted his attention to agriculture—taking charge
of the farm of Villa, in the neighbourhood of Lima.
His health having temporarily broken down there,
he made a voyage to the interior, to the province
of Jauja.   In this rich part of Peru his stay was
turned to good account by a pamphlet,[1] which he
published, containing his observations on its wealth
of minerals, and on the railways, that by this route
might cross the Andes, as well as open up the interior resources of the Republic.   In that *brochure*
he discusses the subject of peopling the valleys of
the Amazon, and argues against the error of supposing this ought to be done, as far as Peru is con-

---

[1] " Estudios sobre la Provincia de Jauja," por Don Manuel
Pardo. Lima : imprenta de la Epoca, por Jose E. del Campo,
Calle de la Rifa, Num. 58, 1862.

cerned, by medium of that part of the mighty river, which flows through much of Brazil. Because, he observes, all the Brazilian towns that exist from the frontier of Peru to the mouth of the Amazon can send to the European markets the same products as those of Peru; and it is not likely they would do otherwise than impede shipments from the latter. Moreover, he gives thanks to Providence for the failure of exertions on part of the Peruvian Government to found colonies there. Such immigrants should come by the railways from the western side. He puts the probable difficulty in a very strong light as regards the contingency of a lot of English, Yankees, and Germans,—say to the amount of five thousand,—having arrived within the last five years on Peruvian territory, at Nanta, on the banks of the Ucayali. These, in five years, would amount to twenty-five or thirty thousand adventurers, who would have become masters of our navigable rivers. So that with the impassable Andes between us, and without any railways, to make these people obey our laws would be out of the question.

The further purpose of the pamphlet is to advocate a railway from Lima to Jauja, which is considered the most salubrious province of Peru, and where magic cures of the aggravated form of *phthisis pulmonalis* (consumption) have been effected. It may be seen by the map, that the Oroya line, now in progress, is the first step towards accomplishing this great work, originally suggested by Don Manuel Pardo.

In 1864, whilst General Pezet was President of Peru, not only were amicable relations suspended between that country and Spain, but a declaration of war had been made. During the period that the Spaniards held the Chincha Islands, of which they had taken possession, a loan was tried to be raised in Europe, and Manuel Pardo was one of those commissioned to negotiate it. Under the circumstances this was no easy job to do. But good fortune stepped in. The Spaniards abandoned the Chincha Islands, the guano of which was the only available resource of guarantee at the period; and the loan was effected.

From Pezet's time, during the Dictatorship of Colonel Prado, as President (which was inaugurated on the 28th December, 1865), we find Don Manuel Pardo, at the age of thirty-one, occupying the post of Minister of Hacienda[1] in the Government of Prado. Here Don Manuel's executive genius soon showed itself. He suppressed some unlawful pensions; put down pawning-houses (Montes de Piedad) that had been wrongly established; regulated salaries that were paid to persons who had no right to them; reformed all the Custom-houses of the Republic; and did away with a thousand other similar abuses. These were no easy tasks to accomplish in such an

[1] Finance Minister.

entourage as the Dictator Prado had in his Administration.

On the 2nd of May, 1866, when the Spaniards bombarded Calláo, amongst the defenders of his country at the batteries was the then Minister, Don Manuel Pardo; and, after the day's siege, he was to be found helping the wounded in their transit to Lima.

At the time of the yellow fever in Calláo, in 1868, Don Manuel Pardo was president of the Beneficencia, or Benevolent Society, in Lima; and nothing could exceed the exertions of his humanity, and philanthropy in trying to alleviate the scourge. The people of Lima presented him with a gold medal on the 1st of January, 1869, as a proof of their appreciation of his services, duriug the dreadful time of the previous year. In 1869 he accepted the post of Alcalde (or Mayor) of the Municipality of Lima; and whilst in this office, the sanatory condition of the city was very much improved. In that year, likewise, the first National Exhibition, which took place in the School of Arts and Sciences at Lima, was organized by Senor Pardo. Hence sprung the idea of the Grand Exhibition, already described, which was opened on the 1st of July, 1872.

The result of all these was the earnest conviction, that made the people believe, he was the best man to be a President. For in spite of the extensive influence of the old spirit of Spanish Hidalgo-ism, that is engrafted with the military rule, the people of Peru are now opening their eyes to the fact of their having been for centuries suffering from such tyranny.

The circumstances, under which Don Manuel Pardo assumed the reins of Government, were of a condition involving no small series of difficulties. The ship of the State had just come out of a dreadful hurricane of the three days described in the last chapter; and the scattered elements of the two previous administrations were no small obstacles still in the way. In fact, Senor Pardo was in a position somewhat similar to that described by John Bright at a meeting in Birmingham last year, when he said, in excuse for mistakes that may have been made,—" The course of the wisest and best of men in the Government of a great country, which is so encumbered with the errors of the past, is one full of difficulty." If such be the case in reference to England with its stable Government, how much more so is it as regards Peru, particularly whilst the Executive is still, with his vessel amongst rocks and breakers,—only visible through the dreadful elemental turmoil from which, by aid of Divine Providence, she has recently escaped.

On the morning of the 2nd of August, 1872, the Plaza Bolivar was again crowded. But the bearing of the people was very different from what it had

been on the last day of their presence here, when
the Congress was driven out by the armed force of
the Dictator Gutierrez. Now every man had a
hopeful, joyous look, and the diminished sprinkling
of military forces about showed what a change
had taken place.

At about two o'clock the new Citizen President,
Don Manuel Pardo, drove up in his private carriage, and was received with enthusiastic acclama-
tions. The entrance way to the Congress Chambers, where Senators and Deputies were congre-
gated, was crowded to an inconvenient extent.
The boxes on either side were filled with the
officials of the Government, as well as the Diplomatic representatives, Ministers, Chargés d'Affaires,
and Consuls of foreign nations. As the President
elect came up to the chair, to which he
was introduced by the retiring Vice-President,
Colonel Zeballos, he was greeted by a tremendous shout of applause from the outside,
which was taken up by many of the citizens
within. It was the first time I had the pleasure
of seeing President Pardo; and this first sight
gave me a very favourable impression of him.
For whilst the soldier, Zeballos read his own
account of giving up the reins of Government, his
hands trembled and shook like the leaves of a
tree in a heavy wind; whereas, when President
Pardo commenced his discourse to the National
Congress, on receiving command of the Republic,

he delivered his address in a most manly, though gentle, tone,—sufficiently loud to be heard by every one in the Congress Hall,—and without the slightest symptom of excitement, or emotion.

This address touched merely on the subjects that, in his judgment, would require the attention of the Executive—congratulating the people on the result of the popular suffrage as evidenced in the recent elections, and pointing out how near the recent military rebellion had been to interrupt and extinguish the peaceful progress of the country. He then referred to the perfect conformity of opinion existing to-day between the people and their lawful representatives, which would be of itself a sufficient guarantee, that the public sentiment and ideas should find the most faithful interpretation in their wisdom. After that he went into a few specialities,—as of municipal reform, electoral organization, responsibility of public functionaries, insufficiency of penal legislation, reorganization of the reduced army, punishment of those who were engaged in the late rebellion, and an inquiry into the finances of the country, as soon as he could make himself master of sufficient data for such an investigation. This would be done with the object of reducing the national expenses as much as possible; and until the financial condition of the country was known, he recommended that no new works should be begun. From these he should except expenses referring to popular instruction;

for the education of the people would be the true source of the nation's greatness.   He did not pretend to make out a " pompous programme," but to ask from the Congress their help in realizing a " practical Republic,"—a " Republic of Liberty." This was not *his* programme, he added, but that which he had received from the Nation.

The discourse, of which the foregoing is but an abstract, was read after his Excellency had taken the oath; and its practical points were frequently applauded by the spectators, who were outside the gangway bar.

Not very long afterwards, President Pardo addressed a special message to Congress, in which was shown the necessity of increased taxation; and although the Legislature was expected to have been closed at the end of November, I find an opening of the Extraordinary Session on the 9th of December.   President Pardo, in his speech reopening the assembly, declares this to be forced on the Government by the exceptional circumstances, which had to be done at the inauguration of their sittings in August last.   Here he gave an account of what had been accomplished by the Executive in the interim.   Part of it was putting into practice two important laws passed by Congress —the one concerning military conscription, and the other organizing the National Guard.   The most important portion of this message, however, referred to the financial state of the country, on which his

Excellency observed, " The situation, as the
Congress is aware, may be stated in two pro-
positions. The proceeds of the guano, which up
to the present time have sufficed for the internal
administration of the country, will be swallowed
up in attending to the foreign debt, when the new
loan for completion of the public works shall be
realized ; and the ordinary revenue of the State is
barely sufficient to meet half the expenses. To
permanently cover this deficit is, and always will
be, the only serious mode of veritably and defi-
nitely solving the uncertainties of our economic
situation,—of supporting our credit in foreign
countries,—of promoting order and regularity in
the public administration,—and finally of giving a
methodic impulse to commerce and industry by
freeing us from the disturbances, which the unforeseen economic operations of the Government
have always produced. And although the revenue
from the guano be not completely hypothecated
by exterior obligations, it would always be one
of the noblest of patriotic tasks to endeavour, that
the State should draw its existence from natural
sources. Not only to avoid unprofitably consum-
ing transitory riches, but principally to prevent
conflicts, which at unexpected moments give rise to
ruinous complications. If this might occur under
certain circumstances, it is hard to conceive, what
objection there could be not to consider the subject
when we find ourselves abandoned to our own

resources, and obliged to look for the means of existence amongst ourselves."

I have made this long extract to show the practical mind of President Pardo, and how in all his labours his one controlling idea is to make his country independent.

Some person has answered, when asked for antecedents about the life of President Pardo, " Read his first message to Congress, and from that judge of the man."   Without expressing a fear that it might have turned out otherwise, I am very happy at having to record that the message given at the closing of the august body, on Monday the 12th of May, is one of the most important documents of which the history of Peru can give record.   It was eloquent, impressive, chaste in style, and replete with sound sense, as well as exponent of the fact, that the first speech of President Pardo had not been " a bombastic programme."   It commenced with a tribute of respect, as a testimony of the gratitude of the country to the Congress of 1872, for the intelligence, elevated patriotism, and application which it gave to its labours.   " In the political system," he said, addressing the members, " in the moral system, in the religious system, in the economic system, in each sphere of social activity, you found a grave situation to consider, a great obstacle to avoid, or an imperious necessity to satisfy."   He then sketched how the previous Government, undermined by its own errors, and sacrificed by its own children, had sunk, along with itself, constitutionalism in the Republic;— how the army was demoralized,—the administration relaxed by abuse,—and all the general confusion ensued, which existed at the period of the cataclasm, in July of last year. The President mentioned these " as the principal characteristics of the situation which we inherited; one of those situations in which Providence proves the virtues of a people; and it is for this that it bears in its bosom the lightnings of the tempest, and the future of the nations. Peru has given a new proof that He was able to save her, and she has been saved—thanks to the unequivocal protection of the All-Powerful, and the harmony of will and effort, with which the public authorities and the people have acted—the former interpreting the aspirations of the latter, and the latter helping the former with all their might."

This is so unlike the rant of Gutierrez—so sound, so practical, so sensible, that I must ask my readers to accompany me in another extract:—

" Peru, in her administrative march, found herself involved in the complicated crisis which I have just described, and is now undergoing a salutary change, in which new ideas, new sentiments, and new aspirations are creating new political forces, and opening up new prospects. This transformation, which we can call the resurrection of the public spirit, has exhibited that in

all its fulness; when the bonds which confined it
disappeared, the public evil was distinguished from
the public good by criticizing the wants of the
country, which knows them because it feels them.
It entered with warmth into the struggle in aid of
this good, which is its own—increasing a hundred-
fold the elements of intelligence and will, whose
concourse is necessary in the passing of great
crises—teaching and strengthening with them the
Constitutional authorities, who are the representatives,—and constituting, in a word, a new political
system, to which the feeling of legality, whereon
public liberty reposes to-day, will serve as an
immovable base."

I only purpose to make one more extract
(although the whole is worthy of being recorded)
to show how the Peruvian Congress, as well as
the President, is not forgetful of its foreign lia-
bilities :—" You began by respecting the rights of
our foreign creditors, and you have not considered
for your internal necessities, the proceeds of the
guano which is compromised abroad. By this act
you have saved our credit, and you have found
means to cover the deficit in the charge for railways, without adding to the public burden, but, on
the contrary, obtaining concessions to the contracts already celebrated."

His Excellency then reviewed many of the laws
that had been passed in the Session, but these did
not include the whole of a large list that were

submitted to the Extraordinary Meeting of Congress before alluded to, and proclaimed in the chief square of Lima on the 28th of November.

A sad picture, though unfortunately a true one, referring to the state of affairs at the period about which it was written, and equally applicable to many years afterwards, is that drawn by Mr. Markham:[1]—"But the great drag upon the public treasury is the enormous army of 15,000 men for a population under two millions, with 2,000 officers,—those who are unattached being still retained on full pay. This will give some idea of the number of families who are living in luxury and idleness on the public money, and of the distress which will follow the sudden stoppage of their incomes, which is inevitable when the guano comes to an end. It will be an embarrassing and difficult question for some future Government to decide upon the proper measures for the disposal of an unwieldy army, and a crowd of hungry, beggared officers."

The measures introduced by President Pardo seem to me to have a much more efficient tendency to accomplish the end in view, than those suggestions of General Miller, recorded by Mr Markham, to establish military colonies in the forests to the eastward of the Andes. The conversion of the military element, amongst South Americans, into an agricultural one, I look upon as nothing but an ex-

[1] Op. cit. chap. xviii. p. 308. Published in 1862.

cessively forlorn hope. It was tried at Santiago del Estero, in the Argentine Republic, by General Don Antonino Taboada, and proved a miserable failure. The semi-civilized life of the soldier, serving under a military despotism, is about the worst school from which could be expected a Cincinnati style of reformation. But, this despotism being, as it is now in Peru, deprived of its *materiel* source—in fact, knocked on the head, and paralyzed—the plans of President Pardo to introduce education and encourage emigration are most likely, not only to enrich the country by developing its inexhaustible resources, but to create a new order of things, —fostered and sustained by a fresh and intelligent population.

CHAPTER XIX.

STARTING from the temporary station of the Oroya
Railroad at Calláo, quite close to the Guadaloupe
Hospital, we very soon skirt by the river Rimac,
and enter into the valley of that name. Not far
from the station is the first chacra (or small farm)
passed,—that of Mirinaves, lately purchased by
Mr. Henry Meiggs.   This valley, we are told by
Senor Don Manuel Pardo,[1] terminates when we get
up to Coca-chacra, the fifth station on the line,
a distance of 44¾ miles from Lima, and a height

[1] In his pamphlet of "Studies on the Province of Jauja,"
p. 23.

of 4,588 feet above the level of the sea. As we
go along, the track passes right through the
centre of one of the old castles of some Yunca
chief, and continues alongside of the river the
whole way to the station at Lima.   A little farther
on, and beyond the right side of the rails as we
ascend, are several others of a like kind, being
masses of broken *adobones*, or large mud bricks,—
all the rooms of which are filled with clay. Around
here, as between this road and that of the Lima
and Calláo Railroad—which runs parallel at about
a mile of distance,—the land is cultivated, but on
the river-side the grass has the character of rushes.
On the opposite bank of the Rimac, and where I
see the train going down on the line to Ancon, there
is another chacra, with a row of trees extending
from it to Lima.   But what tiny things they seem,
when contrasted with the towering rock-masses
above them—some of the mountains, no doubt,
which Prescott tells us were " teeming with gold."

I have always been of opinion, that the surest
way to disparage anything, in a common-sense
point of view—be it a nation, country, institution,
or idea—is to write twaddle[*] about it. Bowling
along this road, in sight of a splashy water-dribble,
that trickles over some gravel, and which I am
told is the river Rimac, my thoughts revert to

---

[*] Twaddle, in Webster's Dictionary, is defined " silly talk ;
senseless verbiage ; gabble ; fustian :" either or all of which may
appear equally applicable in this case.

what the illustrious historian Prescott has been made to sanction under his name—although in reality the early Spanish historians, whose works he consulted at Madrid, must be held accountable for it.[1]   After the execution of Atahualpa, and indeed at the time that Peru might be considered as perfectly reduced under Pizarro, the latter was at Pacha-Cámac, whereat he had been reconciling differences with Don Pedro Alvarado, the gallant officer who had served under Cortés with such renown in the war of Mexico, but who here in Peru had been recently a rival of Pizarro. He had explored for treasure in Quito, and, having failed, came into what Pizarro no doubt considered his own hunting-grounds of Peru. But everything being peaceably settled by Alvarado coming to visit Pizarro at Pacha-Cámac, the latter turned his attention to fixing the site of a new capital for this vast colonial empire. "Cuzco," says Prescott, "withdrawn among the mountains, was almost too far removed from the sea-coast for a *commercial* people." I have italicized the penultimate word of this sentence, because it is the first time that I have heard the Spanish marauders who invaded Peru designated a "commercial people."

It was, nevertheless, desirable to settle somewhere near a port, and Pizarro's first thoughts turned to the place he was at—Pacha-Cámac. But on further examination he found, or rather the

---

[1] "History of the Conquest of Peru," p. 237.

.officers, whom he sent to explore, discovered, in the neighbouring valley of Rimac, a place that was deemed more *à propos*. This Rimac has been already mentioned as the locale of the Delphic Oracle. The officers reported,[4] "Through the valley flowed *a broad stream*, which, like *a great artery*, was made, as usual by the natives,[5] to supply a thousand finer veins, that meandered through the beautiful meadows."

We are further told that "on this river Pizarro fixed the site of his new capital at somewhat less than two leagues distant from its mouth, which *expanded into a commodious haven for the commerce that the prophetic eye of the founder saw would one day float on its waters.*" Other reasons were given, with which I have no desire to dispute. But this one only confirms my justification for repeating the word " twaddle." Such of my readers as have seen how much the Rimac expands into Calláo will appreciate the sentiment; and those who have not may do so from looking at the Rimac passing by Lima in its fullest state during the month of March, as well as knowing that a few hundred yards from its mouth it never reaches

[4] Op. cit. p. 238.

[5] This must mean the Yuncas, as we have no account of any of the Inca people being here at the time spoken of. Moreover, the reigning Inca, who temporarily succeeded Atahualpa, placed on the throne by Pizarro—i.e. Manco, the legitimate son of Huayna Capac—accompanied Pizarro on this last journey from Cuzco only as far as Jauja, or Xauxa. Hence appears to me strong circumstantial evidence that the Incas did not keep up their executive in the valleys after they had subdued them.

to the knees of a horse during nine months of the year. I pass over the fudge about the " prophetic eye of Pizarro " in a *commercial* point of view, so soon after the murder of Atahualpa, and merely add, referring to *the expansion* of the Rimac into the Bay of Callao, that, to use the words of Dr. Baxley, " it would be more just to regard the Gulf of Mexico as the expanded mouth of the Mississippi River, than the Bay of Callao as that of the Rimac."

" The natives " of whom Prescott speaks had already made aqueducts through all these valleys interior to that which bore the name of the river, namely, of Ati, Huachipa, Lurigancha, and Amancãos. Yet he tells us nothing of them. The Rimac is said* to take its origin from a well, situated about two leagues beyond the hacienda (sugar-cane farm) of Casapatea, near the foot of the Cordillera of Huaro-chiri, close to which it is joined by two other rivulets. A league farther on, another small stream flows in at the Quebrada (ravine) of Tingo; farther, another at Cacaray, and then a fifth at Roccha. Passing San Mateo de Dios, by Viso, Machucana, Puruchay, and Surco, it receives many affluents—one being re-nowned for its dreadful disease, " the Verrugas,"—and arriving at San Pedro de Mama, about a mile beyond Chosica, it forms a confluence with a larger river, which is also known as the Rimac, and which comes from the Cordillera of Acobamba. Hence to

* According to Don Ambrosio Cerdau's pamphlet, already quoted.

Lima the number of aqueducts which it contributes to fertilize the land, increases as it reaches the capital, and nearly under the mountain of Cocayo, quite close and interior to Lima, it is put into contribution for the districts of Nasca, Carapongo, Pariache, Huanchiqualas, and Huachipa. . From this point, likewise, as well as below the city, it supplies water to the extensive valley of Huatica, at present divided into three districts—namely, Maranga, Magdalena, and La Legua. I have already described the valley of Huatica, with its old monumental accessories. Our business now is to go up the Oroya railway.

Before arriving at the Monserrat station, in Lima, we pass by the Camal, or public shambles, where, close to the track, one sees no more attractive sight than the blood of slaughtered animals, with pigs feeding upon it. Not much farther off is the station, at which you cannot fail to recognize in everything about a difference from what are the general attributes of a Peruvian institution. Here all is life and activity—some stationary engines doing their work—a locomotive roaring' like a mammoth bull, enchained and goaded, as if it wanted to get off and tear its way without stop or hindrance through Cordilleras and over Andes;— passengers getting their tickets;—luggage and cargo arriving; and the general hubbub and fuss of a train about to start. For it is near to eight o'clock in the morning. The hour approaches;

' The American locomotives do not whistle; they may be said to roar, like the continuous bellow of a lion or a bull.

the fuss increases, but subsides as the outer door
shuts;—the conductor, Mr. H. O. Denning, cries
out interrogatively, " All aboard?" and, looking
up and down to see that everything is right, waves
his hand to the engine-driver, and jumps up. The
engine gives one great spasmodic roar, and—with
the tolling of its bell—away we glide.

Past the river on our left side, as it flows downwards to the sea, its many little gravel-islets covered
with turkey-buzzards, which have plenty to browse
upon, and an uninterrupted line of black liquid
cloacine matter, overtopped by houses, on the right.
Wherever there is space between the rails and the
river, as well as on dry spots in the middle of the
stream, and on the opposite side, adjoining the
Ancon railway station, we see heaps of garbage,
on which the tutelary birds of Peru, just mentioned, are enjoying themselves. We pass under
the first arch of the bridge, leading from the
Principal Plaza, the Government Palace, and from
the larger portion of Lima to the other side, where
the chief features are the Alameda, or public walk,
the bull-fight circus, and the Ancon railway station.
Then beneath another bridge, just finished, looking
very fresh as well as colossal in its development.
This latter is the Balta bridge, so called from its
having been got up during the time of the late President Balta. It was just finished at the time of
his assassination. Cloacine on the right-hand side,
still as we go along. Now we skirt what appears
to have been either a half-swallowed-up building,

as of barracks, or an extensive catacomb trying to struggle to the upper air.   Then, at some height over our track, shoot up crosses and monoliths over a long wall, indicating the cemetery.   After these we are in the country.

A melancholy-looking mill is sighted, and an equally sad-appearing hacienda.   On one of the small spurs to the right is a white house, surrounded by white walls.   This is the national powder-magazine.   A little farther on we stop at Quiroz—the first station out of, and nearly five miles from, Lima.   The only thing to be noticed here is a quarry on the left-hand side, from which has been taken all the stone for the Monserrat station, as well as for the protecting wall on the river-side.   From Quiroz we travel on a track parallel with the old road, leading to the Sierra passes.   Through this part of the valley much cotton is cultivated.   There are also, in several of the small ravines which we skirt, ruins of Indian towns, of huacas, and of what seem to me large fortresses.   We pass likewise the remains of an old Spanish town, called Loma Larga, and a hacienda with numerous cattle—cows and horses—belonging to Senor Mariacho.

As we stop for a few minutes at the station of Santa Clara, distant 11½ miles from Lima, we recognize an increase in the quantity of cotton cultivated at the hacienda of Mr. Bryce, with a most comfortable-looking house on the premises.   From Santa Clara to La Chosica we have an hour's run. This part of the track brings us along the edge of the river, the tortuous course of which is followed by the rails. Here we are amongst the mountains, going — through ravines, with such short tracks, that the locomotive seems as if about rushing against a mighty mountain mass, till it turns a corner, and you are still gliding by the purling little Rimac. On either side as we progress can be discerned the rents in these Cordilleras, made by earthquakes, ancient as well as modern. Immense boulders of rock, some of them from fifty to sixty tons in weight, are lying scattered on the limited plateaux between the rails and the river,—no doubt the result of volcanic agency. Others, such as these, are hanging up on the sides of the hills, at heights varying from one to four thousand feet, and seeming as if they required only the slightest touch to send them crashing into the valleys below.

At Chosica, where there is an excellent hotel, passengers bound upwards stop for breakfast, and, in the time of my visit, it had excellent accommodation, under the management of Colonel Fisher. So as I had come up (for a few days of the pure air that was sure to be here), in company with my exploring friend, Mr. J. B. Steer, we leave the passengers to eat their breakfasts, and continue their route, whilst we proceed on a few archæological inquiries in the neighbourhood.

Not more than about six to eight hundred yards farther on than the station, and behind the house

of Senor Garcia, we came to a place about twenty
feet high over the ordinary mule-road. A few
feet higher up, and on the mountain-side is a large
collection of boulder-stones, built up like walls to
the height of four to six feet in some places,—a
foot or two in others,—but all having the appearance of having suffered from an earthquake, or the
rolling down of large stones from the mountain-
top. Scrambling amongst these, we soon make
out caves, or vaults, parts of which are exposed to
the light, by having had taken off some of the flag-
stones, which covered the tops. Removing a few
more flags, Mr. Steer descends into one, and finds
in it a skull, with arm and leg bones. Examination of others gives like results. Then, observing one or two flat spots, on which we stood,
to be hollow, we sent for shovels and pick-axe.
With both of these alternately Mr. Steer worked
energetically during the succeeding three days. Our
efforts to get help from the natives was perfectly
useless. They won't work, as a general rule,—no
matter what you pay them. In labour like this
they have no sympathy, for they cannot understand its *rationale*.

The result of Mr. Steer's labours consisted in
exhuming half a dozen bodies enwrapped with
cloth, and tied round, as in the accompanying
illustration. In some of the grave-vaults there
were one, two, or three bodies—all in the squatting
posture, with bent knees and hips, as is seen in
the figure of the child. Whether children or not,

BODIES TAKEN OUT OF VAULTS AT CHOSICA.

they were all wrapped up with the same care. The graves were generally from six to seven feet long, four feet wide, and from four to five feet in height. They were built of stone, and some of them nicely plastered inside. Many of these communicated with each other by narrow passages. On unwrapping the swathes, they were found to have the heads carefully bound round with cotton flock—in some cases the hair retaining its plait, whilst there were folds of cloth rolled round over the cotton. Amongst other things turned out with these bodies were a few pairs of silver and copper nippers, such as the Indians are known to have used for pulling out the beard;—a small comb made of wood, containing twenty-five separate teeth, artistically put together with thread weaving;—small beads fashioned out of bones, coloured with something like cinnabar, and having the appearance of red coral;—pieces of cotton cloth, light coloured, as well as dyed brown;—long copper pins, with heavy deposits of sulphates on them, that were used for pinning the cloth wrapping the bodies;—nuts;—a curious specimen of bivalve shell complete, and which Mr. Steer tells me is not now-a-days to be seen in Peru;—skulls of children, with the copper stain between the teeth, as if of the Obolus;—a ball of cotton thread; some feathers, evidently very old; between thirty and forty skulls.   Amongst the last-named lot was the skull of a mouse; several nuts, with the kernels rattling inside; and one of these latter having about an inch in length of a small quill protruding from it. We remarked, that in every case the men had a sling bound round the head, and the women as invariably a small piece of cotton flock, with a spindle in the hand.

After accomplishing as much as we could at the Chosica burying-ground, we turned downwards on the railway track towards Lima, and at about the same distance from the hotel as that last described, we found a somewhat similar city of the dead. This is called Parárá,* and is in the Quebrada, or ravine of Yanacotá. It is on a small

---

* The name was given to me by a native of the Chosica valley. In a paper on the Aymara Indians, by Professor Forbes, read before the Ethnological Society, on the 20th June, 1870, and at page 52, the word Parárá, in the Aymara, is said to signify a pair of corn-grinding stones, such as we see numbers of in this place.

plateau, about fifty feet above the railway track, between which latter and the ruins run two of the sierra roads. Ascending, I look up and see, at a height of five hundred feet or more, the mountain side faced with bits of stone walls, that are relics of the ledges or terraces made for cultivation. The questions at once rise up into my mind as to whether these terraces are so old as to have necessitated their use before the valley had vegetable mould washed down into it ?—or were the valleys themselves likewise cultivated at the same period ? Because here beneath us we have fields of clover and of rice, although the lower ground is not more than a mile across.

PART RUINS OF GRAVES AT PARARA.

That the Spaniards were at this place is evident from the fact of our observing two square blocks

made of stone and adobe—each a foot high, and one
over the other—the upper one being several inches
narrower than the lower. This piece of architecture
was for the purpose of supporting a cross.   Their
visits hither may be also assumed by the openings
in many of the grave-vaults, which in some places
are in three tiers, one over another.   Amongst the
ruins is one burial-place, twenty-four feet long and
eighteen feet wide, divided into three compart-
ments cross-wise, with walls of eighteen inches
thick intervening.   At the corner of each of these
dividing walls, down at the base, there is a small
aperture of about eight inches square—the object
of which it is impossible to guess at, unless it
were intended to allow the spirits of the dead to
hold communion with one another.   Each com-
partment has two small square niches in the wall,
—most probably to hold their idols.   Two of the
vaults had been completely exposed, but the third
only partially.   Looking into it I found a space of
fourteen feet long, four wide, and five deep, built
of stone, and plastered with adobe mortar.   Some
fragments of bones inside showed that it had been
once the resting-place of the dead.   In its outside
architecture it had an eave along the top wall—
a style of building not now seen in Peru, but of
which Mr. Steer tells me he has observed much, in
the Moyabamba and Chachapoyo valleys, on the
other side of the Andes.

Walking through this necropolis, or rather

climbing over the stones, I cannot help being struck with the absence of anything like a passage or street. The graves were built with very great care likewise. The chief features of the place, besides a few skulls which I took out of one of the vaults, together with a pair of sandals, were the number of grinding-stones, evidently for crushing corn, with a round boulder beside each, to be worked by the hand. One of these may be seen to the left of the grave-vault in the accompanying sketch, taken for me by Mr. John Schumaker. Some cotton flock was lying about, and bits of crockery-ware in many places. But no plan of a town could be traced—scramble wherever I would—no streets,—no doors to houses,—no apertures in the walls, save those that had been made by the searchers after treasure here—or by earthquakes, that must have sent down from the mountain the large boulders, of a mingled lime-stone and granite that abound everywhere in dreadful confusion. The grinding-stone, found here at Parárá, is the same as that mentioned by Stevenson,[*] for bruising corn with,—" a large stone, somewhat hollowed in the middle, called a *batan*. The bruiser or *mano* (handle) is curved on one side, and is moved by pressing the ends alternately." He adds, " I have been the more particular in describing this rude mill, because it was undoubtedly used by the ancient Peruvians,—having

* Op. cit. vol. i. p. 369.

been found buried with them in their huacas, and
because it may serve some curious investigator in
comparing the manners of these people with those
of other nations. By the same implements they
pulverized their ores for the extraction of gold and
silver."

Looking from these ruins, across the valley
and the intervening river, I see another place
somewhat similar to Parárí. So I get down to
the track where my horse is waiting, and, taking
a retrograde trip towards the hotel, cross one of
the excellent swinging bridges that have been
put up, wherever required on the Rimac, by Mr.
Meiggs. From this there is a road leading downwards in the direction of Lima, as well as another
upwards to Santa Eulalia. But the former is now
my route. Questioning a native whom I met,
after a few hundred yards' ride, he tells me the
name of the Quebrada here is Cocha-Huakra—not
Cochachacra, be it observed, which is the next
station to Chosica, but eleven miles farther on.
Of the ruins he knew nothing in reference to their
name; I therefore give them the title of the
Quebrada, i.e. Cocha-Huakra. The relics of walls,
terraces, and enclosures, extend here over a
considerable space. But what strikes me with
wonder is the enormous size of the boulders—
amongst which the place is literally honey-
combed with burying-caves. As I had with me
a negro boy, kindly furnished along with some

horses by Mr. Cilley, Superintendent of the Oroya line, I sent him "down amongst the dead men" in a few of those where I had discovered some skulls.

A large water rush from the western Cordillera, in 1869, had swept away a considerable portion of the walls. Nothing of life was visible in the place, except a few lizards,—miserable brown reptiles—seeming not only as if they had been generated out of the stone and gravel, but had nothing else to live upon.

As I was about returning, there came down, quite gently at first, but lasting for three hours after I reached the hotel, a regular autumn shower. Not at all like the misty, murky, drizzling atmospheric spasm, which it would be little short of profanity to designate rain, that we are accustomed to in Calláo and Lima, but soon becoming heavy, pattering wet, which obliged me to change my clothes on return to the hotel. Colonel Fisher tells me it rains like this only three to four times during the year at Chosica. Whilst this evening's shower was falling, a brilliant rainbow was visible over the eastern Cordillera, as I went along, —the atmosphere every moment becoming colder and more refreshing:—thus promising an agreeable morning for my projected ride of next day, by the long terraces of Moyabamba, and to the village of Santa Eulalia.

CHAPTER XX.

APRIL 25th.—Up early,—as the rising sun is just glinting on the mountain-tops, and after my coffee, on horseback for the morning ride. This time I go across the bridge in front of the hotel, and, turning to the right behind the chacra of Senor Montana, pass along by the Moyabamba terraces on the road to Santa Eulalia. These are described to me by Mr. Steer, who ascended them, as similar to those mentioned by Prescott:[1] "Terraces were raised on the steep sides of the Cordilleras, and as the different elevations had the effect of difference of latitude, they exhibited in regular

[1] Op. cit. p. 3.

gradation every variety of vegetable form, from the stimulated growth of the tropics to the temperate products of a northern clime. An industrious population settled along the lofty regions of the plateaux; and towns and hamlets, clustering amidst orchards and wide-spreading gardens, seemed suspended in the air, far above the ordinary elevation of the clouds."

Although by a note to this Arcadian description Mr. Prescott observes that "the plains of Quito are at the height of nine to ten thousand feet

STONE HATCHET FROM MOYABAMBA.

above the level of the sea, whilst other valleys or plateaux in this vast group of mountains still reach a higher elevation," the system of terraces which I see at Moyabamba is the same as of those at Cuzco and Quito. But I do not believe these here were ever done by the Incas. On the contrary, the old Peruvians, amongst whose graves we have been exploring, and of whose antiquity of centuries before the Incas' times we have so many proofs, were, I doubt not, the builders of them—that is, either the Yunca race, or their predecessors.

The terraces extend along the mountain-side for a length of beyond two miles, and rise one above the other to the height of more than a hundred feet, each plateau being not exceeding from two to three yards in width. From the basement upwards they are divided by transverse walls. One part of our road goes through a cutting in a stone wall, which, although not more than forty yards in length from the mountain bluff to the river, is, at the part through which we pass, from three to four yards in thickness. In this place Mr. Steer rooted out a few skulls and some bones, together with a stone hatchet, from a vault-grave, that had been built square, but which previous to our find was opened by some marauders.

Continuing on this road I pass some, and am met by others, of the mountaineers, with their wives; who travel generally in company with a troupe of horses, donkeys, or cattle. This morning I overtake a herd of nearly two hundred,— chiefly mules and horses—all in single file on account of the narrowness of the roadway. The mountain women are entirely different, in type and general dress, from the ordinary Cholo of the lower country, as if they belonged to a different race.   As brown as a berry in the face, yet having a little tinge of the roseate in the complexion—legs bronzed as the face, but failing the delicate tint.   They are generally dressed in a coarse cotton skirt, which scarcely reaches down to the calf of the leg.   A straw hat and a pair of sandals are included in the toilette, which is completed by an apron.   This last is the most remarkable portion of the costume; for instead of being worn as aprons generally are, in front, to keep the gown from being soiled, this hangs on the left side.   It is believed to be put in that position, as a symbol of mourning for some famous ancestor.

At the end of the Moyabamba road there is a gateway, passing through which the way to the right leads to San Pedro-de-Mama, and that to the left to Santa Eulalia.   San Pedro was a Spanish town, for there are remains of an old chapel here.   Wherever the Spaniards settled, they planted a cross, and built a chapel.   But this one, as well as the houses all round, are in a state of as perfect wreck and ruin as the old Indian towns, although presenting the relics of a very different, and inferior kind of architecture.   To get at it I must cross a bridge over the river, which at this point forms a confluence with the Rimac, and whereof I have already written as bearing the same name.   But there is nothing worth looking at; so I return over the bridge, and, going up

the Santa Eulalia road, enjoy more than a mile
and a half of one of the most charming of rides.

Through orchards of guavas, oranges, paltas,
and chirimoyas—across little purling rivulets that
are tributaries to the Rimac—with bright flowers
gleaming in the sunshine, and birds singing everywhere. Much of this road is up and down a solid
rock—no signs of Macadamization about. But
as I am the whole way protected from the sun,
by the trees forming an arch overhead, the effect
is most delicious. It is rendered doubly so by the
refreshing breeze that is blowing; indeed, it is more
of half a gale than a breeze, as several times my
coloured valet had to dismount his horse to pick
up my hat, blown off by the wind.

The whole village of Santa Eulalia seems to be
concentrated in the plaza or square. Here is a
chapel—about as gloomy and semi-ruinous a specimen of a religious house as I have seen in any part
of the world. At right angles with this, on the right
corner of the plaza, is the residence of the Curé;
and at each of the other three corners of the same
is a little wooden house, resembling the upper half
of a sentry-box. In the latter masses are said by
coadjutor padres on days of great religious ceremonies. I went to visit the Curé, and, dismounting,
walked into the house, for the door was wide
open. No one was visible within; but I crossed a
patio, or square, behind, and found him at breakfast. He was getting through an attack of that

dreadful disease, the verrugas, and appeared but the shadow of a man. We had our cigar, and a little chat after the meal was concluded. I learned that a league farther on was another village called Payi;—that in the intermediate space as well as on each side of the road, over which I had recently passed, was a considerable population;—and that Santa Eulalia, where I now am, is the head-quarters of the parish. Twelve leagues distant from this is the first of the large lakes that are found high up in the Andes. It is called Huas-Cacoche; and hence, it seems, "*esta en proyecto*"[2] to bring water to the Rimac, as the latter river is becoming every year more and more incompetent for a sufficient supply to the azequias of the chacras, devoted to cultivation.

We visited the chapel together, and I found the inside to be nothing better than was promised by the exterior. All of the altars—five in number—appear undergoing process of repair. Two small ladders and several planks of wood are stowed away in one corner. Whilst a few tawdrily-done-up statues of saints are thrown carelessly in a heap in the other.

The breeze grew stronger as I rode back to the hotel—better pleased with the most refreshing trip through luxuriant tropical vegetation, than I have been on any similar excursion, since I first

---

[2] "There is in project."

quitted the shores of England nearly twenty-three years ago.

There is no place about Lima, that I could recommend the stranger to, a more agreeable change, than that of Chosica. If he have anything of a taste for archæology, he will have a splendid mine to work on and explore; and I regretted very much my time being so limited, that I could only do very little on the outskirts of the rich collection, which might be made at this neighbourhood, of the relics of Peru from the time of her ancient civilization.

From Chosica onwards the road becomes a regular up-hill work; "for here," observes Mr. Magee, "the four per cent. grades commence, although they do not make it necessary to leave the valley of the Rimac until San Bartolomé, thirteen miles farther, is reached." Some five or six miles beyond Chosica we pass over the first of the iron bridges, the Cupiche, before and after which is a series of curvatures along the river's bank. In this course the river at the present time of the year (February), in consequence of the heavy rains at night from San Bartolomé upwards, is a rushing current—falling, tumbling, jumping, foaming, gurgling over big boulders in its bed,—communicating a sensation of freshness, in the sight and sound of it. The mountains about on both sides present the appearance of having undergone a disintegration of their solidity, as they seem, for the most part, to have been shaken by some subterranean convulsion. We are travelling along (as I learn from Mr. Sweet, the resident engineer, who is a fellow-passenger,) "on a grade of four per cent. or 211 feet per mile, and with a minimum radius of curvature of 300 feet."

From the first iron bridge at Cupiche, to the second at Coracona, (which is considerably larger), we are on the right side of the Rimac, or opposite to that on which we have journeyed hither from Lima. Our next stopping-place is Coca-Chacra, nearly forty-five miles from the City of Kings, and 4,588 feet above the level of the sea. This is an old—a very old—Spanish-built town, with a church that has no roof. Indeed, the sacred building, with its frowsy-looking little bell-tower, seems leaning over, as if it had at one time got an earthquake warning, or was appealing mutely against one of these convulsions doing anything to hurt such a trifling minnow amongst the mountain Tritons all around.

At the valley through which the Rimac passes beneath Coca-Chacra,—for the town is a considerable height over the river's bed,—I saw and heard some of the first birds I met with on this route.[*] Doves, as well as small items of the feathered race here, and a few red-breasts; but all with a melancholy style of chirrup, as if out of their element. For

* Except those mentioned on the road to Santa Eulalia, which is a few miles out of the railway track.

they have no broad plains to disport in, and little
or nothing but a view of barren mountains on
either side. The doves too ! Can any one fancy their
being endowed with the sweet bliss of " billing
and cooing " amongst these gloomy rock masses, as
doves are accredited to do in more genial climes ?

From Coca-Chacra to San Bartolomé, only two
miles farther on, we have still the same grade of four
per cent. Now we are in the neighbourhood of
where the appalling mortality happened on this
road, and of which I have to say a few words.

The " Oroya fever," as it was called, from the
simple circumstance of its having occurred on this
line (although more than a hundred miles distant
from the terminus at the little town of Oroya),[1]
caused a dreadful mortality here during the years
of 1870 and 1871—amongst the Chilian labourers
more especially. Its first ravages were experienced
in the neighbourhood of where they were preparing
for the iron bridges at Cupiche, and Carocona.
The records of deaths in the Guadaloupe Hospital
at Callúo, from this fever, are almost incredible. It
was of the Tertiana, or intermittent type, but nearly
always accompanied with fatal liver derangement,
from which scarcely one in a hundred recovered.
That it could have nothing to do with marsh malaria
may be assumed from the fact of the height of the
position. Mr. Sweet, the resident engineer, places
Coca-Chacra at 4,888 feet above the level of the

---

[1] Situated at the junction of the Jauja and Yauli rivers.

sea. From this spot the worst cases came; yet, according to Carriére and Blake, we are told that malaria never ascends beyond—in Italy from 400 to 500 feet; America (Apalachia), 3,000 feet; West Indies, 1,400 to 2,200 feet; California, 1,000 feet; Western Africa, 1,500 to 2,000 feet.

Perhaps, in the absence of malaria, we may attribute the fever in no small degree to the principle laid down by Dr. Oldham in a recent work on malaria, namely, "to the rapid extraction of animal heat." "Sudden change of temperature from heat to cold," he says, "is mentioned in the history of nearly every epidemic of malarious disease." And again, "It is, moreover, almost universally allowed that relapses of malarious fever are produced by exposure to chill."

Dr. Oldham's theory (after some years of careful observation, whilst serving in India) is this:—that malaria, as a specific poison, does not exist; but that the cause of the diseases attributed to it is chill, or, in other words, the absence of animal heat. Again he adds, that he found the extreme susceptibility to cold (which is caused by long exposure to great heat), intensifies the predisposition to the diseases referred to—thus causing their great prevalence in hot climates,—and that a further effect of great heat upon the system, more especially in the white races, is by lowering the vital powers to render the type of disease more grave."

My reason for deeming this theory to be proved

by the Oroya fever, may be thus briefly explained.
The greater number of persons afflicted up here
were men who, after working at their navvy
work all day—sometimes beneath a roasting sun,
but nearly always in a temperature of not less than
90° Fahrenheit,—then " intensified the predisposition " to the disease—such a predisposition being
strengthened by the fact that they were all unac-
climatized foreigners—and " lowered the vital
powers " by swallowing indiscriminate quantities
of Pisco, the intoxicating spirit made from sugar-
cane.   This liquoring with the Chilians went on
sometimes through the whole night, concurrent
with their gambling.   They cared nothing for sleep
so long as the infatuation of cards could be in-
dulged in, or until this state of things obliged them
to be sent down to the Guadaloupe Hospital in
Calláo, to add a few more items to the mortality.

Besides the fever, there is another dreadful
disease in these neighbourhoods, called the Verrugas,[*] which seems as much indigenous to the
place as the *goître* is to the valleys of the Alps or
Pyrenees.   Whether it comes or not from the use
of water containing earthy salts, is hardly decided
amongst the medical men up here.   It is, however,
a very nasty disease, breaking out all over the
body sometimes, not even excepting the face, in
large warty excrescences.   Until these come out,
and sometimes after they appear, the system un-

* Verrugas is the Spanish word for wart or excrescence.

dergoes a depressed state of all the functions, and its complication with the Oroya fever is very distressing.

We are told by Stevenson[*] that "Verrugas warts of a peculiar kind are common in some of the valleys of the coast." During my residence in Peru I never heard of their being known anywhere except up the valley of the Rimac. There I saw it at Santa Eulalia, already mentioned in the case of the Curé, as well as at Surco, a little beyond the Verrugas river.

On my first visit to San Bartolomé[']] I remained on the hill-top for one night as the guest of Captain Heath, who was in charge of the camp here, and with him I went to visit the hospital. This is called Esperanza. It is situated at the upper end of the valley, and, like all such establishments organized by Mr. Meiggs, is deficient in nothing that can conduce to the comfort of those cared within. It has 153 beds, but at the time of my visit there were only seventy-five patients in it. Amongst them were some very nasty cases of verrugas, as of pulmonary affections with the Chilians.

"The height of San Bartolomé," Mr. Magee says, "is 4,910 feet above sea level. I know of no other road," he continues, "that, starting from the sea, rises to this height in forty-six miles' distance."

[*] Op. cit. vol. i. p. 347.
['] The Indian name of this place is Urabamba.

CUTTING OF RAILWAY TRACK AT SAN BARTOLOMÉ.

Here we find the first of these retrograde developments, of which there are several others required on the track to the summit of the Andes. The engine, when it stops opposite the station, is detached from the carriages. Then, advancing to a turn-table, it is brought round on to another track; now it comes back parallel to the line by which we came up, until, connected by switches with what on the ascent to this was the hindmost carriage of the train, it makes a détour through the hundred feet cutting in the limestone rock, and then progressing up the mountain-side, still on the incline of four per cent., goes on towards Surco.

Few things on my journey up here gave me so much pleasure as an inspection of the 480 to 500 Chinese that were working at this camp. They had got a large galpon, or wooden shed, to sleep in; it is, in fact, a wooden house, enclosed and excellently ventilated—their sleeping-places being arranged in the style of sailors' bunks on board a ship. It is not more than a few hundred yards from Captain Heath's house, on the top of the hill. The flooring is wooden, raised four feet above the ground; and to the capital arrangements of this residence is due no small amount of the contentment of the Chinamen, as well as their good condition. Some friends of mine, amongst the rest my fellow-explorer, Mr. Steer, had previously told me that San Bartolomé was the only place in which

they had seen fat Chinamen in Peru. This was
not surprising, for during their dinner-time, I saw
them regaling on rice, and beef in great plenty.
Before starting in the morning for their work,
they all get bread and tea, and the whole arrangements here plainly indicate, that John Chinaman
would have little to complain of, if he were treated
everywhere in Peru as he is on the Oroya railway
line by the employés of Mr. Meiggs.

From San Bartolomé—although a distance of
only six miles to Surco,—the railway cuttings have
to be made in such a roundabout way, that the
journey is more than doubled. I may here explain
that from San Bartolomé to Lima the rate of fall
in the river Rimac is generally three to five per
cent., and the track of the railway line, alongside
of it, varies its grade from two to two and a half
per cent. as far as Chosica. From Chosica up to
this place (San Bartolomé) the rail is generally four
per cent. grade. But farther upwards, the fall of
the river becoming from ten to twelve per cent.,
—and I believe before getting to Surco as much as
fifteen per cent.,—it may be inferred how impossible it would be to follow the river's track, without
these retrograde movements of a zigzag character,
so to speak, of which I have written in the previous
page.

Our course from San Bartolomé, winding
through the cutting, then skirting the little
village of San Bartolomé, or Urabamba, with

its old grey church, and a considerable arborescence, is very pretty. Whilst coming round again we see the station in the valley underneath us. One cannot help feeling a sort of solemn awe at the steadiness with which the locomotive goes on here,—

> "And break-neck pathway seeking
> 　　Along the mountain's verge,
> The Condor's shriek outshrieking,
> 　　His course can surely urge.
>
> "Alps, Andes, Himalaya,
> 　　Defiant seemed to stand,
> Each range a giant slayer
> 　　Of steps 'twixt land and land."

Rushing through a tunnel, and coming out on a declivity several hundred feet between us and the river Rimac which rolls below, we pull up at the station of the iron bridge which crosses the Verrugas streamlet.

RAILWAY BRIDGE OVER VERRUGAS RIVER.

This is a bridge of iron, according to the Fink plan (as I learn from Mr. Sweet), with piers of 252 feet high, and a total length of 525 feet. It is, in fact, the highest bridge in the world, being 260 feet from the base.

From Verrugas to Surco, the chief notable work on the line is a tunnel through a precipitous side of the mountain, about 575 feet above the bed of the river. In some of this we have a curve of 395 feet radius. Through the tunnel just mentioned the rock was very hard, and tough—scoring glass like a diamond. A considerable part of the cutting was worked by the diamond drill. Up to this the Rimac river has furnished, with its fall of from 200 to 400 feet per mile, excellent water power, alongside of all the tunnels, for compressing air. At the period of my last visit, in April, 1873, the road was in working order as far as Succuta bridge,—a little beyond Surco, or nearly sixty miles from Lima.

On the line from San Bartolomé to Surco, by the mule track over the mountains, you can pass near the locales of Songo and Pucushani, besides many other places with the Spanish names of Cuesta Blanca, Esperanza, and such like. All up this way there are excellent swinging suspension bridges over the rivers, with iron fasten- . ings, put up by Mr. Meiggs. The scenery varies very little up here as you go along. Mountains on each side. The river still tumbling, rolling, splashing, and rushing,—sometimes at a depth of from three to four hundred feet below the narrow ledge on which your horse or mule may be picking his steps, as you occasionally meet a troop of mules, or asses, laden with produce from the interior, and bound to Lima. In other places (although these are very few), you come to spots of beauty like that of the valley of Pongo, in which, on my first visit, there was an encampment.

Creeping up the mountain-side from this, we turn round the remains of one of those terrace arrangements, built of enormous stones, and puzzling us by their colossal size to guess by what mechanical appliances they were put here. This is above the road, and underneath, near the river-side are heaps of rubble—one of them in a horse-shoe form—that might be the relics of human habitations.

Near to Pucushani, and standing close to the bank, I am reminded by the thundering down of the river—for now it is at its fullest height—of what Hawk's Eye in one of Fenimore Cooper's novels said of Glen's Falls on the Hudson, when speaking of the perversity of the water:—" For it falls by no rule at all; sometimes it leaps; sometimes it tumbles; then it skips; here it shoots; in one place it is as white as snow, and in another it is as green as grass, or as brown as a berry. Hereabouts it pitches into deep hollows, that rumble and quake the earth, and thereaway it ripples and sings like a brook—fashioning whirlpools and gullies in the old stone as if 'twere no harder than the trodden clay. The whole design of the river seems disconcerted. First it runs smoothly, as if meaning to go down the descent as things were ordered; then it angles about and faces the shores; nor are there places wanting where it looks backward, as if unwilling to leave the wilderness and mingle with the salt."

Just such is the Rimac, in the months of December and January.

CHAPTER XXI.

AFTER passing the camp at Pucushani, we go on through the same kind of scenery as that described in the last chapter, till we cross the river again near Aposungo. From this it is not far to Surco —a small town of one street. The houses being chiefly stone-built, and with sloping roofs of straw, whilst having in the *tout-ensemble* of walls, doors, windows and roofs, such an appearance of rustiness, as if, in some remote age, they had been pushed up out of the earth by volcanic agency. There is a chapel on the right-hand side of the street, which is of the same colour as the houses.

" At Surco," observes Mr. Sweet, C.E., " there is another development, similar to the one already mentioned (that is, the retrograde track at San Bartolomé), which reaches the pampa of Machucana, at an altitude of 7,500 feet. On this portion there will be three bridges, the longest 240 feet, and about 2,500 lineal feet of tunnels."

From Surco forwards, the first thing to attract me was the hospital of San Juan—very high above the road—which at this point runs through the valley. It is at an altitude of 350 feet, more or less, overtopping the river. In a sanitary point of view it appears in an excellent position; and this is verified by the fact, that there are no cases of Oroya fever nor Verrugas here, except what have been transplanted, or brought up by parties who absorbed the poison lower down, in its own locale. Being already somewhat tired with this my first journey amongst the Cordilleras, I did not care to go out of my road, as I would have to do to see this institution, much as I desired to have a look at the *ménage*. It was under the care of Doctor Kenny, Director of Hospitals, and Medical Inspector of the Oroya line. I have no doubt of its being, from the cyric on which it is built, far superior in that most important matter of hygiene to any hospital of Lima or Calláo. So much so, indeed, that I cannot avoid considering what a desecration it would be to the purity of the mountain air, to

send any fever or other patient hence down to
Calláo.

To Machucana from this we cross and recross
the river again; and at much of this part of the
route the thundering of the torrent causes quite
a remarkable echo amongst the rocks. The track
on which I am travelling is the same mountain
pathway all along, till about one mile before
reaching Machucana, I find myself in a little valley
on a road with stone walls at each side, and being
no more than four to five yards across. The
stones in these walls, if not " hoary," are " rusty "
with age; for they in many places show the outside mossy-looking rust, which is significant of
the action of water on iron-stone, or pyrites.

The town, or village, of Machucana is very
similar to Surco,—alike in its one street, its dreary
volcanic aspect, its sombre chapel, and its Indian
population. On the day of my arrival—it was
the 6th of January, " La Fiesta de los Reyes," the
Feast of the Kings—I was for a considerable time
impressed with the almost " audible silence " of
the place. I had been lying down on the sofa at
the house of Mr. Bogue, Mr. Meiggs' principal
engineer—when suddenly there arose a combination of yelling, screaming, and vociferating,
accompanied with the tinkling of some stringed
instrument. So discordant was the uproar that
I went to the door to find out its sources.
There were about half-a-dozen women near one

of the doors on the opposite side of the street. Besides these were three men,—one scraping a fiddle,—another blowing into a most untuneful pipe,—and the third with a bottle in his hand, to which he was paying unremitting devotion. All the women were engaged in the same pursuit —passing bottles round from hand to mouth— and the whole company may be described as emphatically drunk. Three of the men—to represent the kings I supposed—were decked up in the most outrageously common style of tinsel, and with spangled ponchos. The fiddler was so stupidly intoxicated as to be able only to scratch out such discordance as, I believe, never was elicited from catgut by hrose-hair since the violin was invented, as traditionally reported, by Ravana, King of Ceylon, 5000 B.C. To complete the grotesqueness of the ceremony, there was a harper, who held his instrument upside down, and tinkled away with far more energy, than harmony. In fact, the whole dis-concert was sublimely hideous, and did not impress me much with the sanctity of their religious ceremonies at Machucana.

Here we are at a height of 8,000 feet above the level of the sea, and the Cordilleras at either side about 3,000 to 4,000 feet from the base to summit. Now we commence to see the snow in small quantities on the mountain-tops, indicative of our approaching the Andes : those

SAN MATEO VILLAGE ON OROYA RAILROAD.

[Vol. II. p. 73

> " Palaces of nature, whose vast walls
>   Have pinnacled in clouds their snowy scalps,
>   And throned eternity in icy halls
>   Of vast sublimity."

At Machucana we are only nine leagues from the highest point of that part of the Andes through which the railway line runs. The peak at the indicated part is 16,330 feet above the level of the sea ; but at a depth of 680 feet from the top, there is a tunnel to run 3,850 feet in length, and at an altitude of 15,650 feet.

After Machucana, there is a line of retrograde development, where the Parac river falls into the Rimac. The wildness and savagery of scenery up here is indescribable ; and how the people live in such an out-of-the-way town as San Mateo is a problem not easy to be solved. Here, no doubt, there is a sort of refreshment for the traveller coming over the Andes ; but it must be a cheerless one. It is, however, very comfortable at the house of Mr. Meiggs' engineer, seen with its commodious verandahs in the centre of the view.

From Machucana, the plan of the road is thus sketched out by Mr. Sweet, C.E. :—To Chicla, a distance of twenty-five miles—where there is another development of the retrograde class. The valley of Chicla is at an altitude of 12,000 feet above the level of the sea.

Between San Mateo and Chicla, the line passes through a horrible gorge, to which the title of " Los

Infernillos"[1] has been given by the Spaniards. "The river here," says Mr. Magee, "passes for some distance between two walls of rock that rise perpendicularly to heights variously estimated at 1,000 to 1,500 feet. For a considerable way it comes down a flight of stairs or falls, roaring like a small Niagara. The line leaves a tunnel, crosses the river on a bridge of 160 feet span, and at a height of 165 feet above the water, entering another tunnel."

From Casapalca across the summit, and to the Rio de Visca, a tributary of the Amazon, the track although between certain points, yet is made up generally of a succession of curves.

From the final station at the same place already mentioned, Oroya, 140 miles from Lima, it is considered a distance of 250 miles to the navigable waters of the Amazon. This, however, is a point not yet decided on. We have had so many of these rivers in the Amazon valley examined by Mr. Markham, Mr. Squier, Mr. Chandless, Senor Raimondi, Admiral Trotter, Senor Malinowski (the chief engineer of the Oroya line), and a host of others, that we may hope to know before long whether this line can be continued, so as to make the Uyacali, or other stream, connect it with the Amazon, and thus be solved the problem of junction between the Atlantic and Pacific. One thing, at all events, is very

---

[1] The little hells.

WATERFALL OF LOS INFIERNILLOS (LITTLE HELLS).

[Vol. II. p. 77.

satisfactory—that by the Arequipa line to Cuzco, as well as this Oroya line to the other side of the Andes, the Peruvian Government is losing no time in assisting some of the greatest facts of the age. But the most important of these will be the bringing of passengers from Callao on the Pacific, across the Andes, to the Amazon—great highway of the Atlantic,—even at fifteen miles an hour,—and doing the whole journey in the space of from twenty to thirty hours.

Whilst we are still up in the regions of the Condor, I may ask my readers to glance at the map. By which they can see, that from the Oroya, branch lines may be run to the Cerro del Pasco mines—the richest silver-mines in the world—in a northerly direction, or to the south to the city of Jauja, which boasts of an atmosphere that is infallible for the cure of consumption. This is the place about which such an excellent treatise has been written by the present President of the Republic, and to which I have recently alluded.[1]

"On a simple inspection of the map," says Senor Don Ernesto Malinowski, the engineer in chief, "we can notice the importance of the position called Oroya, to satisfy all the exigencies of a general head-quarters position at the other side of the Cordillera. From thence branches can be made in three principal directions, and evidently

---

[1] *Vide* chap. xix. p. 370.

the most direct way from Lima to Oroya—that by the valley of the Rimac—is the preferable one. A project departing from Lima, and passing by San Damian, would likewise have the advantage of terminating at Oroya. But it may be observed that such a route would necessitate a considerable roundabout, and a double expense of all transported material, not only with the distance from Lima to Lurin, but also with about eight leagues that it would be incumbent to pass on the very peak of the Cordillera, without gaining altitude.

"The road by the valley of the Chancay offers still greater inconveniences. It is certain that by this, the important mining district of Cerro de Pasco might be brought nearer the coast, and its distance from Lima the same, or a little less than by the Oroya. But then it would be necessary to sacrifice the wooded districts of Chanchamayo, and the valley of Jauja, whereof the products would have to be recharged, perhaps more than thirty leagues of additional transport, to arrive at Lima or Callao. The impossibility of taking the line," concludes Senor Malinowski, "by any other direction than one of these three, will therefore justify our selection, for the convenience of the most direct route from Lima to Oroya will be probably manifest."

The engineering difficulties of this road are inconceivable to any one who has not been amongst them. Mr. Magee tells me there are parts where,

RAVINE ON OROYA RAILROAD TRACK.

Vol. II p. 70.

" if it had not been for benches or shelves on the rocks, the places would be inaccessible to bipeds." One part of embankment near the Verrugas bridge contains 90,000 cubic feet of material; whilst the quantity of cuttings, blastings, and tunnellings that had, and still have, to be made is prodigious. When I was leaving there last May, there were 850 mules and 150 horses in the employ of the company, making a transportation cost of 3,000 soles (45*d*. each sole) per day. All the plant for the building of the road, in advance of track, is necessarily obliged to be transported by mules.[a]

Looking over the excellent and exhaustive pamphlet of Dr Raimondi on the province of Loreto,[b] I find that some of the rivers, as the Rio Mayo and the Huallaga, likely to be interested in the future continuation of the Oroya railroad, run through that province. The Huallaga river debouches into the Maranon, as the Amazon is styled to the west of Nanta. At the latter place comes out the Ucayali river, which, having its source from the combined streams of the Apurimac, the Uribamba, and the Tambo, flows in nearly its whole course through the Loreto province. The limit of navigation up the Huallaga is now to a place called Chenuci, beyond Yurimaguas, and not at all far distant from the fertile Peruvian

[b] " Apuntes sobre la Provincia Litoral de Loreto." Por Antonio Raimondi, Professor de Historia Natural de la Facultad de Medicina. Lima, 1862.

valleys of Chachapoyas, and Moyabamba. It was here that Mr. Steer landed when he made the voyage up from Para. Thence, going south to Tarapoto, he turned north to Moyabamba city, from which he tracked his course S.W. to Chachapoyas, making a large collection of rare birds through its Eden-like valley—passing Balsas, Cajamarca, and thence by Guzmango to the port of Malabrigo, on the Pacific.

No part of Senor Raimondi's book seems to me more interesting than that where he describes the different tribes of wild Indians, amongst whom he spent several years. Their name is legion, and their titles are so polysyllabic that I pass many. Of the Campas, he says,[1] " They are a tribe likewise known by the title of the Antis, and occupy a large extent of territory, comprised between the river St. Ann, from the mountains of Cuzco, and the river Chanchamayo, from the mountains of Tarma,—living on the banks of the rivers St. Ann, Tambo, and their affluents. The Campas form a nation, numerous, brave, and warlike. They are distinguished from the Piros by their language, as by their not having the custom to paint their teeth, which, on the contrary, are beautiful and white. Besides, they wear a tunic[2] longer than that of the Piros, which is different likewise in its colour—that of the Campas in-

<hr>

[1] Op. cit. p. 117.   [2] Cushma.

CITY OF JAUJA (THE XAUXA OF PRESCOTT).

[Vol. II. p. 81.

clining to yellow or golden. The tunic of the Campas reaches down to the ankle."

Then follows a philological dissertation on the superior beauty of the Campas over the Piros idiom—which I confess, with what is supposed to be the skull of a Campas man before me, I am slow to appreciate. " The Campas who inhabit the mountains of Chanchamayo," he tells us, " are very hostile, and no friendly relations can be entered into with them." Those of the valley of St. Ann, in the department of Cuzco, are, however, tractable—Mr. Raimondi having been hospitably treated by them in 1858.

SKULL FROM CAMPAS.

I cannot say whether the skull, which is here illustrated, belongs to the Campas tribe, or whether it is of the trachycephalic, dolicho-

cephalic, scaphocephalic, or any other jaw-break-
ing cephalic type; for I claim no status in
craniology, although having picked up nearly a
thousand skulls during my two years in Peru;
but the original of this is at Lima, in the possession of Mr. Bryant, of the mint, and from it
Mr. Richardson, the photographer, took the sketch.
That it comes from a height of 12,000 feet above
the level of the sea I have no reason to doubt; for
that is the given altitude of the place, named
Campas, where it was picked up.

SKULL FROM NEAR SURCO.

In describing the Conibos, who live in different parts of the Uyacali valley, Senor Raimondi[*]
gives an account of the custom by which this

* Op. cit. p. 119.

abnormal head-formation is caused :—" The Conibos have peculiar characteristics amongst them.
With others, they have the barbarous fashion
of flattening the heads of their children with
two small pieces of thin board—one of which is
applied to the forehead, and another behind—in
such a manner that the front of the head is pushed

SKULL FROM HUANCANI.

down, and the head enlarged posteriorly, resembling the skulls that are sometimes turned out of
the burial-grounds (huacas) in the sierras. In the
mission of Sarayaco, I had the opportunity of
seeing a child, which its mother had brought to
be baptized, and which, besides having the head
enlarged behind, had at the same time a rounded
projection on the frontal bone; the latter being
much depressed outside the prominence. Not
understanding how a projection could be de-

veloped in a skull flattened by a board, I asked the mother if the board employed to flatten the head of this child was a smooth surface, and she answered me that there was a considerable-sized hole in it. Thus with facility could be explained the protuberance in question—the cranium having become developed in the part corresponding to the hole, from not finding itself compressed there by the flat board."

I know not if Mr. Raimondi made any inquiries as to what was the *rationale*—if such a word can be used—of this barbaric deformity amongst them. For he gives us no account of it. These Combos, he further tells us, with the Setebos and Sipibos— all three being often confounded one with the other—make holes in the wings of their noses, to suspend little silver drops from them, which some- times come down as far as the upper lip. They are, moreover, remarkable for the roughness and raspiness of their skins, which is in no small degree attributable to mosquitos and sand-flies, as well as to a sort of permanent eruption on the cuticle.

CHAPTER XXII.

RETURNED from my trip up the Oroya line, I made
the following entry in my note-book :—

" Amongst the Cordilleras of the Peruvian Andes
—those vast upheavals of the old volcanic periods,
—and whether seated on a pinnacle, wandering
through a valley, or scrambling on mule-back up
and down a precipitous gorge, I can see little of
what is associated, in my mind's eye, with Byron's
expression of

'The wild pomp of mountain majesty.'

Call it grand, sublime, picturesque, romantic, or
what you please, but outside of very few spots,

where one meets cordial hospitality (as I have had
it invariably from the railway officials employed
by Mr. Meiggs), the permanent impression, which
these dark masses of Cyclopean mountain gave
me, was of their being the most superlatively uncomfortable places to be obliged to pass a night
in."

Between Lima and the port of Huacho, seventy
to eighty miles distant by land, a. railway was inaugurated in a short time after the late President
Balta came to be at the head of affairs in Peru.   It
was undertaken from a contract given to Senor Don
Modesto Busadre, a citizen of Lima, on the 19th of
August, 1867.   This, however, was transferred
to Senor Don Waldo Grana, one of the directors of
the Bank of Peru, in March, 1870, and on 19th of
following month in same year it was opened to the
public as far as Ancon, distant about eighteen miles
from Lima, and already constituted the favourite
bathing-place of the late President Balta.

Although Stevenson devotes several pages[1] to
Ancon, Pasamayo, Chancay, and Huacho, strange to
say he never mentions their crowded grave-yards.
Hence I am led to infer that the excavations which
are seen everywhere in these districts must
have been made since he was there.   From Paz
Soldan's geographical map, I should guess Ancon to
be in the Caraballyo district, although even its name

---

[1] Op. cit., vol. i. chap. xv.

is not mentioned by him.*   To reach it from Lima
we have to go by the train from a station on the
side of Rimac opposite to that of the Oroya line.
Our first few miles, through the suburbs and past
haciendas, or sugar-cane farms, bring us to the
station called "Las Infantas;"—then across the
little rivulet of Chillon,—past another stopping-
place, Puento de las Piedras,—by some old ruins
of adobe construction,—through a Golgotha of
skulls and other bones,—and into the little wooden
village of Ancon.

At present (I wrote of it in January, 1872) it is
the head-quarters of President Balta, where he
has four to five thousand troops in improvised
barracks.   It has a very spacious hotel, and the
soil being of fine sand, in each street there is a
wooden *trottoir* to the houses.   One of the finest
residences in the town is that of Senor Grana.
There is a mole here, and now we find two Peruvian
men-of-war in the harbour.   It is an uncommonly
pretty little cove—the waters literally crammed with
fish ; the air alive with pelicans, penguins, sea gulls,
and other piscatorial birds, that seem to have all the
game to themselves.   Not a vestige of vegetation,
save two stunted palm-trees in the upper street, and
a few flowers in the hotel verandah.   Smooth sand

---

* There is no mention of these places by Cieza de Leon, as he
jumps from Huaman, or La Barranca, by saying, "One day's
journey further on brings us to the valley of Huara, whence we
pass to that of Lima." Op. cit. p. 248.

is in the bay, and a capitally-arranged bathing-
house down at the end of the strand, which at
this point is overtopped by a hillock of from
seven to eight hundred feet in height, and de-
clining gradually in its altitude, as it stretches
out about a mile to the corner of the harbour's
mouth. At this point excellent sport is to be had,
as there are generally several seals and sea-lions
basking on the rocks.

Turning my back to the hotel, and riding to
the distance of half a mile (to begin with)—then
going on two or three miles farther, and—finally
making a circuit of six to eight miles, my journey is
all through burial-ground. Skulls, legs, arms, and
the whole anatomy of the human body are about.
Legs attached to pelvis, and bent up, still with
mummified skin on them; arms in the same state;
relics of plaited straw, forming coffin-swathes;
pieces of net, of cloth, of cotton-flock, and many
other such accompaniments of the funeral accessories. Some water-crofts, of a very superior
quality, have been obtained out of the graves
at Ancon. Of those there are three different
forms, in places separated at short distance from
each other, but each style having its defined
outline of locale. As to the shape of the graves,
there are some of inverted cylinder form, like
that of a limekiln, the insides of which are lined
with masonry work. In those the body is placed
in the upright position. There is also the ordinary

longitudinal grave, in which the corpse is put right in contact with the earth. Likewise the grave cut square to a depth of six to eight feet, at the top of which, or within one to two feet of the ground, is a roofing or covering over of mat-work, placed on wooden rafters. In one of these last-mentioned I saw three bodies, all wrapped up together, being man, woman, and child. In this case the faces were swathed with llama wool instead of cotton, as is usually seen in ordinary ones. Here too I turned out relics of fishing-nets, with some needles for manufacturing them, —varieties of cloth,—tapestry, and work-bags resembling ladies' reticules.

WATER-CROFTS EXCAVATED AT ANCON.

Not a vestige of vegetation being about, nor sign of relic of the terraces mentioned by Prescott, the first difficult problem to be solved is—whence came these hundreds, and thousands of people, who are

buried in Ancon, or how did they make out a living
whilst on the earth ?   I sent a collection of skulls,
with their accessories of cloth, fishing-nets, and so
forth, from Ancon to the Anthropological Institute
of London ; and in less than two days between
this and Pasamayo, only fourteen miles farther
down the sea-shore, I had gathered 384 skulls,
with specimens of pottery, for Professor Agassiz,
which he took away in the United States exploring-
ship " Hassler," brought by him down from
Callao for the purpose.[3]

The railway from Ancon to Chancay—all of this
Huacho line that is yet accomplished—is certainly
not very much to be commended to nervous
people. Its track is on the side of a soft-sand hill
—sand of the same quality and of a like material
as the Médanos heaps bordering the Arequipa
track,[4] and therefore having no cohesive nature.
Thus it is as far as the extensive burial-ground of
Pasamayo—a place which has nothing to mark it as
a necropolis, save the hundreds and thousands of
skulls that have been turned up by the seekers after
gold, and silver. The burial-ground here has more
than half a mile of railway cutting passing through it.
It extends up the face of the hill from the sea-shore
to the height of about 800 feet, and, being from
half to three-quarters of a mile in breadth, some
idea may be formed of its extent. With the aid of

[3] *Vide* Appendix B.   [4] Chap. v. p. 81.

a few assistants I got several skulls from it, together with some specimens of a not very superior style of crockery-ware, in the shape of saucers. Amongst the peculiarities of these skulls were several with sutures in the frontal bones, like those

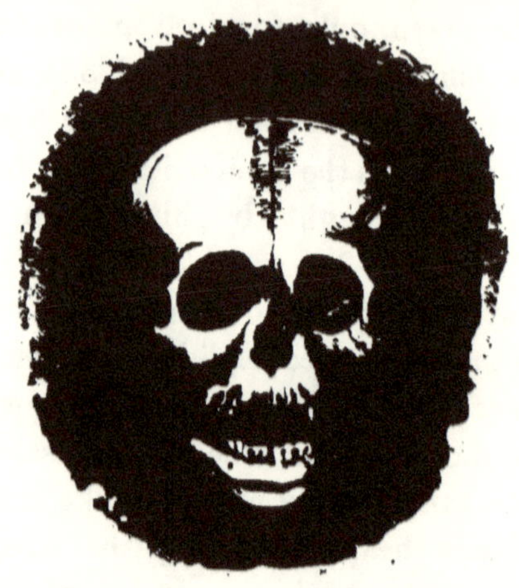

SKULL WITH SUTURE IN FRONTAL BONE, FROM PASAMAYO.

which I afterwards procured at Pacha-Cámac. In order to be sure that these were not remains of people killed in battle, or by any accidental casualty, I organized some extensive diggings, from which were taken out skeletons, accompanied with cloth and crockery-ware, much of the latter crumbling into dust the moment it was exposed to the external air. Another resemblance to those found at Pacha-Cámac consisted in the small pieces of copper between the teeth, as if for the Charon obolus, and one or two had plates of copper on the head. I must confess myself puzzled more and more to guess whence these people were brought to be buried, and by what means, for, previous to the railway on this line, there was only a bridle pathway to and from Lima.

From the graveyard to the station of Pasamayo we have about a mile. Here there is a small valley, in which is a sugar-cane establishment, and through this runs the river of Pasamayo, generally a small stream—but, coming as it does from the Cordilleras, a rushing, roaring torrent when the wet season is in. There is an excellent trestle-bridge for the line across Pasamayo river, and five miles farther on, having gone through many ruins of old walls,—of bones lying about—and of a multitude of archæological relics, enough to occupy the most industrious of students for some months, we arrive at Chancay.

LLAMA WOOL ORNAMENT FROM PASAMAYO BURIAL-GROUND. FROM THE COLLECTION OF SENOR ESPANTOSO, AT LIMA.

I stayed for several days in this little village occupying the pretty house of Senor Grana; and

CHOLO INDIANS

CHOLO INDIANS SITTING DOWN.

from my note-book I take the following extract :—

November 1st, 1872.—Wandering through the streets of Chancay,—wading amongst the heavy sand of the principal square, or Plaza de Armas, is very fatiguing work in the relaxing atmosphere down here. Although it is not yet one o'clock, the Matriz, or parish chapel, is locked; for, strange to say, every place of worship in Peru is hermetically scaled to the outer world after midday. As I walk along, I cannot help being struck with the intense expression of indolence in the faces of the people, and the palpable signs of irreparable decay in the buildings. Perhaps they are cause and effect. Whether it is at shop doors, plying the needle at a tailor's, or the awl at a shoemaker's, they are all doing it with an air of lassitude, that signifies how little they care about this world or the next. The condition of the town, as regards heaps of garbage lying about, unfinished houses that seem to have been started into building half a century ago, with the unwashed faces everywhere, prove one part of the last-named proposition. The dilapidated condition of the chapels, of which there are three, with the number of bats and the mouldy smells inside, prove the second—for I managed, by hunting out the sacristans, to get into each.

Attached to the chapel of San Francisco, with its tower of a few rotten branches and bits of mud, that never could have had strength to support the smallest bell, is a hospital—the very atmosphere, (if I may call it so,) inside of which is enough to qualify a man to be a patient for such an institution anywhere in the world. The portions allotted to male and female patients are divided by high walls; but as there is nothing in it now but dirt, and decay, we have to be satisfied with speculating as to what the town, the chapels, and the hospital might have been in times gone by. For we can get no data about them from any person. There is a market-place by which we pass, but the only tenants of it at two p.m., are a few turkey-buzzards, employed in their daily occupation of clearing decks. Close by is an immense large door at each side of a corner, by which entrance is to be had into a general store, and this door is about the size of the main passage to the General Post Office at St. Martin's-le-Grand, in London.

Here, as elsewhere, I have been presented with earthenware, so old—so very old, the donors say—in fact, as old as the conquest! In every town of Peru that I have visited I have rarely found the owners of prehistoric crockery-ware to be able to comprehend, that it could date farther back than the time of the Inca's subjugation.

The limit of Peruvian antiquity to the period of Pizarro's invasion is followed by Stevenson[*] also, where he says he has drunk, at Patavilca and

* Op. cit., vol. i. p. 373.

Cajamarca, chicha that had been found "interred in jars in the huacas, or burying-places, where it must have remained upwards of three centuries." Again[*]:—"Owing to the nitrous quality of the sand, and to its almost perfect dryness, the bodies are quite entire, and not the least defaced, although many of them have been buried *at least three centuries.*"

Probably five to six times three centuries multiplied would be nearer the mark in "many of them." The limit of three centuries may imply that all these things were done by some spiritual inspiration, just before the Spaniards came, that they might fall into the hands of their conquerors. I showed some of the proceeds of my excavations to Professor Agassiz, and he assured me of the impossibility of calculating, without better data than we have as yet, whether they were aged more thousands of years, than the owners credit them for centuries.

Crossing the brow of the first hill, entering Chancay town, and stretching towards the sea, I see the remains of a two-yards-thick wall, constructed of adobones. On the face of this hill, pointing to the line of railway from Ancon, are two stone ditches, perfectly parallel and symmetrical, about 100 yards apart, and running from bottom to top to a height of about 300 yards. Between these are other lines of stones displaced—perhaps the ruins of some of the old terraces. All about this

* Op. cit., vol. i. p. 415.

place, at the base of the hill looking towards Chancay, as well as on the side in front of the sea, is full of graves;—some built up with stone walls, through which the railway cutting has gone;—others lined inside with mud-bricks of no formation more than that of a heap of clay and water moulded up in the hands and (as shapeless as an African yam) allowed to dry in the sun. Large quantities of broken crockery-ware, some of which was of excellent material, and beautiful design, lay scattered about.

Over the hills of Chancay we find a large quantity of small stones—such as might have made terraces or walls—of a different geological formation from the rock here, and therefore proving that they have been transported. These are covered over with lichen. On to the sand of the bay of Chancay fall several small streams of the purest water, coming out of the bank at a height of eighteen to twenty feet. I cannot doubt that this is infiltrated from the interior Cordilleras.

A few days previous to my coming down I received a letter from my friend, the Rev. Kenelm Vaughan, whom I had recommended to try the air of Chancay, as I had heard it highly spoken of in reference to such a delicate pulmonary condition as he was labouring under. Dated 30th of October, he writes :—" I am come to the conclusion that Chancay is a great city of the dead, or has been an immense ossuary of Peru; for, go where you will, on mountain-top, on level plain, or by the sea-side, you meet at every turn skulls and bones of all descriptions. Never was I in such a sepulchral spot in my life. Were it not for one thing, which is all to me (the blessed sacrament of which I am guardian here), I should soon be in my dying agonies, and my bones perhaps come to be knocking about like that poor Chinaman who was inhumed by the seaside a few nights ago."

During one day of my stoppage, I rode over a few leagues to a hacienda, formerly owned by the late President Balta, and now tenanted by his son Don Ricardo. Rearing of pigs seemed to be the chief feature of the farm. A few leagues farther on, and in valleys apparently shut in from communication with the world, are stone walls, adobe ruins, excavations, with skulls and all kinds of bones lying about.

Some of those people who attribute the first colonizing of Peru to Chinese, try to make out that Ancon is derived from Hong-Kong, and Chancay from Shanghae. I do not intend to argue on this subject.

The road hence to Huacho, although only sixteen leagues farther north, according to Paz Soldan, must be very difficult of accomplishment. So as the railroad goes no farther than Chancay, I deem it better to return *via* Lima to Calláo, and take one of the excellent steamers of the Pacific Company for our trip farther north. I do this on board the steamship "Quito," with the most genial of Commanders, Captain Bird.

By referring to Dr. Tschudi's book,[1] I find that he visited Huacho during his residence at Lima in the year 1841. His chief occupation there, during a six weeks' residence, was to augment his ichthyological collection, and to make himself "*well acquainted with the environs of Huacho.*" From several hundred specimens of fish he made a fine collection, of about a hundred and twenty different species. These were put into a cask with brandy, which was allowed to evaporate in the sun's heat on the mole at Calláo. A second collection shared no better fate, for on arrival in Europe it proved utterly useless.[2]

"Huacho," the Doctor tells us, "is a large village, which, since the War of Independence, has received the title of city. It has more than 5000 inhabitants, of whom four-fifths are Indians, and the rest Mestizos. Very few whites have settled here. Among them I met an old lame Spaniard, Don Simon, who, at the beginning of the present century, accompanied the celebrated Alexander Von Humboldt to the beds of salt, situated a few miles to the south. In relating, with enthusiastic

---

[1] "Travels in Peru during the years 1838—1842, on the Coast, in the Sierras, &c." By Dr. J. T. Von Tschudi. Translated from the German by Thomasina Ross. London : David Bogue, Fleet Street, 1847.

[2] Op. cit. p. 211.

pleasure, his recollections of the youthful and indefatigable traveller, he told me that some years ago he had read the book which Humboldt wrote on America, and he added, with great simplicity : '*Pero Senor, ahi hé perdido los estribos.*'"[*]

The rest of the Doctor's observations about this place refer to the Cholos' mode of bringing poultry to Lima—of the women plaiting straw hats and mats, which are also sold in Lima—of a Padre that had such a love for his hounds, that separation from them was his great grief when he was dying, and he called to his negro servant for a pair of buckskin hunting gloves, and desired to have them drawn on. Further, he tells us of the immorality of the clergymen here—and of the filth of the native burying-ground. At the end of his six weeks, he ascertains that "the environs of Huacho abound in fine fruit gardens and productive Indian farms." But not a word about its antiquities. Perhaps this should not be wondered at when we find, as may be seen hereafter, that his descriptions of many other places are nearly, word for word, from Garcilasso de la Vega, and the various romancers.

From Callao to Huacho by sea is only sixty-five miles. Viewed from the harbour—for I had not

---

[*] Literally—"But there, sir, I lost the stirrups." Meaning that he did not understand it. The Spanish phrase, "Perder los estribos," signifies to get confused or embarrassed.

time to go on shore, as the steamer stops only a short time here to land passengers and mails—the town appears, almost a mile off, to the left of the landing-place. Little of it can be seen except of a group of houses, having the steeples of three or four chapels sticking up—one of them with a dome nearly as large as St. Paul's in London. Around the landing-place is a considerable fringe of green vegetation—evidencing cultivation. A small mole here begins at the first cutting of the Sayan railway. Another railway is about to start from this to the salt-mines, sixteen miles distant. Senor Paz Soldan tells us little more about Huacho than that there is "a huaca, or burial-ground, near to this town, and about which the people relate a thousand fables."

What a pity that some of these fables have not been investigated, to test their foundation of truth, or prove their falsehood!

CHAPTER XXIII.

THE coast voyage from Calláo up to Huacho has
the same monotonous feature as lower down—
dark brown rock, occasionally set off by patches of
white, that may be guano, soda, or possibly lime-
stone. Now and then a little patch of green; but
this is most perceptible as a kind of fringe near
the burial-ground of Pasamayo, and there little
farther than the extent which is marked by the
necropolis boundaries.

Going north or south from Calláo, on board any
of the Pacific Company's commodious steamers, I
must confess that the Cholo element, invariably on
decks, is not one of the most agreeable accompani-

Front view of Ceremonial Court Dress of Cuys-Mancu, the last King of the Yuncas, in the Valley of Rimac, and lineal Descendant of the Cuys-Mancu mentioned by Garcillaso de la Vega (cap. xxxii. p. 212) as reigning at Pacha-Cámac when that place was taken possession of by the Inca Pachacutec. Taken out of a Royal Huaca, or burial-ground, at Huacno, sixty miles north of Lima, and now in possession of Professor Don Antonio Raimondi in that city.

ments. Here, this morning (the 20th of November, 1872), going along from my room to the Captain's, and so late as nine a.m., I have to pick my steps daintily, amongst many who are still bundled up in their coverlets on deck. Much care is needed, as the ship is rolling, not to come in contact with any of the chamber commodities which each family has with them, and, above all, to look sharp about the same state of affairs that Dickens describes of the Mississippi steamers, namely, "the deck paved with oysters."   This last-mentioned custom is one of the most disagreeable accompaniments of Cholo society wherever you meet it. For it is not only confined to the decks, but penetrates to the cabin, and is remorselessly carried on during meal-times. In railway carriages, or in the chapels, you cannot escape it. It follows you not only in the streets, squares, and at the theatres, but sometimes in- trudes into the drawing-rooms of the best society. At a hotel it is completely tyrannical, because there every one is supposed to have liberty to do as he pleases. Therefore it is not an unusual thing to see on the walls of the bedroom in the hotel where you sleep, sure evidence of the Cholo's previous occupation of your quarters. It is, in fact, simply disgusting.

I cannot feel at all satisfied at Dr. Tschudi's leaving Huacho, after his six weeks' residence, without being able to tell us something more of it than of his ichthyological collections—of its fruit-gardens,—and of its productive Indian farms. That Huacho has still materials for further explorations —like nearly every inch of Peruvian territory on the sea-coast—is evident from the feather state-dress which was lent to me by Dr. Raimondi of Lima, to illustrate the antiquities of Peru. It was taken out of a burial mound here. The art that has been used in the manufacture of this is wonderful. The lappets hanging down from each shoulder, as well as the circle which embraces the forehead, are of one piece of fabric continuous with the broad flap that falls down the back. On this last-named is designed the figure of what is supposed to represent a fish, or reptile—the two eyes of which are made of red feathers—all the remaining part of the plumage being black, or white. But the most wonderful part of this work is, that the small feathers are so grafted, as it were, on a ground of cotton cloth, that the greatest force of my fingers could not pull one of them out.

The *Polayna*, or gaiter, which was intermingled with bright red and yellow colours, is turned up-side down in the photograph. This is a cloth of nearly half an inch in thickness, and such as is worn to-day by the Indians who cross the Cordilleras. All of these were found in the same grave at Huacho.

It was at Huacho, Stevenson tells us,[1] he heard for the first time " the oral tradition " of the first

____

[1] Op. cit. vol. i. p. 395.

Inca, Manco Capac,—about a white man found on the coast by a Caçique, or head of a tribe, named Cocapac—as of this white man answering the question put to him by signs of "who are

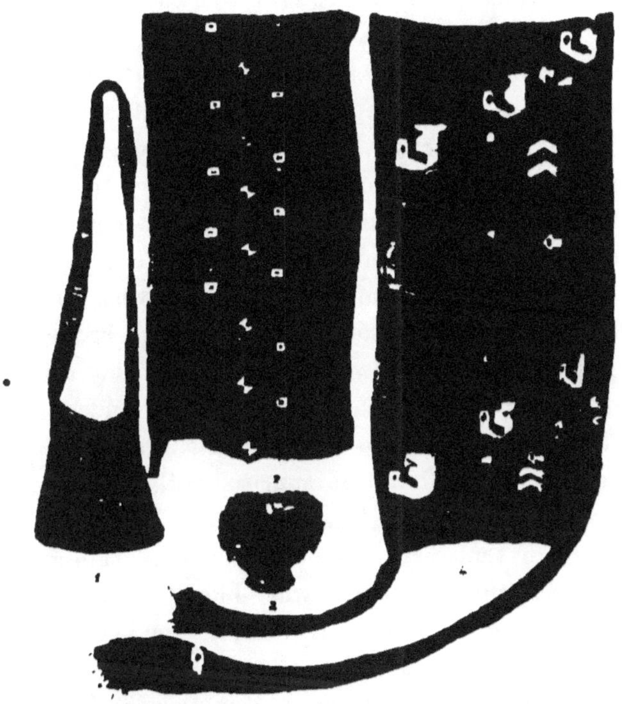

GAITER, CLOTH, BAG, ETC., FOUND AT HUACHO.

you?" and his reply that he was an Englishman. This son of Albion, taken to Cocapac's house, fell in love with his daughter, and married her, we may suppose. At all events, "the stranger lived with him (Cocapac) till the daughter of the caçique (the same Cocapac) bore him a son and a daughter, and then died."

To make the story short, Cocapac, who seems to have been considerably in advance of the age in which he lived, brought the boy, whom he had called Ingasman Cocapac—and how natural to the trusting mind seems the abbreviation to the pet name of Manco Capac?—together with the girl, Mama Oclce, across the Andes to Cuzco, a trifle of six hundred miles or so. Here a large tribe of Indians resided, whom Cocapac tried to persuade that their god, the Sun, had sent them two of his children to make them happy and to govern them. But the two new comers were not at once brought on the scene. They were crammed to play their part. The Indians had to go for them under the pilotage of Cocapac to a certain mountain, where they would be found at sunrise, with their hair like the rays of the Sun, and their faces of the colour of that orb. Yet the Indians, thinking probably that Cocapac was like the lady of Gengulphus' "coming it rather too strong," arrived at the conclusion that the pair were a wizard and a witch, and sent them down to Rimac Malca, the plain on which Lima stands. Whence it may be seen how easy travelling over the Andes was in those days, even before the Incas had made their great highways, or Mr. Meiggs had commenced his railroads. The old man, however,

* *Vide* "Ingoldsby Legends."

followed them, though probably not on a velocipede —for the distance is about 200 leagues from Cuzco to the Lima valley, and over Andes covered with perpetual snow, some of it being from 15,000 to 16,000 feet above the level of the sea.

He next took them to Lake Titicaca, to do which he had to recross the Andes again—over the like high mountains, and to a greater distance than Cuzco. Here Cocapac came to another tribe of Indians, on whom he tried the same game as at Cuzco. These were more amenable; for when they went to the lake, as they were told to do, at sunrise, they found the Viracochas (which I suppose was the fancy name for the brother and sister), and they immediately declared them to be children of their god, and their supreme governors. Then continuing the play—I don't know well whether to call it a farce or a pantomime—Cocapac told the people that the Viracocha Ingasman, Cocapac (which possibly may be translated as Cock-of-the walk Englishman), had determined to search for the place where he was to reside. He requested they would take their arms and follow him, saying that, wherever he struck his golden rod, or sceptre into the ground, that was the spot where he chose to remain. The young man and woman directed their course to the plain of Cuzco, where, having arrived, the golden staff went into the earth. The first Indians, previously incredulous, surprised by the reappearance of the Viracochas, and overawed by the numbers that accompanied them, acknowledged them as their Lord, and the children of their God. "Thus, say the Indians,"—Mr. Stevenson concludes with the same gravity as he narrates the whole story,—"was the·power of the Incas established, and many of them have said that, as I was an Englishman, I was of their family." No doubt. Yet perhaps they might have added aside,—"but belonging to the Marines!"

From what I have seen of the Indians along the coast of Peru, I believe this oral tradition at Huacho was no more than a *crambe repetita* of the same fable put forward by Montesinos, Sarmiento;[2] Garcilasso de la Vega, and a host of other Spanish fabulists.

In order to point out the discrepancies, as well as resemblances, between this oral tradition,

---

[2] It will be a comfort to those who have doubts about much of the fabulous history of Peru, to read the following extract from the *Athenæum* of July 5th, 1873:—"Señor Gonzalez de la Rosa, a learned Peruvian, who is preparing editions of some important Spanish manuscripts for the press, has made an interesting discovery respecting one of Mr. Prescott's principal authorities in his 'Conquest of Peru.' Hardly any author is more frequently quoted in that work than 'Sarmiento,' whom Mr. Prescott supposed to be a writer, who had himself been long in Peru, and an eye-witness of the scenes he described. Señor de la Rosa is able to prove that the manuscript in question is really the second part of the 'Chronicle of Peru,' by Cieza de Leon (hitherto supposed to be lost); that Sarmiento was a lawyer and President of the Council of the Indies, who was never in America in his life; and that the document is merely endorsed as having been sent to him."

recorded by Stevenson, of what he heard about sixty years ago, and that published by Garcilasso de la Vega in A.D. 1609, or more than 200 years previous, I quote an extract from the latter, which is given in Rivero's work :[4]—"The Peruvians believed that the Sun, a tutelar divinity of their empire, had sent his own sons to reform and instruct them, of whom the descendants were their Incas or emperors. Previous to the arrival of these children of the Sun, Peru, like the other territories of the New World, was found, according to tradition, divided into several nations or independent tribes, wandering or fixed, rude and ferocious, whose unteachable and warlike disposition prompted them to battle continually among themselves. Ignorant of all industry and culture,[5] knowing no law of morality [which, it might have been added, they were subsequently taught by the Incas, who all had their own sisters for wives] nor any social compact, wandering through the forests [this may be supposed to refer to the forests on the coast of Peru, that, according to Rivero, "present trees, which almost serve as props to the vault of heaven"]—more resembling the brutes than the human race,—subjected to the inclemency

[4] Op. cit. p. 43.

[5] Meant, no doubt, for the prehistoric Peruvians, who built the temple of Pacha-Cámac, the grand fortresses of Huatica, and the city of Chan-Chan, and whose works of art are chronicled in this volume.

of the elements and to the molestations and evils consequent upon this savage state,—none teaching them that they might better their condition. Such was their state when the merciful father, the Sun, placed two of his children on the lake of Titicaca [it may thus be seen that Garcilasso disdains to recognize the people of the coast having anything to do with the primary migration], and told them that they might go where they wished and wheresoever they pleased ; they might stop to eat and to sleep. The Sun likewise commanded them to place in the ground a small wedge of gold which he gave them, informing them that where that wedge would sink at one blow, and go into the earth, there he wished them to stop and make their residence and court.

Arrived at the valley of Cuzco, after having vainly tried the prescribed operation through all the roads where they had travelled, they found themselves on the ridge of Huanaucauri, and there endeavoured anew to sink the wedge, which went in with so much facility at the first blow, that they saw it no more. Then said the man to his sister and wife, ' In this valley our father the Sun commands us to stop and make it our seat and residence to accomplish his will. It is necessary that we take different ways, and that each should attempt to draw together and attract these people, to indoctrinate them, and accomplish the good which our father the Sun commands.'

From the ridge of Huanaucauri the man went to the north, and the woman to the south, and harangued the multitudes, exhorting them to unite and to receive, as gifts from heaven, the counsels and instructions which they condescended to give by order of their father the Sun. Fascinated by their appearance, and confirmed by the respect with which these extraordinary beings inspired them, the wandering tribes [no doubt some of the savages before described] followed them to the valley of Cuzco, where they laid the foundation of a city. This region was the central district of these tribes, and its name, according to Garcilasso, in the language of the Incas, signifies *Navel.* And it is certain, according to the traditions of the natives, that as the navel is the source whence the infant receives life and growth in the womb, the plane* (plain ?) of Cuzco was the nucleus of civilization, and the focus of light for the State, founded by Manco Capac and Mama Oello-Huaco, as the celestial couple were called."

We are further told that Manco Capac taught the men agriculture, industry, and the useful arts, with laws, as well as political and social perfection, whilst Mama Oello "taught the women the art of spinning, weaving, and dyeing,—and at the same time the domestic virtues becoming grace, chastity, and conjugal fidelity."

The arrival of Manco Capac from Lake Titicaca,

* *Sic* in Senor Rivero's book.

Garcilasso tells us, took place in A.D. 1021, or little more than eight hundred years ago. From the few excavations I have been able to make, I am disposed to think that "agriculture, industry, and the arts," ornamental as well as useful, were known to the Peruvian races before that time, as well as that Mama Oello teaching the arts of "spinning, dyeing, and weaving," to the women, was a sort of bringing coals to Newcastle.

Garcilasso de la Vega gives account of only fourteen Incas between A.D. 1021, Manco Capac, and A.D. 1533, when Atahualpa, the last of them, was murdered by order of Pizarro in the public square of Cajamarca. Whereas Montesinos records a hundred and one (101) Incas—and although he begins them with Manco Capac's father, he traces the first appearance of that personage to an emigrant from some place abroad, who, after killing two of his brothers, proclaimed himself as a son of the Sun. The following is part of the rhapsody of Montesinos:—
"Peru was populated five hundred years after the deluge. Its first inhabitants flowed in abundantly'[1] [what a pity we are not told how they flowed, what they flowed upon, or wherefrom they flowed at all!] towards the valley of Cuzco, conducted by four brothers named Ayar-Manco-Topa, Ayar-Cachi-Topa, Ayar-Anca-Topa, and Ayar-Ucha-Topa, who were accompanied by their sisters and

[1] Rivero's Work, op. cit. p. 52.

wives [wife and sister being one and the same person, I hope it is understood], named Mama Cora, Hipa Huacum, Mama Huacum, and Pilca Huacum. The eldest of the brothers mounted to the summit of a ridge and threw with his sling a stone to each of the four quarters of the world, thus taking possession of the soil for himself and his family. He afterwards gave a name to each one of the quarters which he had reached with his sling, calling that beyond the south Colla, beyond the north Tahua, beyond the east Antituyu, beyond the west Contisuyu, and for that reason the Indians called their kings Tahuantin Súyu Capac, i. e. lord of the four quarters of the globe. The youngest of the brothers, who, according to tradition, was at the same time the most skilful and hardy, wishing to enjoy alone the plentitude of power, rid himself of two of his brothers by enclosing one of them in a cave, and throwing the other into a deep hole, and then caused the third to fly to a distant province. The fratricide consoled his sisters [they must have been very amiable, these ladies, as well as susceptible of consolation, to have taken to it under the circumstances] and told them that they must consider him as the only child or son of the Sun, and obey him as such. He commanded his kinsmen to level the ground and make houses of stone. Such was the origin of the city of Cuzco.* The neighbouring

* Montesinos supposes that the name of Cuzco is derived

nations followed the example of the vassals or subjects of Ayar-Ucha-Topa, and founded populations
in the vicinity of this city. For sixty years did
this first king govern (whom Indian traditions also
called Puhua Manco), leaving the throne to his
eldest son, Manco Capac, the fruit of his union with
his sister, Mama Cora."

Upon this I have only to observe, that Montesinos must have spent his fifteen years rather
unprofitably in Peru not to be able to get up a
better thing . than such a clumsy story. He
" studied antiquities with so much zeal," says
Rivero, " that none equalled him in archæological
knowledge." If his account of the foundation of
the Inca empire be a specimen of his research, I
for one should be much inclined to set him down
as a concocter of myths. In spite of a somewhat
similar opinion given by Rivero, although not so
emphatic, the latter says that " the relations of
Montesinos in a later period of Peruvian history
present a degree of authenticity superior to that of
Garcilasso de la Vega,"—from which I come to the
conclusion that scarcely a single word said by
either of them is to be believed.

The account given by Pedro de Cieza de Leon of
the first origin of the Incas is simply that whilst the
Devil was playing his pranks " with the people in

from Cosca, an Indian word which signifies " to level," or from
these heaps of earth, called Coscos, which were found in the
environs.

the provinces of the Collas, and in the valleys of
the Yuncas," two brothers rose up [he does not say
whether from the lake, the provinces, or the
valleys], the name of one of whom was " Manco
Coapac."[9] The marvels and fables repeated by
the Indians about these men were to have been
published by Cieza de Leon. But the second,
third, and fourth parts of his work, have not come
to light—the third and fourth being in MSS. in
the library at Madrid—and the second mislaid.[10]

Yet, devoid of its mythical tomfoolery, the
tradition of Stevenson, about some white man
wanderer having settled in Peru, is worthy of
being discussed. Particularly when we find that a
somewhat similar legend exists about white men
in Brazil,[1] before its discovery by the Portuguese.
Another white man, " a bearded white man,[2] has
been accredited by ·the Mexicans as a legislator
called Quatzalcoati, the high-priest of Cholula,
chief of a religious sect, as well as legislator. He
preached peace to men and prohibited all sacrifices
to the Deity, excepting the firstfruits. These three
white men, together with another—bearded likewise,—and having a triplicate of aliases, Bochica,
Nemquetheba, or Subé, recognized as a legislator
by the Muysca Indians of the plains of Cundina-

[9] Cieza de Leon's Op. cit. p. 136.
[10] This is the book erroneously attributed to Sarmiento. Look
back to note at page 108.
[1] Stevenson's Op. cit. vol. i. p. 397.
[2] Stephenson's Op. cit. p. 65.

marca, should not be passed over in the still unsettled question as to the origin of the early Peruvian race. It seems to me outside the point, the argument of Stevenson that the Inca laws did not "bear any resemblance to those of any of the northern governments, except setting aside lineal descent, the papal, where the spiritual authority is exercised by the King (query Pope ?) of Rome."[1] Because, in the times when such incidents may be supposed to have taken place, it was not at all probable that such adventurers, as those spoken of, should bring with them the laws or religion of the countries whence they came. We are more likely to approach to whatever truth may be in these traditions, by comparing the arts and manufactures to be discovered in the burial-mounds, than by any reasoning of analogy in " religion and legislature."

A few miles from Huacho stands the small town of Huaura, which is the capital of the province of Chancay. This place has got a considerable number of sugar-cane factories, and of course plantations in the neighbourhood to correspond. By the side of Huaura goes out into the sea a river of the same name, which has its origin so far up in the Andes as Cajatambo. This and the Pasamayo already mentioned are the only two rivers of the province. The Cajatambo source of the Huaura I give on the authority of Mariano Felipe Paz

<hr>

[1] Stevenson's Op. cit. vol. i. p. 399.

Soldan,[4] whereas Dr. Tschudi says it is formed
by the union of two rivers. The larger of the two
rises in the Cordillera of Paria, and flows through
the wild ravine of Chiu Chiu. The smaller river,
called the Rio Chico de Sayan, rises from a lake
of considerable size in the Altos de Hunquimarcu.
Both unite below the village of Sayan.

The map which accompanies this book makes
me incline to believe the correctness of Doctor
Tschudi's account. For it will be seen there is a
considerable difference in the relative positions
of Cajatambo and Huaura;—the river Barranca,
higher up the coast, being the one that rises near
Cajatambo. Except for geographical accuracy, it
is not, however, of much consequence.

Between Huacho and Supé we pass a point
called Atahuanqui, close to which are two enormous mounds, resembling those of the Campana,
and San Miguel in the Huatica valley. We are
not near enough to make out by a glass whether
they are burial (huacas) or fortress mounds.

Supé is about 120 miles north of Calláo, and is
the northern boundary of the jurisdiction of that
port. It is a very quiet spot as regards the
condition of the sea, and therefore easy for landing.
The chief exports hence are cotton, wool, and occasionally a little silver ore. From Lima, through
Chancay and Huacho as far as this, a general
feature of the farm places is the feeding of pigs.

[4] "Geography of Peru," p. 321.

Before coming to Supé we pass by the island of San Martin, parallel and interior to which we get glimpses of the Beagle mountains, marked on the chart as 4000 feet high. In the neighbour-hood of Supé are many mounds, of which nothing is known; and on the top of a small hill you can see the remnants of an old city. Ask a Peruvian about them, and he will tell you they are of the Inca period. Whereas the fact is they are of a prehistoric people, of whom all other possible traces were swept away by the Incas, except the grand old ruins that they could not destroy.

About two miles and a half beyond Supé we pass Barranca, where we see some bathing-boxes on the shore. This is the bathing-place for Patavilca, Paramunca, and Barrancas, all of which are most interesting for exploration. Here, according to Garcilasso de la Vega, we are coming on the territory of the great Chimoo, who offered more resistance to the Incas than any other of the coast rulers.[a] Close to where we are now, I can see two streams pouring down from the bank into the sea—a very rare sight along the Peruvian coast. Up to this the last-named has the same forbidding aspect which it

[a] Yet Salcamayhua says, "The Inca Pachacuti marched to the country of the Chimoo, where was Chimu Capac, the chief of the Yuncas, *who submitted, and did all that was required of him.*" Rites and Laws of the Incas, translated by Clements R. Markham, C.B. Page 94.

presents all along—cindery-looking islets, stretches
of sand—now and then a patch of verdure, which
one cannot help pitying, in its sickly appearance,
knowing, as we do, that it never receives a drop
of rain—ranges of mountains at different heights,
—with intervening gaps, and conical tops. Behind
these is a dense cloud, through which we occasionally get a view of an Andine peak,—at once assert-
ing its supremacy. Still, with the "one step from
the sublime to the ridiculous," the Cholos on
board paying their devotions to the deck, or to
the oilcloth on the cabin-floor.

Four leagues to the north of Supé we pass what
is styled the hacienda of Paramunca—a large
sugar-cane establishment. This, no doubt, derives
its name from Paramanca, or Paramunca, the place
reputed by Garcilasso de la Vega, and believed in by
Mr. Markham, Dr. Tschudi, and all previous writers
about Peru, as the locale where the Incas erected
a fortress to celebrate the conquest of the Chimoo
monarch, and the subjugation of his territories.
In Dr. Tschudi's work * is a note, which contra-

* "According to some ancient authors, Paramanca was built
by King Chimu (this ought to be the king of Chimoo, as his
territory was called, the last great monarch being Chucha
Machoon as a frontier fortress against the neighbouring
nations." The Doctor adds, "There is some foundation for
this view of the subject, as Chima Caucha (Chucha Machoon),
long before he was attacked by Capac Yupanqui, carried on war
most fiercely with Cuys Mancu, King of Pacha-Cámac, and
Chuquiz Mancu, King of Runahuanac (the present Limahuana.)"
Op. cit. p. 219.

dicts this idea, and seems to me the proper view of the case. For an English gentleman who was on board, and who resides at Paramunca hacienda, told me he saw no difference from each other, in any of the buildings here, as regards their seeming antiquity, appearance, and style of structure. "They are," he added, "exactly like the mounds in the Huatica valley." Of these I had shown him the sketches.

The dispute between Dr. Unanue and Dr. Tschudi as to this fortress being built to commemorate the peace between the Inca, and the conquered, is scarcely worth discussing. The Spaniards, at all events, by giving the neighbourhood the title of Barranca, or the bank— by which name we are also directed to it in Garcilasso de la Vega—have managed to confound the whole of the surroundings. There is a small river of Patavilca running into the sea near the hacienda. The fortress is built on an isolated small hill, to which some writers have given the title of "Cerro de la Horca," or Gallows Hill. Because here, they say, was kept a prison by somebody at some time or another. The mode of punishment, for capital offences, was by flinging the condemned from the top, about 300 feet high, and with a precipitous face to the sea, down on some sharp rocks that are underneath. If this be correct, it must destroy any claim made for the Incas as to their having had it in their programme. For they surely came

to preach "benevolence and suavity," according to
their historians. The word Paramanca, Tschudi
tells us, means in the Quichua, "rain-pot" [1]—a
title difficult to understand in a part of the coast,
where rain is not known, except a few times during
a century.

It is but fair to add that Senor Don Mariano
Felipe Paz Soldan, in his "Geography of Peru," [2]
speaks of these ruins as entirely belonging to the
Chimoo period. He mentions the fortress, which
is quadrangular,—its walls of large adobe (tapia),
and measuring 300 yards in length by 200 in
breadth. Within it are other squares, with bastions and passages of narrow ways—in fact, the
same style of building as we saw at Huatica
valley, and as we shall see in a few days at Chan-
Chan, near Trujillo. These stone circles that we
observe on the sharp rock, he speaks of as the
prisons of the Chimoo king, from which criminals
were thrown.

Of the fortress here, Stevenson remarks :[3]—
"About five miles from Patavilca, and a hundred and
twenty from Lima, is a place called Paramonga, or
the Fortaleza [the latter being no doubt the
Spanish title for it]. The ruins of a fortified
palace of very great extent are here visible; the
walls are of tempered clay, about six feet thick.

[1] *Para* (rain), *manca* (pot).
[2] Op. cit. p. 233.
[3] Op. cit. vol. ii. p. 22.

The principal building stood on an eminence, but the walls were continued to the foot of it like regular circumvallations; the ascent winded round the hill like a labyrinth, having many angles, which probably served as outworks to defend the place. It is supposed to have belonged to the Chimu, or King of Mansichi, and was a frontier palace during the time of the Incas [or more probably during the period of the Inca invasion]. The oral traditions of the Indians say that at this place the Chimu did homage to Pachacutec, the tenth Inca."

Oral tradition is therefore antagonistic to Garcilasso de la Vega's history, which tells us that Pachacutec (who was the ninth, and not the tenth, Inca) never came here at all; for the war against the Chimoo people was carried on by his son, Yunpanqui, who was the tenth Inca. In this neighbourhood much treasure has been also excavated—all of which must have been concealed by the prehistoric Indians, as we have no evidence of the Incas having ever occupied this part of Peru after they subdued it.

From Supé to the next stopping-place we have a trip of fifty-four miles. This is what we find on Fitzroy's Admiralty Chart marked down as "Guarmey,"—on the Pacific Steam Navigation Company's list "Huarmey," and which is spoken of by Garcilasso de la Vega (as repeated by Mr. Markham) as "Huallmi."

There is a very excellent bay here, and the ruins
of an old fort on a mound in front of where our
steamer is anchored; but no other sign of human
habitation. In the harbour is one small rocky
islet. On our way up to this from Supé, we
passed a place, thirty miles to the south, called
Callejones (the blind alleys)—though whence the
derivation of the word I am at a loss to conjecture,—
and in which Captain Bird tells me he is never at
a loss for a mark to tell him his exact position, be
it clear or cloudy. For always in the same spot,
between his steamer and the shore, there is a flock
of birds on the water. This has been his experience for two years.

From Guarmey a captain of the port comes off,
although it is difficult to guess what are the
precise duties of such an official in the place.
There are some few huts up in one corner of the
harbour, seeming at first sight as if they had
been chiselled out of the adjoining rock, from their
similarity of colour. The chief produce hence
is maize and a small quantity of potatoes. But
the wonder to any one, who goes no nearer than
the deck of the steamer, is where they grow the
maize and potatoes in question; as not a vestige
of verdure is visible anywhere. I am told, that
behind the hills is a real town of Guarmey, or
Huallmi, with a population of about a thousand
inhabitants; and thereabouts possibly may be
found the agricultural districts.

Fifty-four miles farther north, we find ourselves in the Bay of Casma, protected by very high precipitous rocks on the south side; and having a rough beach, with an angry sea to the north. The town here is built in the south-eastern corner of the bay. It owns an iron mole of considerable length, which has for some years past been rendered perfectly useless and unapproachable, from the silting up of sand at the mouth of the river by which it stands, and whereby boats cannot of course approach. The town, which is behind the mole, has a large church with a huge dome on it. This is at present the native outlet from the city of Huaraz, to which latter Mr. Henry Meiggs has a railway in progress from the Bay of Chimbote farther on.

Sumanco Bay, twenty-two miles north of Casma, presents the same desolate appearance of every place on this coast. It is, however, a very extensive harbour, the chief signs of life—besides the boisterous crying out of some boatmen that are coming to the steamer for cargo—being of a few pelicans, and penguins that are about. At the southern corner is a small excuse for a village, in which there is an exceedingly comfortable-looking house belonging to Mr. Henry Swayne, of Lima, who has a large sugar plantation some eight or ten leagues to the interior. Behind this house is visible the green of the Sumanco valley, apparently stretching to the southward. Into this bay falls a small river, or rather a rivulet, called the Nepeña. The bay here is from six to eight miles across; and to the north side there is only a spit of sand—a few miles in width—separating it from Chimbote. Our steamer, however, is obliged to make a small détour past some of the bald, and hump-backed looking islets, such as we have been passing all the way up to this from Callao.

Chimbote[1] is another large bay, with a very

CHOLO MAN AT CHIMBOTE.

extensive sand plateau between it and the Cordilleras. The appearance of the mole, with the fresh-

[1] Paz Soldan's "Geography of Peru" does not mention Casma, Sumanco, or Chimbote.

ness and comfort of all the houses occupied by the
staff, working for the railway here, gives it quite
an attractive inducement to go ashore.   At this
bay there are soundings of five fathoms of water
not   more   than   300   yards   from   the   beach.
Although, up to the time of occupation by the
railway people, it was nothing but a deserted and
barren spot, it has now extensive stores, dwelling-
houses, workshops, and the inevitable consequence
—a Peruvian Custom-house.

CHOLO WOMAN.

The first notion of a railway between the coast
and Huaraz—from Santa or Chimbote—appears
to have been a proposal of Mr. John Edmonson

in the year 1864. From this date till the final contract, confirmed to Mr. Henry Meiggs on the 31st of October, 1871, there were several other attempts made in the same direction. The names of Senor Don Eugenio Higueras, as of Senores Valdea, Vellano, and Derteano, appear amongst the number of those, whose proposals ended *in nubibus*. In like manner terminated a decree of the minister, Santa Maria (during the Balta Presidency), to have the Lima and Huacho rail-road—as yet only done to Chancay—extended on to Huaraz.

It was on the report of the engineers on this line, given in to Government on the 16th of September, 1871, that the contract of Mr. Meiggs was founded. The road is being carried on, like all the other works of this great contractor, with energy and the best of execution.

The Cholo labouring classes here present the same features as they do all along the coast from Iquique to Payta. The illustrations in this chapter will give an idea of their physical type.

CHAPTER XXIV.

Twenty miles north of Chimbote, we come to Santa, another spacious bay, in its general features somewhat resembling the former as well as like to Sumanco. The houses of Santa have quite a homely look about them, and the green fringe of its spacious valley comes down to the water's edge in a thick cluster.

Santa is one of the provinces of the department of what was formerly called Ancachs, but which, since 1839, has been entitled Huaylas,—from the name of a place where was fought a battle that

destroyed the power of General Santa Cruz.[1]
Whether it ever had another name than this I
cannot say, for of its history I can trace no further
back than Garcilasso de la Vega, and he says about
it,[2]—" The inhabitants of Sancta [the real Spanish
' holy ' name] showed themselves more warlike
than those of Huallmi and Parmunca, by going to
meet the enemy [the Inca Yupanqui] and defend
their country. They fought with much spirit and
strength on every time when they had opportunity
to fight. For a considerable time they resisted
successfully the efforts of their invaders. They
gained even the respect of their enemies from their
valour, and raised very considerably the hopes of
their Curaça, the Grand Chimu."

The exports hence are chiefly maize, cotton, a little alfalfa, and a considerable amount
of rice. The town has a population of about
fifteen hundred, and the country all around
is studded with ruins of burial-grounds, fortresses, palaces, castles, and every kind of
building which comes under the generic title of
Huaca. In the bay are two small islands—one
of which is called the Corcobado, or crooked-
backed—the other is only a trifle of something
volcanic.

From Santa to the Guanape islands—one of the
chief treasure-groups in the matter of guano—our

---

[1] Soldan's "Geography of Peru," p. 227.
[2] Op. cit. cap. xxxii. p. 113.

course was about west by north, and the distance thirty-two miles. As we did not arrive till eight p.m., and the steamers only call with passengers and mails, I could not see much of the islands. The moon was shining brightly, and the masts of forty to fifty vessels, being loaded with guano, were distinctly visible—part against the brown island, and part set off by the moonlit blue sky. There are 500 Chinamen occupied here, who are employed by the Guano Loading Company, that has a contract with Messrs. Dreyfus Brothers and Co., of Paris, the lessees of these islands from the Peruvian Government.   Of the guano produce, Mr. Heaton, late British Vice-Consul at the Guanape islands, has furnished me with the following details :—

"The deposits in the Guanape islands were first worked in the early part of 1869, since which time till present date, 30th September, 1871, 838,853 tons (more or less) of guano have been shipped.

"The dimensions of the north island are—

		Metres.
Length	. . .	1,050
Breadth	. . .	700

"The quantity of guano left on this island at present date is very small, being about 12,000 to 15,000 tons.

"The dimensions of the south island are—

	Metres.
Length . .	690
Breadth	570
Height of top of guano above sea level . .	160
Height of base of guano in present working .	120
Distance between north and south islands .	2,800

"The quantity of guano still on this south island may be estimated at about 450,000 tons."

PENGUIN FOUND UNDER GUANO AT GUANAPE [*]

The Guanape islands, as well as the Chincha, give their evidence of the antiquity of life in Peru. At a depth of thirty-two feet under the guano here has been found the body of a flattened Penguin, with a piece of cloth underneath, given to me by Captain Bird. Several idols have been discovered here likewise, and the Chinese

[*] This was put upright when the sketch was taken. In its flattened position it is only half an inch in thickness, from the enormous weight and length of time of the superincumbent pressure.

workmen have turned up gold ornaments, which, of course, were at once appropriated and partitioned, according to their ordinary usages in cases of treasure trove.

Fifty miles farther on, again bound north, we find ourselves in the awful roadstead of Huanchaco. This certainly cannot be the place about which some writer in " Household Words "[1] chaunts of,—

> " Where the smooth Pacific swells
> Beneath an arch of blue,"—

for to-day, the 1st of December, 1872, the smooth Pacific is more like to the Bay of Biscay after a good south-western has been clawing it for some days, or to the harbour of Lagos, on the West Coast of Africa, during a tornado. The " arch of blue " must be somewhere behind the scenes, for the view from the steamer's deck is exactly like the view from the centre of London, or Westminster bridge during a November fog. However, as my time is limited, I must make the venture to get on shore. Captain Bird tells me the *lancheros* are very expert; although only a week had passed since such a boat as they use here was upset in the surf at Eten (farther up the coast), and five persons drowned. The sea at the last-mentioned place, I am told, is not half so bad as at Huanchaco; and this is very comforting to know. From my note-book of this period I make the following extract:—

" *Trujillo, December, 1st.*—Coming ashore this

[1] Vol. v. p. 54.

morning at Huanchaco, I was disposed for a reflection, such as I have more than once found myself employed in elsewhere—referring to places, disturbed like the waters of this port. The cogitation almost resolved itself into a conviction, that when such ports along the sea-coast of Peru were formed, they must have been fashioned by the Creator of the universe with the intention—that none of the residents inside should ever come out, or that any people from the outer world abroad should ever go in. But the boatmen did their work in excellent style, and I was put on shore without being sprinkled by a drop of water. In effecting the landing I must try to explain how it was done. From the moment that the boat shoved off from the ship, the men on board seemed to know every wave and roller around. They did not rush right through these, or the craft would have been swamped. But by means of clever steering, and what I cannot help calling scientific dodging of the tremendous breakers—now with the boat's side lying parallel to the surging wave— now with her head to the coming in of an immense mass, over which the launch was made to float like a duck—and after half-an-hour of this kind of thing,· with a spurt, as we got inside the breakers, we were pulled on to the beach. A number of helping hands being ready, she was hauled up high and dry."

Huanchaco is a miserable, dirty rancheria (collection of ranchos or huts) ;—the front shore space having a large shed on it for temporary

Custom-house purposes, with the Pacific Navigation Company's offices on the right hand, and the captain of the port's office in front of where we are landed. There is a melancholy-looking church, with an empty bell-tower on a rising ground in front. But, walking up a street, large black letters, forming the word "Hotel," painted on a flaunting white calico flag, lured me at once to ask for my breakfast. I was told that no breakfast could be had at the hotel; the fonda being the place for that. I confess that I did not regret this information, for without any reference to the old story of sour grapes, the hotel was anything but attractive. The fonda, round the corner, did not show much more agreeable appearance, as far as cleanliness was concerned. The floor was damp—the chairs ricketty,—on the tables in the dining-room were what might have been either slices from dirty sheets, or relics of towels from the Inca times—and out of either no kind of conviction could realize table-cloths. However, a good appetite makes one resolved to look on these matters as secondary, particularly as soon as a well-cooked Churasco [*] was served up by the Chinaman attendant. This fonda is entirely under Chinese *ménage*, which may perhaps account for the combination of dirt and good cooking.

Huanchaco has only a few hundred houses—each one seeming more dilapidated than its neighbour—and all having that shaky condition of walls

[*] South American beef-steak.

STUCCO WORK FROM RUIN-WALLS OF CHAN-CHAN.

so suggestive of impotency against earthquakes.
Many of the houses here are empty, and on subsequently inquiring the cause at Trujillo, I was
informed that these are owned by the gentry
from that place, who come down in large numbers
to bathe during summer.

In as short time as I could after breakfast,
I was *en route* to Trujillo, in a carriage kindly
sent down for me by Mr. Blackwood. I could
not think, however, of going to visit Pizarro's
city,[*] without having a look at the ruins of
Chan-Chan (the name of the Chimoo capital),
more particularly as the high road, from Huanchaco to Trujillo, passes right through the middle
of them. All that I had learned about Chimu (or
Chimoo, as it is pronounced) from Paz Soldan—
after mentioning the name of the capital, Chan-
Chan—is that the king of these parts held sway
over the coast from Supé to Tumbez (nearly one-
half of the coast territory of Peru) when he was
come down upon by the Inca ;—that the ruins consist of two magnificent palaces, and many houses,
over a space of five leagues square ;'—that it has
remnants of splendid walls as well as of aqueducts
and other engineering works for bringing waters
to the artificial meadows ;—of cultivated grounds ;

* Trujillo was founded by Francisco Pizarro in A.D. 1535,
and was given this name as an honour to his native town of
Trujillo in the province of Estramadura, Spain.

' Mariano Eduardo Rivero says " *the ruins of Chimu* (?) cover
a space of three quarters of a league, exclusive of the great
squares." Op. cit. p. 264.

of relics of their idolatrous worship,—with impregnable fortresses to sustain their sovereignty. In fact, such a description of generalization as I suppose to have been written by a man who never visited the place at all.

The road, from Huanchaco to Trujillo, is nearly ten miles in length, and at about seven miles from Huanchaco, we are inside of Chan-Chan. This road goes right through a causeway,[*] about four feet above the ground, and leading from one great mass of ruins to another,—ruins of what have been either forts, castles, or palaces, although they get the title of Huacas. That to the right is the Huaca del Toledo (of which the original Indian name was Llomayoahan), and that to the left is entitled the Huaca del Obispo (or Huaca of the Bishop), its Indian nomenclature not known. I was met here by Mr. Blackwood, Colonel La Rosa, and Mr. Hugh Carrige, C.E., who accompanied me in my wanderings amongst the relics of this great old city. The whole distance from Huanchaco is marked by bits of walls, remnants of houses, and broken pottery, strewed along, so that it seems to me very difficult to distinguish the limits of the inhabited part of this valley.

Several hours' wandering amongst the lofty broken walls and ruins of houses in Chan-Chan—on horses kindly furnished by Mr. Blackwood—gave

---

[*] Colonel La Rosa informed me that there is a tunnel beneath this causeway.

me only a confused idea of its extent.   But Colonel
La Rosa, although an old explorer here, could not
point out what were palaces or what were not.
Neither could any of our party distinguish them.
Those large square enclosures, shut in by walls
(wedge-shaped) of adobe, twenty to twenty-
five feet high, have nothing of an entrance into
them that could be defined to be a palace gate.
There are no less than half a dozen of these
amongst the ruins.   Within some of them are
large square mounds of burying-chambers, many
of which have been opened and rifled of their
contents.   These are all plastered at the ceilings.
Besides the two so-called huacas, already mentioned, there is another on the left side of the
road, to which the Spaniards gave the title of
" La Misa," or the Mass, but the Indian name
whereof is Yomayugari.

On many of the walls, particularly on the left
side of the road, is some excellent stucco-work.
This may be considered chiefly so as regards the
material of which it is made, more than any
reference to its style of art.   For there is not a
single grain of disintegration in the parts that
surround the walls of a chamber—although it is
half an inch high above the ordinary plaster on
which it is done,—nor the slightest item of impair-
ment in its integrity during the many centuries it
has stood exposed to the elements.

The highest enclosures—those of adobe brick
up to thirty feet, and with a base of fifteen feet,

or five yards'—must have cost an immense amount of labour, and needed a large number of hands for their erection. These high walls are all on the right-hand side of the city as you advance to Trujillo, between that town and the Huaca of Llomayoahan.[1] Inside of some of them, besides the square mounds, are narrow passages not more than a yard in width. In others are squares, wherein are visible, though now filled with clay, the outlines of water tracks. But such things as Rivero speaks of,[2]—"adobes, often of twelve yards long and five or six broad in the lower part of the wall"—do not exist. On this side, too, appears the greater number of what we can recognize as burial-mounds. In some of these are stairs of adobe. One of such I counted with fifteen steps, each of about a yard from end to end. The greater number of these stairs are double— that is to say, like the steps on each side of many a hall door—but the walls and structures to which they mount are so much destroyed that it is diffi- cult even to guess at what might have been their original intention.

Several of the burial-vaults having been ran- sacked, the stones and adobes constituting their

* Mariano Eduardo Rivero (op. cit. p. 265) speaks of these walls as fifty yards (a hundred and fifty feet) high—a very great exaggeration.

[1] Alias Toledo.

[2] Op. cit. p. 265.

structure are lying about.   In some of these the
ceilings are not only plastered, but whitewashed.
From them treasures of gold and silver as well as
works of art have been taken.   One of those little
silver cylinders, exactly similar in shape and material to that I have already shown as found at

SILVER CYLINDER FROM A BURIAL-PLACE AT CHAN-CHAN.

Icæ,[3] is now in my possession, and was given to
me by Mr. Blackwood.[4] In another of these burial-
places, entitled the Huaca de la Concha (or Huaca
of the Shell)—its Indian name is Mansuvillaga—
several gold idols have been dug out, and amongst
them were found mantles of silk interwoven with
gold and silver thread.   It almost gives me the
primary symptoms of tertian fever to be told that
the iconoclasts, who discovered these, tore them

[3] *Vide* chap. vii. p. 122.
[4] In this the figures are stamped, being convex on the front.
It may be observed, the Lunar Zodiac is again represented here
in the stars on the cross.

up for the sake of the precious metals which they
contained, thus illustrating what Virgil apostro-
phized two thousand years ago :—

> " Auri sacra fames !
>   Quid non mortalia pectora cogis ?"

So far as the palaces are concerned (of which
Mariano Rivero, Bollaert, Markham, and Paz

WATER-CROFT WITH SERPENT DESIGNS, FRONT VIEW.

Soldan write), I regret that I could find no traces
of them, nor was Colonel La Rosa able to point
them out. They might have been any of these
big mounds inside the square enclosures, which in
their present state bear as much resemblance to the
ruins of a police-barrack as to those of a palace.
From the excavations here several excellent specimens of pottery have been given to me by Mr.

Blackwood—amongst them two remarkable ones
—of which the first shows the symbol of serpent
worship, and the second is of a face having more

SAME WATER-CROFT, SIDE VIEW.

of the Aryan or Phœnician type than of the Indian.
But the general impression left by the ruins of
Chan-Chan can be only described as an agglome-
ration of walls—squares of mounds—gable ends
of houses—lines of water channels—deep excavations[1] (from 20 to 30 feet in profundity, and 70
to 100 feet square) lined with small stones, and a
general crowding-up of adobe ruins everywhere.

[1] These are supposed by Colonel La Rosa to have been
granaries.

CHAPTER XXV.

In his "Geography of Peru," [1] Senor Paz Soldan says that this beautiful city of Trujillo, which is of an oval or elliptical form, and completely walled in, has been frequently damaged by earthquakes, as well as by water inundations from the mountains. The latter were especially strong in the years 1701, 1720, and 1728. So late as in 1816, and previously in 1725 and 1759, occurred dreadful earthquakes, the severest of these having destroyed the whole of the chapels in the town except one. They, however, are all right now. That which was preserved is Pizarro's chapel—the first after

[1] Page 214.

you enter the gate of the city from the Huanchaco road.   The relics of the Indian town of Mansiché —by some writers confounded with Trujillo—are passed about half a mile to the westward of this gate, and near to where we observe a not very sprightly style of chapel.   Over this entrance outside is painted on a white ground, in black letters, and set off by the brightest of bright blue walls adjoining, the following inscription, which I translate from the Spanish :—"Trujillo was the first capital that in Peru proclaimed emancipation, on the 29th of December, 1820."

The wall enclosing Trujillo, with its several gates, and bastions, was built in A.D. 1686, and this is the only city in Peru, except Lima, that is inclosed by walls.   But, like these of the capital, being in process of demolition (as I have already noticed, under the magic sway of the railway king, Mr. Henry Meiggs), those at Trujillo are also in progress of being pulled down for the railway that is to cross to the valley of Chicama, from the neighbouring port of Salaverry—an enterprise which is in the hands of Senor Larranage, of Lima, and under the engineering charge of Mr. Hugh Carrigo, C.E.

There are nine chapels in Trujillo, including the cathedral,—a very spacious building in the principal plaza.   Besides these, there is a theatre and a large market-place.   Trujillo has likewise its bank. The streets in general are wider than they are usually found in Peruvian towns, but they communicate the same *dolce far niente* sensation that is met almost everywhere in South America. Its present population does not exceed five to six thousand inhabitants. Indeed, it seems very much of a stationary city, without any change from century to century.

Trujillo has had, in its colonial days, five orders of monks—1st, of San Francisco; 2nd, San Domingo, founded in the time of Pizarro, or at the first erection of the city; 3rd, of Our Lady of Mercy; 4th, the monks of San Augustine, established on 25th October, 1558; and of Religious Hospitality, in 1680. All of these orders are now suppressed.

There are, however, still in Trujillo two communities of religious ladies—namely, that of Santa Clara and that of the Carmelites. The first was founded in A.D. 1587, and the second in A.D. 1724. Their large rents are said to have diminished very much of late years; and although each of their establishments (surrounded by walls of eighteen to twenty feet high) seems sufficiently extensive to hold some thousands of inmates, the Santa Clara has only nineteen *religieuses* inside its walls. Of the number of Carmelites I could obtain no information.

In the neighbourhood of Trujillo are two small towns of Indians—one that of Moché, with a

population of about 2000.   It is a league and a
half south of the city, and within half a mile of the
sea.   The inhabitants are the market-gardeners
for Trujillo, as it is from their little farms that

TINTED SHROUD IN WHICH A FŒTUS WAS ENROLLED AND BURIED AT CHAN-CHAN.

the town is supplied with maize, melons, alfalfa,
potatoes, and other vegetables.   To the north-east
of Moché is another small village—that of Huamán, with a population of from 200 to 250, horti-
culturists, like the Mochénos.   The river of Moché,

which is tho chief source of water supply to
Trujillo, falls into the sea between Huamán and
Moché.   Besides this there are two other streams
in the province of Trujillo—one of Chicama,
which runs from the heights of Cajamarca, and
the other that of Virú, Birú, or Pirú (from which,
somehow or other, the Republic is said to derive
its name).   This last-mentioned rises from a Cordillera called Conchucos.   Whilst at Trujillo I cannot avoid observing how active were the Spaniards
at the period of the conquest.   The butchery of
Atahualpa occurred in 1533; Lima and Trujillo
were founded in the same year of 1535, or two
years after; and yet we find Pedro de Cieza de
Leon not very long after, visiting this neighbourhood, and telling us of the Spaniards with their
orchards, vines, figs, pomegranates, and many
other fruits of Spain.—But he only devotes one
page of his book to Trujillo, and in this only a
single mention is made of the ": Valley of Chimu."[1]

The remnants of the Indian tribes here, of
whom I have written as located at Mansiché,
Moché, and Huamán, have exactly the same
physical type of the Cholos that are seen all
along the coast.   You cannot, for any bribe or
consideration of reward, induce these people to
dig for huacas, or for such treasures as are buried
with the dead, at any period except that of full
moon.   Because, they say, that at all other seasons

[1] Op. cit. p. 244.

the huacas, as well as gold and silver, sink beyond their reach. This is more particularly observed with reference to such of these, as whistle at the side on which the bird's head is designed, when water is poured into the opposite.

At a place called Conaché, about two leagues and a half to the north-east of Trujillo, Mr. Black-wood had an extensive cochineal plantation. For many years the farm produced above 125 bales, of a quintal and a half (or 150 lbs.) to each bale of the insect. In the year 1871, when the great floods did so much damage all along this part of the coast, there was an inundation from the mountains on the farm of Mr. Black-wood, which destroyed 17,000 dollars' worth of cochineal, with its cactus plant, in a few hours. The most curious feature of this deluge was of its being followed, before the water finally sank into the earth or evaporated, by millions of a small cricket-like reptile—locust, probably—which devoured everything green as fast as it sprang up. The de-struction of these plagues was a very difficult matter.

A pair of fresh horses having been procured, I rode out with Mr. Blackwood to see the remains of the Temple of the Sun on the day after we had been at Chan-Chan. It is situated about a mile and a half to the eastward of Trujillo—placed right under the shadow of a hill, nearly a thousand feet high, and this hill to the eastward, so as to prevent the sun from having a gleam on it till the day is well advanced. It is of exactly the same style of architecture as those fortress mounds described in the Huatica valley,[1] of large adobones in some parts, and of small adobes in others; a mass of parapets and of declivities, built up with adobes, and filled with clay; being about ninety feet high, but more than a hundred yards in length, and from sixty to seventy in breadth. On the side facing the south, and at a height of about seventy feet, is the first plateau, which I guessed to be twenty yards in width. From this the elevation to the top is brought up in ledges or terraces—each one like the step of a flight of stairs—but separately high enough for a man of ordinary height to stand with his feet clear of the head beneath him. Whether this was a fortress or a castle, I cannot say. Neither can I believe that it was ever a Temple of the Sun. The base of it is not distant more than a few hundred yards from the hill, which shuts out the morning sunshine.

Making a tour of observation, after going up to the top and coming down again, we saw an opening made at the eastern side looking towards the mountain. This being near enough to the ground, Mr. Blackwood crept in, and I followed —for it was only three to four feet high. We penetrated to about four yards' distance on our hands and knees, when by groping we found that

[1] *Vide* chaps. xiii. xiv.

we could stand up. We learnt nothing by our
expedition, except, through the aid of a match,
to see a few partial excavations made from an
enlarged space in which we found ourselves,—and
still the darkness proving that no opening had
been made towards the light. Our matches
roused the bats, whose fluttering soon drove us
out of their territory.

Between this great building and the mountain
adjoining—indeed, built into it—we see traces of
a wall, which may perhaps be part of the four-yards-
wide wall spoken of by Rivero. Hereabouts the
ground is literally paved with bits of broken
crockery-ware. In part of this, too, we see where
these immense heaps of drifting sand ' have buried
the portion of ruins which join the mountain. I
cannot recognize any evidence of its having been a
Temple of the Sun, or a convent of virgins. If it were
held as such by the Incas, the question again arises,
Who built up some rooms with adobes, and filled
others with clay? That this was done by the
Incas does not seem at all probable ; that it was
effected by the Spaniards, after the conquest, appears
equally unlikely. I am also puzzled to know what
the conquerors had to conquer here—for except in
these grand old mounds, or fortresses, that might
have been built ages before the coming of
Pizarro, there is no evidence of his having had
anything to subdue in the valley of the Chimoos,

' Médanos.

near Chan-Chan, than there was in the valley of the Yuncas at Rimac.

Trujillo, though having much of the monotonous square-square-ism of Spanish-built towns, has an excellent road from its gate to Huanchaco. The first half-mile of that comprises a boulevard, or alameda, with trees on either side, and seats at different distances. Those terminate as we get near to Mansiché.

Returning to Huanchaco to proceed northward, I find the sea still very much agitated, but nothing like what it was the day that I entered. The port of Salaverry, two leagues south, and whence is to proceed the railroad to the valley of Chicama, is said to be quieter than this of Huanchaco. More rough, at all events, it would be impossible to find it. The whole of this voyage up to San José appears rather boisterous; but this can scarcely be wondered at, as it is all an open roadstead. The valley of Chicama extends thirty leagues interior to Trujillo, and the Cordilleras all around are rich in silver ore.

South of Trújillo, in the direction of the Piru river, is another large building, twice the size of that I saw with Mr. Blackwood, which is also reputed to have been a Temple of the Sun. It is called San Juan, but my faith being already shaken in the reputed Temples of the Sun on the Pacific Coast, I did not care to go and look at it.

It was quite a comforting piece of information

to be told that the city of Trujillo is very well conducted as regards its population—little or no crime being ever committed in it. Indeed, I am assured that, in the possibility of bad people (*malas gentes*) venturing in here, they are at once stamped out by the moral force of the popular indignation. Of what form this takes I am not cognizant.

It appears to me somewhat curious that no notice of these ruins of Chan-Chan is made in any of the six quarto volumes by the brothers Ulloa, although much space is dedicated in the second of these to a description of Trujillo, its ecclesiastical discipline, and its haciendas.

" Trujillo," says Stevenson,' " is noted for its Quixotic nobility; it is often said that the body of the celebrated Don was buried here. I have frequently," he continues, " seen in the house of a Mulatto or a Zambo a full-length portrait of the individual, who by a kind of *faux-pas* caused them to emerge from the African race and sable colour, and of whom they speak with as much respect as the Montaneses do of Don Pelayo, whose descendants they all pretend to be, or as any nobleman of England would do of Ptolemy or Alexander, if he fancied that he could trace his pedigree either to the Egyptian astronomer, or the Macedonian hero."

Leaving aside the genealogical fancy in the last

* Op. cit. vol. ii. p. 117.

sentence, I cannot avoid coming to the conclusion that to the belief of Don Quixote being buried in Trujillo may be traced no inconsiderable part of the romantic gasconading, written about this and many adjacent parts of Peru. Indeed, the life of the famous Knight of La Mancha has many episodes in it, not more absurd than much that is recorded about the Incas. Cervantes seems to have been the chief model of the majority of writers in the early times.

CHAPTER XXVI.

During my stay at Trujillo, I obtained through
Mr. Blackwood, from the municipal records of the
city, copy of a document highly interesting to all
persons who care about the archæology of Peru.

This is a "copy of the accounts that are found
in the book of Fifths of the Treasury in the years
1577 and 1578 (nearly three hundred years ago),
referring to the huaca of Toledo." Of its authenticity Mr. Blackwood assures me there can be no
doubt, as his own brother took it from the original
in the archives of the Trujillo Municipality.
Speaking of this, Don Mariano Edward Rivero[1]
says "There is a tradition that in the huaca (of

[1] Op. cit. p. 269.

Toledo) there were two treasures, known as the great and little *peje*,[1] that the first is still buried, and the second has been found at Toledo."

Here, then, is the inventory of the smaller of these that has turned up :—

"Copy of the entries that are found in the book of Fifths of the Treasury in the years 1577 and 1578, referring to the huaca of Toledo."

FIRST.

"In Trujillo, Peru, on the 22nd of July, 1577, Don Garcia Gutierrez de Toledo presented himself at this royal treasury, to give in to the royal chest a fifth. He brought a bar of gold, 19 carats ley, and weighing 2,400 dollars, of which the fifth being 708 dollars, together with 1½ per cent. to the Chief Assayer, were deposited in the royal box.

" WEIGHT.

"2,400 dollars.   Fifths, 708 dollars.
Francisco Camu.   Juan de Vergara."

SECOND.

" In Trujillo, Peru, on the 12th of December, 1577, Don Garcia Gutierrez Toledo again presented himself with the fifths of other treasure, that he had got out of the huaca, which he held registered, and which is in the jurisdiction of this city. As follows :—

---

[1] *Peje* is Spanish for *fish*.

Bars of gold.	Ley in Carats.	Weight of bar in Spanish dollars.	Value of fifth and of percentage [1¼] to Assayer.
1	19	1,200	354
1	19	900	190 4ts.
1	19	1,050	222 2ts.
1	19	2,400	708
1	19	1,800	481
1	15	1,568	332
Gold dollars . .		8,918	2,287 6ts.

" So that the said bars being of the weight and value of 8,918 Spanish gold dollars, three belong to his Majesty for his royal fifth, and 1¼ per cent. to the Assayer, 2,287 dollars and six timinos,' which are paid into the royal chest in equivalent money.   F. C.   J. DE V."

THIRD.

" In Trujillo, Peru, on the 7th of January, 1578, came again Don Garcia Gutierrez de Toledo, with his fifths of large bars and plates of gold of the following different leys, out of the huaca, which he holds in the jurisdiction of this city :—

Numbers of bars.	Ley.	Weight in dollars.	Fifths.	
16	16 carats	20,800	4,272	0
19	20 ,,	26,240	5,500	0
49	17 ,,	61,952	13,248	0
13	19 ,,	19,200	5,654	0
18	15 ,,	25,088	5,312	0
115		153,280	33,986	0

" From which these 115 small bars being of the weight of 153,280 dollars of gold, the royal fifth

' Eighth of a drachm.

belonging to his Majesty, with 1½ per cent. to the Assayer, Don Garcia Gutierrez de Toledo has paid into the royal box, of the same value and the same ley.

"F. C.   J. DE V."

FOURTH.

"In Trujillo, Peru, on the 8th of March, 1578, Don Garcia Gutierrez de Toledo came to present the fifths of division of the following gold that he had taken out of his huaca, registered in the jurisdiction of this city :—

	Ley.	Weight in gold dollars.	Fifths.
1	16 carats	650	158 4ts.
1	20 ,,	820	171 7ts.
1	17 ,,	968	207 ,,
1	17 ,,	448	103 4ts.
1	20 ,,	1,640	343 6½ts.
1	15 ,,	748	166 0
1	19 ,,	1,200	354 ,,
1	19 ,,	900	190 4ts.
1	14 ,,	1,568	334 ,,
1	18 ,,	1,920	407 ,,
2	21 ,,	3,840	815 0
2	20 ,,	3,280	687 4ts.
2	14 ,,	3,136	668 0
16		21,118	4,607 1½

"Therefore these sixteen bars of gold, of different leys, amount in value to 21,118 gold dollars, and there belong to his Majesty, as the royal fifth, together with 1½ per cent. for the Assayer, 4,607 dollars and one real of gold, which tho said Garcia Gutierrez do Toledo brought and paid into tho royal box, in the same money and ley as represented tho duties of every bar."

FIFTH.

" In Trujillo, on tho 5th of April, 1578, Don Garcia Gutierrez do Toledo brought to the royal chest different ornaments of gold that he had taken out of tho huaca, which he has registered in the jurisdiction of this city, some being little bells of gold, and patterns of corn-heads, and other things, all of which, being examined by the Master Assayer, were proved to be of gold of 14 carats, and to weigh 6,272 dollars in gold, which gave to the royal fifth of his Majesty, with tho $1\frac{1}{2}$ per cent. commission to tho Assayer, a sum of 1,336 gold dollars, which the' said Garcia Gutierrez do Toledo paid into tho treasury-box of his Majesty, being of tho same gold as to ley and value of the original sum.

" J. C.   J. DE V."

SIXTH.

" In Trujillo, on the 20th of April, 1578, Don Garcia Gutierrez do Toledo came with three small bars of 20 carat gold, which weighed 4,170 dollars, of which tho royal fifth, with tho Assayer's $1\frac{1}{2}$ per cent., amounted to 884 dollars of gold— the last-named sum being paid into his Majesty's royal box here by tho said Garcia Gutierrez do Toledo.   J. C.   J. DE V."

SEVENTH.

"In Trujillo, on the 12th of July, 1578, Don Garcia Gutierrez de Toledo came with the fifths of forty-seven bars of gold of different leys, which he had taken out of the huaca he holds registered in the jurisdiction of this city, as follows :—

Numbers of bars.	Ley.	Weight in dollars.	Fifths.
3	15 carats	6,272	1,328
5	20 „	8,320	1,768
5	18 „	7,680	1,630
4	14 „	6,272	1,336
3	19 „	4,800	1,416
9	17 „	15,488	3,312
10	20 „	13,120	2,750
8	21 „	15,306	3,262
47		77,312	16,802

"So that 77,312 dollars being the weight and value in gold of this parcel, the same coming as the royal fifth to his Majesty, with 1½ per cent. to the Assayer, amounts to 16,802 dollars in gold, which sum has been paid to-day into the royal box by Garcia Gutierrez de Toledo as the fifth of a treasure that he had taken out of a huaca registered to him within the jurisdiction of this city—said fifth being of the same value and of a like ley in proportion to each bar."

EIGHTH.

"On the same day, as aforesaid, Garcia Gutierrez de Toledo came back again with a fifth to the royal box of another portion of gold, and ornaments of corn-heads, and pieces of effigies of animals, which were seen by the Master Assayer, who was present, and who said—that having proved and tested them, he found them to be gold of 14 carats—all these ornaments, and having weighed them, they amounted to 4,704 dollars' weight of gold, of which belonged to his Majesty the royal fifth, 1,002 dollars, with 1¼ per cent. for the Assayer—said sum being put into the royal box by Garcia Gutierrez de Toledo as being of like nature and ley.

"J. C.   J. DE V."

	Gold dollars of Fifths.	Gold dollars value of treasure found.
No. 1	708	2,400 00
„ 2	2,287 6 tims.	8,918 00
„ 3	33,996	153,280 00
„ 4	4,607 1 tim.	21,118 00
„ 5	1,336	6,272
„ 6	884	4,170
„ 7	16,802	77,312
„ 8	1,002	4,704
	61,622	278,174
	16	16
	369,732	1,669,044
	616,221 6	2,781,740
	$985,953 6	$4,450,784
Royal Fifths deducted .		985,953 6
Remain . .		3,464,830 2

The native name—Quichua, no doubt—of this huaca was, as I have previously noted, Llomayoahuan; and we are told of it by Rivero, that the gold taken out here produced to the King, as a fifth only, 135,547 Castellanos, or Spanish dollars.[a] Whereas this document tells a different tale. He also mentions that, when Don Antonio Chayque pointed out the locale of the treasure, one portion of his agreement with Don Diego Piñeda, at the time Chief Magistrate, was to the effect that part of it should be allotted for the benefit of the Indians of Mansiché and Huamán. But it appears that, having robbed it of great wealth, the agreement was violated by the Spaniards. The Caçique then pretended (but why pretend, Senor Rivero, if the result be what you state?) that he knew of a still greater treasure that he could discover—to obtain which they gave him 42,187 dollars, raised by a tax charged on the inhabitants in favour of the Indians before named. Of this very little of the principal now remains, partly from the calamities of the times, and partly from the unfaithful administration of the protectors of the Indians, or the collectors of taxes. So says Feijoo de Sosa, and his statement is endorsed by Rivero. Therefore the Caçique's was no pretension, in spite of a previous violation on the side of the Christian contracting party.

That effigies of different animals of gold were found here from time to time, even after this great haul, I am assured by Colonel La Rosa. Mantles also adorned with square pieces of gold, as well as robes made with feathers of divers

[a] Op. cit. p. 268.

colours, were also dug up; but there is not the slightest foundation to believe that a single one of these things was ever deposited here by the Incas, or by any of the Inca people. For the strongest supposition is that they were made by the predecessors of the Incas, the great Chimoo race that inhabited the valleys from Supé to Tumbez.

If, however, the little *peje*, or the small fish, amounted, as appears from this, to the value of 3,464,830 dollars in gold, and that the larger one is not yet found, I think my readers will be of opinion it is worth looking after. That an attempt was made to get it is evident from what is set forth in a quarto MSS. of about sixty-nine pages that I have before me.

Brown and moulded with age though it be, each leaf has the royal arms of Carolus III., and bears date 1774—1775 on the stamp, to which (seeming to have been subsequently printed) are added the dates 1781—1783,—more than 200 years, it may be scarcely necessary to add, after the labours of Toledo. This latter was at the time that Don José Antonio de Axecho, a Spanish nobleman of the distinguished order of Charles III., was sub-delegated for the royal rent of tobacco, and in other high official positions in the territories of Chile, Peru, and La Plata. The manuscript sets forth that Don Francisco Solano Chayhuac Caramucha, principal Caçique and Governor of the parishes and valley of Chimoo, the towns of Mansiche and Guanchaco (Huanchaco is the modern spelling), near Trujillo, presented himself to the superior Government in the month of September, 1776, with ten of the principal Indian men of his jurisdiction, and some of other reductions, asking licence for the discovery of various treasures and mines, that were hidden from the times of the Gentilidad (Pagans), according to the traditions they had in their families. This petition extended over forty pages, and set forth that the chief benefit they intended by the discovery was only that which it would bring to the royal treasury of his Majesty, and, secondarily, to the Indians themselves.

I must here acknowledge that this statement (with my belief of the *morale* of "the poor Indian whose untutored mind," and the rest of it) shook my faith in the purpose set forth. A perusal of the whole document, however, leads me to the opinion, that the representation of the Caçique could hardly have been of his own originating. Because by it we find that seven of his countrymen died in prison, where they had been confined with him for eight years. Outside of this melancholy fact, the document gives us no details save rambling repetitions about the treasure, and the usual stereotyped technicalities of a document penned by a notary public. But that the MSS. in question refers to the *peje grande* not yet discovered I have no doubt.

Of this grand old place of Chan-Chan, subdued by the Inca Yupanqui (son of Pachacutec), we as yet know little more than what is recorded by Garcilasso de la Vega. Yet Cieza de Leon writes of these people having "submitted to the rule of the Incas,"[3] whilst Salcumayhua's account gives us to understand the Chimoos submitted without any fight at all.[4] The conquest of the territory governed over at the time by the great King of Chimoo—the Curaca, Chucha-Machoon—was, according to Garcilasso, a long fight for the Inca, although he was helped by several allies—the kings lower down—those of the Chincha, Canete, Pacha-Cúmac, and Rimac. Unless in Rivero, little or no notice of this place is taken by any of the score of writers on Peru.

I regret that my stay at this interesting place was necessarily short; but I trust that the Peruvian Government is now wakened to the knowledge of how much hidden store of archæological wealth there is still to be brought to light, through the length and breadth of the Republic.

Again bound northward, we have to accompany the steamer in its trip to Maccabee islands—thirty-two miles seaward from Huanchaco—and whence the chief Peruvian guano product for the next few years is to be obtained. These islands are three in number. It may be seen from the sketch

---

[3] Op. cit. p. 245.
[4] "Rites and Laws of the Incas," p. 94.

accompanying, that two of them are joined together by a bridge put up by the Guano Loading Company. The chief residence of the working officials is on the island to the right—that to the left being

the principal guano deposit. A small quantity of shipping was here at the time of our visit, for I believe it is not the intention of the Government to have this worked, so long as the supply lasts in Guanape. These islands are included within the jurisdiction of Trujillo, although their name is not even noticed in Paz Soldan's " Geography of Peru."

As to the guano of Maccabee, I received for my first trade report the following information from Mr. F. Heaton, at the period British Vice-Consul

for the Guanapes and Maccabees.   It was dated in
September, 1871 :—

"*Maccabee Islands.*—Those islands were first
opened in September, 1870, but the rate of shipment has been small in comparison with that of
the Guanapes.   These are situated about sixty
miles to north of Guanape, and about eight miles
from the mainland, off the port of Malabrigo.
The rock at these islands is not so high as in the
Guanapes, being only thirty metres, and the height
of the top of the guano above sea-level seventy-
two metres, consequently the work of shipment is
much easier than at the Guanape islands.

" The quantity of guano still on these islands
may be estimated at 400,000 tons."

From Maccabee we turn again towards the
Peruvian coast—to one of those wild, exposed
roadsteads, called Malabrigo (bad shelter), and
certainly well deserving the name.   This is nine
miles distant from the Maccabees.   On the beach
here is a large cluster of brown houses, of the
same colour as the rock.   Interior to this is the
very extensive hacienda, or sugar-cane plantation,
of Mr. Albrecht, a German gentleman of Lima,
who was kind enough to invite me to see his
works, which, I regretted, want of time prevented
my doing.   I believe the machinery on this establishment is some of the most efficient on the coast.
The towns of Escope and Paysan are interior.
Rum, sugar, cotton, and minerals are exported
hence.

The next stopping-place, forty-two miles farther on, is Pacasmayo,—somewhat like the usual rough, open roadsteads that we have all along the coast, but sheltered considerably by a southern promontory that runs out some distance to the sea. It has a very spacious bay, the chief foreground of which shows the large rice and cotton-packing mill of Senor Fuentes, with a pretty dome on the top, and not far from it the spacious store premises of Senor Ferreyra. The offices and residence occupied by *employés* of Mr. Henry Meiggs' railway from Pacasmayo to Guadaloupe, and to Cajamarca, are in the first-named building, between the cotton-packing machinery and the rice mill. Here for some days I enjoyed the hospitality of Messrs. Maynadier and Ewing, whilst from this I was able to explore some portion of the interior country. The town of Pacasmayo has not more than from 1500 to 2000 inhabitants, and, excepting the two houses I have mentioned, the residences are of the same ramshackle description as those already mentioned of Huanchaco.

During my first night's stay at Pacasmayo, the braying of asses, crowing of cocks, and barking of dogs, from bedtime till sunrise, made the night hideous. I believe there is a donkey kept at every house in Pacasmayo, and three or four dogs to every donkey. Yet, judging of the canine tribe, whilst strolling through the little village in the daytime, one would scarcely think there could be a bark amongst the lot of them.

In the course of this ramble,—passing behind Senor Ferreyra's store to the back of the chapel, and along a narrow street, gradually ascending all the time,—I soon found myself in company with eight or ten turkey-buzzards on the top of a hill, overlooking the town and the harbour. Sandy desert to the east and south—a very great distance between me and the Cordilleras—some few ships out in the harbour—the railway station at the northern side of the town, and the hospital directly east. From this position the houses of Ferreyra and Fuentes have quite an imposing appearance. The chapel is small, and I regret to say not so clean in its interior, as it is tawdry in its ornamentation. Quite near to the summit I saw a heap of adobe masses of unshaped bricks similar in form to those I picked up at Chancay—some of the latter forming walls in a cutting of twelve feet deep on the Huacho railway line.

After vainly searching about some time for what Dr. Heath, the hospital surgeon, told me I should find on the top-cliff—namely, relics of the old Inca road that led hence to Ascope—and skirted along the cliff—I went down the hill to the hospital. This is an excellent institution, like all those built by Mr. Meiggs, with capacity of accommodating forty to fifty patients. A well-furnished pharmacy is attached. Dr. Heath showed me a roomful of prehistoric crockery-ware, that had been excavated from a burial-

ground in some places not twenty yards from the
hospital door; and yet no signs of grave or graveyard was about.   In this neighbourhood, as all
along the railroad track for forty miles, we see
large mounds of the fine sand such as we saw on
the Pisco and Ica, as well as the Mollenda and
Arequipa, railroads.   Mr. Maynadier tells me these
Medanos accumulate at the rate of 100 (one
hundred) cubic feet in the year.

My first trip up this line was made at the end
of last year to the distance of thirty-six miles, the
extreme of the trackway—namely, Monte Grande
—being at the time between two bridges—one at
Papai, then finished, and the other only done to its
buttresses at Yonan—both to cross the Jejetepeque'
river.[8]   This is reputed to be formed by the junction of three minor streams—the Magdalena, the
Payaguas, and the Puchito.   Besides being crossed
in the line to Magdalena, it is traversed—such a
winding course has it got—again on the railway to
Guadaloupe, which diverges from the Magdalena
track at a distance of five miles beyond San Pedro,
where the junction is called the Calasniqui station.

Not very far from San Pedro, and before coming up to the junction, my attention was called

---

[7] From the Quichua, *Jejete* (hidden) *peque* (water), in consequence of the quantity of arborescence that enshrouds its banks.

[8] This, no doubt, is the fino river mentioned by Cieza de Leon,
as flowing through the Pacasmayo valley, when he journeyed
from San Miguel (Piura) to Trujillo.   Op. cit. p. 238.

by Mr. Ewing to the remarkable hill of Chocofan,
which was surrounded by high adobe walls in two
ranges of height—one being a few hundred feet
above the other. Of course I had no time or opportunity to examine it; but it was the first I had
seen of those thus mentioned by Mr. Squier : [9]—
" The usual mode of fortification in Peru consisted in throwing up a series of embankments
around the summits of isolated hills—a practice
which was common enough with the ancient Celts,
and which is still preserved amongst the Australian and Polynesian islanders."

Of these I have observed only two instances
along the coast neighbourhood—namely, that
which I now mention, and another subsequently,
interior to Chiclayo—so that I cannot coincide
with Ulloa in respect to their number that " one
scarcely meets a mountain without them." The
two I speak of are in the same province—that
of Chiclayo, of which Senor Paz Soldan[1] tells,
that " this province is bounded on the north
by Lambayeque, and on the south by Trujillos."
He does not at all mention the existence of such a
locale as Pacasmayo; yet my readers, on looking
at the map, will see the relative bearing of these
parts.

About two miles past Calasniqui we skirt an

<hr>

[9] " Ancient Monuments of the Mississippi Valley." By Squier
and Davis, Smithsonian Institute, New York.

[1] " Geography of Peru," p. 233.

immense extent of adobe relics—the ruins of an
Indian town called Pitura—near to which, on both
sides, and for an extent almost inconceivable, the
ground is literally carpeted with bits of broken
crockery-ware, such as the drinking-vases or
pitchers were made of. Farther on the line continues the same, and for the distance of about five
miles, till we get near to where a slit is visible
high up in the mountain. To this the Spaniards
gave the name of Ventanillas (or little window).
Here the whole valley is thickly covered with remnants of walls, significant of ruined dwellings.
Therefore the wonder suggests itself—this place,
being so densely inhabited, could not have been
cultivated for purposes of agriculture; and if this
be granted, then how did the inhabitants live?

Progressing, we find a cutting through a large
wall from three to four yards in thickness, running
across the valley, from the base of a hill to the
river's side. This may probably have been put up
to resist Inca invasion, as it shuts out the road to
Cajamarca,—or it may have been a division between two Indian tribes.

As we were crossing this valley, an incident,
which our conductor tells me is not uncommon,
happened to a few of our fellow-passengers. In
fact, on this line, as it is not yet opened for traffic,
there can scarcely be said to be passengers in the
orthodox meaning of the word. For although
the locomotive runs up and down every day, it

only brings open carts with rolling stock, as well
as the workmen on the line, accompanied by their
wives and families. Those who have not an order
from the agent at Pacasmayo, as testifying to their
belonging to the works, are always charged their
passage. "Amongst our fellow-travellers to-day,
November 27th" (I find in my note-book), " was
the most miserable, ragged-looking specimen of
Indian humanity I have ever seen—scowling face,
seeming never to have been washed,—a pair of
worn-out sandals, and a large bag well filled, the
contents of which nobody knew. Two boys of the
same type carried bags of the like fashion, and
they climbed up on the truck where I had fixed a
chair for myself, just as the train was about to
start.

A considerable number of persons being on each
of the trucks, no notice was taken of any person
till the time for collecting the tickets came. The
passengers consisted of navvies going to work, of
women bringing up food to their husbands, of
others selling chicha, and of some of the artisans
and engineers of the line. We had got into one
of those horribly desolate, barren stretches of
desert in the valley, when the ticket-collecting
time arrived, and our "poor Indian," was
asked for his ticket. He had none, he said,
with a whine in Spanish. "Money, then,"
said the ticket collector. None of that either.
No time was lost in the driver's attending to

a whistle from the guard, and the engine was stopped.   Then he was told that, as he was trying to deceive the company, he and his two boys with their three bags should at once get off the cars, when he might find his way either to Pacasmayo— whence he came—fifteen miles back, or forward to wherever he was going.   He tried to plead—even began to whimper about his poverty ; and I myself was judging that the guard was too harsh in pushing him, with his luggage, down on the ground.   But he had scarcely lighted, and before there was time for his two boys and the three bags to be sent after him, when he took out of his pocket a small bag, as dirty-looking as himself, and full of silver.   So paying the money, he was allowed to get up and continue his journey.   I must confess that my sentiments of commiseration towards him were at once changed, and for the moment, I could scarcely see any harm in leaving this shabby fellow to muse for a short time amongst the Condors. Like all the other valleys from Piura to this, as well as hence down the coast to Pisco, Cieza de Leon tells us that "here there were great build- ings for the Inca's use, and where the Temple of the Sun was erected,"[1] of which I regret to say there is not the slightest evidence in the part of the valley through which I travelled.

[1] Op. cit. p. 241.

CHAPTER XXVII.

At the end of the first valley we come to a sharp
curve, near a place called the Rio Seco; and on
the side of the hill facing west, I observe that
excavations have been extensively made in a burial-
mound, which at first sight resembled a portion of
the adjacent rock, so like were they in colour.
Mr. Ewing tells me some excellent specimens of
pottery were got out of here, and—he was informed
by several of the explorers, who were workmen on
the railway—not a few specimens of silver and
gold likewise. There is a large *débris* of trees all
through the way we have come, and a hacienda
here, named Tolon, was swept away, as well as
much property destroyed, by a mountain inundation
in 1826.

A little over twenty miles from Pacasmayo, we

cross the Papai iron bridge ; and only about a mile
farther on I saw a large stone boulder, almost
square, with hieroglyphic figures carved thereon.
The locomotive having been stopped for a few
minutes to allow me to inspect it, I come to the
conclusion that these figures are not chiselled in,
but like what Senor Rivero[1] describes of the
Dighton Rock at South Carolina, " to have been
made by picking with the point of some fine iron
implement."

Beyond Papai bridge, we pass through the ruins
of Chingallo to Monte Grande, where there is a
temporary station, and thence by horseback on
through the valley of Templeros,[2] to the Yonan
Pass of the Jequetepeque.

The opposite side of the river—at what is called
the Yonan Pass, is an accumulation of boulders, of
various sizes, one over the other to the height of
almost forty feet, and all carved over in every
direction. Figures of cats, foxes, dogs, serpents,
star-fish, centipedes, fowls, birds, fishes, and
square-headed men—some of the last-named holding what seem to be battle-axes in their hands.
Of this place nobody here knows anything, except
that there is a locale near to it called San Juan,
and another, not far away, styled Santa Clara.
If the Spaniards did nothing more, they sedulously
tried to wipe out all the old Indian names, and

[1] "Peruvian Antiquities," p. 21.
[2] So styled from some species of a sensitive plant that is here.

ENGRAVED ROCKS AT YONAN PASS OF RIVER JEJETEPEQUE.

(Vol. II. p. 174.

substitute holy ones instead. This might have been praiseworthy, did not all South American history teach us that to erect a cross upon a hill,—to build a chapel where convenient,—and to give a place that had an Indian title the name of some saint, was generally the extent of their Christianity.

Here is a locale most interesting to any future archæological explorer. In one of these stones I observed three mortar-shaped holes, eleven inches in diameter, and two feet and a half in depth. Those had been evidently excavated here, and were well triturated by frequent use of something being pounded within. Dr. Heath, Mr. Ewing, and myself mounted as near to the top of them as we could get; and these stones, some of them calculated to be from forty to fifty tons in weight, seem to be all in separate blocks; but whether moved here artificially or not I cannot say.

Not far from Santa Clara, on the hacienda of Chuquimango (I am told by Senor. Casimiri Razuri, of San Pedro), there is one immense mass of flat rock, supported on three pillars or buttresses, that are believed to have been arranged by some Druidical giants of past ages.

From the side next to the river, of where lies this collection of carved stones, there is the remnant of a large four-yards-thick stone wall, across the little valley—indeed, the term " ravine " would be more appropriate to it. This wall stretches down

ENGRAVED ROCKS AT YUNAN PASS OF RIVER JEJETEPIQUE.

[Vol. II. p. 176.

miles; from which seven miles farther on will bring us to Chilete,[3] one of the richest silver districts in Peru. From that to La Vina, nine miles; and from there to Magdalena five. The railway concession of Mr. Meiggs only extends as far as Magdalena, whence exists a short distance, although it is a high Cordillera, between Magdalena and Cajamarca—the Cordillera, which I believe, limited the occupation of the Inca people in the sea-coast direction.

After reaching Magdalena it is hoped the line will be continued on to Cajamarca. There are few parts of Stevenson's or of any other work on Peru that I desired to study with so much interest as that which relates to the incidents of Pizarro's first *coup de grâce* at Cajamarca, in which we find details of the death of the Inca, Atahualpa.[4] Prescott never was in South America; his account is, therefore, derived only from the Spanish writers whose works he studied at Madrid. Stevenson spent a considerable time in Cajamarca, and the "historical sketch," of the events whereof I am

[3] Latest news from Peru brings wonderful accounts of the richness of this mine.

[4] Atahualpa is styled Atabaliba by Francisco Xeres (secretary to the Conqueror Francisco Pizarro), and he is entitled Atabaliva by Hernando Pizarro in his letter to the Royal Audience of Santo Domingo. *Vide* Mr. Markham's "Report on the Discovery of Peru." Printed for the Hakluyt Society, 1872.

writing, he thus premises:[5]—"The residence of Atahualpa at this place was accidental, as will appear from the following historical sketch, which I have endeavoured to make as correct as possible, with the assistance of the works of Garcilasso, Gomara, Zarate, and others, collated with the oral traditions of the Indians of this province, and particularly the Caçique Astopilco, as well as those of Quito."

With this combination of literary research and "oral tradition," one would expect, at all events, a resemblance to the probable in the so-called historical sketch; yet we find the whole story an incongruity of Munchausenisms, and impossibilities, as the reader, no doubt, will find if he accompany me in its analysis.

The accidental circumstance of Atahualpa being at Cajamarca—in these times a kind of Harrogate or Buxton of the Incas, on account of its famous mineral springs—was by reason of stopping here till a *ruse* of his planning had succeeded to depose his brother Huascar from the throne of Cuzco, to which he had been appointed by the father of both—Huayna Capac—the throne of Quito having been left to Atahualpa. The *casus belli* between the brothers was said to owe its origin to the fact that Huascar was the legitimate descendant of the Inca, and Atahualpa only the illegitimate. However, the latter succeeded in

* Op. cit. vol. ii. p. 143.

the first move, and his brother Huascar was prisoner at Andamarca, about forty leagues from Pacha-Cámac, at the time that Pizarro came on to Cajamarca. It may be almost supposed that they ate and drank gold in these days, when we are told that at the baths where Atahualpa resided,[6] —and to which Pizarro sent his troops to loot as soon as operations had commenced—" the weight of gold at the baths, *and accounted for*, amounted to 15,000 ounces." Doubtless some trifle may be considered as " *not* accounted for "—at the baths !

After his famous exploits at Tumbez, " Francisco Pizarro pushed forward to Cajamarca, where he arrived with 160 soldiers."[7] To omit the preliminaries of speeches,—the golden goblets,—the seats covered with gold to sit down on,—and the presents of gold with which Hernando Pizarro and Hernando de Soto, ambassadors for the conqueror, returned to the camp, we are told,[8] " On the following day Pizarro placed his cavalry, composed of sixty men, on each side of the square of Caxamarca, behind some high walls; in the centre of the square he had built a small breastwork, behind which he placed his two field-pieces, and behind these 100 men, and they awaited the arrival of the Inca."

[6] Op. cit. vol. ii. p. 157.
[7] Op. cit. vol. ii. p. 145.
[8] Op. cit. vol. ii. p. 149.

N 2

" High walls on each side of the square" are most unusual things in Peru, and the carelessness of allowing a breastwork, to be run up in one night, shows lack of watchful organization amongst the Inca people.

But " Atahualpa made his appearance on a throne of gold, carried on the shoulders of his courtiers and favourites, with a guard of 8,000 of his soldiers in front, 8,000 on each side, and 8,000 more in the rear, besides an immense number of nobles and attendants." Let us put down the number, though " immense," of the last-named as 1,000, and here we have 25,000 warriors coming out to hold a parley with a soldier and a few priests, who had only 160 soldiers with them. The friar Vicente Valverde delivered a long speech—what Stevenson calls a " most extraordinary harangue "—very few words of which, even when translated, were intelligible to Atahualpa. The latter, however, tried to answer, and asked who had informed Valverde of what he had heard from the interpreter. Whereupon Valverde gave his breviary to Atahualpa, and told him, through Felipe, that that book informed him of all that he wanted to know respecting the true God. The Inca folded over the leaves, examined the book, placed it against his ear, and listened. Then he said, " It is false, it cannot and does not speak ; " when he let it fall. At this Valverde cried out, " To arms, Christians ! these infidel dogs have insulted the minister of your Redeemer. The word of God is thrown under foot. Revenge! Revenge!"[*]

Then "the soldiers rushed on their unsuspecting victims" [fancy a rush of 160 men on 25,000, or one man surrounding 160 of the Incaites]; "Pizarro flew to Atahualpa, well aware that the preservation of his life was of the utmost importance. But upwards of 20,000 Indians fell" [so that each of Pizarro's 160 men killed for his own share 125 of the Indians, who surely must have been unarmed, or such shamble's work as this could never have occurred. And if it did come off as related, the incredulous may ask, is it possible for the most active of men to get through slaughtering 125 antagonists in one *mêlée?* Additional particulars of the incident are given to us by Francisco Xeres, Secretary to the Conqueror Pizarro, who, we may imagine, was not distant from the slaughter. He says :[1]—

"The battle only lasted about half an hour, for the sun had already set when it commenced."

In this case the term slaughter would seem more appropriate than battle, or such a result

[*] Op. cit. vol. ii. p. 157.

[1] "Reports on the Discoveries of Peru." Papers translated and edited by Clements R. Markham, C.B.   London : printed for the Hakluyt Society, 1872.   Page 58.

could not have taken place. Let us consider another calculation :—

Given—20,000 Indians killed by 160 Spaniards in about half an hour: we find that each of Pizarro's soldiers, massacring 125 of the natives, must have knocked them off at the rate of four men and one-sixth per minute. That even such work was a trifle to the mind of Senor Xeres, may appear from his reflections in the same page, where he observes, "If the night had not come on, few out of the 30,000 men that came would be left. It is the opinion of some who have seen armies in the field, that there were more than 40,000 men."

Not the least wonderful thing in this great feat of Pizarro's appears, that the only casualty to his forces was that one horse got a slight wound.

This is the romance which we are expected to take as "an historical sketch" of the first great blow of Pizarro in the conquest of Peru.

On the return journey I had an addition to my fellow-travellers, in the Bishop of Chachapayo, together with the Prefect of Cajamarca and his wife. Amongst the suite of the latter were a parrot and a tiger-cat. The whole valley of Jejetepeque abounds in deer.

I saw, whilst at Yonan, a case of that horrible disease called *Utah* (a kind of lupus, cancer, phagœdenic ulcer). It is believed, Dr. Heat tells me, to result from the bite of a venomous fly.

Returning to Pacasmayo, I proceeded on the next morning to see the fair of Guadaloupe. This commences on the 28th of November and ends on the 8th of December—the festival (in

AGRICULTURAL IMPLEMENTS FROM HUARAL.

the Roman Catholic Church) of the Immaculate Conception.

Our route to Guadaloupe is by branching off in a northerly direction, where I have indicated the railway junction at Calisnique, whence we proceed and pass by a miserable little town, called Gultambo, quite close to an iron bridge of 630 feet in length that crosses the river Jejetepeque.

But I do not reach Guadaloupe on the day of starting, for I stop at Talambo, where I am to be the guest of Senor Don B. Salcedo y Ruiz for the night, at one of the most extensive haciendas in Peru.

The house, stores, cotton-pressing machinery and sugar-cane apparatus are situated to the left of a road, on the opposite side of which is the dwelling.   In fact, the residence stands between the railway track—for as yet there is no station here—and the roadway leading down from the mountains to the fair of Guadaloupe, which is about three miles farther on.   Down they come —the visitors to the fair—in troops of dozens and scores from Cajamarca, Chachapoya, Chota, Jaen, Seladin—bringing such a variety of things for sale—ropes made of grass, potatoes, cheeses, biscuits (the last-named from Cajamarca and very celebrated), saddle-bags, hats, horse-covers, shawls, tobacco, ponchos, gaiters, medicinal herbs, and a lot of other matters to exchange for foreign goods. From so far north as Sechura and Piura—and even north-west from Quito, the capital of Ecuador— they come to the fair of Guadaloupe.   Troops of horses, mules, and asses—the two last chiefly carrying the cargo.   These, from Cajamarca direction at least, are generally hired at two reals (about 7*d.*) per day for a horse, and one real for an ass,—with the obligation not only to feed and care for the animal on the route, but to return him unimpaired to his owner.

Before proceeding to Guadaloupe, Senor Salcedo kindly presented me with some result of the archæological collections of the neighbourhood, from a place about three leagues distant, named Huabal. But the whole country around here is full of such relics, requiring only to be sought for. Mounted on magnificent horses, Senor Salcedo and

PREHISTORIC POTTERY FROM HUACAS AT HUABAL.

I made a visit to the ruins of what I conceive to be a fortress, resembling those at Canete, Huatica, and behind Trujillo. This is about six miles distant to the south of his establishment. All the road thereto was like that up the other railway, literally covered with ruins and bits of walls. The fort had three squares inside of a larger square, and about half a dozen burying-mounds, or huacas, were around. At this fort was a deep dyke, protected by a yard-thick wall of stones that led from the ramparts to about fifty yards distant, to where an azequia still exists—a water-course that Senor Salcedo tells me has its origin in the Jequetepeque river, and extends in a bed of twenty-one miles' length, falling again of course into the river when it has served the purpose for which it was made —namely, of watering the lands. Of this place I could not ascertain the name. Portion of the wall—of adobones' material—in front of this old fort is still there, twenty feet high, and having a foundation of stones, whilst above the earth it is fifteen feet across. We pass alongside the cutting of an old azequia—not used now—fifteen to twenty feet deep in parts, and nine to twelve feet across.

On our way back by another route, we rode through a cutting in one of these long straight walls such as I have described near Ventanillas, on the Magdalena railroad. The whole of the district through which we travelled this morning for several hours, as well as over miles and miles around, is covered with relics of stone-built houses—of adobe buildings—of neglected azequias—of burial-mounds where the bodies were put in with the huacas or pottery-ware. In several of these mounds excavations have been made,—evidenced from skulls and bones lying about. The illustration of the copper utensils accompanying this chapter shows likewise

that all these implements, when buried, were
wrapped up in cotton cloth, for they all have
still some of its fibre sticking to them.

In none of these things—or, in fact, nowhere, as
far as regards my exploration—can I recognize
anything of Incaite prestige as it is trumpeted by
its advocates.   Every yard of my journeyings
proves that these districts must have been densely

PREHISTORIC POTTERY FROM HUACA AT HUABAL.

populated.   But, then, how did these people sub-
sist?   By commerce, or otherwise?   If the topographical condition of affairs were the same in
their days as it is now, certainly not by agricultural or horticultural pursuits, for one-tenth of
the population, proved by the ruins to have existed,
could not be subsisted by land cultivation.

From this hacienda of Senor Salcedo y Ruiz, at Talambo reputedly arose the germs, in 1860, of the Spanish war against the Pacific Republics in 1866, which was commenced by bombardment of the Spanish fleet against Valparaiso in March of the same year.   This was followed by a similar course of action, although with very dissimilar results, in the attack on Callao of the succeeding 2nd of May in the same year.   The question[1] ostensibly proceeded out of some disagreeable occurrences, that took place on this hacienda, in a matter of 300 Spanish immigrants, who had been brought out from the Basque country by the father of the present occupier.   Through an invitation, whereof a copy is before me, the Guipuzcoa[2] agriculturists (of which province in Spain Senor Salcedo was a native) were offered something of an Elysium in Talambo.   They were told that, once out there, land and means of cultivating cotton, sugar-cane, rice, cochineal, wheat, coffee—in fact, every luxury—would be given to them ;—that a priest to be their comfort in religion, and a doctor to help their bodily ailments, would be always in attendance ;—that, in fact, Talambo was to be a Paradise.   Influenced, perhaps, by the enthusiasm which this bright picture painted, they did not observe that the same paper obliged them to a

[1] " La Cuestion Talambo, ante La America." Lima : Imprenta del Comercio, 1864.

[2] Province in Vascongadas.   Lat. 43° 6′ N., 2° 10′ W.

term of service of eight years with the owner of
the Talambo estate; and that, on the second year
of their coming out, the products of their labour
in the matter of cotton would have to be divided
—one half for themselves, and the other half
for "their partner, Senor Salcedo." The
agricultural matters of wheat, maize, and potatoes would go to their support, with the pro-
vision that out of these, after the third year,
a contribution of 4 per cent. should be levied
for expenses of the chaplain, doctor, and major-
domo.

Possibly some of these 300 immigrants knew
that, at the time of their contract, cotton was very
much enhanced in value, on account of the existence at the period of the civil war in the United
States. But, at all events, it appears that as soon
as they came out they broke their agreement
—although free passage was given at Senor
Salcedo's expense—a very common occurrence, as
I happen to know to my cost, in South America.
Then the Peruvian authorities were appealed to,
after the chief Spanish mutineer took hold of
Senor Salcedo's horse, with its master on its back,
whilst the others threw stones at him as he went
along the high road. A row ensued in the patio
(or yard) of Talambo House; several Spaniards and
one Peruvian being killed in the *mêlée*. To this
succeeded the disbanding of the whole colony—
diplomatic expostulations in Lima and Madrid,—

and the final result of the bombardments already alluded to.

There is a considerable number of Chinese at the hacienda now; but the establishment does not present any features of prosperity.

WHISTLING WATER-CROFT.

I may add, as explanation of the foregoing title, that when water is poured into the tube at the left-hand side of this water-croft, the whistling sound comes from the head of the bird on the right.

CHAPTER XXVIII.

As soon as our horses could be saddled, on the morning succeeding my visit to Talambo, Senor Salcedo and I set out for a visit to Guadaloupe fair. The crowds were still pouring down by the road from Cajamarca, and on our way we met some groups returning with cases of brandy, and bundles of other civilizing influences, which they had exchanged for their products, strapped on to the backs of their mules. This, too, although it was only the 29th of November, and the fair could be scarcely said to have been initiated.

The road here is a very excellent one; through the village of Chepen, with a considerable population, and past the hacienda of Surifico. Although the houses in Chepen are now only a very miserable collection of huts, it must have been a place of no small note in prehistoric times. For only a few weeks previous to my final departure from Lima, I saw exhibited for sale there, in the Calle Ayacucho, a collection amounting to eighty of some of the most highly-finished specimens of pottery, that had been exhumed from burial-mounds at Chepen.[1]

The hacienda of Surifico outside of Chepen had a short time previous been purchased by President Balta; but it was again bought from his Excellency by Mr. Henry Meiggs. It is therefore now in proper order, having large crops of sugar-cane, with excellent gates and fences.

Between Surifico and Guadaloupe we pass by an establishment, comprising a manufactory for sugar and distillery for rum, over the principal gate of which was such a large wooden cross as one seldom sees, except at a more holy kind of building. In a quarter of a mile after, we were in the streets of Guadaloupe. Although it was very considerably crowded, as I might have expected from the numbers I saw coming in during the two days previous and the morning of my visit, I was assured this was nothing to what it would present in a few days after—the ensuing Saturday and Sunday more particularly. We rode up to the Plaza Principal, or principal square of the

---

[1] Yet no mention of this *locale* is made either by Ondegardo, Cieza de Leon, Garcilasso de la Vega, or any writer previous.

town, where tents were being fitted up with sides and roofs of mats, attached to poles stuck in the ground. In many of these gambling with roulette tables was already commenced. Round and about were listless groups,—some selling and others drinking chicha. At the stands already constructed were offered for sale alforjas (saddle-bags), shawls and ponchos, brought down from the Cordilleras. These last named are of a quality very inferior to those we find on the eastern side of the Andes in the Argentine Republic.

The band of one of the Peruvian regiments was playing in the plaza, opposite to the chapel. I was anxious to see the inside of this church, because, from the religious date (8th of December), on which is the principal bearing of the fair, I inferred it must have some holy origin. The interior does not differ from the general aspect of South American chapels, outside of Lima, being damp and chilly. The altar seems unfinished, though on the top of it is the identical statue of the Virgin, on account of which this fair had been established. In fact, it was intended by the Spanish clergy, who founded it, more in the light of a pilgrimage than a trade meeting; but, in the degeneracy of the age, its sacred character has merged into the commercial.

The tradition about it is as follows:—Many years ago—no one here, not even the oldest chronicler, can tell how many—the Curé of the

district had to speak to his congregation about
the neglect to which the statue of the Virgin was
subjected in the matter of offerings. Neither ornaments nor clothing were given, and the old ones
seemed wearing away. Repeatedly they were
warned and threatened of what the consequences
might be; but they heeded not, till one morning
the statue was missing from its accustomed niche.
Contributions were, therefore, soon poured in by
the simple congregation to appease the divine wrath,
that had manifested itself in the supernatural disappearance of the statue. A searching investigation was made, but nothing discovered for some
days, although every hour the Curé still impressed
the indispensability of increasing the offerings.
On the third day, and after a solemn procession had been made, the statue was discovered
on an isolated rock about 300 feet high, and to
which previously there had been no ascent known
to be attempted. The succeeding Sunday found
it again in its place, on the altar, although
nobody had seen it removed. And from time to
time, till its fame spread far and near, it came to
make disappearances, and returns without any
visible aid—these being generally suspected, by
the sceptical mind, to depend on the Curé's sensations about the lack or abundance of contributions.

Another account of this miraculous statue tells,
that it was originally brought to this place by

the early Spanish missionaries, and transported on the back of a mule. Somehow or other, the mule strayed away, losing the case in which the statue was contained, and subsequently losing itself, for the animal never turned up afterwards. But the case with the statue in it was picked up on the identical spot where the chapel is built in this square. In the neighbourhood the town of Guadaloupe was founded.

And such a town as it is, to be sure! Surrounded by clumps of hills—on tops of several of which are relics of old times—pieces of walls, and masses of ruins. Its component parts, of the general run of streets, present a collection of dirty people, rolled up in filthy clothes, and peering out of tottering houses into abominable by-ways. On one or two of the houses you see a daub of whitewash, as if a spasmodic idea of cleanliness came like a flash of lightning to somebody. But all the surroundings seem so strongly to protest against such a thing, that it is a palpable failure. At the corner of the plaza, adjoining one of these streets, was a large advertisement-sheet, like that at Mollendo, big enough for Covent Garden, or the Italian Opera House, announcing a theatrical performance to-night, the 29th of November, that had been performed with great success on the previous Thursday. The idea of a theatre in such a place startled me for a moment, and after again contemplating the surroundings, I could not help a suspicion that the " Dead March in Saul" would most probably be the opening overture of the performance.

There is one redeeming quality in Guadaloupe—that is, the house and store of Colonel Don José Bernardo Goyburu, at the right-hand angle of the plaza from the chapel. Here I saw, in the proprietor, a man of business, who has on his farm cultivated coffee, for which he got a premium in the Lima Exhibition of 1869, and a gold medal in the London Exhibition of 1871. He is likewise introducing the silkworm cultivation, as the mulberry grows in abundance through the Jequetepeque valley; and he showed me some very healthy cocoons, upon which he was experimenting.[1]

The only features of what on the continent of Europe are recognized as fairs consisted of a few asses and pigs, that were tethered not far from the railway station as I returned to Pacasmayo.

From my note-book on the day of departure from Pacasmayo, I extract,—" Dec. 1st. Although I feel very grateful for the kind, affable, and agreeable hospitality of Messrs. Maynadier and Ewing, I am afraid that I must speak the truth about the village behind their residence. 'The

---

[1] I regret having heard, on the day after I left Guadaloupe, of one of the gallant old colonel's legs being broken, by the kick of a horse, in his patio.

litter of the rose-leaves and the noise of the nightingales' were once mentioned by George Robins as the only drawbacks to a splendid property he had put up for auction. The litter here in the streets, and the nightly noises of which I have already written, must bring to my mind this story of the world-famed auctioneer, on the principle of ' *Les extrêmes se touchent.*'"

Before starting, I again examined the two roads pointed out to me by Dr. Heath as of Inca making, and found them only simple trackings in the sand from Pacasmayo hill-top southward towards Malabrigo. In one place there is a cutting through a four-feet-deep heap of rubble, but the sand, (accumulation of Médanos) has obliterated all other pathways in the surroundings.

Again searching through the works of Paz Soldan for some mention of this place, and finding nothing in the index, I am glad to discover that he does notice it, under the slice of statistics which he gives about the province of Chiclayo,[1] in the following words :—" In the district of San Pedro stands the port of Pacasmayo, in which is made some maritime commerce."

A few days after my first visit to Pacasmayo, one of the *lancheros*, who fell asleep in his boat whilst alongside a ship, let his head fall over the boat's side, and in a lurch of the vessel against the launch, his skull was broken. Never after could

[1] "Geography of Peru," vol. i. p. 224.

any one be got to make a voyage or pull an oar in *that* craft; it was consequently hauled up on the beach, and condemned as derelict.

Cotton and rice were formerly the chief exports from Pacasmayo, as indeed from nearly all the northern ports of Peru; but the sugar-cane cultivation is found to be more profitable, and is therefore coming to be generally adopted.

From Pacasmayo, still going northward, I must ask my reader to make this journey with me overland to the port of Eten, beyond thirty-five miles distance. My passage between these two places was in reality made from Eten to Pacasmayo on horseback, kindly procured for me by our worthy Vice-Consul at San José, Mr. Wm. Fry. But the whole district is most uninteresting and uninviting. Except at a distance of about two leagues north of Pacasmayo, where I find ruins of exactly the same kind as those in the Huatica valley, and behind Trujillo. Close to a precipitous bank of nearly 300 feet high, overlooking a large extent of the Jejetepeque valley, are the ruins of a very large city, with two huge fortresses. In their style of architecture they are exactly the same as the so-called huaca of Toledo at Chan-Chan, the buildings in Huatica and Cañete valleys. I had no spirit to examine them, for it was nearly ten o'clock in the day, with a roasting sun, and I had been riding all night from Eten. Through a country of arid sand, pebbles, and rocks—of the bleached bones of cows and horses marking the roadway—of nothing to comfort or alleviate one's thirst or hunger, if likely to perish, —and of everything suggestive of the African desert. When crossing the mouth of the river Jequetepeque, and for a mile or two on either side, the whole beach is covered with *débris* of tree stems and branches swept down from the valleys. After the water here, none is to be met with for nearly ten leagues, till we arrive at Lagunas, where there is a pretty considerable-sized village, with a Governor in it. There is a little port, called Cheropee, one league to the south of Lagunas.

The latter village is reported to have about 600 inhabitants, and around the lakes we find some scanty vegetation, but little or none of cultivation, except a few fields of Indian corn, and some pumpkins. Farther on we pass a place called Mocupe, having only a few houses in it. The valley behind Lagunas has still its old Indian name of Rafang. Near to this is a district entitled Calanacoche, and we pass the Rio de Lobos (or river of seals). Several points of mountains here are designated " Corcovado," or hump-backed.

CHAPTER XXIX.

During the year before last (1871) there was published at Lima a "Collection of Laws, Decrees, Contracts, and other Documents relative to the Railways of Peru."[1] From this I find that in April, 1867, a presentation was made to the Government by Senor Don Juan Cossio, of Lima, repeating a proposal that had been made in the previous February of 1866, asking permission to make a railway between the small bay of Pimentel and the town of Chiclayo, with a ramification to Lambayeque. To this, in the next month of May, 1867, succeeded a despatch

[1] For a copy of which—three volumes bound in one—I am indebted to the courtesy of Mr. John H. Meiggs. The work was compiled by directions and at cost of his brother, Mr. Henry Meiggs.

to President Balta from Senor Don Jose Antonio
Garcia y Garcia, in which it is suggested that
neither the more spacious port of San José nor the
smaller bay of Pimentel is fit for introducing the
railway system into the rich valleys of Lambayeque,
and Chiclayo, but that the port of Eten is the proper
place for such an initiative.   Moreover, Senor
Garcia guaranteed that the necessary capital was
ready to be invested for the building of a railway
as well as for the construction of a mole at Eten,
if his Excellency would decree the suppression of
San José as a " puerto mayor," or Custom-house
port, and have it transferred to Eten.

In compliance with this, on the 25th of August,
1871, was issued the decree for transferring the
Custom-house from San José to Eten, and ordain-
ing that it should take effect from 1st of March,
1872.   A company was formed in October, 1867, for
constructing the Eten line.   This, in its first concession, was only provided to go through the towns
of Eten, Monsefu, Chiclayo, and Lambayeque, until,
by decree of June 7th, 1868, it was prolonged ten
miles farther north to Ferrañafe, one of the most
important rice-producing districts of the province
of Lambayeque.   At the end of 1871 it was opened
to Chiclayo, and rapid progress had been made
with the mole.

At the time of my visit about to be described,
I found an excellently-arranged station, works,
manager's residence, and goods stores at the port

of Eten, the whole line being under the management of Mr. John Daly, from whom I received every courtesy during my short stay. The mole, which is being erected on screw piles, and is to be of a length of 2500 feet, was put down to the length of 1927 feet in November last, and is no doubt completed before this time. The station here is very well adapted to the needs of traffic, being 1200 feet by 600.

On the day of my arrival Mr. Daly kindly brought me on a special engine, in company with Mr. Hindle, C.E., Government Engineer, and Mr. Cole, C.E., of the Pimentel line, along the whole of the railroad from Eten to Ferrañafe. Our first visit was to the town of Eten, of which Senor Paz Soldan says,[1] "Eten is distant from the sea seven leagues. Its people are a pure race, who take much care to have no intermixture. They allow no idle persons in their community. Eten signifies in their language *the place where the sun rises.*' It is said that in Lima a Chinese and a native of Eten understand each other perfectly." Equally misleading is the account of its position by Mr. Spruce, who says, " The town stands on a steep hill (*morro*) close to the sea."[2]

If either of these were at any time correct, the town of Eten must have undergone some remark-

---

[1] "Geography of Peru," vol. i. p. 223.

[2] See note in Mr. Markham's translation of the " Travels of Pedro de Cieza de Leon," p. 44.

able transitions, since Senor Soldan or Mr. Spruce knew it; for on the morning of my visit there it was about a mile to a mile and a half distant from the sea, and nearly three miles north of the station wherefrom we started.

I saw as many idle people in Eten as in other Peruvian towns, and no one could confirm the Chinese affinity. The story of the primitive settlers here is, that they were wandering from some place of which the chroniclers give no record, and that, being wearied out, they came to a resolution to stop and make their location in the next place where they would find themselves, on the rising of the sun. It was a very wise resolve this, for, supposing them to have come from the East, as some persons think probable, less than two miles farther would have brought them into the Pacific Ocean. So here they stopped, and called the place Eten,' which signifies, as we are told, " where the sun rises."

A walk through the town of Eten impressed me with an indescribable *je ne sais quoi* to know more of the people, than I could pick up from my short visit. I entered several of the houses—saw their occupants working at mats, hats, shawls, quilts, and cigar-cases, and was impressed with a greater dignity of physique, as of manner, than I have met elsewhere

---

' It might not be an uninteresting point of philological inquiry to ascertain the difference, or similarity, of the *Unde Deriratum* of this place, and the college of Eton, near her Majesty's palace of Windsor.

in Peru. Instead of believing them to be in any way connected with the Chinese, I confess myself at first impressed with the idea of their being descended from the last remnants of the Inca people, and to have immigrated hither from Cajamarca.

Of these people Stevenson says,[3] " The town of Eten stands on a sandy plain [it is not a sandy plain,—for the country round is dotted with fields of clover and sugar-cane], and is entirely inhabited by Indians. Those are the only people who speak the Chimu dialect, which is the original language of the coast of Peru, and so different from the Quichua, that I could not understand a single word, nor trace any analogy between them, and beyond the limits of their own town their language is unintelligible. They do not allow any persons but Indians to reside amongst them,[4] and a traveller is only suffered to remain three days in the town; but the Alcaldes always take care that he be provided with whatever he may require." The difference in the dress from that of other Indians, as described by Mr. Stevenson, I did not recognize, except in the matter of the mourning. This is mentioned by him as "a kind of long black or blue tunic without sleeves, girt round the waist."

---

[3] Op. cit. vol. ii. p. 187.

[4] This is not correct; as there was a German or Swiss, I forget which, and whose name has escaped my memory, who had a store there, for three years previous, within half a square of the chapel in the Plaza when I visited Eten in November, 1872.

The mourning may, as is said by some, be for Atahualpa, but I think it is far more likely to be for the original great man of the Chimoo valley, the King Chucha Machoon.

If it be correct that they do not speak the language of the Incas, of course my first reasoning on the subject falls to the ground, because I had suspected their Inca descent for the following causes :—

1st.—Their physical type. It might be an accident;—but, if so, it is a very curious coincidence, —that I saw women in the streets of Eten, with form and figure, exactly resembling those painted in Montero's great picture of the funeral of Atahualpa. Mayhap the models of Montero are only imaginary, or artistic ; possibly it can be proved so ; but that does not alter the fact. As they are in the painting, so they exist at Eten—with their Roman noses, swarthy complexions, long black hair, and robust figures.

2nd.—The women at Eten all wear mourning outside of doors, and have worn it during all the time that is known of their history. This consists of a black garment of petticoat, gown, or skirt, whichever it may be called, with a white shawl thrown over. Therefore, probably in mourning for Atahualpa, or possibly for the last Chimoo king.

3rd.—I have been informed by a resident for three years (the European before-mentioned), that brothers and sisters live in marital connexion, as we are told all the Incas did from the first down to the last.

4th.—An indistinct remembrance is in my recollection of one of the Inca kings (although I fail to call to mind which it was) having devoted much of his time to making straw hats, in the periods of his recreation. The Etenites manufacture straw hats, mats, cigar-cases from straw, and quilts from cotton. This is their chief business here. The quilts are worked in raised patterns of flowers, although in a very inferior style, to that in which the same kind of thing is executed in what are called *colchas*, by the women of Santiago del Estero, in the Argentine Republic.

5th.—The implied devotion to the Sun in the idea of their halting at his rising, and the mystery about their speaking a different language from the other Indians, are matters of problematical speculation, well worthy of an archæologist to investigate.

They cultivate the ground very partially, and chiefly for sugar-cane growth. Their cane mills are of the most ordinary kind, called *trapiches*, worked by bullocks, or horses. They have the same style of one shaft, low sloping car, with solid wooden wheels, that may be' seen in many parts of the south of Ireland to draw turf upon. In fact, there is little attractive about the Etenites, except the mystery of their origin.

Not more than two miles from the town of Eten, and along the line to the north of it, is another large village, at which we stop to have a look around. This is called Monsefu, and I am told the inhabitants of Eten hold no communion with them, nor they with the Etenites. Perhaps in some matters this holds good, but in commercial and social points I know it does not; for I saw, during the period of one of the ordinary trains passing by, that they were going in no inconsiderable numbers, from one town to another. Monsefu is like the usual run of old settlements of Spanish foundation all along this coast, that seem to have been built for the chief purpose of falling into wreck and ruin. It has its principal plaza or square, Matriz or parish church, and the remnants of some old triumphal arches built centuries ago. Its chief trade is the manufacture of *alforjas*, or saddle-bags; and these of Monsefu are famous over all Peru. At some time in the year there is a fair here, like that of Guadaloupe, but of the period I am not certain.

A few hundred yards outside of the town I visited a copper-foundry, whereat they manufacture sugar-pans, used at the haciendas down the coast. These are made out of old bells, and bits of copper picked up everywhere. The sugar-boiling pots are sold at the rate of five reals (about two shillings) per pound weight; and as the material from which they are fabricated is bought cheaply, it ought to be a profitable business. But the place lacks the stir of life seen in our

English manufacturing places. In fact, a woman with a baby—three men, one of whom was making a cigaretta, and two were smoking, constituted all of the executive of the establishment whom we saw, and the foundry itself was in a state of repose.

Monsefu must have undergone a great transformation since Stevenson visited it, as he describes[1] " the village of Monsefu a remarkably handsome place; the houses are very neatly built, with wide corridors in front, and whitewashed; several streams of water cross the principal street."

Neither corridors, whitewash, nor streams of water put in appearance during my visit to the town,—the chief features of which were a broken-down church in one corner of the principal plaza, and two half-ruined triumphal arches, entering from the western side, in two different cuadras.

From this station we go north six miles to Chiclayo, the capital of the province, and a city of considerable population. Its church,—in the principal plaza of course,—seems to have suffered much in the war of the late President Balta against Prado during 1868. There is some story about Balta, or perhaps one of his warriors, having ensconced himself up in the bell-tower, from which cause the edifice was submitted to a peppering from without. An excellent hotel is at Chiclayo—the Hotel de Globo—kept by a

[1] Op. cit. vol. ii. p. 180.

German, and at which we had a capital break-fast. The station is about a quarter of a mile distant from the principal plaza, and to get there we have to go under a triumphal arch, in better repair, or perhaps, more properly speaking, in considerably less decay, than those at Monsefu.

ANCIENT AGRICULTURAL IMPLEMENTS FROM POMALCA.

From Chiclayo (still with our special engine), we make almost a semicircular *détour* of the city, to go out on a branch line which is being laid down to Patapu—the hacienda or sugar-cane plantation of a German gentleman, Mr. Solf. This brings us through a country rich in Indian remains. Mr. Daly, having an eye to the profit of the railway, points out to me how there are three branches off this line to three different sugar-cane farms before we are a league outside the city. I am afraid to confess that I paid more attention to Mr. Hindle's description of some relics that he stopped at a small farm-house to obtain for me, and which were taken out of a burying-mound quite close to a place called Pomalca. These consisted of what appear to have been, for the most part, agricultural implements. They were all covered over with a thick, bright green crust, as of sulphate of copper, and with this were mixed up the remnants of cotton threads of the cloth, in which they had been rolled. That which counts fourth from the left side struck me as somewhat resembling the Roman *scrinium*. It was of telescopic arrangement,—of two parts,—one fitting into the other, and reversed, was the shape of a horse's hoof. Cloth fragments, with needles and buttons, as well as a pair of small tweezers, were inside. This last-named is such as we know to have been used for plucking out hair of eyebrows, whiskers, and moustaches.

On our way a little further we passed the large hill of Pomalca,—having the same style of defences of high walls as those described at Chocofan, interior to Pacasmayo. The country around here is full of burial-mounds. This subsidiary line turns to the left by a station called Cambo, and crosses the Lambayeque river, through Tuman (a hacienda recently purchased by President Pardo), proceeding on to Patupa. At the time of my visit they were only in progress with the bridge as far as the southern side of the river. Coming back, I observe that the northern aspect of the large hill, on which I saw the fortifications this morning, is considerably covered over with ruins of walls and houses.

From Chiclayo, again northward, we pass a pantheon, or burying-ground, about half a mile outside of the town, and then through a broad and well-cultivated country. I have seen in no part of South America, alfalfa (South American clover) to equal, in the rich green fatness of its stalks and leaves, the alfalfa which I saw growing here. Along this part of the road the valley is so extensive, that in much of it one can see no Cordillera,—the view inland being bounded by horizon.

From Chiclayo to Lambayeque, the distance is only seven miles, and here we come to another town of the stereotyped model—plaza principal, with church and a market-place,—the last-named being an open shed with a matting roof. This place of Lambayeque is a wonderful locale to think of any person making his permanent residence in, when we come to consider a few features of its history. In 1791 it was nearly all swept away by a torrent of water from the mountains. The same thing occurred in 1828, when Lambayeque, from a town, was declared a city. In the year 1870, or three years before the period of my visit, a similar catastrophe occurred, and it was believed this last was the most destructive of all. Houses were swept down by the current, which went over the sides of the Lambayeque river, and several persons drowned, independent of the furniture destroyed. Cattle were carried away, and rice-fields rendered useless. Such of the people as saved their lives, did so by escaping to a neighbouring sand-hill of about 300 feet high; and there they had to bivouac in the open air for several weeks till the water subsided. In one place the river cut right through one of these *Médnas*, which was about sixty feet high, and that extended for a mile or so across the valley, in front of the river's outlet. At the time of my visit the marks of water, on the outside of the large chapel, were from six to eight feet in height; and through the streets are still remnants of walls leaning down, —evidences of roofs washed away,—broken doors hanging on their hinges,—and much appearance of ruin, that seems to be as recent as if the inundation had only taken place yesterday.

There is a geographical error in Mr. Stevenson's work referring to this locale which I must correct. He says:[a]—" Lambayeque is the capital of the province. It is situated about two leagues from the sea and four from its seaport, called Pacasmayo,—where the river of this name enters the Pacific, partly by which river, and partly by the river Lambayeque, the town and surrounding

[a] Op. cit. vol. ii. p. 181.

country are watered." In rectification of this I have to observe that San José is the present seaport of Lambayeque, distant only two leagues from the last-named. But if Pacasmayo ever were the seaport of Lambayeque, it could not have changed its position, which at the period of my visit by nearest route was thirty leagues by land, and nearly fifty miles from Lambayeque by sea. There is no river of Pacasmayo except a very tiny stream; for that which waters the valley between the two districts just mentioned is the Jejetepeque.

From Lambayeque the train goes north to Ferrañafe, where there are four large rice-preparing establishments, and which stands in the centre of a well-cultivated district. This is ten miles from the former town. All the country through the last-mentioned route is laid out in small farms of mango as well as orange-trees, plantations of Guayaquil bamboo, and rice-fields. The population of Ferrañafe is calculated at from three to four thousand. I am told the average annual export of rice from Lambayeque is fifty-five to sixty-five thousand fanegas (each fanega being 150 lbs.).

Farther north than this it is difficult to travel, unless we go on horseback—a thing which I recommend every one, who consults his comfort, to avoid as much as he can in the country parts of Peru. In the neighbourhood of San José and Lambayeque, there is a large quantity of deer. Indeed, some years ago Senor Delgado, of Lima, who owns a small kingdom of territory to the north of this, sent out a pack of deerhounds from England; but from neglect, or perhaps from the climate, they soon died. Senor Delgado's property up here is represented to me to be 180 square leagues in extent.

Farther still to the north, including no small stretch westward towards the ocean, is the district of Sechura, with its desert of thirty-two square leagues, on which wild horses, mules, and asses are said to exist in multitudes. Up in this direction, too, is the city of Piura—the first founded in Peru by Don Francisco Pizarro, in 1531, or nearly two years before the butchering at Cujamarca.* I believe it is not in exactly the same spot as stood the original San Miguel de Piura. But it does not matter much, from being of little importance to the equilibrium of affairs in the world. Moreover, its churches, and chief public buildings were almost annihilated by an earthquake in 1855.

My observations in Peru being principally confined to the coast, I have still two places to look at. So, returning as far as Lambayeque by train from Ferrañafe, I take horse, sent over to me by our worthy Vice-Consul, Mr. Fry, and go to visit San José, the seaport of Lambayeque. This ride is over a pampas of sand for two leagues, with the

* *Vide* chap. xxvii. p. 517.

same profusion of burial-mounds that I note everywhere. For a mile outside of the last-named city, and after crossing the river, the road is through a pretty grove of algarroba trees; and then we get into a heavy sand, which seems to assert its supremacy. Inasmuch as, after passing the river neighbourhood, there is not a vestige of anything in the shape of vegetation on the road to San José. Barrenness of sand, rock, and clay all through! Several donkeys, laden with loads of alfalfa, form part of our travelling *cortége*, some of these loads weighing 500 lbs. In fact, the poor animal is so smothered up with his cargo, that nothing is visible except the pair of ears and the face. Many of the burial-grounds along here have been dug into. These can scarcely be called mounds, for they are not more than an elevation, and without any form, of about a yard higher than the circumjacent road, precisely as they are all over the coast from Arica, nearly eleven hundred miles away.

At San José, I find the following in my note-book—November 20th, 1872:—

" A single glance at the tumble-down appearance of this as well as nearly all the towns, I have visited along the coast, makes me think these places must have undergone a very material change since Mr. Stevenson wrote, 'The villages along the coast have a very neat appearance; the houses are but one story high, with a capacious corridor in front.   Some of them are supported by pillars, made of sun-dried bricks, whilst others are composed of bundles of canes, lashed together, and covered with clay, with arches made of the same material.   The whole front is whitewashed, and a comfortable promenade is produced under the grotesque piazzas ; a range of seats sometimes extending the length of ten or twelve houses ; and here, in the cool of summer evening, the villagers sit, or lay their mats on the ground and sleep.' "[1]

I have copied this out for the purpose of saying that I have seen nothing of such an Arcadian neatness on the whole coast of more than eleven hundred miles over which I have been.   The houses at San José, with the exception of one or two, are the most miserable and uncomfortable of residences. They are the same at Etén, Lambayeque, Pacasmáyo, Huauchaco, Chancáy—everywhere along the coast down to Arica (excepting, of course, Calláo and Chorillos).   No whitewash, and no arches, no comfortable promenade, excepting what is built by the foreigners who are residents of the coast districts, or by the Peruvians of the higher classes. " Lo, the poor Indian " is still the same as he has been from the beginning ; and, however good or humane he may be, he does not seem at all to take to soap or whitewash.

[1] Op. cit. vol. ii. p. 18.

CHAPTER XXX.

"To compare little things with great" ("*parvula
componere magnis*"), the town of San José bears
a somewhat similar relation to Lambayeque in
topographical position, as Calláo does to Lima.

The distances, by steamer, of the ports from
Pacasmáyo northwards are—from the last-named
to Etén, thirty-two miles; from Etén to Pimentel,
seven; and from Pimentel to San José, five.

To land at San José, the safest mode, be it from
steamer or sailing-ship, is in a *balsa*—the same
kind of craft that Prescott tells us the Indians of
the coast of Peru navigated with at the time
of Pizarro's first coming out here. Although I
had seen *balsas* on the beach down at Chimboté,
as well as at Huancháco and Pacasmáyo, I first

witnessed them afloat at San José. They are
great cumbersome-looking things, quite quadrangular,[1] and without the least appearance of
anything in the shape of sailing qualities—composed of eight to ten trunks of cabbage or cork-
tree (which grows in Guayaquil), lashed side
to side. These form a floating mass of thirty to
thirty-five feet in length, and from twelve to
fifteen feet across. The *balsa* is propelled by a
large square lugger sail, and steered by three or
four men at different parts of the craft, using large
paddle-shaped pieces of wood for helm power.
The Cholo sailors, who manage these, seem to be a
rough set, as I am taking observations alongside
our steamer. Mr. Fry tells me they come from
Sechura district, not far from Payta. Whilst we
are talking about them, one jumps into the sea from
a *balsa* to fish up the stomach and entrails of a
cow, that had just been thrown overboard by our
butcher, who is preparing the daily meat for the
ship. Others of them, while waiting for the cargo
and passengers to go ashore, are fishing in the
bay with hook and bait,—hauling up quantities of
a small fish resembling bream, to which they
give the title of *Mojarilla* in Spanish. But the

---

[1] These are a different form from the balsas described by
Zarate as " the shape of a hand stretched out, with the length of
the fingers diminishing from the centre." *Vide* " Reports on the
Discovery of Peru," by Clement R. Markham, Esq. Printed
for the Hakluyt Society, 1872. Note to page 14.

Indians call it *Guajolitas*. The cook turned out a delicious dish of it for breakfast.

Undoubted signs of the "Painter" this morning, in the roadstead of San José, show that it is not confined to Calláo. Mr. Fry tells me that, even on shore during the "Painter" time here, silver, as well as white paint, is turned black by the fumes, and the people are afflicted with headaches. No doubt the same sulphuretted hydrogen gas, from submarine volcanic action, although in a modified form, that we have at Calláo. At San José we are more than 400 miles farther north than, as well as the same distance from, Calláo.

After breakfast I go on shore with Mr. Fry, on one of his *balsas*. As soon as the craft is under weigh, a number of planks, of an inch thick each, are passed down in the spaces to the depth of four to five feet, between the trunks of the cabbage-wood; and these are so regulated as to influence the steering qualities in reference to the point from which the wind is blowing. The motion is very pleasant, neither rolling nor pitching; but rising gently over the comparatively calm water this morning. Topping the breakers, and keeping full sail on, the balsa brings us right up to the shore, and as soon as it touches *terra firma*, we are secured by aid on shore from being drawn back through backward action of the wave force. One of these balsas is estimated, Mr. Fry tells me, as worth 700 Peruvian soles, or about 140*l*.

As soon as the cargo is discharged, the ropes, that bind together the different stems of which the balsa is composed, are unlashed, and these trees are rolled up high and dry upon the beach, where they remain till next wanted. This is indispensable as regards their efficiency, for if they were allowed to remain in the water, the light, absorbent structure, of which they are composed, would become saturated with the liquid, and hence their floating powers be lost.

Before the port privileges connected with the Custom-house were transferred hence to Etén, San José had 1200 inhabitants. Now (in December, 1872) it has not more than six to seven hundred. It is difficult to be described. Every house in the town, save two, seems to be leaning against its neighbouring house to keep it up. These two are side by side, but sturdy—the houses of Mr. Fry and of Mr. Solf, of Patapa. The majority of the population belong to the soft— I can scarcely call it " fair "—sex, and generally partake of the dumpy order. From the verandah of Mr. Fry's house I note several of them going through the streets, all barefooted, and in the very superlative of *degagée* as regards their dress—the long black hair flowing down to their hips.

The Lambayeque river debouches into the sea by three small mouths, at distances of from a mile and a half to three miles above San José. Rice, sugar, cotton, tobacco, coffee, orchilla (which comes from Piura), and cascarilla bark from some place more to the interior are the chief exports from San José. Through the streets in many places I see groups of donkeys, that appear to be enjoying, to the greatest intensity, the satisfaction of doing nothing.

Before dinner, on the day of my going ashore at San José, Mr. Fry had ordered two horses, one of which was for the use of Mr. Feeley, a resident Irish gentleman here, who kindly volunteered to be my *chaperon* on a short ride. This was to about five miles, directly north of San José, to what is called the Huaca of Chatuna. Our way was through a large flat of land with rushy and shrubby vegetation, having breaks (quebradas) here and there—evidences of where the water had left its mark during the last great inundation from Lambayeque in 1870. On our road we passed three or four large mounds, and after about an hour and a half of journey reached the ruins—not of a huaca or burial-mound, but of an enormous square fortress. The main building I tracked 180 yards across, or in the direction facing the sea, whilst between the latter and the building ran a long wall at a distance as nearly as I could calculate of 200 yards. Behind these are three enclosures at spaces of forty to fifty yards between each intervening wall. These walls are from three to four yards in thickness. Terraces and bastions to it, exactly like those at Cañete, Huatica, and behind Trujillo. Mounting up to the top in this, as well as the others already mentioned down the coast, presents no difficulty. For the broken walls and the filling up with clay permit an ascent even on horseback to be made with facility. On the top, and standing on a yard-thick wall, I saw that one of the large rooms had been emptied of its clay; and there stood out revealed a chamber of twenty yards square, and plastered in excellent style.

Behind the fortress, at a distance of about a mile, were the ruins of a large town, which I suppose we may likewise call Chatuna; and the view from the top of this great building embraced the country far and away beyond Lambayeque, even to the valleys extending northwards to Ferrañafe, and southwards to Chiclayo.

The sketch of San Miguel, or any part of the Huatica valley,—of the so-called Temple of the Sun behind Trujillo,—and of several others that I could enumerate, would serve for this of Chatuna. So that we have evidence not only of "persistence of type in the skulls of the pure races of Indians," as Professor Busk expresses it,[*] but we have persistence of type in the architecture of those people. For the burial-mounds, as well as the forts and fortresses, are of the same style along the coast from Arica to this—be the founders of

<hr>

[*] *Vide* Appendix A.

them Chinchas, Yuncas, or Chimoos.   In art, too,
can be recognized a similarity of fashion, as we see
little or no difference between the pottery-ware
that comes from Arica, and that which is obtained
here at San José, though a thousand miles apart.
The silver cylinder from Ica also resembles that
from Chan-Chan, places nearly as remote from
each other as San José and Arica.

I cannot leave this great old monument of prehistoric times in Peru without asking—though
with little hope of an answer—if the world be
still expected to believe of the people, who worked
these arts, and consummated this architecture,
the stories that are told of them by the early
Spanish historians.   The tale related by Garcilasso de la Vega, of the polytheism of the ancient
Indians, is written so as to persuade us into the
belief, that few of the primitive races were tame,
whilst the greater number might be compared to
wild beasts.   Everything animate and inanimate
was worshipped by them—from the whales in the
sea to the bats on the shore—from the emeralds
in the mountain mines to the shells on the
whitened beach—from the tiger in the forest to
the frog in the marshes.   In one of his chapters
he gives us details about their human sacrifices,
that seem to me a little *de trop* of the disgusting, as well as the improbable, to be more than
casually noticed.   Worse than beasts they are
described in their houses, their morals, their

customs, and general modes of living. They were cannibals according to Cieza de Leon. In the preface to his book, Garcilasso says that he " writes only about the Empires of the Incas, without entering into other monarchies, as he knows nothing about them." Of course this could not refer to the old monarchies of the pre-Incaite people, for of them he seems to know a great deal, as he tells us about their bestialities, in his ninth to fourteenth chapters. We must cease to wonder that they went perfectly naked except in regions where the cold obliged them to use covering, and that they cohabited indiscriminately with mothers, sisters, and daughters—in fact, played the very deuce with everything till the Incas came, specially sent by Divine Providence, to convert them from their idolatry to the worship of the Sun. Garcilasso laments, as a proof of the savagery of the Indians, that they remained seventy-one years, after their conquest by the Incas, without being converted to the new faith, or being convinced that they were conquered for their good. I may add this is not a rare occurrence in the history of mankind, as such a lesson has seldom been kindly taken to by humanity in any part of the world.

The reader who has accompanied me to this will see that, from my explorations along the coast of Peru, I cannot believe that a single item of Inca civilization is manifested in the archæo-

logical remains that exist in such profusion there.
I confine my observations simply to the coast
district, which shows only what the Incas have
undone—not what they did.

Not more than forty-five miles from San José, in
a north-westerly direction, is the more southern
of the two guano islands of Lobos—not yet
worked on by the Peruvian Government. These
islands are reported to me to contain from one to
two million tons of guano. It is considered to
be of a superior quality.

Still on the track towards north, from San José
to Payta is a voyage of 150 miles. The coast
being along the sandy desert of Sechura, it is
better to make the journey in the mail-steamer
from Calláo.

Accordingly, on the 14th of May last, I
started on my return to England on board
the Pacific Company's steam-ship "Santiago,"
with the attentive and courteous Captain W. J.
Barber. From Calláo to Payta there is nothing
to be noticed, as we are out of sight of land
nearly the whole of this two days' trip. We
have our usual contingent of pleasant cabin
passengers, with a deck-load of Cholós—men,
women, and children—whose strongly-smelling
beds and dirty blankets on the main deck do not
add much to the comfort of the passage. But
they all left us at Payta.

Like many other places on the coast, the neighbourhood of this port is as barren as barren can be. Not a vestige of verdure is visible anywhere. The only Englishman resident here is the much-respected British Vice-Consul, Mr. Blacker, whose courteous hospitality does away with much of the grating influence of the place. Payta is chiefly important from its being the basis of telegraphic communication in Peru. Hence to Lima telegraphic despatches can be sent to connect with the mail-steamers, and the Government of President Pardo is about to continue it on to Panama, so as thereby to secure, *viâ* Colon and Jamaica, communication with Europe and the United States. In this, as in her railways, Peru again proves how she is progressing.

Payta has not more than 4000 inhabitants. It owns, however, one of the smoothest and most secure bays on the Pacific Coast. From here to Piura is a distance of forty miles. The river Chiva empties itself into the sea about fifteen miles north of Payta, and thence has to be brought all the water used by the inhabitants of the town. To places like Payta, of which there are numbers on the Peruvian coast, the invention of Mr. Wilson to obtain fresh water from salt will be an incalculable advantage.

" *May* 17.—Last night we passed Tumbez, where Pizarro first landed with his handful of Spanish adventurers, and this morning we are skirting by Saint Helena Point, and Puerto Viejo, whence the

SEA-SHORE VIEW OF PAITA.

Heliotype

giants are reported to have come down to Pacha-
Cámac."

In the reign of the twelfth Inca, Ayatarco Capac,
we are told by Mariano Edward Rivero, "Giants
having entered Peru, they populated Huaytara,
Quinoa, Punto de Santa Elena, and Puerto
Viejo, and built a sumptuous palace in Pacha-
Cámac, using instruments of iron. As they were
given up to unnatural crimes, divine wrath annihilated them with a rain of fire, although a part of
them were enabled to escape by Cuzco. Ayatarco
Capac went out to meet them, and dispersed them
about Limatambo."

If this were not such an awkwardly constructed
piece of fee-faw-fum, I might ask, How is it that
Senor Rivero is able to give us such a minute item
of detail as that about the instruments of iron, and
yet does not say a word as to the old names of
Santa Helena and Puerto Viejo, which, as a point
of geographical curiosity, if nothing more, would
prove interesting to the inquiring part of the
world?

Straining my vision to get a glimpse of the
shore, I cannot help wondering if there were any
Pacific *balsa* Navigating Company in those days.
Or if the Gogs and Magogs were of the seven-
leagued-booted tribe, they might, by the aid of
walking-sticks of cabbage palm, have footed it
over the Sechura desert and down along the coast
to Pacha Cámac. More wonderful things than

such a feat are recorded by many of the ancient chroniclers of Peru.

As we approach the bay of Guayaquil, and come near the territory of the Republic of Ecuador, I am reminded that, according to a report made by the Reverend Father Woolf to the Government of Ecuador, there are extensive fossil remains of the Tertiary and Quaternary epochs on the coast of Manabi, and near to Punin. Besides the mastodon, the fossil horse is found, proving that in prehistoric times such animals existed there, although they became extinct, and the present race was introduced by the Spaniards.

The only part of Ecuadorian coast which is approached by the steamer, that does not go into Guayaquil, is Cape San Lorenzo, in lat. 1° 3′ S., long. 80° 56′ W. At this place is a small village, where they make the so-called Panama hats. Not far hence, or about twelve miles as the crow flies, is the town of Manta. Indeed, at San Lorenzo and Monte Christo, not far distant, the chief manufacture of hats from Ecuador is found; and these are exported from Manta. It was quite a refreshing sight to us, who had so long been accustomed to the barren coast of Peru, to see the bright green arborescence at San Lorenzo down to the water's edge.

On the 20th we are entering the Bay of Panama, —which might be called a bay of islands—the old city of buccaneers still keeping up its prestige for bloodshed.   Only the day previous to our landing there had been a constitutional fight for the Presidency, and sixty men of one regiment were shot down by another regiment of the army in the public streets.   Of course it was done with the object that the Republic should live.[3]   The number of persons killed in this revolution amounted nearly to two hundred.   Several marines from the United States' war-steamer "Pensacola," then in the harbour, were on shore to protect the railway station and the Custom-house, whilst the town seemed anything at all but comforting.   I made a short visit to the Grand Hotel—called so, I believe, more from its great dimensions than its comforts—had a few minutes' chat with Dr. Long, the United States' Consul, and Mr. Boyd, of the *Star* and *Herald*. Then drove in the same omnibus that brought us up from the wharf back to the railway station. When seated in the carriage, and as the train moved to cross the isthmus to Colon, I began to feel rather tranquillized at hoping that I was bidding farewell to the shores of the Pacific.

Before starting for the other side I tried to obtain some information about the progress of the idea to be worked out in the Inter-oceanic Canal, which I have no doubt will one day join the Pacific and Atlantic here.   The part which Peru has already taken in this matter reflects the highest credit on the administration of President Pardo; for I find,

[3] "Viva la Republica!"

by the Lima official newspaper of January last, the
following Protocol on this subject, entered into
between the Minister for Foreign Affairs of the
Government of Peru and the Minister resident at
Lima of the United States of Colombia :—

PROTOCOL of a Conference held between the Peruvian Minister for Foreign Affairs and the
resident Ambassador of Colombia relative to
an Inter-oceanic Canal.

JOSE DE LA RIVA AGUERO, Peruvian Minister for
Foreign Affairs, and TEODORO VALENZUELA, resident
Minister of Colombia, having met in the Foreign
Office, with the object of taking into consideration
the projected work of an Inter-oceanic Canal, the
first said :—

The Government of Peru has regarded with
interest the plan of an inter-oceanic canal across
the isthmus, which divides the two continents of
America, and believes that such a work will affect
not only civilization and the commerce of the world
in general, but in a special manner the political
and commercial interests of Peru.   Inspired by this
idea, in the treaties which were celebrated with the
Republics of Costa Rica and Nicaragua in 1857,
certain stipulations were inserted, tending to the
establishment of an inter-oceanic highway, but unfortunately this agreement was not ratified, and the
grand work remained a mere project.   But that
now, knowing that this question is being debated

afresh, he should wish Senor Valenzuela to be good enough to tell him, if the Colombian Government had celebrated any treaty with any other Government or any private company whatever, for the carrying out of the work, and if in case such an agreement had not been entered into, they were disposed to enter into a negotiation with Peru, either to undertake the work jointly, or with the help of all the Spanish American Republics which are interested in its completion, or at least with the participation of Peru, giving her the share in the profits and advantages to which her help might entitle her.

The Colombian Minister replied :—

That it was very satisfactory to him to see that the Peruvian Government understood so well the importance of an inter-oceanic canal, the results of which would doubtless be favourable to Peru, taking into consideration the daily increasing importance of its principal port, Callao, and the rapid progress of Peruvian commerce in the last few years.

That the Colombian Government was not at present bound by any treaty in the affair, although a few years ago two understandings were come to with the United States of America for the excavation of the canal; and the last was even approved of by the Congress of Colombia with certain modifications. The Congress of the United States had no opportunity of discussing it, and in the meantime the period for the exchange of ratifications had passed.

Therefore Colombia has entire liberty of action in the matter, with regard to which there is at present no other practical fact worthy of mention than the permission granted to the American Government to send exploring parties into the territories of the States of Cauca and Panama—explorations which are about to be repeated, as has been announced by the press.

Colombia is therefore disposed to treat with Peru, and would see with the greatest pleasure this great undertaking, which would be the most important work of our age, carried out with the intervention of that Republic and the remainder of America; but if such a thing were not possible she would be inclined to give to Peru whatever intervention the latter might take in the work—giving her of course a share of the profits and advantages to which her participation might entitle her.

Colombia perfectly understands that the community of interests which a canal would establish between her and the Republics that might take part in the undertaking, would be a powerful and durable link in the chain of close union with which she desires to be bound to her sisters.

The Foreign Minister of Peru then said :—

That in view of the frank and friendly disposition which animates the Colombian Government, and taking into consideration the fact set forth by

Senor Valenzuela, that an American exploring expedition was about to visit the isthmus, his Government would like to add some competent persons to it, in order that they might be informed of the practicability and cost of the work, if such an addition to this Commission could be possibly made, and meanwhile—that is to say, until such intelligence had been obtained, which would be duly communicated to the Colombian Government —the preliminary negotiations relative to the work could go on.

The Colombian Minister observed that he accepted, in the name of his Government, the idea of sending a party of engineers to join the American exploring party, and whose admission the Colombian Government would be glad to recommend. They would, besides, furnish every assistance in their power in order to further the ends of the Commission, considering it as sent by themselves, hoping that the Minister would be good enough to let him know in time the names of the parties who might be selected by his Government.

The interview being at an end, it was resolved to draw up the present Protocol, which has been signed in duplicate.

J. DE LA RIVA AGUERO.
TEODORO VALENZUELA.

Not very long before I left Peru, a Commission, consisting of Port-Captain Don Camillo Carillo, and Engineer Don Francisco Paz Soldan, was appointed by President Pardo to make the exploring survey in connexion with this inter-oceanic canal, as proposed in the last part of the Protocol. They were, unfortunately, too late to join the United States' party under Captain Selfridge, and were obliged to return without making the survey across, owing to the rainy season having come down upon them with unusual severity. But their report[4] is such an excellent one, and reflects so much credit on its authors, that I must give a synopsis. Whether the Lesseps of the Colombian Canal, to unite the Pacific and Atlantic, may accomplish the inter-communication in our day or not it is difficult to guess; but I coincide in the general belief that the thing is only a work of time—to sever the small ligature of the Panama isthmus or neighbourhood, and separate the northern from the southern continent of America.

The Bay of Cupica, in 6° 43″ N. Lat., and 77° 38″ W. Long., was the base of operations, on the Pacific side, of both the United States and the Peruvian explorers. Messrs. Carrillo and Paz Soldan's report says :—

The Bay of Cupica is an immense roadstead, limited on the north by the Punta de Cruces, and on the south by the Cabo Solano, and is distant about 180 miles from Panama. It contains several

<hr>

[4] For which I am indebted to the Supplement to the *South Pacific Times*, Callao, July 10th, 1873.

small inlets, the most northerly of which takes its name from the bay itself, the others being called respectively Chicocora, Limon, Tebada, Nabuga, and Jella, which is the most southerly. Half a dozen huts, built of palm-posts and with a roof made of the leaves of the same tree, compose the village of Cupica, which contains, between negroes and Indians, some twenty or thirty inhabitants.

Finding, when they arrived here, that Captain Selfridge had returned in consequence of the rains having already begun—in fact, they passed him in the steamer "Tuscarora" between Panama and Cupica—they very courageously determined not to go back without doing something; and so they attempted an exploration of the isthmus by the river Napipi, which was the first route selected by the American Commission of 1871. Of this last-mentioned survey, a memoir of its practicability was presented by Commander Selfridge to the United States' Secretary of the Navy, and was published by him with his report to Congress in December of same year. The Peruvian explorers went from the inlet of Cupica to that of Limon, where the path begins, that leads from the Pacific to the river Napipi. From Cupica to Limon the distance is six miles, and had to be done in canoes. They described Limon as well sheltered from all winds, with a good anchorage, and plenty of water. Some of the difficulties of tropical exploration may be understood, by those who have not been amongst them, from the following extract out of the report :—

"Thirty-five minutes after leaving the Bay of Limon, the highest part of the track (190 metres) is reached, and from this point it descends to the head-waters of the Limon, distant about five minutes' walk. The path lies along the right-hand side of the Limon gorge ; and while going over it, you never see the river for a single moment, although the noise of the waters is clearly heard at different points. The road is not more than 200 metres above the river; but, nevertheless, from the thickness of the wood one is unable to distinguish it, nor could we make out the ravine through which the river runs. Vegetation had obstructed the path in many places ; and the axe-men had to march a-head in order to clear the ground before we could run the levels."

Although forty minutes are necessary after leaving the sea to reach the source of the Limon river, the horizontal distance between these points is only 1,730 metres,—the source being at the height of 173 metres above the level of the sea.

But the road which has to be got over is so broken and fatiguing, that the traveller has got to look where he is going to step before putting his foot down, as the ground is made up of an infinity of roots crossing each other in all directions and at different heights,—the undulations containing the red argillaceous clay which covers all the road, forming with the help of this regular steps, which must be mounted with caution in order to avoid falls.

The description of the Napipi and its fords I pass over. The time of survey appears to have been very infelicitously chosen, as in one part of the river, the Vado del Yucal, " the natives of the country assured us that during dry weather the Vado was nearly dry, though the expedition had to swim across it the day they broke up the Yucal camp."

They only succeeded in getting as far as Antado —a height of eighty-one metres above the level of the Pacific, and a horizontal distance of 12,417 metres from Limon Bay. The difficulty of obtaining canoes, however, prevented their going as far as the Atrato, although such a communication by canoes is only possible in the rainy season. But I can easily understand how impracticable and impossible it is to make observations or fix instruments on the banks of a tropical river during the rainy season, when I recall to mind how we had to turn back from Hamarua in the steamship "Pleiad," during exploration of the Niger-Tshadda-Binne in 1854-55.[1]

After returning to Panama, they learned that Captain Selfridge had done his recent explorations

---

[1] *Vide* Author's account of this exploration, Longman's "Travellers' Library," 1855.

from the little bay of Chiri-Chiri, one of the many inlets which the great bay of Cupica contains. This was attempted for the following reasons :—

It would appear that there is in that part a spur of the mountain which begins to pass the Cordillera. It is 700 feet high, and consequently of a greater altitude than the heights of Limon. When this summit is passed, the direction of the Dogado river, which is an affluent of the Napipi, was followed to the confluence of both rivers. The course of the canal then descends to the Atrato, on the right bank of the Napipi—that is to say, the same side on which the Dogado flows into the Napipi.

The river Bojaya, as well as the Napipi, is a tributary of the Atrato, and its waters may perhaps serve to feed the canal. The tunnel which has been suggested by way of the Dogado will be at least two miles shorter than the one proposed in 1871 by Captain Selfridge on the Napipi and Limon route: that is to say, that the tunnel in the new plan will be three miles long, the whole canal being twenty-eight miles, or three miles shorter than that projected to start from Limon Bay. The probable cost of the work may be set down at 75,000,000 of dollars. The new plan for the canal contains eighteen locks, the descent to the Pacific being much easier than by the Limon Bay route.

To an un-engineering mind, like mine, the idea of a tunnel, five miles long, and of a canal with eighteen locks for inter-oceanic communications, seems to partake of the impossible. The following was Captain Selfridge's first report in 1871 :—

To take advantage of navigation on the Atrato river, and of the waters of the Napipi, one of its affluents, and then to perforate the isthmus of Napipi, descending to the Pacific by the valley of the Limon river. The canal, exclusive of these rivers, would be thirty-one miles long. There was supposed to be enough water to allow ten ships daily to pass through the canal.

Its proposed dimensions are :—Depth of water, 26 feet; width, 129 feet. The bottom of the canal at the summit would be 130 feet above the level of the sea, and as the starting-point at the confluence of the Napipi with the Atrato is at an elevation of forty, it would be necessary to ascend ninety feet. This would be done by means of nine locks, each ten feet above the other.

In order to pass the Cordillera, a tunnel is proposed 9010 yards long—more than five miles—and to descend from this tunnel to the Pacific there would be thirteen locks, each of ten feet fall, and 436 feet in length ; but as the horizontal distance is only 4000 feet, these thirteen locks would be in three parallel lines, and the ships would pass these thirteen locks, which would seem like a ladder with so many rungs. The width of each proposed lock would be sixty feet, and the dimensions of the tunnel seventy feet wide, and 120 feet high. The transverse section of the roof would be elliptic, so that no more material might be taken out than would be necessary to allow a ship to pass through. This would be an economy in the construction of the tunnel, though on the other hand it would diminish the solidity of the work, as elliptical roofs are not calculated to bear heavy weights, above all on the sides, and a circular section would be much safer.

Besides these, with pumping apparatus to raise the water from the lower to the upper locks, " the estimated cost of the works, excavation of the canal, locks, tunnel, improvements in the Atrato, a mole, a lighthouse, warehouses, dredges, pumps, &c., including twenty-five per cent. for unforeseen expenses, is $123,000,000.　The American Captain sees the following advantage in this route over all others which have been surveyed :—

" 1st. That the canal would be excavated almost wholly in solid rock; and that when the work was concluded, there would be no necessity of embankments to strengthen its sides, nor of dredges to be constantly scooping out the mud.

" 2nd. That it is thus easier to form a closer estimate of the cost of the work.

" 3rd. The healthiness of the region as compared with other parts which have been surveyed.

" 4th. That the most difficult part of the canal

—that is to say, the tunnel on the Pacific side—is almost on its shore, thus rendering the introduction of workmen, machinery, &c., very easy.

"5th. The relatively low price of the work, and, finally, the safety and size of the ports in which the canal terminates, in the bays of Limon or Cupica in the Pacific, and the gulf of Darien in the Atlantic."

The Peruvian explorers commence their objections to Captain Selfridge's plan as follows :—

In the first place, it appears to us that the dimensions he proposes for the canal do not and will still less suffice, later on, the growing requirements of the maritime commerce of the world, as the size of the tunnel and locks are barely sufficient to allow passage to the steamers which at present come to the Pacific from Europe,—taking the " Aconcagua " as a sample, of which the dimensions are:—length, 437 feet ; beam, 41 ; drawing 26 feet of water.   The dimensions of an inter-oceanic canal should, in our opinion, be greater than those which are adapted to satisfy the actual needs of navigation, for it is well known that the size of ships built is continually on the increase, and this should be taken into account when fixing the dimensions of the canal, which should be sufficient for the present and the future.   The water drawn by large steamers varies from 25 to 30 feet— and the depth of 26 feet which Captain Selfridge gives to his canal, if sufficient for the present, may not be so for the future. Our opinion is that the canal should be constructed of greater dimensions than that required by the largest merchant steamer afloat, excluding of course the "Great Eastern," which is a phenomenon. The canal should also be sufficiently broad to allow two vessels to pass in opposite directions, so that neither should have to wait till the other had passed. It is true that the estimate of Captain Selfridge is relatively low; but we must find, not the cheapest route, but that which best meets the wants of commerce.

We should prefer the estimate to be two or three times greater, for a rational and practical solution, without a tunnel five miles long, nor three parallel lines of locks, which would cause great delay in the passage of ships through the canal.

There is a great deal of sound sense in the foregoing, as well as in the succeeding observations referring to the difficulties in travelling here —not taken into account by Captain Selfridge. For tunnelling in this part of the world must be very different from what it has been in Mont Cenis, and the Hoosac in the United States. Further, the Peruvian Commissioners state:—

"Any plan which comprises tunnels and a large number of locks cannot be considered as the best, as analogous results have been obtained by other explorers, such as Garella, Capt. Kelly, &c.

The first proposed a canal through the isthmus of Panama by means of a tunnel of 5350 metres and thirty-five locks—and the second a canal without locks, and a tunnel of 4827 metres through the isthmus of Darien, taking advantage of the waters of the Truando which flow into the Atrato. Its dimensions were to be—breadth, 200 feet; depth, thirty feet—and its estimated cost 781½ millions of francs. Consequently, the result obtained by the isthmus of Napipi is not an improvement—this route presenting natural difficulties, which cannot be overcome save by the tunnel and locks proposed by Capt. Selfridge. We are of opinion that other routes should be surveyed before choosing that of Napipi, which really presents no more acceptable solution of the problem than those chosen by other explorers."

On the subject of other routes, and of that one suggested, nearly parallel with the Panama line of railway, they observe :—

"Considering that the highest point of the Panama railroad is only eighty-five metres above the level of the sea, and that the distance from sea to sea is only sixty kilometres, we can do no less than recommend a serious survey of that part of the isthmus before accepting a plan which contains tunnels and a large number of locks. The difficulties in this route are swampiness, and the great difference in the tides in the Pacific and the Atlantic. The high equinoctial tides in Panama rise six metres, whilst in Colon they only rise forty centimetres; and, finally, the insecurity of the port of Colon during a hurricane, and the small depth of water in the bay of Panama."

Of that by the isthmus of Nicaragua, they say :—

The route by the isthmus of Nicaragua also offers great advantages, for although the isthmus is here 150 kilometres wide, it has the immense lake of Nicaragua in its centre; this is 476 kilometres long by fifty-five wide, having an average depth of fifty-five metres; while its height above the level of the sea is only forty metres. Many plans have been proposed to utilize this as well as the waters of the San Juan river and Lake Mangua, but it would appear that the descents from these lakes to the Pacific present difficulties which have not yet been solved.

For any future Commission to explore the isthmus, it is recommended they should leave Calláo in the month of December, so as to arrive in that month, or early in January, as it appears the only dry months here are from December to April. After speaking of difficulties caused by the rainy season, and appending the plan of the 12½ kilometres which they levelled, they thus conclude :—

Amongst the recent explorations which have been made on the isthmus of Darien from the

gulf of San Miguel in the Pacific to the mouth
of the Atrato, we find those of Messrs. Lacharme
and Puydt; the first made a survey of the
inland in 1866, and found the highest elevation
that would have to be passed was fifty-five
metres.

Mr. Puydt found, on his expedition in 1865,
that the summit was at forty-five metres, following
a route very near that of Lacharme; both took
advantage of the lower part of the river Tuyra,
which flows into the gulf of San Miguel. None
of these observations were made with the level,
but with barometers, and consequently can only be
looked upon as simple explorations. Captain
Selfridge caused these routes to be surveyed in
1871, and from barometrical observations practised
under his direction, it seems that the highest
point in the ground gone over by Lacharme is at
an elevation of 125 metres, and that of Puydt
more than 200 metres; the country lying between
the Tuyra, and the summit being intercepted by a
number of hills of different heights. At the
termination of this report, this Commission can
only express their regret that they have not been
able to practise a more extensive survey, on
account of the limited time at their disposal; but
they think, nevertheless, that the description they
have made of the work done by them will give an
exact idea of the nature of the ground explored,
and of the difficulties which the isthmus of Napipi

presents to the opening of a great international canal.

CAMILO N. CARRILLO.

FRANCISCO PAZ SOLDAN.

Lima, 18th June, 1873.

As I desire the present chapter may be of some information to future explorers of this great work, I deem this an appropriate place for inserting news of a passage about which no notice seems to have been taken. This I cut out of an issue of Mr. Boyd's paper, the *Panama Star and Herald*, during some time last year :—

Senor Jose Maria Hernandez, long a resident of the small village of Terable, on the banks of the Bayano river, and well known in Panama for his intelligence and respectability, having on his arrival here heard talk of a canal across Darien, asserts that the Indians had shown him a pass over the Cordilleras, which is not so high as the Ancon hill near Panama. He makes the journey to the shores of the Atlantic in two days, and offers to conduct any individual or party who wishes to survey the route. The distance on the map in a straight line is about fifteen miles.[*]

The present railroad between Panama and Colon is said to have cost the life of a negro for every sleeper on the tracks. The line is laid down

---

[*] The latest work I am aware of about Panama was written by Mr. Bidwell, who was Vice-Consul out here, and which was published, I believe, in 1868, by Messrs. Chapman and Hall.

with as many curves as if it had been traced by a Brobdignagian serpent. I did not care to take any observations of the passage across it—for all its luxuriance of tropical vegetation was a matter with which I had been surfeited for the last twenty-three years. And to me, I confess, the pleasantest thing on the Panama railroad was the sniff of the Atlantic Ocean, as we glided by the Chagres river, and came into the bustling life and activity of the station at Colon. Next to this was the joy of getting on board the royal mail-steamer " Tagus," bound for Plymouth, Cherbourg, and Southampton.

CHAPTER XXXI.

In all that I have written of observations during
my two years' residence in Peru, I have had before my mind the principles enunciated by Professor Tyndall in his addresses during his recent
lecturing tour through the United States.   In one
of his " Lectures on Light," he says to his
audience :—" Keep your sympathetic eye on the
originator of knowledge.   Give him the freedom
necessary for his researches, not overloading him
either with the duties of tuition or of administration—not demanding from him *so-called practical
results*—above all things avoiding the question
which ignorance so often addresses—' *What is the
use of your work?*'   Let him *make truth his object,
however impracticable for the time being that truth*

may appear. If you cast your bread thus upon the waters, then be assured it will return to you, though it may be after many days."

Declaring my faith in the excellence of this doctrine, I regret having to affirm as no more than a matter of truth—even without "a so-called practical result"—that since I began to study Peruvian History nearly three years back, nine-tenths of the works which I have read contain more of "the Bounderby balderdash and bluster" than of "the Gradgrind facts, sir!"[1] And yet, whatever history is written, it ought to contain facts rather than balderdash and bluster. The more I read, the more the muddle increases. I have already pointed out much of the anachronisms put forth by Garcilasso de la Vega. Senor Mariano Paz Soldan, in the preface to his "Geographical Atlas of Peru," commenting on the works of Barth, Speke, and Livingstone, in Africa, as of other travellers elsewhere, asks, "What are the serious works we have on Peru? Apart from a few like those of Mr. Pentland, and two or three others, all the rest *are full of errors*—fruits of the levity with which they discuss everything without looking at causes attentively, or taking good reports, or for want of indispensable knowledge. It is necessary, then, that our youth should convince themselves how it is only by using efforts they can arrive at a ⋆knowledge of their

[1] "Hard Times." By Charles Dickens.

country, and that the era has arrived when they should commence national scientific studies, that, as we have said, are the only ones by which can be attained a knowledge of Peru."

This morsel of special pleading might be more intelligible on the part of Senor Soldan, if he himself in his works—more especially in the " Geography of Peru"—did not follow the path which he cautions future workers to avoid; for he has put down the wildest utterances of the erroneous statements made by the old Spanish writers, and printed them as facts, when a little inquiry must have proved their error, and falsehood.

Senor Don Mariano Edward Rivero, too, at the time his work was compiled, as well as published, held the post of Director of the National Museum at Lima.   From thence we may imagine he set off with Dr. John James Von Tschudi to carry out a great design.   In the preface to their united book on Peruvian antiquities [2] the reader is entertained with the following apologies for not having sooner done their contemplated work :— "There were many obstacles opposed to the successful accomplishment of our enterprise," says Senor Rivero.   This was "to examine the archæological monuments of the Incas [for Senor Rivero goes no further back than to the period

* Translated into English from the original Spanish by Francis L. Hawks, D.D., LL.D.   New York : Putnam and Co., 1853.

of what he styles the "code which governed the ancient Peruvian nation, dictated by its founder, Manco Capac"], to obtain an exact knowledge of their idiom, religion, laws, sciences, and customs, as well as all that relates to the empire of the Andes."

The Director of the National Museum at Lima —doubtless knowing nothing of the grand old monuments of the prehistoric Yuncas within walking distance of him in the Huatica valley— makes up his courage to overcome the obstacles previously alluded to, which are thus heroically set forth :—

" 1st.—The political dissensions which have succeeded each other, keeping the country in constant alarm.

" 2nd.—The diversities of the climate, the bad and, indeed, impassable roads of the coast, and the Cordilleras, the dangers to be overcome in visiting long-abandoned sites, the close thick forests, in which Nature with such prodigality shows her profusion and fertilizing power." In what way does the reader think this power is manifested in Peru? Simply, Senor Rivero tells us, by " presenting trees which almost serve as props to the vault of heaven."

After this, the third obstacle being complained of as a total want of itinerary, is such a piece of bathos that, looking at the part of Peru, so full of monuments, through which I wandered, and with scarcely a shrub in it, I must pause for a moment.

I confess that the discomforts as well as inconveniences of Peruvian travel and exploration cannot be exaggerated. But, in a common-sense point of view, I may ask, Why need Senor Rivero jump from Lima into those mythological forests " supporting the vault of heaven," which (though perhaps not quite so intensified) may be supposed to exist at the other side of the Andes, contiguous to the Amazonian valley, or northwards towards Ecuador? Or why not some equally patriotic Peruvian examine the hundreds of graveyards, huacas, fortresses, ruined towns, castles and temples throughout the valleys from Arica up to San José—a coast distance of nearly eleven hundred miles? I regret that the only answer that seems to me could be given to such a question is, that Senor Rivero's ideas could not stretch, or probably did not care to do so, beyond what he styles " the code which governed the ancient Peruvian nation, dictated by its founder, Manco Capac." So ancient, forsooth, that he tells us,[1] " Manco Capac began to reign in the year 1021 and died in 1062, after reigning forty years."

" The authority of the Peruvian monarchs exceeded," again observes Rivero,[4] " as we have already hinted in our preceding chapter, that of the most powerful kings of the earth. ' The very

---

[1] Op. cit. p. 49.　　　　[4] Op. cit. p. 174.

birds will suspend their flight in the air if I command it,' said Atahualpa to the Spaniards in his
hyperbolical language."   In the succeeding page
we are told, by an extract from Sarmiento,* of some
episodes in the regal journeys of the Incas in the
following stuff:—" From all parts the multitude
hastened to contemplate their monarch, and when
he raised the curtains of the litter or palanquin,
in which he travelled, to allow them to see him,
the vociferations with which the multitude congratulated him and besought heaven's favour in
his behalf were so great that we are told [and of
course expected to believe it, I should say] the
motion of the air caused these birds which were
flying over to fall to the ground."   This extract
from Sarmiento is given by Senor Rivero as a rehash from Prescott, and "its claim to probability is
founded on the assurance by Plutarch, that a similar
occurrence took place in Greece when the Roman
herald proclaimed the liberty of the Greeks."

On which I have merely to observe, it would be
better we had no account of the Incas at all, than
that such nonsense as this should be foisted on
us as historical.   Narrative loses all its value when
bedaubed with anachronisms of this kind.   I have
already commented on what Prescott copies from
one of the Spanish historians about the victory

* Believing the recent discovery of Senor Gonzalez de la Rosa,
mentioned previously, this must be attributed to Don Pedro
Cieza de Leon.

achieved at Puno by "Saint Michael and his legions, seen high in the air above the combatants, contending with the arch-enemy of man, and cheering on the Christians by their example."   The devil is again brought into play at Pacha-Cámac by Senor Inca Garcilasso de la Vega.   All through the work of Cieza de Leon we have doings, not of one devil, but of multitudes.   And with these and like illustrations of the great glory of the Inca period, I find the old writer Montesinos, whilst gasconading about the pure worship of the Sun, and the extension of edifices for the priestesses or virgins of the Solar God, still confessing that, during the reign of the ninetieth monarch (Inti-Capac, Maita Pachacutec VII.), and " when was completed the fourth millenary cycle since the deluge, customs were so corrupted, vices so abominable, the links of society so decayed, so little were the law and the royal power respected, that the country bid fair to be destroyed little by little."   Here I may be told that this is one of the stories for which Montesinos got the title of " liar of the first magnitude."   Perhaps so.

It was after this Augustus that the first title of Inca was given.   Montesinos tells us of the giants already mentioned as coming from Santa Helena to build Pacha-Cámac, and speaks of many of the Incas sending down from Cuzco to have the temple of Pacha-Cámac repaired.   But he never mentions the name of Pachacutec, the conqueror of the coast valleys ; and nearly all his statements are at variance with those of Garcilasso de la Vega.

Such romance as the foregoing is all recopied by Rivero, the Director of the National Museum of Lima, and I cannot help thinking it a great loss of time to publish it instead of carrying on the explorations of which I have written, for I have no doubt they would throw an immense amount of light on the little we know of prehistoric Peru. I believe the mounds, huacas, cemeteries, and fortresses already mentioned by me are of an age, hundreds if not thousands of years, anterior to the period of the Incas—of whose connexion with the valley of the Rimac we have no reliable historical proof whatever. I am, moreover, disposed to the faith, that when proper investigations are made, it will be ascertained that the builders of those things, of which we have now only the relics, will be proved, by the treasures of art found entombed with their people, to have been very far removed from the barbarism which is attributed to them by all the Inca worshippers.

Turning for awhile to another work of Dr. Tschudi's,* separate from that which he published in connexion with Senor Rivero, we are told in the

* "Travels in Peru during the Years 1838—1842 ; on the Coast, in the Sierra, across the Cordilleras and the Andes, into the Primeval Forests." By Dr. J. J. Von Tschudi. Translated from the German by Thomasina Ross. London : David Bogue, Fleet Street, 1847.

preface that, " disclaiming any intention of making one of those travelling romances with which the tourist literature of the day is overstocked, the author has confined himself to a plain description of facts and things as they came within the sphere of his observation."   And yet the Doctor tells us, amongst other things, of a reputed incident connected with the fate of Atahualpa, not on the authority of any one, I should suppose, but of " his own observation," in the following words : '—" A quantity of gold, which the Inca ordered to be collected in Caxamarca and its vicinity, when piled up on the floor of the cell, did not reach above halfway to the given mark.   The Inca then despatched messengers to Cuzco, to obtain from the royal treasury the gold required to make up the deficiency ; and, accordingly, eleven thousand llamas were despatched from Cuzco to Caxamarca, each laden with a hundred pounds of gold."   We have heard of this before, although never within the sphere of any author's observation.

Speaking of the lands of the Incas, and their aqueducts for agricultural purposes, he says,[1] " The Spaniards having destroyed the conduits, the reservoirs dried up, and the soil became barren. Many of these conduits were subterraneous, and it is now no longer possible to find them.   In some places they were constructed with pipes of gold, which the Spaniards eagerly seized as

[1] Op. cit. p. 325.   [2] Op. cit. p. 495.

valuable booty."   And again: *—"In the royal palace of Cuzco, and in the Temple of the Sun, a fusion of gold and silver was used for cement between the stones.   This was, however, employed only as a luxury—" But enough of such—what shall I say?—in the mildest of phrases, " trash "—that idea of gold and silver fused together, and put for mortar between stones in a building *as a luxury !*

It is useless to search for truth amongst the old Spanish chroniclers; for in many things, observes Rivero, " the commentaries of Garcilasso de la Vega are in direct contradiction to the statements of several of his predecessors and contemporaries,— amongst them Acosta, Fray Marcos de Niza, Pedro Cieza de Leon, Montesinos, Francesco Lopez de Gomara Balboa, Zarate, and others. The same may be said of several of his successors—it being easy to convince one's self by a comparison of the text, that the dates and allegations are erroneous not through ignorance or scantiness of information, but through the partiality of the author, who omits or falsifies all which tends to oppose his views."

This scathing criticism would be very refreshing to an impartial searcher after the truth, if he could avoid feeling that its author, Senor Manuel Edward Rivero, seems to have been born before the period when was introduced the old adage of "those who live in glass houses should not throw stones."

* Op. cit. p. 496.

It is therefore a pitiful thing to reflect that the latest account of Peru which the English reading public can be said to possess is that contained in the last edition of "Chambers' Cyclopædia."[1] This gives the old history about the Incas, almost literally from Prescott, with a geographical and statistical sketch down as far as 1864. In it we are referred for information regarding Pre-Incarial times to Mr. Bollaert's " Antiquities, Ethnology, &c., of South America."[2]

It is a very unpleasant thing for me to feel obliged to state that my friend, the gentleman just named, has fallen into more than one error in this work, which I deem it incumbent *pro bono publico* to set right. This I do only because I feel he will appreciate the doctrine of Professor Tyndall, enunciated at the beginning of this chapter— "truth being my object"—and feeling that, with such a distinguished author on South American affairs as is Mr. Bollaert, " the truth can never be impracticable."

In the frontispiece of his book is a head with large ear-lobes, entitled " Chimu, King of Manseriche, or Trujillo, Peru." Here we have three errors to begin with.

1. Chimu (or Chimoo, as a good authority in Peru spells the word for me) was the name of the tribe of people over whom the king reigned, and

[1] Vol. vii. p. 435.
[2] Trübner and Co., London, 1860.

not the name of the king himself. The last monarch of this country conquered by Yupanqui was Chucha Machoon. His name is preserved in the archives of the Municipality of Trujillo.

2. There is no such place in the neighbourhood as Manseriche. But there is a Mansiche, part of the suburbs of Chan-Chan, between the latter and Trujillo, though it has no appearance of ever having been large enough to be entitled to a king.

3. Or Trujillo? I may ask how could an old Indian locale have an *alias* of a new town— particularly when they are built on separate locations. Trujillo, as I have already mentioned, was founded by Pizarro, and never had another name.

In the same book we are told [2] of the " conquest of the coast territory belonging to the Chimu, or Chincu, whose capital was at Trujillo." No such place as Trujillo existed at the time the Chimoo people were conquered. The capital then was Chan-Chan, between the port of Huanchaco and where Trujillo now stands. This is the geographical truth.

Again Mr. Bollaert says : [1]—" The Incas' army entered the country of an old enemy, that of the powerful Chincu, or Chimu, who possessed the valleys of Pamunca, Huallim, and Huarapa (Trujillo), 8° 10′ S. near Quambacho, the Incas defeated the last Chimu of Trujillo." So that here we are puzzled to know how in the days of " the last

* P. 138.   * P. 131.

Chimu of Trujillo"—the last, in fact, of a place that did not exist—there could have been a double *alias*, i. e. of Manseriche, and of Huarapa.   It seems to me rather difficult to learn the archæology, or history of the place from this confusion.

What Mr. Markham has written about Peru is done in a vigorous and manly style, showing much perspicuity, save in the one thing of bringing the Inca dominions too near to the coast. That the Incas conquered the seaboard valleys I admit; that we have any reliable historical proof of their ever having occupied these valleys, I emphatically deny.   And I do so from having rigidly followed out the canons of criticism laid down in Mr. Markham's paper read before the Royal Geographical Society* about the "Geographical positions of the tribes which formed the Empire of the Yucas."   In this he states that as regards most modern travellers, amongst whom he enumerates Rivero, Von Tschudi, Paz Soldan, Squier, Bollaert, Wilson, Forbes, and many others, "he never relies on them for any statement not based on personal observation."

* *Vide* vol. xli., "Journal of the Royal Geographical Society," p. 281.

CHAPTER XXXII.

In searching after the origin of the primitive Peruvian people, it may be imagined from my ideas, already expressed, of their great antiquity, I do not care to dwell even for a moment on the fabulous story of the first pair.having been sent by the father of the universe—the Sun—out of Lake Titicaca with a small wedge of gold, and orders to stop where it would sink into the ground. Every one knows it is reputed to have sunk at Cuzco.

Mr. G. Smith, the famous decipherer of Assyrian manuscripts,[1] observes :—"The histories of almost all ancient peoples show at their commencement a number of mythological stories,

[1] In one of his letters to the *Daily Telegraph*.

which are of great interest with regard to any inquiries into their origin and history." This, no doubt, is true; but in Peru the idea has been limited to the Inca period, anterior to which we are ignorant of anything that does not chime in with the changes rung on the Incaite monarchy.

The theory of the orginal immigration (referring to the coast provinces at least) from the Celestial Empire by way of Behring's Straits finds more advocates than De Guignes, Paraney, or Senor Newmann de Monaco. It is supported and advocated by Senor Mariano Rivero,—admitted as possible by Senor Mariano Felipe Paz Soldan, —and even " suggested as probable " by the illustrious Baron von Humboldt.

I find it, however, difficult to reconcile the great differences of physique in the Cholo of Peru, whom we have to-day, and the Chinaman such as I see him coming out of the ship at Calláo, as bearing on one and the same source. Unless, indeed, we can attribute these discrepancies to the influence of climate, expressed by Mr. Wallace Wood,[2] who institutes what might be considered something of a like parallel. " If you plant a certain seed," he says, " in the valley of the Thames, you have a fine drum-head cabbage; but plant the same seed in the valley of the Mississippi, and in a few years it grows to a tall weed, like a mullein stalk. And the men who have in these regions grown up from

[2] In " Mother Earth's Biography."

the same human seed—the Saxon race—are not less different in their natures than the cabbage and the colewort. The beginning of European history shows us a number of human beings alike in their disposition, habits, and culture, wafted by nature like seeds up from the Indus, and the plateau of Frau, and across the Caucasus mountains, spreading in divergent streams out over the great Asiatic peninsula upon the shores of the North Sea, and upon that of the Atlantic, and down upon the three sides of the Mediterranean. Here on these coasts the seed took root. It is the waters which have made these lands what they are; and it is the continued influence of these waters, and of the soil and of the air, which has shaped the character of these people, who in the commencement were so homogeneous."

During my residence at Rosario, in 1867, I read in the *Revista* of Buenos Ayres a series of articles by Dr. Lopez, of Monte Video, intended to prove that the Quichua language (which he styles the Keshua) was not only of Pelasgic origin, but that the Incas of Peru were of Greek descent. This has been contradicted by Mr. Bollaert, in my last work about the Argentine Republic.[1] But my investigations since that period, trifling though they be, amongst Peruvian antiquities make me inclined to have this matter a little more discussed

[1] "The Parana," &c., chap. ix. p. 71. Published by Stanford, Charing Cross, London, 1868.

before coming to any dogmatic opinion on the subject, chiefly on account of what has recently come to light of the researches amongst the ruins of Homer's Troy.

From the labours of Dr. Henry Schliemann,[1] on his excavations of the ancient cities of Ilium, it appears he has found traces of the prehistoric peoples in regular strata. In one part of his explorations of the Acropolis—a portion of which had been partially searched into by Mr. Calvert, of the Dardanelles—he found the ruins of different ages in strata of comparative regularity, and his account of this finding is so interesting as having, to a certain extent, a similitude to Peruvian excavations, that I am induced to copy it. " I found the ruins of historic times," he says, "reaching generally only to a depth of one and a half metres,[2] and nowhere deeper than two metres. In a depth of from two to four metres there were no stones, and the calcined ruins left no doubt, that for ages immediately preceding prehistoric times there had been only wooden houses here. Presently I shall speak of the objects found in those different layers of ruins, and particularly of the religious symbols, which prove that the inhabitants had been of Arian race. At a depth of four to seven metres there was an entire absence of metal, and I found

_____

[1] Vide *New York Herald*, Dec. 21st, 1873.

[2] Dr. Schliemann advises the general reader to count the metre at forty inches English.

a very great quantity of stone implements of all kinds, finer pottery, all the houses built of small stones united with earth, and evidence that the inhabitants were Arians."

In the Peruvian burial-grounds the finer pottery is always found at the greater depth, and the houses built of small stones intermixed with earth constituted a feature in part of my excavations at Chaucay, forty miles north of Lima.

" At a depth of from seven to ten metres," continues the Doctor, "I found all the houses built of unburned brick; inhabitants of Arian race; very many copper weapons and instruments, although implements are for the most part of black stone (diorit). At a depth of ten metres we came upon immense masses of large stones, and I at once believed that I had reached the ruins of Troy."

The " houses built of unburned brick" and the " copper implements" at once suggest speculation, in which, however, I am as yet cautious to indulge.

But the Doctor goes on with what he styles " cutting in earnest," and certainly the description of it shows with what wonderful energy it was carried out. At one metre below the surface, whilst searching for the Temple of Minerva, he came upon a relic of Greek art—a fine sculptured marble of the time of Lysimachus, representing Phœbus Apollo in female attire, with the disc of the sun on his head, and supported on four horses of beautiful workmanship. He also brought to light a Greek inscription on a slab, weighing upwards of a ton, that stood probably in a temple, which, to judge from the sculptured figure, was that of Apollo. Then he finds a wall, built of huge stones joined with clay, two metres in thickness and three in height, which, as the layers of rubbish below it distinctly show, had been built on the slope. These approximate to the general dimensions in height and thickness of the walls we meet in Peru.

"Below and above this wall," he continues, "I find masses of that splendid black pottery, which resembles so much the Etruscan terra-cottas, and which I find here exclusively in the two inches immediately above the virgin soil, and at a depth of from fourteen to sixteen inches below the surface." No inconsiderable quantity, I may add, of excellent pottery, resembling Etruscan ware, forms part of the magnificent collection of Peruvian antiquities owned by Senor Don Miceno Espantoso, of Lima.

Then through what he supposes part of the city wall and Priam's tower, he brings us to traces of the people, and of their utensils, of which the Doctor says, " In common with all their successors at this place, until the beginning of our era, and perhaps later, they (i. e. the Trojans, who built on the primitive soil their houses of stones joined with clay) have found objects of terra-

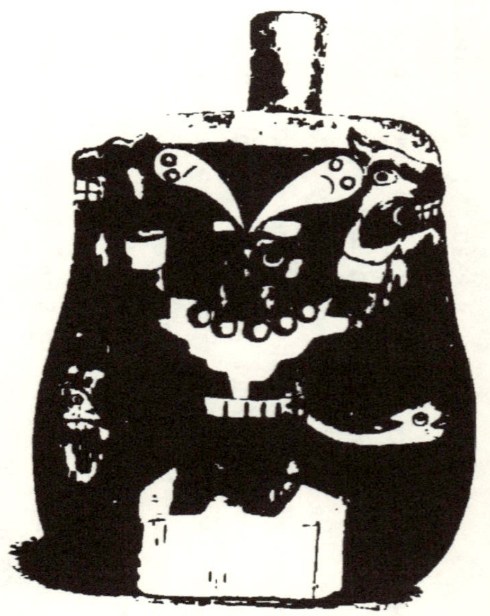

PERUVIAN PRE-HISTORIC EARTHENWARE, FROM SENOR ESPANTOSOS' COLLECTION.

[Vol. II. p. 296.

cotta in the form of volcanoes, and carousels, with
and without ornaments. Some similar terra-cottas
without ornaments are in the museum at Athens,
and two ornamented ones which are found in the
terra wares of Italy are in the museum of Parma ;
but these are the only examples I have ever seen
in any museum. Here I find them by thousands,
and about half are ornamented. These terra-
cottas, found at a height of two metres above the
virgin soil, represent the sun with his rays ; sometimes stars are intermingled with the rays—or the
sun in the centre of a cross. Copper nails, seventeen centimetres long, were found on the virgin
soil. There was no trace of metal weapons or implements ; but the nails are a sufficient evidence
that these people knew and worked the metal
copper, and of course weapons existed."

In what follows one might imagine Doctor
Schliemann was describing much of what I have
illustrated in this work about Peru, more particularly of the mill-stones found at Chosica—of the
double red goblets from Chan-Chan—and of the
bowls with tubes on each side from Canete. He
writes, "I found many small saws of flint stone,
four and a half to five centimetres in length, and
hand mill-stones of lava thirty-three centimetres
long by seventeen broad, *in the form of an egg cut
in its length into two halves.* With little exception,

____

' The very shape of the mill-stone found at Parara. See
chap. xix. p. 50.

all the terra-cotta vessels I found in the layers of rubbish of the Trojans are broken, and but few can be put together. Everything in the nature of pottery was destroyed by the huge stones that fell into the ruin ; but I possess all the pieces of some black vessels, and of one double red goblet. Of a dozen more of these I have only the central part, though sufficient to show what they were. Without exception, all the terra-cottas of the Trojans of which I have found pieces, and particularly the black urns with Assyrian ornamentation—the shining black bowls with a tube on each side—the very small round black pots which represent the human face (and of which I have one nearly perfect), as well as the larger vessels and bowls with tubes on each side for suspension—and sometimes with three feet—all attest the opulence, the fine taste, and the art of their possessors."

This description, I again repeat, would be applicable to exactly the same class of objects that, by one casualty or another, are daily being turned out of Peruvian mounds, and that I regret to say are likewise daily being destroyed by the iconoclasts into whose hands they come.

Besides a similarity in works of art, there is a like relation as regards the palaces and dwellings. This is more particularly evident in the size of the walls—"built of stones joined with clay "—and of four to six metres in thickness. The ancient symbol of the cross with a crotchet at the end of

PERUVIAN PRE-HISTORIC EARTHENWARE, FROM SENOR ESPANTOSOS' COLLECTION.

The figure No. 2 represents "El Desempenador" ("the Destroyer of Pain"). This official's business was to hammer the breath out of a man or woman who might have been given over by the doctors as incurable.

each limb enables the Doctor to say that the
Trojans were Arians. Take the crotchets away,
and what can be said of the cross on the silver
cylinder found at Chan-Chan?' "It appears to
me certain," adds the Doctor, "that both the
simple cross and the other (the one with crotchets
at the end) were symbols of the highest religious
importance with the Arian race, at a time when
the people now known as Celts, Germans, Per-
sians, Pelasgians, Hindoos, Helluces, Slavonians,

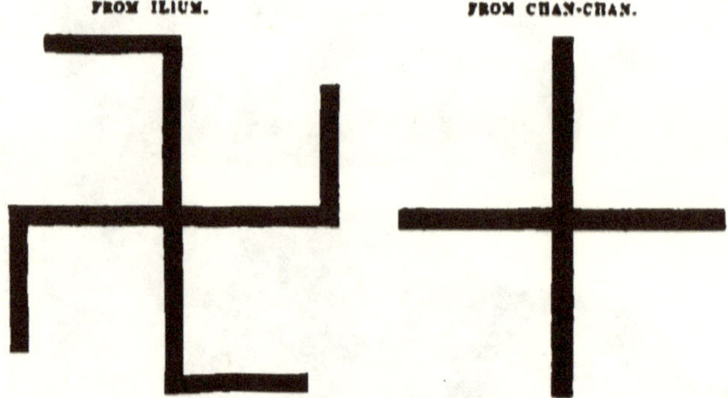

CROSSES WITH AND WITHOUT CROTCHETS.

were still one nation and spoke one common
language—and both of those symbols I have found
in their most definite form on large numbers of
the small terra-cottas taken by me from the
lowest stratum of rubbish on the site of Troy."

Prehistoric times terminated, the Doctor observes, "when the accumulation of rubbish had
reached about two metres below the surface of

' *Vide* chap. xxiv. p. 139.

the mound; for at that depth I came upon Hellenic masonry of large hewn stones, joined without any binding material, and above them house-walls of brickwork or stone joined with cement or lime." The hewn stones joined without cement may be said to have their corresponding state in the Inca period in Peru.

I think that I have shown sufficient similarity between the results of explorations in Ilium and in Peru, to justify archæologists in not coming to any conclusion on the original source of the Peruvian races until a more minute examination is made into the unbounded stores for research, so profusely spread over all Peruvian territory.

These excavations done by Dr. Schliemann may be hoped to have some bearings on the following point from Mr. Bollaert's " Peruvian Antiquities " : *—" It is observed by the authors of the indigenous races, that the rock caves with their fantastic relief are of Buddhist origin, more chaste in style than the idols of the present worshippers of Shiva, and belong to a period of Indian history, classical for art and poetry, from 500 b.c. to about 300 a.d.   By a strange coincidence it is the same period in which Phidias, Praxiteles, Lysippus, and the Roman artists of Augustus and Trojan flourished in Europe.   If we follow Montesinos, this was about the period of Peruvian history."

The coincidence of the same period of Roman

* Op. cit. p. 125.

history, or rather the same epoch of its fame in
art and poetry, being synchronous with a like
condition of affairs in Peru, according to Montesinos, makes the resemblance between the copper
implements and pottery-ware now being dug out
of Ilium to those I got from the Peruvian huacas
still more remarkable, and therefore more worthy
of further inquiry.[*]

Some few years ago a writer in a Buenos Ayres
paper (*El Orden*, February, 1868) came out with
the statement that " the Incas of Peru had for
many years made paper for the Romans; and it is
said of them (meaning of course the Incas) as it is
said of the lords of the world (the Romans, no
doubt), that they adopted the manners and customs
of such people as were submitted to their dominions."   This may appear not an unusual
episode of riding the Inca idea to death by such a

---

[*] A journal of Bogota, New Granada, the *America*, announces
a discovery so strange that confirmation is required before giving
credence to it.   Don Joaquim de Costa is reported to have found,
on one of his estates, a monumental stone, erected by a small
colony of Phœnicians from Sidonia, in the year IX. or X. of
the reign of Hiram, contemporary of Solomon, about ten centuries before the Christian era.   The block has an inscription of
eight lines, written in fine characters, but without separation of
words or punctuation.   The translation is said to be that those
men of the land of Canaan embarked from the port of Azion-
gaber (Boy-Akubal), and having sailed for twelve months from
the country of Egypt (Africa), carried away by currents, had
landed at Guayaquil, in Peru.   The stone is said to bear the
name of the voyagers.

wild statement of paper-making in Peru for transmission to the Roman empire in Italy.

Before concluding this chapter, I desire to refer to a recent discovery in the Sandwich Islands, which may involve still more the yet undecided question as to the extent of ancient civilization, and the unknown relations of different lands to each other. An American writer[1] tells us that the island of Hawaii has in it the remains of a City of Refuge, wherein, once · that criminals had fled there, they had a perfect sanctuary. "This was a vast enclosure, of which the stone walls were twenty feet thick at the base, and fifteen feet high; an oblong square, a thousand and forty feet one way, and a fraction under seven hundred feet the other. Within this enclosure in early times has been three rude temples, each two hundred and ten feet long by one hundred wide, and thirteen feet high."

After visiting Pacha-Cámac, Chan-Chan, and Chatuna, one feels on reflecting over this almost as if amongst Peruvian architecture. And the idea is increased on turning over the next page,[2] when we read,—"The walls of the temple are a study. The same food for speculation that is offered the visitor to the Pyramids of Egypt he will find here—the mystery of how they were

---

[1] "Roughing it," p. 526. By Mark Twain. Hartford County, American Publishing Company, 1872.

[2] Page 528.

constructed by a people unacquainted with science and mechanics."

The mystery of which the author speaks here I cannot help regarding as an inference without foundation. It is met everywhere amongst the ruins of Peru. Therefore it appears little better than scholastic cant to write of buildings, done by people who knew nothing of science and mechanics, when the very works themselves proclaim, that, without such a knowledge, they never could have been erected.

"The natives *have*," he continues, "no invention of their own for hoisting heavy weights; they *had* no beasts of burden, and they *have* never shown any knowledge of the properties of the lever. Yet some of the lava blocks, quarried out, brought over rough, broken ground, and built into this wall, six or seven feet from the ground, are of prodigious size, and would weigh tons. How did they transport, and how raise them?"

The *have* and *had*, which I here put into italics out of the foregoing extract, will show that Mr. Clemens writes of these works done by parties whom he calls by the generalizing term of "natives;" and his inductions are based upon the very doubtful supposition that the works in question were accomplished by the ancestors, speaking ethnologically,—of the present natives. Because, forsooth, those now residing in the Sandwich Islands know nothing of the properties of the lever, the builders of the old temples could not know them.   No Peruvian in the present day would be able to tell, even by what power, or from what source were brought the millions of tons of clay that fill up the large rooms in the fortresses of Campana, and San Miguel, at a distance of four miles outside of Lima.   So that, before asking how they did these works, let us try and find out who they were that did them.

SEGMENT OF ONE OF THE WALLS IN RUINS OF CHAN-CHAN.

Description of the architecture of these relics of walls at Hawaii possesses another phase of interest : '—" Both the inner and outer surfaces of the walls present a smooth front, and are very creditable specimens of masonry.   The blocks are of all manner of shapes and sizes, but yet are fixed

' Op. cit. p. 528.

together with the neatest exactness. The gradual
narrowing wall from the base upwards is accurately preserved. No cement was used, but the
edifice is firm and compact, and is capable of re-
sisting storm and decay for centuries. Who built
this temple ? and how was it built ? and when ?
are mysteries that may never be unravelled."

Such a fashion of architecture as the gradual
narrowing from the base upwards is exactly what
we find in the wall buildings of the Huatica
valley, as well as in those of the Chan-Chan relics
near Trujillo.

Investigations shall, I hope, be still pursued
in this interesting subject, of which I regret
having been able to do no more than touch on the
outskirts. But I trust to live to see proved—
the opinion of Mr. Baldwin, before alluded to,' in
addition to which he states,—" The civilized life of
the ancient Mexicans and Central Americans may
have had its original beginning somewhere in South
America (perhaps in Peru ?), for they seem more
closely related to the ancient South Americans
than to the wild Indians north of the Mexican
border. But the peculiar development of it represented by the ruins must have begun in the
region where they are found. I find myself more
and more inclined," he continues, " to the opinion
that the aboriginal South Americans are the oldest
people on this continent." And the explorations

' Chap. vii. p. 105.

made by me—chiefly those in the Huatica valley,
as well as Chosica—predispose me very strongly
to concur with the faith of Mr. Baldwin.

The surest way to confirm this, as well as to
educe proofs of the Peruvian races and their early
civilization, is to examine the mounds, huacas,
burial-grounds, and such buildings, for treasures
to illustrate the anthropology of the old inhabitants.
If I did not feel that a good thing cannot be said too
often, I should dread being accused of tautology
in again repeating [s] the opinion of one of the most
experienced archæological explorers of South
America, Mr. Squier :—" The mounds and their
contents, as disclosed by the mattock and the
spade, serve to reflect light more particularly
upon their customs and the conditions of the arts
amongst the nations who built them. Within
these mounds we must look for the *only authentic*
remains of their builders. They are the principal
depositories of ancient art." To which I may add,
whilst omitting the sentiment about " hiding from
the profane gaze of invading races the altars of
the ancient people," that the researches of such
men as the recent explorers of Homer's Ilium
(Dr. Schliemann), and of the Assyrian ruins (Mr.
Smith), can throw more light on the old races of
Peru, than millions of volumes with such gasco-
nade and romance as we are treated to in the works
written about that part of South America.

* Vide chap. viii. p. 131.

CHAPTER XXXIII.

To consider on whom should devolve the primary
duty to rectify the lack of exertion in exploration,
as well as to go deeper into further investigations,
I feel that the general public will agree with me,
we should expect a beginning from the Peruvian
Government and the Peruvian people.

Quite as applicable to the people and Government of Peru, as if addressed to themselves, are
the sentiments of Mr. Gladstone to the meeting of
Welshmen at Mold in August of this year, when
he said " there is no greater folly circulating upon
the earth, either at this moment or at any other
time, than the disposition to undervalue the past,
and to break those links which unite the human

beings of the present day with the generations that have passed away and been called to their account. If we wish really to promote the progress of civilization, never let us neglect, never let us undervalue, never let us cease to reverence the past. Rely upon it the man who does not worthily estimate his own dead forefathers, will himself do very little to add credit or honour to his country."

No persons ought to be more interested in the history of their own country than the natives themselves. It may be seen not only what an Augean stable of error and falsehood must be cleaned out, but the history of Peru,—of her early races,—their arts,—civilization,—and general ethnology, has yet to be written.

I am very glad, however, at having it in my power to recognize a new spirit rising up in Peru, amongst private individuals as well as in the Government, to do something in this matter. Once created, the idea requires to be fostered with energy to make it a progressive fact, and to give it the help of the authorities. The light of scientific knowledge is needed for its manipulation, and its pursuit should be carried on in the same spirit, that has actuated the Smithsonian Institute of the United States with Mr. Squier, and that has guided the London *Daily Telegraph* with Mr. Smith.

In the middle of last year there appeared in one

of the Lima newspapers[1] an interesting article on Antiquities, in which public attention was called to the important matter of studying the archæology of Peru. "The most glorious part of our history," it said, "is doubtless that anterior to the colonial epoch. And about the period referred to, we possess very few data, on account of the paucity of interest inspired through bibliographic and archæological details, as well amongst native writers, as with the Government. From such a carelessness it results that there are not a few foreigners who know more of our ancient history than we ourselves know. The huacas of the Incas (?), within which are hidden precious treasures for the studious man, are being gradually crumbled away, without any person taking an interest by making inquiry into their contents. Only the searchers urged by a desire to seek gold explore, whilst they reject with disdain the multitude of art-treasures and objects of curiosity to be found."

Knowing, as I do personally, the writer of this article, although not having asked for permission to give his name, and cognizant as I am of his being amongst the first rank of *literati* in Peru, I trust that he, being yet a young man, will follow up in this good cause. Not, however, as regards the huacas of the Incas (!), not

_____

[1] *La Republica*, 17th June, 1872.

one of which can be proved to be on the coast
of Peru, but the mounds of the prehistoric
races, of whose relics I have given some slight
account in this book. I believe that such stories
as those of Dr. Tschudi about " the gold and silver
mortar," and the gold conduit-pipes, have had
no small amount to do with " the searchers
urged by a desire to seek gold,"—on which the
Inca delusion has been fostered, to an amount
of exaggerated extravagance which is almost
childish.

La Republica[2] goes on :—" Similar carelessness
is exercised with reference to documents that treat
of times before the Independence days : without
understanding their merit, they are sold at a low
price to the costermongers' shops, or allowed to
rot under the action of time and moths. We have
palpable examples of what we talk about in all our
libraries—from the Government book-stores as
well as those of the convents, and many private
ones besides.

" Meantime we want a history, let it be of however medium a performance, for lack of elements
to compile it, *without crude errors, or scandalous
omissions.*   To gather all these materials that up
to the present day are dispersed, and publish them
as bases of a great work—this is what ought to
be done, and what actually belongs to the mission

[2] The author of this paper was, at the time of its having been
written, Editor of *La Republica*.

of the present generation. History exacts, before all other things, the aid of archæology and bibliography, particularly in countries like Peru, where the darkness of early ages is joined to the disorder of the Colonial epoch.

" It would be advisable that the Supreme Government, in imitation of countries a little more advanced, should foster and protect the taste for studies of this class. The expenses, that would be required, are insignificant compared to the results. There is not a road, city, nor town in Peru in which there does not exist monumental ruins that excite the interest of the traveller. *We are ignorant of the Inca civilization, when the remains of the old Imperial dynasty are presented to us in the past.*"

I may add, there appears to me no more characteristic incident of the "disorder of the Colonial spirit" than its having still continued harping on the " Inca civilization" and the " old Imperial dynasty" without inquiry as to whether these were delusions, or realities.

The article continues :—" Our indolence or laziness makes a notable contrast with the observing spirit of the foreigner, who comes from long distances to explore our territory. His endeavours are duly recompensed. The work of Markham, ' Cuzco and Lima,' enjoys an almost universal reputation through its erudite observations. A clever North American writer, Mr. Squier, has published in the United States and in Europe a series of articles about the ancient Peruvian monuments, which have brought him very high compliments from many literary and scientific societies. Only a few days back the celebrated Professor Agassiz, in passing by Peru, has collected with extraordinary activity a large quantity of *Incarial works of art*, to show them to the European public as treasures of inestimable value.

" Why continue ? Have we not seen a distinguished personage from the North, surrounded with some labourers, and in company with his wife, in the ruins of Pacha-Cámac, during some days, removing carcases and accumulating objects, that, if not worth anything in a material point of view, serve as so many lights to guide us in the study of a glorious epoch ? Well, then, more and more honourable will it be for Peru to unite such things as these in a national museum.

" In the midst of ignorance and preoccupations that still dominate in certain classes of the people, there will be found some to find fault with us because we dedicate our second editorial to this subject instead of to a political one. But we are confident that the enlightened class will not be of that opinion.

" We live in an age of progress, in which it is necessary to correct our errors, and offer stimulents to the study of serious things. With this object we suggest to the Government,—

" 1st. That, in every future railway contract, shall be imposed on the contractors the obligation to bring to certain persons appointed by Government works of art, manufactures, and all curious objects of antiquity in general that will be found during the progress of the works.

" 2nd. The organization of a public museum, appointing intelligent *employés* that will be obliged to write a memoir on each of the subjects entrusted to them.

" 3rd. To help whatever persons may desire to remove huacas under certain conditions, that will obviate the complete ruin of such monuments, giving them premiums in proportion to the objects they may collect, and appointing qualified persons for this examination.

" 4th. To promote *réunions* between those who possess antiquities and historical documents of Peru, or who desire to write on their importance. The premium which the Government will give to the best writers and explorers will serve to stimulate many to the cultivation of a branch utterly neglected up to the present time."

I at once availed myself of the opportunity which this excellent paper afforded to translate it for the *South Pacific Times* ' of Calláo, and sent it, with a letter of comment, for publication. In part of the latter I committed an error, from being under the

---

' Vide *South Pacific Times*, vol. i. No. 5, June 22nd, 1872.

impression that "the distinguished personage from the North" was intended for Professor Agassiz and his wife, who, I knew, had not been at Pacha-Cámac; and I mentioned that I had obtained for that gentleman 384 skulls, with other curiosities, from the burial-grounds at Ancon, Pasamayo, and Chancay, and that this collection was given by me to the Professor, with the object of being presented to various museums in the United States, more especially that of Cambridge, Massachusetts, which had been endowed with a large sum by the late Mr. Peabody, principally for the preservation of Indian curiosities.

To this I added, " At some future time I hope to have the opportunity of explaining the reason of my belief, that these belong to prehistoric times —in fact, to a period long antecedent to that of the Incas.

" To preserve such relics in the country, no doubt a national museum would be indispensable. There is not much time to be lost on the subject, for, as you truly remark, ' the huacas are being destroyed, little by little, without any person taking the trouble to examine them.'

" An Archæological Society, established on the four bases which you propose, would be the best means to preserve your antiquities ; but such a thing must be initiated either by the Government or by some scientific corporation in Lima ; and although it may seem presumptuous in a stranger to make the first step, I offer, in the cosmopolitan spirit of our nineteenth century brotherhood, to give my small services as a fellowlabourer.

"With such an intention I take the liberty to offer two suggestions in addition to your four,—

"1st.—That an appropriate site for such a museum would be the little town of Magdalena, only a few miles from the capital, and now being connected with it by means of a railway. According to Don Mariano Rivero, in his work on 'Peruvian Antiquities,' it appears 'Tradition relates that the celebrated temple of the Idol Rimac, in the valley of Huatica, was contiguous to Limatamba, and that the destroyed town has passed into that of Magdalena. There exists a large number of huacas, of different sizes—some being more than fifty yards in length and fifteen yards in height —from Limatamba to Marenga.'

"2nd.—To begin the work by the establishment of a society, somewhat similar to that which exists in Liverpool, under the title of the Naturalists' Field Club, in connexion with the Literary and Philosophical Society of that city. The Naturalists' Field Club, as its name indicates, does all its operations in the country. The members, consisting of ladies and gentlemen, meet together at each other's houses on appointed days, and proceed to study botany, geology, and natural history— to make their scientific studies a thing of re-

creation—to instruct one another, and whilst finding, in the words of Shakspeare, 'Sermons in
stones, books in the running brooks, and good in
everything,' to enjoy the amenities of social inter-
course, as well as invigorate their constitutions by
the fresh country air."

I must explain here that, at the time I suggested
the site of Magdalena for a museum, I was as ignorant, as I believe the majority of Peruvians are to
the present moment, of the large monuments in
its neighbourhood and all around the valley of
Huatica [1] (whereof Magdalena forms the centre)
—believing them to be no more than Rivero described them (although I now cannot imagine that
he ever visited there), "some being more than fifty
yards in length and fifteen yards in height from
Limatamba to Marengo."

In the same paper of *La Republica*, June 17th,
in which my letter was published, appeared the
following :—

"To Senor Dr. THOMAS J. HUTCHINSON.

"SIR,—The foregoing letter, which you have
addressed to us to-day, obliges us to occupy ourselves anew with a matter so important as the
archæology of Peru.

"You will believe that we do it with true pleasure, since you, Senor Hutchinson, to whom the

[1] *Vide* chaps. xiii. and xiv.

country already owes some services, are the first
to hasten in response to the call made in favour of
our country, and of science.

"' In the midst of ignorance and of preoccupations that still rule amongst certain classes of the
people,' says the article to which you refer, ' there
shall not be wanting some persons who will judge
us dispassionately, because in our second editorial
we do not give place to a political point, and we
are certain that educated persons will not be of
this opinion.'

"The letter before us shows that we have not
been mistaken.   The idea of exploring the huacas
in aid of knowledge and civilization, as of esta-
blishing a national museum, has found echo, and
can claim distinguished supporters.

"You know it.   In all the extent of America
there is no country which has materials to excite
the curiosity of the archæologist and the studious
man as that of Peru, with its monuments of antiquity spread all over the extent of its territory,
attesting the former existence of a powerful and
civilized Empire.

" By an anomaly which can scarcely be credited,
hardly any one takes an interest in examining these
ruins, *wherein is written the true history of old times in
this Continent.*   Has not the period arrived to put
the work in hand ?   Will it not be easy to organize
a society with this object ?   Will not the Government lend its aid to this new association for

whatever means it requires to advance the work? Undoubtedly, yes.

"The idea is launched. You offer your useful co-operation. It is necessary, then, to commence the work. If we have not associations such as that of Liverpool, and others which you cite, the University body, the School of Medicine, the Literary Club, and all intelligent persons will, for their own pleasure as well as for duty, give a helping hand to the work. In the confession that you are a stranger, you merit more honour, and it places us more under the obligation of gratitude to you.

"Before finishing, we have to say that, in mentioning a distinguished personage from the North, surrounded by some labourers, and accompanied by his wife, in the ruins of Pacha-Cámac during many days, removing carcases and accumulating objects of curiosity, we referred to Mr. Squier, whose studies of the ancient monuments of Peru, published in *Frank Leslie's Illustrated Paper* at New York, made such a brilliant exit in Europe and New York.

"Always attentive, as *La Republica* will be, to accept writings of this class, which have a noble and elevated end, we hope you will continue to send us your important observations.

"Remaining, dear sir, your obedient humble servant,   "THE EDITOR."

But neither the School of Medicine, nor the

Literary Club, took any initiative in the matter. In fact, no step was made on the subject, as the political caldron of Peruvian politics was, at the period, about getting into a seething state for the dreadful catastrophe of the last week of July already described.[*]

As soon, however, as President Pardo was called to the position of First Magistrate of the Republic, he took in hand the complete reorganization of the whole system. The military and municipal discipline being once arranged, and the most important of all—the financial condition of the State—having been set to rights, as much as it was in his power to do, he then turned his attention to the matters expressed in a Decree of which the following is a translation :—

" SOCIETY OF FINE ARTS.

" MANUEL PARDO, Constitutional President of the Republic,—

" Considering: That it is necessary to provide for the preservation of the Exhibition Palace, which is not only one of the most splendid monuments of the capital, but a point of *réunion* and recreation for a large section of our society, and an excellent practical school for the nation :

" That it is convenient to give to its spacious saloons a profitable application, in harmony with its structure, and with the object of its creation:

[*] *Vide* chap. xvii. pp. 1 to 20.

" Be it decreed :

" 1st. The formation of a society, to be denominated that of the ' Fine Arts,' to charge of which will be handed over the preservation, and administration of the palace, and its dependencies, as well as the direction of a museum, of a school of painting and sculpture, and of a conservatory of music, to be established therein.

" 2nd. This society shall consist of twenty-five members.

" The following are named to form part of it:— Senores Don Ignacio Osma, Don José Antonio Barrenechea, Don José Bresani, Don Miceno Espantoso, Don Manuel Atanacio Fuentes, Don Antonio Raymondi, Don Ernesto Malinouski, Dr. T. J. Hutchinson, Don Gaspar de la Puente, and Don Pedro Correa, authorizing them to select the thirteen other members, and to form and present to the Government the statutes of the society.

" 3rd. The saloons of the Exhibition Palace will be destined to the establishment of a general museum, to a school of painting, and sculpture, and to a conservatory of music.

" 4th. The funds of the Society of Fine Arts shall be the products of the Exhibition Palace, and the sums that may be voted in the budget for its preservation, and for the establishment and support of the museum of the school of painting and sculpture, and of the conservatory of music.

" To be communicated, registered, and published.

" Given in the Government House, at Lima, this 17th day of December, 1872.

" M. PARDO.
" F. ROSAS."

The statutes accompanying the rules and regulations of the Society of Fine Arts are too long to quote here. But they explain its objects in the second section as follows :—

" Article 6th. The society will occupy itself—

"1st. With the care and protection of the Exhibition Palace, its parks, and other dependencies; procuring for the public, in exchange for moderate prices of admission, recreations and diversions in harmony with the nature of its institution; and organizing periodical exhibitions of flowers, fruits, animals, machines, and industrial matters, whether native or foreign.

"2nd. To organize, enrich, and preserve a museum of objects of utility as well as interest, whether native or foreign, and before all of Peruvian antiquities,—procuring collections of historical objects, native to the country, of instruments, utensils, machines, and so forth.

"3rd. To create and support an academy of drawing, of painting, and of sculpture, promoting the teaching of these arts, as well as procuring paintings and original statues, or copies, of celebrated masters, to form special museums of such objects.

U 2

" 5th. For the establishment of a conservatory of music that will encourage the teaching of this art, applied principally to composition and to singing, procuring collections of foreign classical compositions, as well as those that are in Peru, although they may not merit such a character; to promote philharmonic *réunions*, concerts, festivals, and everything that can tend to popularize and refine the taste for music."

Such a society has a noble field for its operations in Peru; and although, as the president, Senor Don J. A. Barrenechea, in his despatch to the minister accompanying the statutes for approbation, observed, " it does not flatter itself that it can be organized in a day, still it hopes eventually to be founded on solid bases, such as in other countries are only proved to be the result of great labours, rich elements, and the slow course of time."

" Rich elements " in Peru existing to a degree that may be characterized as inexhaustible; let us hope that labour and time will do the rest.

CHAPTER XXXIV.

THE first year of President Pardo's accession to political power was marked by some excellent measures—chiefly those proposed to Congress—of which I am about to make brief notice.

In the month of October were published the bases of an Immigration Society, to be divided into six sections, each of which was to take special charge of the immigration from the following countries—viz., France, Italy, Spain, Portugal, Austria, Germany, and Great Britain. This was organized, and nothing more; as it only professed to establish agencies in the countries specified, for paying the passages of immigrants, and providing the means of their establishment in the territories of the Republic, be it by contract or otherwise. Immigration to Peru, or to any South American Republics, is a matter requiring more serious thought, as well as more advantages than are usually offered to the immigrant, before it can be put in competition amongst the northern races of Europe, with immigration to the British colonies, or to the United States.

The following is the text of the law of immigration which was passed by Congress a few weeks before my departure from Peru :—

"MANUEL PARDO,

" CONSTITUTIONAL PRESIDENT OF THE REPUBLIC.

" *Inasmuch as*

" THE CONGRESS OF THE PERUVIAN REPUBLIC,

" *Considering :*

" It being unquestionable that immigration contributes to the prosperity of nations,

" Has passed the following law :—

" The Executive Power is hereby authorized,

" 1st. To expend the sum of one hundred thousand soles a year for the encouragement of European immigration, on the basis which may be most suitable to each nation, and to each labouring class.

" 2nd. To distribute to the immigrants irrigated lands belonging to the nation.

" 3rd. The colonists will be obliged to reimburse the Treasury for the expenses, save those of transport, which they may occasion, according to the conditions the Government may fix.

"Let it be communicated to the Executive Power, so that the necessary measures for carrying it out may be taken.

"Given in the Hall of the Sessions of Congress in Lima, on the 29th of April, 1873.

"Manuel F. Benavides, President of the Senate, Felix Manzanares, Secretary; Jose S. Tejeda, President of the Chamber of Deputies, José M. Gonzalez, Secretary.

"Be it therefore printed, published, and circulated, and let it be duly complied with.

"Given in the Government House in Lima on the 28th of April, 1873.   "M. Pardo."

As far as immigration of the agricultural classes is concerned, I cannot speak in favour of Peru, for the simple reason that the fiscal lands available for cultivation are nearly all in the Amazon valley, and therefore out of reach of the ordinary emigrant. If carpenters, or other mechanics, wish to go to Peru, where they never need be a moment idle, and where they will get excellent wages,[1] they will find, amongst the reforms introduced by President Pardo, one that will be of greater benefit to them, as well as to the country, than a dozen Acts of Parliament. This refers to the doing away with what is called the matriculation paper, which

[1] I must add, too, the cost of living is very high in Peru.

every mechanic hitherto was obliged to take out. It was payment for licence to work at his trade, granted to him so as that he should consider himself subject to the laws of the Peruvian Constitution, with, of course, the advantages ceded by any treaty between his own Government and Peru. A mechanic working without a licence, or matricula, was considered a sort of poacher.

In this latter light, was held William How, an English ship carpenter, who came to my Consulate one day to complain that he had been taken prisoner and put on board a Peruvian man-of-war, with orders to work, and of his being badly treated on account of refusal to comply. I sent him at once to our Minister at Lima, the Hon. William Stafford Jerningham, who took the matter up very strenuously, as the case of ill-treatment of a British subject. After some time the particulars of the affair, which it is not necessary to reprint, appeared in the official newspaper, joined to an opinion of the Fiscal (chief law officer), Senor Paz Soldan. This was addressed to the President of the Republic, and amongst other matters pointed out :—

Foreigners, as well as citizens, are free to follow in the Republic every kind of commerce, industry, or work, on paying the respective licence, which assures and protects them in this right. In order to exercise any of the learned professions, one is required to present a university diploma, and prove besides the possession of the necessary skill and practice which is required.

Individuals, not natives of Peru, who desire to navigate Peruvian ships, must undergo the examination decreed on the 4th of August, 1840.

Another of the same year, dated 20th September, declares the individuals who compose the matricula to be exempt from the payment of *contribucion personal* (a poll-tax). But this tax was abolished by a law of Congress.

The regulations of the matricula allow entire liberty to those who wish to inscribe their names, without being able to compel any, but only those, who put their names on the marine register, had the right to navigate, and exercise any other industry connected with the sea. Each department is allowed to have its roll of ship carpenters and caulkers, to the number which may be thought convenient. The non-matriculated artisans may freely exercise their calling in the towns where they reside, but not in Government work, except in the absence of matriculated tradesmen. It is, therefore, clear that the regulations require no matriculation on the part of any person, nor is there the slightest excuse for obliging any one to do so. Fishery and navigation are the only industries which cannot be freely followed, and those who are not matriculated can exercise these occupations in the ports in which they reside.

I consider it is very useful to foreigners coming

to Peru to know the actual status of affairs in points of this kind; and I therefore continue the opinion of Senor Paz Soldan :—

The State must pay the passage of such carpenters, and blacksmiths, as matriculate in the ports of Arica, Calláo, or Paita. Those who matriculate are exempt from all kinds of personal tax, as long as they serve in the mercantile marine, or are embarked aboard of the Custom-House cutters or other ships belonging to the navy (see the 6th and 13th clauses of the law, dated 18th January, 1848).

This law, which was passed for the protection of the Merchant Marine, does not recognize the exclusive right of fishing, which formerly belonged to those who matriculated, and which had been abolished by subsequent acts of Congress. The 483rd article of the Civil Code declares "that the right to fish is common to the natives of the country," and the community of right destroys every privilege.

Citizenship in Peru is obligatory on no one; nor is it denied without a just cause. To effect it there is first required, the desire and request of the foreigner; the wish to be naturalized as a Peruvian must be first expressed; he must be twenty-one years of age, and possess some profession or trade, besides which he must be inscribed on the Civil List in the form prescribed by law. (35th Article of the Constitution.)

The 19th Article of the Civil Register regulations sets forth the formalities, which are excessively easy and liberal, wherewith such an inscription is to be made.

There have been established, and are in operation at the present time, many mercantile companies; many industrial, farming, manufacturing saltpetre, mining, navigation, irrigation, and railway undertakings, whose promoters, owners, and agents are not citizens of Peru.

Many other persons, belonging to different countries, have entered into contracts with the Government, concerning various works, and have solicited and obtained the concessions of privileges, in whose quiet possession they still are. It may be said that the greater part of the riches of Peru, and the most lucrative enterprises are in the hands of foreigners, without their having been called on to take out their papers as citizens.

Foreign capital which has been spent in taking advantages of the various kinds of riches that the country possesses, can reckon on every assurance of legal guarantees; regarding many of these the nation has assured them interest, which is a favour that has seldom been granted to the natives of the country. The advantages and protection which foreigners find in Peru have led some of them to believe, that they were in a better position, and even more privileged, than our own people. On this account some have pretended that political disturbances should not affect them, or that the

State should indemnify them for the losses which are the result of civil conflicts; in short, that there should be for them a special legislation, which in their own country they cannot find, and which they would look for in vain.

These are facts which are patent and known to all; they are more decisive and conclusive than any reasons that could be brought forward, to prove that foreigners possess in Peru every guarantee, that can be desired in the following of their trade, and the employment of their capital. Contracts entered into with them are scrupulously carried out, and justice is done when a proper claim is presented; they are, on this account, content with Peru and with her Government.

If they even suffer in person or interests, it is not from the fault of the administration, but because passions, vices, and crimes are common to men and peoples ; it is a fatal leprosy, which affects the human race, spread over the face of the globe.

Between the Government of Peru and that of her Britannic Majesty there exists a treaty of friendship, commerce, and navigation, in which the rights, guarantees, and protection, which the subjects and citizens of both countries are to enjoy when residing in either territory, are declared. But the ordinary laws of Peru concede to British subjects greater and more extensive rights than are set down in that treaty. They can freely enter Peru, reside where they like, leave it, get married, make a will, and dispose of their property as they wish, or, dying intestate, their heirs are protected. They can inherit real or personal property, obtain exclusive privileges, carry on manufactories, or establish any kind of industry, but subject to the same laws.

England, so justly praised for liberty, and the good sense of her people, who offer admirable examples in all walks of life, has not been so generous with foreigners, who, according to a recent writer, are barely tolerated.[2] There foreigners could neither possess real estate, nor inherit gifts, legacies, or any kind of personal property until they were authorized to do so by a statute of the 4th of August, 1844, which still kept in force the old prohibition of not being able to possess real estate. The Fiscal has gone into the foregoing explanations to satisfy the desires of the Honourable Chargé d'Affaires of her Britannic Majesty on the one hand; they are favourable to his industrious countrymen who come to live in this country, bringing with them as capital, their trades, economy, and work under the protection of our laws. On the other hand, they are for the benefit of the country itself, and principally because at the time, when a law affecting foreign emigration has been passed, emigrants may be aware of the guarantees, rights, liberties, and pro-

---

[2] If Mr. Soldan resided much in England, he would be disabused of this error.

tection which they may hope for on arriving in
Peruvian territory."

The most cogent part of this important document is, however, in the final recommendation,
which I am informed has, since its suggestion,
been passed into a law by Congress:—

"In conformity with what is declared in the
Constitution, and according to the laws of the
Republic, your Excellency may declare:—

"1st. That all the blacksmiths, carpenters,
caulkers, and other workmen, either native or
foreign, who may come to reside, or who actually
reside in the ports, greater and less, of the
Republic, to carry on their trade, either afloat or
on shore, cannot be obliged to serve on board the
national ships, nor yet on works undertaken by
the State; nor shall they be required to inscribe
their names in the guilds, whatever may be their
character.

"2nd. That the inscriptions and matriculations should be voluntary, and whatever work
should be required for the foregoing shall be paid
for according to contract, to the artisans who may
be called upon to execute it.

"3rd. That all decrees, rules, orders, and
regulations to the contrary be abolished, and that
only the published laws and the decrees dictated
in conformity with them shall be strictly observed.

"4th. That the Honourable Chargé d'Affaires
of her Britannic Majesty be replied to, enclosing

him an authorized copy of what your Excellency may decree, as well as the reasons which led to its promulgation. Always excepting that your Excellency should consider the contrary to be in accordance with justice, and in conformity with the national interest."

Besides these, in the month of April this year, 1873, and after some opposition from Congress, the sum of 40,000 soles, or about 8,000*l.*, was voted to bring some schoolmasters for Peru from Europe. In the same month was likewise decreed a similar sum for the increasing of lighthouses on the coast of this Republic, as well as the putting into better discipline, of those that already existed.

In the month of March, the Minister of the Interior, Senor Rosas, sent to Congress a suggestion for the handing over of all the telegraph lines to the Government, as well as for the granting of a subsidy for the Payta and Panama telegraph line. Referring .to these matters the Minister thus concluded :—

With the desire of favouring commerce, which is daily assuming greater proportions among us, and of satisfying the wishes and wants, which at present characterize every civilized people, the Government has decided to ask for authorization to guarantee five per cent. on the probable cost of a submarine cable between Payta and Panama. This guarantee will encourage the promoters, and will cause, before long, a cable to be laid, which will render communication possible with Europe in a few hours. The Government have the greatest hope, that it will in no way affect the public revenue; for if some present sacrifices were required, they would be amply compensated by the activity which the submarine cable would impart to our telegraphic lines, and the increase of commerce and industry which would result.

In order to carry out the foregoing objects, the Government has drawn up the following project, which I have the honour to include to you, and which you will be good enough to make known to the Honourable House of Representatives.   FRANCISCO ROSAS.

"'PROJECT.

"' *The Congress of the Republic considering :*

"' That it would be better for the Public, and the Administrative service, if the Telegraph lines belonged to the Nation :

"' *Hereby decrees :*

"' 1st. The Government are hereby authorized to assume the direction of the Telegraphic lines which exist in the Republic, paying in bonds of the internal debt, bearing six per cent. interest, the difference which may be found to exist between the calculated value of the said lines, and the amount which the actual company owe to the nation. This difference not to exceed S. 350,000.

" ' 2nd. The Government will then proceed to extend the line from Pisco to the port of Iquique, and are hereby authorized to make the necessary disbursements.

" ' 3rd. The Government are authorized to guarantee five per cent. on the capital which may be employed in laying a submarine cable between Panama and Payta, the said capital not exceeding 1,500,000 soles.' "

On the subsequent 19th of June was published in the official gazette of Lima, under the rubrics of his Excellency President Pardo, and Minister Rosas, the plan of bases for the construction and laying of the last-mentioned cable between Payta and Panama, with a guarantee of five per cent. This guarantee was to be for the term of ten years, not on the whole capital that may be employed, but on the sum of 1,500,000 soles. The proposals were to be published, through the legations of the Republic in France, England, and the United States; and amongst the provisions was one to the effect:—

" 16. If the contractor be a foreign citizen, he must renounce all diplomatic intervention in the questions, which may arise about the carrying out the contract. These must be judged and decided according to the laws of this country, and before its own tribunals."

To this is tacked on another plan of bases for the construction, and laying of the cable, without the guarantee of five per cent.

Another project of President Pardo's was the formation of an Irrigation Society—a thing so much needed, in fact so indispensable, in the arid, sandy coast valleys of Peru.

This last-mentioned was sent in April last to the Tribunal of Commerce, after being favourably reported on by the Committee of Accounts, and Credit, and a company was recommended to be formed on the following statutes:—

" 1st. The object of the Society will be the irrigation of lands in the territory of the Republic, either buying lands to irrigate, or undertaking works on their own account, to sell or rent the water which they may be the means of furnishing to the owners of lands which need it; or contracting these works on account of the owners, to be paid annually by them, or on Government account, if the occasion should offer.

"1. The capital of the company will be two millions of Soles (S. 2,000,000), to which the Government will add 400,000*l.* sterling in bonds of 1872.

" 3. The company are empowered to issue bonds at interest not exceeding eight per cent., for double the sum, which may be realized from Government capital, or of the company's with a mortgage of the lands, which the Society may acquire, or of the works which they may conduct.

" 4. The company will pay the sum corresponding to the interest and sinking fund of the Government bonds, after giving the preference to the interest and sinking fund of the mortgage bonds which it may emit.

" 5. The company may augment its capital, as far as it may think convenient, the Government reserving the right to increase or not, proportionally, the sum it may lend in bonds.

" The Tribunal of Commerce will name a commission of competent persons, to draw up and propose, for the approbation of the Government, the definite statutes of the company.

" M. Pardo.

" Jara."

Amongst other incidents of progress in Peru during the past year is an invention by Mr. C. Wilson for procuring fresh water from sea water through direct action of the sun's rays. Every one who has travelled, or resided, in that country will acknowledge the advantage of having this principle carried out, as extensively as possible, on a coast where water is so scarce, and in many parts impossible of being obtained. At Iquique, Pisagua, and all the ports in that neighbourhood, fresh water is procurable only from distillation by steam machinery. At the Literary Club of Lima, in the month of March last, its manipulation was expounded by Mr. Eugenio Plazolles, Engineer, as follows :—

" The apparatus consists of a box of pine wood

x 2

one inch thick, and which is about fourteen feet long, two feet wide, and has an average depth of six inches. The upper part of this box is closed with ordinary glass, which has an inclination of an inch and a half.

At the lower edge of the glass there is a semi-circular canal, destined to receive the fresh water which is condensed on the interior surface of the glass. The salt water is let into the box to about an inch in depth. It is then exposed to the rays of the sun, the heat of which is sufficient to raise it to sixty-five or seventy degrees centigrade. A very active evaporation then begins, and it is proved that a square metre of glass will condense daily two gallons of pure water."

I witnessed the apparatus in operation at Messrs. Dockendorf's stores near the works of the Pacific Steam Navigation Company, and am gratified at considering it a complete success. The Central Board of Government Engineers recommended Mr. Wilson's right for Letters Patent, in regard to this invention, after its utility and perfect adaptability to the climate had been recognized by the Prefecture, the Honourable Municipality of Lima, and the Attorney General of the Supreme Court of Justice.

THE END.

APPENDIX A.

ANTHROPOLOGICAL SOCIETY OF GREAT BRITAIN AND IRELAND.

APRIL 1st, 1873.

Professor BUSK, F.R.S., *President, in the Chair.*

THE minutes of the previous meeting were read and confirmed.

The following new members were announced :—Sir THOMAS GORE BROWNE, K.C.M., Athenæum Club; RICHARD WORSELY, Esq., Reform Club; THOMAS H. GAY, Esq., 103, Victoria Street.

The President having vacated the chair in favour of Sir JOHN LUBBOCK, Bart., read a paper as follows :—

Remarks on a Collection of 150 Ancient Peruvian Skulls, presented to the Anthropological Institute, by T. J. HUTCHINSON, *H.M. Consul at Calláo (with Plates* VII. *and* VIII.*). By Professor* BUSK, *F.R.S.*

THIS important and interesting collection of ancient Peruvian crania was forwarded during the year 1872 by Consul Hutchinson, who has devoted much time, and labour, in the exploration of the ancient burial-places in the country around Calláo.

The first instalment consisted of eight skulls from a "*huaca,*" or ancient burying-ground near Ancon, to the north of Calláo. They are considered by Mr. Hutchinson to be those most likely

of the tribe of Chinchas, or Huancas, or, perhaps—as he surmises
—of Quichuas, or Aymaras; all of which tribes, he states, are
now probably absorbed into the Cholos, a *mestizo*, or mixed race.
At a place called Ica, Mr. Hutchinson had exhumed an earthenware round jar, or jug, containing all the bones of a full-grown
man, and side by side with it were several smaller urns, containing
the bones of children. On exposure to the air these bones fell
to powder, but the urn has been sent. Besides the eight skulls
from the locality above referred to, Mr. Hutchinson sent twelve
more to Dr. J. Barnard Davis, who has forwarded them for exhibition on the present occasion, and it is much to be regretted
that he has not himself been able to attend, to give us his views
concerning them.

The next despatch from Mr. Hutchinson, accompanied with a
letter, dated 26th April, 1872, comprised twelve skulls, with
the lower jaws, which he says were picked up in the same place
of interment, near Ancon, from which the mummified bodies had
been turned up by the Spaniards at the time of the conquest,
or by Peruvians at later dates, when searching for treasure. However this may be, it is curious to find that among these bones,
and other relics from the same place, is the entire hoof of a
mule, which could only have been introduced by the Spaniards,
at or since the invasion of Peru by Pizarro and his followers.
These crania were accompanied by some leg and thigh bones,
with the dried flesh still upon them, showing that the bodies
had been buried in the usual sitting posture. Together with
them, also, were some fragments of fishing nets, and a wooden
club and sword. The site is about twenty miles north of Calláo,
and about a mile only from the sea-shore.

In another communication, dated August 20th, Mr. Hutchinson announced, that he had sent off another collection of from
thirty-six to forty skulls, with the lower jaws, and states that he
had collected the great number of three hundred and sixty-eight
skulls for Professor Agassiz; and noticing that amongst those
here collected, was one with the frontal suture open.

Another letter of September 12th, 1872, announced the sending of five cases of Indo-Peruvian skulls. Of these (cases 1, 2),
fifty-eight were procured from Pasamayo, five miles south of
Chançay, and thirty miles north of Calláo. At this place it is

stated that there are two burial-grounds, close to the sea-shore, and that the surface of the ground for nearly a mile square from the beach, up a sand-hill, is white with skulls and bones derived from bodies which were dug up, no doubt, by the early Spaniards. He remarks, also, that some of the lower jaws from this place are stained with copper on the inside, from a coin which had been placed in the mouth, and one of them, he states, has had a copper plate or skull-cap on the head. A very curious circumstance, when taken in connexion with what we know, was the practice among some Asiatic, and in remote times, even among some Western European peoples, of encasing the skulls of friends or enemies in metal; a subject upon which I offered some remarks on a former occasion, when describing an engraved calvaria from China.[1]

Mr. Hutchinson remarks that among this collection there were also two in which the frontal suture was not closed.

Another case contained twenty-three skulls from Ancon, and Mr. Hutchinson remarks that in that neighbourhood there are three different styles of graves at places situated some distance apart; but, strange to say, here, as at Pasamayo, there are no vestiges of houses.

The burial-places are :—

1. Cylindrical or funnel-shaped graves, lined on the inside with stones, in some of which the bodies appear to have been placed upright.

2. An ordinary longitudinal grave, of the same style as those in our churchyards.

3. A large square excavation, which is roofed with rafters covered over with bamboo matting. In some of these latter Mr. Hutchinson found five or six bodies, including men, women, and children, swathed in clothes, and with the faces covered, some with cotton, others with llama wool.

At Ancon all the graves contain either pottery, or cloth, or pieces of fish-nets, or needles for manufacturing nets, or lace-work, or bags that resemble reticules for ladies.

Another case contained thirty-three skulls from the Cerro del Oro, in the Canéte valley, interior to Cerro Azul, about a

[1] "Ethnological Journal," vol. ii. p. 73, 1869.

hundred miles south of Calláo; and in another wore thirteen skulls from the same place, together with two from Pasamayo, and a few ordinary specimens of prehistoric Peruvian crockery-ware.

Those from Cerro del Oro are from the brow of a hill, which shows evidence of having been densely populated in former times, from the quantity of *adobe* ruins in the neighbourhood. "To the best of my recollection," he says, "it was here that Pizarro and Almagro had their first meeting. And the old road from the Canéte valley to Lima passes by the ruins of the celebrated temple of *Pachacamac*.

"The whole of the Canéte Valley, now covered with sugar plantations, is full of Huacas, or mounds of interment described by Prescott. So also in the valley of the Rimac, as well as that of Huatica, in the districts between Chorillos and Lima, converging seaward to Callao and Ancon. These mounds are for the most part still unexplored. Of some such Prescott writes, 'Vast mounds of an irregular or more frequently oblong shape, penetrated by galleries running at right angles to each other, were raised over the dead, whose dried bodies or mummies have been found in considerable numbers, sometimes erect, but more often in the sitting posture common to the Indian tribes of both Continents. Treasures of great value have also been occasionally drawn from these monumental deposits, and have also stimulated speculators to repeated excavations, with the hopes of similar good fortune.'

"But the skulls which I send," Mr. Hutchinson goes on to say, "are not from *huacas*, but from places of interment such as are described in 'Peruvian Antiquities,' by Don Mariano Eduardo Rivero." [9]

Having thus, for the most part in Mr. Hutchinson's words, described the localities from which the present collection of crania was procured, I will proceed to offer a few remarks upon them regarded craniologically. But since the matter has come more particularly under my attention, I have found that so much has been already written on the subject by others, that very little remains for me to remark without repeating what has been

---

[9] Chap. viii. p. 200 *et seq.* G. Putnam and Co., New York, 1859.

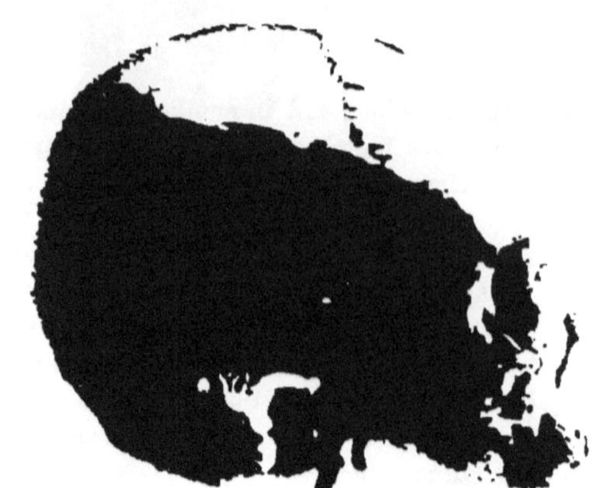

Fig 1

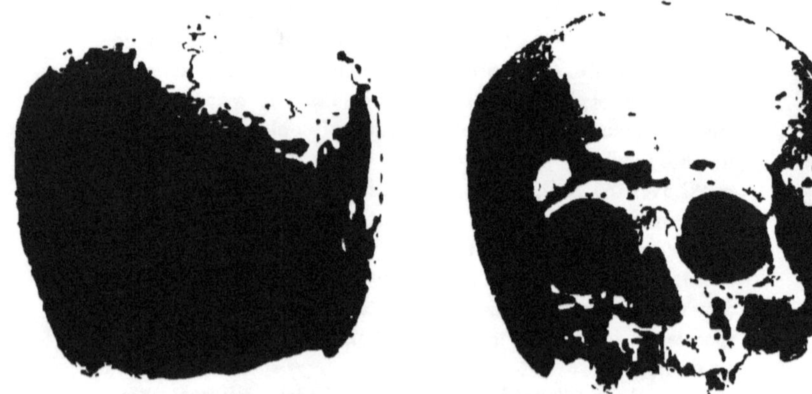

Fig 2

Fig 3

Fig 4

Fig. 5.

Fig 6

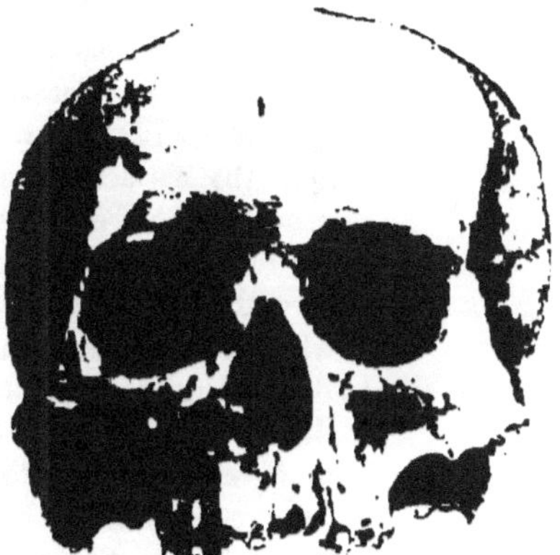

Fig 7

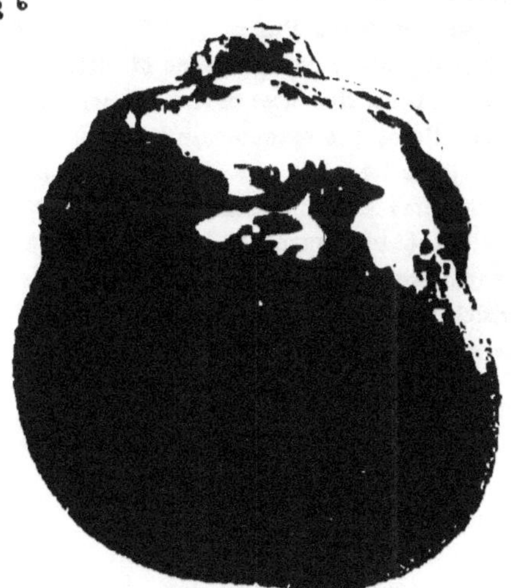

Fig. 8.

SCALE

already published, a general *résumé* of which will be found in Professor Daniel Wilson's "Prehistoric Man," and "On the Cranial Characters of the Peruvian Races of Men," a paper by Mr. C. C. Blake in the second volume of the Transactions of the Ethnological Society for the year 1861-2; a paper which is especially valuable for the copious references to the previous literature on the subject.

Perhaps, however, the most complete view, within a small compass of the subject, as regards these ancient Peruvian races, will be found in Professor D. Wilson's work above cited (p. 225), where he gives an account of his observations, made upon the collection of mummied bodies and crania in the possession of J. H. Blake, Esq., of Boston, and which was brought by him from ancient Peruvian cemeteries on the shore of the Bay of Chacota, near Arica, in latitude 18° 30′ S., which burial-places appear to be of exactly the same kind as those from which Mr. Hutchinson's collections were procured. As Dr. Wilson's work is in our library and readily accessible, there is no occasion for my making any lengthy extracts from it on the present occasion. It may be mentioned, however, that Mr. Blake remarks that "there is no record or tradition, concerning this and similar cemeteries, of the period when they were made use of; and it is by no means certain that they contain the remains of the ancestry of the Indians who now occupy the country."

He remarks also that the colour and texture of the hair are facts of great importance to the ethnologist, as indicating essential differences from the modern Indians in one important respect; and therefore confirming the probability of equally important ethnic differences suggested by other evidence.

With respect to this point Professor Wilson (p. 235) states, that he has repeatedly obtained specimens of hair from Huron graves near Lake Simcoe, the most modern of which cannot be later than the middle of the seventeenth century, yet in all of which the hair retains its black colour and coarse texture, unchanged alike by time and inhumation; and in this respect corresponding with that of the modern Indians of South America, and also of the Chinese and other true Mongols of Asia.

The hair which is so abundant upon many of the crania on the table is, as will be observed, by no means coarse, but rather fine and silky—nor is it truly black, but rather of an auburn tint, whilst on one the hue is reduced to a dirty stone colour. But there is no reason, perhaps, on this account to assume that the hair in both cases was not originally black, exposure in a hot, arid, sandy soil, and in the latter case probably to the weather, being sufficient to account for the change of colour from black to the present tint. But the comparative fineness and coarseness are another and more important matter, and if, upon proper microscopic examination and comparison, the differences stated to exist between the ancient and modern Indian hair should be found really to exist, a strong argument would arise in favour of those, who suppose that the ancient cemeteries may not really contain the remains of the ancestors of the Indian tribes of the present day.

As will at once be perceived, the present collection, taken as a whole, presents a remarkable uniformity of cranial conformation. This is of a strongly brachycephalic type.[*] I have not measured the entire collection, but having selected what appear to be the fairest examples of the various forms, their mean length appears to be about 6.25 ins., and width 5.6 ins., giving a cephalic or latitudinal index of .905, only two falling below .800. In this estimation, however, were included both artificially-compressed and, so far as I can perceive, normally-shaped skulls. Separating these two from each other, the cephalic index of the supposed normally-shaped crania is about .873, the greatest being .935, and the least .812, and of the clearly artificially deformed or flattened ones about .979, the least being .861, and the greatest 1.32.

These figures show how very much the latitudinal index is exalted by fore and aft compression of the skull, and the almost equally great effect in increasing the vertical height will be seen in the fact, that the altitudinal index of the normal skulls is about ·843, the greatest being ·919, and the least ·806, whilst in the compressed ones the altitudinal index rises in the mean to ·878, the greatest being ·919, and the least ·824.

<hr>

[*] Linnæus's term " plagiocephalic " is emphatically descriptive of the more common form of American skull, and may be conveniently used to distinguish the broad head with flattened forehead, so characteristic of the greater part of the American races, as, in fact, it was used by him.

TABLE OF MEASUREMENTS OF ANCIENT PERUVIAN SKULLS.

SPECIMEN	1. General			2. Breadth					3. Radial					
	Length	Breadth	Height	Postorbital	Frontal	Parietal	Occipital	Zygomatic	Frontal	Vertical	Parietal	Occipital	Maxillary	Fronto-Nasal
No. 1 A	6.5	5.5	5.6	3.7	4.7	5.1	4.3	5.3	4.0	4.9	4.8	4.2	4.0	3.6
'' 2 A	6.3	4.7	5.0	3.1	4.0	4.7	3.8	4.6	3.8	4.9	4.4	3.8	3.4	3.3
'' 3 A	6.3	5.1	4.4	3.3	4.1	4.8	4.0		4.2	4.3	4.5	3.4	3.6	3.2
'' 4 A	6.6	5.2	5.4	3.5	4.4	5.0	4.1	5.0	4.3	4.8	4.6	3.8	4.0	3.7
'' 5 A	6.8	5.9	5.0	3.5	4.9	5.0	4.3	5.3	4.6	4.8	4.9	3.6	3.4	3.6
'' 6 A	6.4	5.6	5.5	3.7	4.7	5.4	4.5	5.4	4.3	4.6	4.6	3.6	4.1	3.7
'' 7 A	6.7	5.9	5.3	3.6	4.7	5.7	4.6	5.4	4.1	4.6	4.7	3.1	4.8	3.5
'' 8 A	6.5	5.7	5.5	3.6	4.5	5.5	4.6	5.0	4.1	4.6	4.9	3.8	4.2	3.6
'' 9 A	6.4	5.6	5.6	3.7	4.6	5.8	4.2	5.1	4.3	4.7	4.7	3.7	3.7	3.4
'' 10 A	6.3	5.5	5.5	3.6	4.4	5.4	4.3	5.2	4.4	4.6	4.7	3.2	4.3	3.4
'' 1 B	6.3	5.3	5.6	3.4	4.6	5.7	4.2	5.7	4.3	4.6	4.9	3.9	3.5	3.2
'' 2 B	6.1	5.5	5.5	3.6	4.6	5.1	4.8	5.0	4.3	4.6	4.7	3.5	3.7	3.3
'' 3 B	6.3	5.8	5.7	3.7	4.7	5.6	4.6	5.3	4.3	4.6	4.9	3.5	3.4	3.6
'' 4 B	6.4	5.4	5.3	3.6	4.3	5.3	5.1	5.9	4.1	4.5	4.4	3.7	3.4	3.6
'' 5 B	6.1	6.1	5.3	3.9	5.0	5.4	4.7	5.6	4.3	4.7	4.8	3.6	4.0	3.6
'' 6 B	6.3	6.3	5.7	4.0	5.1	5.9	4.5	5.7	4.6	4.9	5.0	3.8	4.3	3.8
'' 7 B	6.1	6.3	5.7	3.8	5.2	6.1	4.3	5.6	4.6	4.9	4.4	3.5	4.0	3.7
'' 8 B	6.1	6.0	5.4	3.7	5.1	5.9	4.5	5.6	4.5	4.6	4.6	3.3	4.2	3.7
'' 9 B	6.7	5.3	6.3	3.8	4.3	5.2	4.2	4.7	3.8	4.5	4.9	4.2	3.7	3.3
Quaqua V.I	7.3	6.8												
'' V.I	7.3	6.3												
Titicaca														
Perno														

SPECIMEN	4. Circumference	5. Longitudinal Arc				6. Transverse Arc			
		Frontal	Parietal	Occipital	Total	Frontal	Vertical	Parietal	Occipital
No. 1 A	19.8	4.9	5.0	4.6	14.5	11.6	12.9	13.6	12.0
'' 2 A	19.0	4.2	4.6	4.2	12.9	10.3	11.2	12.3	11.0
'' 3 A	19.2	4.4	4.7	4.4	13.5	11.0	12.0	12.5	10.6
'' 4 A	19.4	4.6	4.5	4.0	13.5	11.6	12.3	12.9	11.0
'' 5 A	19.5	4.4	4.8	4.0	13.8	12.7	13.6	14.1	10.9
'' 6 A	19.5	4.0	4.7	4.6	13.8	12.1	12.9	13.3	11.0
'' 7 A	19.0	4.3	4.5	4.5	13.3	11.4	13.1	13.7	11.8
'' 8 A	19.0	4.5	4.8	4.3	13.6	11.6	12.9	13.7	11.4
'' 9 A	19.3	4.5	4.3	4.6	13.8	11.8	13.1	13.7	11.0
'' 10 A	19.0	4.3	5.1	4.2	13.3	12.1	11.7	13.1	10.4
'' 1 B	19.3	4.5	4.1	5.0	13.6	11.2	13.0	14.3	12.3
'' 2 B	18.9	4.6	4.7	4.3	13.6	11.6	12.7	13.2	11.2
'' 3 B	19.3	4.7	4.7	4.4	13.8	11.6	12.9	13.6	11.2
'' 4 B	19.0	4.3	4.4	4.6	13.7	11.0	12.0	13.7	11.4
'' 5 B	19.8	4.6	4.5	4.3	13.4	12.0	13.8	14.1	12.0
'' 6 B	19.4	4.6	4.8	4.2		12.6	13.9	14.1	11.8
'' 7 B	19.7	5.6	6.6	4.3		12.6	14.3	14.3	11.6
'' 8 B	19.6	4.7	4.3	4.3		12.2	13.3	13.5	10.4
'' 9 B	19.3	4.9	4.9	4.5		10.2	12.0	13.5	12.0
Quaqua V.I									
'' V.I									
Titicaca									
Perno									

SPECIMEN	7. Indices				8. Contents		9. Sex
	Latitudinal	Altitudinal	Maxillary	Facial	Capacity	Weight of Brain	Male or Female
						oz. A.	
No. 1 A	846	680	…	4.	73.6	39.5	M.
'' 2 A	765	668	…	5.	67.0	47.5	F.P
'' 3 A	822	709	…	4.	81.0	34.0	M.?
'' 4 A	812	843	…	3.	73.7	40.0	M.
'' 5 A	1010	943	…	2.	72.0	39.9	P.
'' 6 A	875	678	…	6.	85.0	45.5	M.
'' 7 A	1060	912		3.	77.8	42.0	M.P
'' 8 A	880	859		4.	79.28	43.0	M.
'' 9 A	861	845		2.			M.
'' 10 A	874	674		6.	78.0	42.25	M.
'' 1 B	935	903	…	1.	90.0	50.0	M.
'' 2 B	897	657	…	4.	81.0	46.0	M.
'' 3 B	835	919		3.	78.6	41.5	V.
'' 4 B	843	834		4.	71.6	34.5	?
'' 5 B	853	834		4.	80.75	44.0	?
'' 6 B	1000	719		5.	85.5	47.0	—
'' 7 B	1350	934	…	5.	87.5	64.0	—
'' 8 B	848	843	…	5.	87.3	64.0	—
'' 9 B	791	791	…	6.	74.0	41.25	Flong.
Quaqua V.I					85.5	52.5	Flat.
'' V.I					81.5	46.5	Flong.
Titicaca					85.7	16.5	Flong.
Perno					73.8	39.5	Flat.

As regards the comparative cubic capacity of the two kinds of skull, I am not able to speak positively, as, in order to determine this with any accuracy, it will be necessary to separate, so far as is possible, the male and female skulls ; for the reason, first, that the latter are, of course, much less capacious ; and, secondly, that in the case of artificially-deformed skulls, if it be true—as most writers state—that it is only the males who are subjected to treatment, no comparison can be instituted unless the latter are eliminated. But so far as my experiments have gone they would have served to confirm the general opinion, that the compression has no effect in diminishing or enlarging the cranial capacity— nor is it likely that it should. The mean capacity of the larger skulls—which may be regarded as males—appears, so far as I have gone, to be about eighty cubic inches, equivalent to a brain of about forty-five ounces, roughly estimated. This capacity, and the measurements above cited, show that the crania generally are of small size.[*]

It will also be seen, when comparing the numbers I have given with those afforded by Professor Wilson (p. 222), taken from a series of ancient crania from North American mounds and caves, that they very nearly correspond. In the mound skulls the mean length is given as 6·54 inches, and width 5·67, the cephalic index being ·861, and in those from sepulchral caves, as 6·62 × 5·78, with a cephalic index of ·873 ; figures that show clearly enough that even at that distant period there must have been a great similarity between the inhabitants of the western part, at any rate, of North America, and of the seaboard regions of South America, and, it may be added, with the modern inhabitants of the same regions.

Besides these brachycephalic crania, which form the bulk of the present collection, there are a few of a more elongated form ; but these, however few in number, are of especial interest, open- ing up, as they do, the interesting question as to whether there is really more than one type of skull to be found among the ancient Peruvians, and also the still wider one whether there is more than one type peculiar to the American Continent.

As is well known, Dr. Morton was of opinion—and no man's

---

[*] This is in accord with the statements of all observers.

opinion can be more weighty—that there was but one American type of skull—exclusive, of course, of the Esquimaux—and that of strongly brachycephalic form. According to Morton, the Indian skull " is of a decidedly rounded form. The occipital portion is flattened in the upward direction, and the transverse diameter, as measured between the parietal bones, is remarkably wide, and often exceeds the longitudinal line." The forehead is low and receding, and rarely arched,—a feature that is regarded by Humboldt, Lund, and other naturalists, as characteristic of the American race, and serving to distinguish it from the Mongolian. The general question whether a diversity of type exists among the native races of America down to the present day, need not here be discussed ; but I would simply remark that, so far as my own observation of collections goes, there is every reason to believe that the brachycephalic type exemplified in the present collection and shown on a somewhat larger scale, but with precisely the same essential features in the Chinook Indians and in the natives of Vancouver's Island, prevails amongst all the native tribes—at any rate, in the seaboard regions of North and South America—from Nootka Sound round the coast of Patagonia and up the east coast, within the historical period, to the Caribbee Islands ; whether it extended further north on the Atlantic shores in earlier times I do not know.

With regard to the dolichocephalic type of American skull, and the tribes amongst which it exists in North America, I need merely refer you to Professor Wilson's copious data, at the same time expressing my belief that it will be found to prevail—or to have prevailed—throughout the greater part of the central or east central parts of America, both North and South, from Canada to Tierra del Fuego. The whole question is ably stated and argued by Professor D. Wilson, who, with Mr. J. H. Blake and others, is of opinion that, not only are two distinct forms of skull to be found in the ancient cemeteries,—one rounded or globular, and the other elongated,—but also that two distinct types of skull are at the present day to be observed amongst the existing American populations. The evidence to this effect, both as regards the ancient skulls, cited by Professor Wilson, is amply sufficient to decide the point.

The evidence of the existence of a dolichocephalic type

afforded in the present collection is not very abundant, but is, nevertheless, decisive. And if it be true—as is extremely likely —that the practice of artificial deformation of the skull has, in most cases, originated in a desire simply to increase or to add to the natural features, we cannot fail to perceive, in the elongated skulls from Titicaca, that that peculiar kind of deformation has arisen from a desire to add to the attractive features of the peculiarly elongated form of skull, of which several instances are presented in the present collection.

The Director read the following paper :—

On Ancient Peruvian Skulls (with Plate IX.). By J. Barnard Davis, M.D., F.R.S., V.P. Anthropological Institute.

Professor Agassiz during his late travels went to Callao, in Peru, and when there he received great attention from her Britannic Majesty's Consul, Mr. Thomas J. Hutchinson. Mr. Hutchinson made a fine collection of skulls of the ancient Peruvians, and other antiquities from the Peruvian cemeteries during the stay of Professor Agassiz, and presented the whole collection of three hundred and eighty-four skulls, and other articles of pottery, &c., to him for the museum at Cambridge, in the United States. I send a copy of the letter of Professor Agassiz, who states the great value of the collection, and expresses his warm thanks for it.

Another fine collection of Peruvian skulls has been sent to the Anthropological Institute by Consul Hutchinson, which I am informed is being exhibited. I have no doubt it will attract much attention, and will receive considerable elucidation from the observations of craniologists present, particularly from the President. At the request of Consul Hutchinson, I have forwarded a number of articles of Peruvian pottery obtained from the cemeteries, to be exhibited at the same time.

It will not be necessary for me to say anything of consequence respecting the skulls, as this will be done more accurately and more copiously by very competent gentlemen, I have no doubt. I will merely refer to one point—i. e. the so-called *long* skulls of the ancient Peruvians, which was treated more at length in the

"Thesaurus Craniorum," p. 246. It is there stated that Professor Morton, the distinguished American craniologist, in the early period of his researches, considered that there were both natural dolichocephalic and brachycephalic crania among those obtained from the Peruvian cemeteries. He subsequently saw his mistake, and perceived that the longer examples had obtained this character merely from the interference of art. A more recent investigator—Dr. Daniel Wilson, of Toronto, who has acquired a deservedly high reputation in various pursuits, both scientific and literary—has also devoted much attention to craniology. Having the opportunity of examining many collections of Peruvian skulls, particularly that made by Mr. J. H. Blake, now at Boston, in Massachusetts, he has revived the former opinion of Morton.

Dr. Wilson expresses his conclusion upon the subject emphatically in these words: "It is not at all necessary for the confirmation of the opinion reasserted here, that there are two essentially different types of Peruvian crania, to affirm that the form of the elongated skull never owes any of its peculiarities to artificial compression."[a]

The view thus taken by Dr. Wilson, which is that the dolichocephalic Peruvian skulls are of natural form, was combated in the "Thesaurus Craniorum." Since that book was printed I have received ample and perfectly satisfactory evidence as to the truth of the proposition that the longer skulls owe this quality to artificial means. By the politeness of Dr. J. Aitken Meigs, of Philadelphia, I have obtained two Peruvian skulls, which at one period belonged to Dr. Morton's collection, as a specimen of each kind. One of these is brachycephalic, the other is dolichocephalic; but they both present distinct traces of artificial distortion. This fact is conclusive, but, besides, by the politeness of another eminent American man of science, Dr. Jeffrys Wymann, professor of anatomy at Harvard University, this conclusion has been again and still more distinctly established, by an examination of Mr. Blake's collection itself, whence chiefly Dr. Wilson obtained materials for the foundation of his opinion. Dr. Wymann has been so good as to examine

* "Prehistoric Man," 2nd edition, p. 410.

Mr. Blake's collection with its present owner, Dr. Warren, of Boston, and wrote me the result on the very day of his visit. I may here introduce an extract from Professor Wymann's letter:—

"The upshot of the whole is, the crania do not confirm Dr. Wilson's statement. One of Dr. Wilson's points, in fact it is his chief point, is that the skulls are natural because they are symmetrical, and that it is next to impossible that a distorted skull should be other than unsymmetrical. I have carefully examined eight elongated Peruvian crania with reference to this point, and find that they are quite as symmetrical as any ordinary crania; in fact, neither Dr. Warren nor myself could detect any asymmetry in the general outlines. The mode of employing pressure by bandages would indeed be likely to produce symmetry. Curiously enough, it so happens that the skull represented in Fig. 59 of Dr. Wilson's work is the only one in which asymmetry was detected, and in this the most prominent part of the occiput projects farther on the left than on the right side."

This Fig. 59 is given in Dr. Wilson's book as a *natural* dolichocephalic skull; but I informed him, on the publication of the work, that it had obviously been distorted by art. Dr. Wymann goes on to say, "Both Dr. Warren and myself were agreed on this point. In addition, this cranium as well as that of the child (Figs. 60 and 61) in Dr. Wilson's book, presented the usual appearances seen in artificially distorted crania, particularly in the contraction of the circumference of the cranium between the middle and hinder portions. It seems to me, therefore, that the criticisms of Dr. Wilson's statements in the 'Thesaurus Craniorum,' p. 246, are quite correct. I cannot conceive his having arrived at the views he sets forth, and it is rather odd that the skull he has chosen to exemplify his views should be the one, out of the whole, showing (from his own stand-point) the incorrectness of them."

I do not doubt that the extensive collection of skulls sent by my friend Consul Hutchinson will afford ample and conclusive evidence upon the questions here discussed.

I may then at once revert to the Peruvian pottery which I have sent for exhibition on the present occasion. Upon this

I shall say very little, scarcely more than give a catalogue of the specimens exhibited. It will be understood that this pottery is derived from the same tombs, or *huacas*, in which the skulls were met with. It was the practice of the ancient Peruvians to inter with the dead a great variety of objects. Some were of gold and silver, various implements, some of them of other metals, some of textile materials, and a vast diversity of pottery. From this fact, of the interment of such numbers of articles with the dead, it may be inferred with much probability that the Peruvians were not without some hope of a life beyond the tomb. The pottery indicates considerable skill and ingenuity in its execution, for they did not possess the famous and ancient "potter's wheel," a simple machine above their powers of invention. It is all made by hand, and there is no doubt that, like the pottery of the ancient Britons, it was by the labour of the women's delicate fingers that it was produced. It may be noted that none of the Peruvian pottery is thoroughly baked, so as to fuse the body and to render it very hard. On the contrary, it is more like *terra-cotta* than anything else, yet it is baked somewhat more thoroughly than terra-cotta usually is. A large number of the specimens, indeed the majority, exhibit imitations, more or less successful, of animal forms, sometimes of vegetable forms; the large majority typify the human form. It also occasionally occurs that the forms of the vessels have a grotesque character, and at times give expression to the humour of the people who made them. Skill and taste have been abundantly displayed in the modelling of the almost endless designs of these vessels. Much of the pottery is of a black colour, from a metallic oxide introduced into the clay ; other vessels are made of lighter-coloured clays, and all are ornamented in many peculiar styles. Some ornaments, which have been regarded as of classical origin, may at times be found upon Peruvian pottery, such as the *fret* and *scroll*, which were not unknown to the Greeks. These and other accidental coincidences have been employed by some as arguments to support the delusive notion that the Peruvians were of European origin. This kind of erroneous deduction from coincidences has been widely employed in the philosophy of anthropologists, who explain things upon hypothesis. Sometimes it has betrayed even eminent men. I remember being astonished some years ago, to find the very distinguished and accomplished Councillor Thomsen, the founder of the grand Ethnological Museum at Copenhagen, to take this view. Looking at some of the beautiful feather helmets with crests in the museum, made in the Sandwich Islands, he told me that these very helmets proved that the Greeks had had communication with these islands, for here we saw the Greek crested helmet. A common decoration in Peruvian pottery is produced by placing small grotesque animals in different positions on the vessels. The chief use of most of these curiously-formed vessels is considered to have been for holding and for carrying water. As they have handles, they are *water vessels*, articles of vast importance in a climate like that of Peru. From their porous nature they would keep the water cool. A hint has been thrown out that some of them may also have been employed for sipping an infusion of that great exhilarator, the coca (*Erythroxylon coca*), through a silver tube. This is the mode of sipping the *Maté*, or Paraguay tea, but whether the coca be taken in the same way is rather uncertain.

The specimens sent for exhibition are—

Vessels in *Black Ware*.

No. 1. An amphora, with two ears or handles. This closely resembles the amphoræ of the Greeks and Romans. It has been elaborated with great care. The marks of the tool are seen all over its surface.

No. 2. A curious water vessel modelled in the exact form of a gourd, with all its natural prominences. Upon one side is modelled the bust of a woman to form the orifice, with her arms and pendant breasts. Her face, with the ears, eyes, nose, lips, and teeth, are all expressed. In the ears are large ear-rings. The head has been modelled as a separate piece, and been attached to the vase afterwards. The potter's finger marks are seen in this attachment. I believe the gourd is a cast from a clay mould taken from a natural specimen, as there is an appearance of a seam along the middle of the bottom. The woman's head is broad, and brachycephalic according to nature. The nose is depressed, like that of a negro, and the hair is represented in tufts; neither of which is correct to nature, but more for the convenience of the potter. This vase is an admirable

ANCIENT PERUVIAN POTTERY.

piece of pottery. The marks of the modelling tool are very obvious on the neck, but totally absent from the gourd, or cast part, which, in fact, supports the view that the gourd is made from a mould.

No. 3. Water vessel, which has a double tube rising up from the belly to join in a single one for the mouth. This combination of the tubes forms a handle. It is neatly decorated on the sides of the upper part with four grotesque birds, having long bills. The depressed field upon which the birds are placed appears to have been formed by an impression.

No. 4. Another handsome water vessel with the double tube for a handle, resulting in the single mouth. This vase is neatly ornamented with three oval prominences, like olives, conjoined by a cord on each side, each of the series of three being equally conjoined by the cord. On the outer sides at the angles at which the tubes rise a small bird is attached, and a minute monkey at the angle at which the single tube rises. From the marks of seams at the sides, it is probable that the body of this vessel has been made in two halves.

No. 5. Another water vessel, in the form of a depressed globe, which has a prominent spout like that of some teapots. On the opposite side is a grotesque seated figure, having a square head, a prominent nose of *a natural American form*, and a large board, holding a cup upon his knees. A flat handle is formed conjoining the back of the figure with the spout. [See Plate IX., Fig. 1.]

No. 6. A small *whistling vase*, formed of the body of a bird, with long beak. There is a small hole above the bird's head to produce the sound. Wings and feathers are modelled on the sides of the vase.

No. 7. A small cylindrical vase, or urn, with a row of indented ornamentation near the top. This vessel closely resembles some of the ancient British urns. The marks of the tool upon it fully indicate the patient labour by which this pottery has been produced.

No. 8. A vase formed of three conjoined almost cylindrical bodies, which are surmounted by a tube on each side, running into the terminal spout. There is a very minute bird perched at one of the angles of the tubing.

Y 2

Red Pottery.

No. 9. A semi-conical water vessel, with a double tubular handle on one side, ending in a tubular mouth. The flat side of the vessel is elaborately decorated with the squat figure of a man standing, holding two long objects in his outstretched arms. This man is a grotesque, has long canine teeth like the tusks of a boar, a singular helmet on his head, on the front of which is an animal's face, a cravat round his neck with bands falling down before. This may be intended for a Peruvian deity. The whole is coloured black and white in contrasts. There is a dog-tooth border to this sculpture, which terminates in a grinning head at each extremity.

No. 10. Another depressed cylindrical vase, with a teapot spout. A bird has balanced the spout at the opposite end of the handle. This vase is decorated with red lines, having scroll ornaments between them.

No. 11. A vessel much like a bag. Has two ears, and the neck is ornamented with an animal having four feet and a tail. This vessel is decorated by lines running lengthwise, between which are placed wavy lines. It has been coloured white, the decoration being dark red, almost black.

No. 12. Another bag-like vessel, or jug, ornamented at the neck with portions of a man's head. The ears, eyes, nose, and mouth stand out, and the two hands project from the side of the jug. The nose is *natural*, or truly American.

No. 13. A small neat vessel, in shape resembling the body of a squat man with his hands on his knees. He is dressed in a tunic, which is fastened by two strings upon his breast. The wide spout is placed at the back of the head. The head is modelled with great accuracy, and exactly presents the American nose. The vessel may be regarded as exhibiting the model of an ancient Peruvian. [See Plate IX. Fig. 2.]

No. 14. Two minute vases, forming almost a pair, ornamented with black upon white ground, and having ears at the necks.

No. 15. A neat shallow vessel, which is ornamented outside with black in diamonds upon the red ware, and then white lines between. It has a row of three lines, two black and a white line between, inside the neck. Ornamented outside the rim also. This vessel is remarkable from being made of a red pottery, which has numerous minute particles of gold interspersed in it.

No. 16. Another small discoidal vessel, ornamented in a very similar diapered manner. It has, besides, the fret pattern on the extreme circumference. These two vessels are decorated with much elegance.

No. 17. A painted water vessel with handle much fractured. It is a red body painted white at the upper part, and birds drawn upon it in a brown colour.

No. 18. A hemispherical cup.

Anthropologically considered, this exhibition of specimens of ceramic art proves incontestably that the Peruvian potters worked from nature from the Peruvian people themselves, a people who possessed brachycephalic, broad heads, well exemplified in No. 13, and had a nose which occurs only in its pure form as a race characteristic in America, but upon that continent ranges from a high north latitude down to Peru, if not farther south. Since I first observed this peculiar nose, I have long been accustomed to regard it as the true *aboriginal American nose*, which may require a word of explanation. It is an aquiline nose, which distinctly differs from the Roman nose, as well as from that of the Jew. It is at once appreciated by the eye, but perhaps is not so easy to describe in words. No one has depicted it so well as Catlin, who spent so many years of his life in delineating the Indians of America. I possess a large work executed in pencil by his own hand, in which he has drawn facsimiles of all his paintings, and this peculiar nose is represented in the men and the women also of all the tribes. It is, as it were, a crescentic nose, beginning to curve at the upper part, and curved uniformly, or nearly so, to the tip. It is a decidedly handsome feature, of which the native races of America have reason to be proud.

This exhibition also throws much light upon the state of civilization of the ancient Peruvians. It shows that although they were highly advanced in many arts, as weaving, dyeing, metallurgy and the ceramic, in which they had acquired a knowledge of moulding, casting, and producing a very permanent pottery, ornamented with taste in numerous ways, yet they knew nothing of one of the simplest and earliest inventions of man, the potter's wheel. This fact proves conclusively, as far as any negative can do, that they were an aboriginal people, whose industry was not derived from any people of the old world, but was strictly native and indigenous. Nevertheless their skill and their taste were unquestionably highly cultivated. We have likewise obtained evidence of a sufficiently satisfactory character, that their aspirations were not bounded by the horizon of this sublunary world, but extended beyond the tomb. This evidence assuredly is most interesting to us as fellow mortals, and engages our sympathies infinitely more than all besides.

The following paper was read by the author :—

On the Peruvian Pottery sent by Consul HUTCHINSON. *By* JOHN E. PRICE, *F.S.A.*

WITHIN the last few days I have had the opportunity of inspecting the interesting collection of human skulls, pottery, and other relics, sent over from Peru by Consul Hutchinson to the Museum of the Institute. It is fortunate for us, that the description of this marvellous series has fallen to the able hands of our esteemed President and Dr. Barnard Davis, whose collective labours will probably embrace all points of interest, and leave but little else to be said concerning the collection. There are, however, one or two minor points for reflection which have occurred to me, especially with regard to the pottery discovered in the graves at Ancon, to which I would briefly direct your attention.

From the information furnished by Consul Hutchinson, there is but little to assist us in determining any date as to these remains. He mentions, however, that some of the skulls were taken from a place of interment, which after the conquest by Pizarro had been rifled by the Spaniards in their search for treasure: it is to be assumed, therefore, that they belong to a period anterior even to the subjection of the country by the Incas, and represent, indeed, some of the numerous aboriginal tribes. From the Spanish conquest, in the early part of the sixteenth century, history leads us through some four or five centuries of an advanced and flourishing state of civilization to what is usually termed *Pre-Incarial times*—a period of unknown duration, one of which no literature whatever exists, and which save by a careful investigation of the remnants of sculpture„ carvings, and architectnral remains, can only be illustrated by such discoveries as the present. Among all such relics, pottery is one of the most useful for comparison ; for as illustrations of the requirements of domestic life among uncultivated tribes, there are few things more durable or lasting than those of earthenware. Fictile vessels mnst have been among the earliest manufactures of man—a necessity indeed of his existence—a want which must be supplied. Food must be prepared for consumption, and receptacles for water must be had, even in the most primitive condition which can be imagined ; accordingly, the clay usually to hand becomes employed, means are adopted to harden it for wear, and a way becomes opened for the active exercise of human ingenuity in ornamentation and design. A great similarity, though, exists in the simple forms as fabricated by most ancient nations. The specimens before us, primitive though they be, forcibly remind us of classic types, and yet they are such as required no especial training or education in the higher principles of art to fabricate. A vessel is wanted for suspension, to hold water or other liquid, and to allow of being carried from place to place ; the idea, therefore, of such globular vessels with rings on either side the neck, by which to sling or affix to the body, becomes a natural one, and it matters little whether this be represented by those upon the table, by a Roman or mediæval amphora, or the pilgrim's costrel of early English times. I enclose a sketch of two such vessels found some years ago in London, and of about the same dimensions as the largest of those from Ancon ; the similarity is apparent.

The pottery, therefore, may or may not date from a remote antiquity : there is nothing about it decisive in this respect ; it is roughly made, evidently from the native clays, and imperfectly baked. It has been remarked that there is no evidence of the use of the potter's wheel, and I believe it is pretty generally understood that the Indians of South America were unacquainted with this useful invention—a contrivance the origin of which, so far as regards the ancient nations in the East, is lost in obscurity. There seems to be but little attempt at decoration— a few lines in a yellow-tinted pigment appear on some of the

smaller cups, and on others there is a white substance somewhat
analogous to a glaze.   Some such attempt at decoration is usual
with early tribes.   In Nicaragua the natives glaze their pottery
with a kind of varnish lightly rubbed over the vessels, and in
Australia and New Zealand it is customary to smear them with
melted Kauri gum.   The specimens of black Peruvian pottery
exhibited by Dr. Davis hardly come within these observations.
They seem to belong to a different style of art, are many of
them of grotesque form, marvellously light, and of a much finer
kind of pottery than the specimens from Ancou.   The colour of
this blue-black slate-coloured ware may have been derived from
some metallic oxide in the clay, but (what would be still more
curious and interesting) why should not the Peruvian potters
have been acquainted with the principle of suffocating the fire
of their kiln at a certain degree of heat, and thus ensure this
uniformity of colour?   I refer to the smother kilns, as illustrated
by the late Mr. Artis at the Roman potteries of Durobrivæ.

In the present collection there appears but a small proportion
of pottery to the number of the graves which must have been
examined in order to produce so large an array of skulls.   This
is accounted for by Consul Hutchinson from the fact of the
difficulty he found in collecting, packing, and sending a large
quantity; he mentions, however, that most of the sepulchres
contained pottery.   This is a clear illustration of the practice
among the Peruvians of interring such objects with the deceased,
and resembling in this respect the customs of many other nations.
We need hardly refer to its almost universal existence among
the Romans.   In far-off China it has been observed.   Nicolo di
Coti mentions it as existing among many of the Indian tribes.
The Moldavians also, the Caubees, and many others may be
cited.   The objects buried usually comprised articles prized by
the deceased during life, receptacles for food or wine, clothing,
implements of war, with many other things likely to be required
on the last long journey.   Of such interments, a series in New
Granada, Ecquador, Peru, and Chili, with other places in South
America, has been well described by Mr. Bollaert, F.R.G.S., with
many curious details concerning the discoveries made by him
among the huacas of that country.

Among the objects on the table are two pieces of netting;

these seem the most difficult to reconcile with a remote antiquity. The preservation is so good, they are so well made, and bear so striking a resemblance to such fabrics as used in the present day, that one can hardly imagine them as having been interred for centuries, yet it appears to have been usual for such pieces of network to be included among the objects selected for burial. It would be interesting to inquire how far this has been observed in other nations. With tribes like these, situated near the coast, it may have been thought probable by the survivors that such things would be required by the defunct. In Granada, however, and among the Chilchas of South America, the net seems to have been adopted at religious festivals as a symbol of death; one was cast over the principal musical performer as a reminder, even in times of rejoicing, of the proximity of the last enemy. A strange resemblance here to the custom of placing a skeleton among the guests at a banqueting-table in classic times. There are yet many other such matters which might be referred to; for instance, the metal found within the mouths, &c.

Colonel A. LANE FOX exhibited several specimens of ancient Peruvian pottery.

Dr. RICHARD KING exhibited flattened American skulls and drawings illustrative of the method of flattening employed by certain of the native tribes.

DISCUSSION.

Professor HUGHES pointed out that some of the pottery bore evident marks of the potter's wheel, though that may have been of the rudest description; and remarked that it was not safe to infer the non-existence of the potter's wheel from the absence of the usual concentric markings in a few specimens, as it was quite possible they might have been obliterated during subsequent ornamentation, affixing of handles, &c.

Mr. C. HARRISON, F.S.A., exhibited in illustration of these communications twenty-three photographs, being part of the series of photographs from collections from the British Museum, published at his expense by Messrs. Mansell and Co. These photographs represented various antiquities from Peru, principally terra-cotta vases of quaint forms. Among them was a stone seat from the mountain of Hoja, Ecuador; a bronze buckler from Ipijapa, in the same country; a remarkable paddle and staff from a tomb at Yca; stone corbels from the city of Huamanchuco; and vases from Truxillo, Chocope, Cuzco, Lake Titicaca, and other localities.

APPENDIX B.

COPY.

PROFESSOR LS. AGASSIZ TO THE HON. H. M. BRENT,
United States Chargé d'Affaires in Lima.

CALLÁO, *June 1st*, 1872.

MY DEAR SIR.—Before leaving this port, I wish to express to you my most sincere thanks for the friendly reception you have given me, and the many attentions you have extended to me. Your kindness emboldens me to ask another favour of you. The day after my arrival, Dr. Hutchinson, H.B.M. Consul in Calláo, called upon me, and offered to go to Ancon, to have collected for our museum such specimens of Indian antiquities as he could bring together in the short time of our stay in these parts. I accepted the more readily his generous offer, as we possess nothing of the kind in Cambridge, and I am myself too little familiar with the subject, while Dr. Hutchinson has made a special study of it. Yesterday I received from Dr. H. the proceeds of his efforts in my behalf. He has been wonderfully successful, and I carry away, besides 384 skulls and several boxes of earthenware which he has presented to me, a number of other highly valuable articles—indeed, so many specimens that I shall be able to provide several of our institutions of learning in the United States with a very full series of these curious relics. Under the circumstances, I feel embarrassed how properly to acknowledge the services of Dr. Hutchinson, which, as you may perceive, are not only benefiting the institution with which I am connected, but science generally among us. It has therefore occurred to me that you might do a gracious thing by calling upon his Excellency the British

Minister in Lima, and thanking him for the kind offices a British Consul has rendered us, and the valuable collections with which he has enriched our scientific institutions. In so doing you would add one more to the many favours for which I am indebted to you.

With high regard,
Very truly yours,
Ls. Agassiz.

APPENDIX C.

THE ISTHMUS CANAL.

Tue following important communication appeared in the London *Shipping and Mercantile Gazette*, during the month of June last.

Sir,—In your issue of May 31 you give your readers a most interesting account of the proposed undertaking by an American company of joining the Atrato River, in the Gulf of Darien, on the Atlantic side, with the San Juan River, which falls into the sheltered little bay of Tupica, on the Pacific side, in about lat. 4.30 N. There is no doubt important and expensive work to be done to canal the intervening tributary streams, &c., especially the Napipi, but I believe it only wants money and the sacrifice of a thousand lives to complete this water-way in about five years' working time. It will be interesting to many of your readers to know that there has long been a Commercial Canal or water communication between the two oceans at this point. A monk of great activity, Padre of a village near Novita, employed his parishioners to dig a small canal on the Quebrada de la Raspadura, which is a branch of the San Juan, by means of which, when the rains are abundant, canoes laden with cacao passed from sea to sea. This interior communication has existed since 1788, almost unknown to Europe. This small canal of Raspadura, with, I believe, the aid of the Napipi (which flows into the Atrato just below the town of Citera), unites the two oceans. In 1850, Lieutenant Wood, R.N., went over the ground, starting from the Pacific side. He considers that the most elevated part was between 300 and 400 feet, the rapid ascent being from Tupica Bay. On this upper part is comparatively low land, through which a canal may be cut between the partly navigable portion

of the Napipi and the San Juan, on the Bay of Tupica, and that
a road of any kind may readily be made there is shown by the
fact that a boat has been dragged across in a few hours. Lieutenant Wood does not speak of the "Canal of Raspadura,"
which doubtless had been choked up and unused long before his
visit. I was in those regions early in 1853; and although I
took great interest in the matter, having read of that locality
being one of the most feasible for a ship canal, I could not hear
of the then existence of that most extraordinary canal communication. The success of the Suez Canal has intensified the
interest in this American project. The first has diverted
the European traffic to the East in a surprising degree. The
Darien Canal will hope to do the same with the Pacific and
Australian trades. The strait discovered by Magalhaens has
only recently awoke from its sleep of solitude, and is now one of
the most important and most used of our ocean by-ways. Will
the new Darien Canal (when completed) send "Magellan" to
sleep again, or will not its deep-water channels and freedom
from dues always command the West Coast and South Pacific
trades? Before leaving this important subject of the Darien
Canal, I should like to know what difficulties the delta of the
Atrato presents to the navigation of large steamers from the
gulf to the river. Many large rivers running to the sea through
many mouths or outlets present the greatest obstacles to safe
navigation in entering from sea. Doubtless the projectors have
thought of this, and some one in their interest will kindly satisfy
your many readers.

Yours, &c.
EDWIN S. ROBERTS.

38, Great St. Helen's, E.C., June 5, 1873.

Crown Buildings, 188, Fleet Street,
London, October, 1873.

SAMPSON LOW, MARSTON & CO.'S
ANNOUNCEMENTS FOR THE
COMING SEASON.

THE AUTHORIZED VERSION OF THE
FOUR GOSPELS.
WITH THE WHOLE OF THE
MAGNIFICENT ETCHINGS ON STEEL,
AFTER THE
DRAWINGS BY M. BIDA.

THE drawings, etchings, and engravings have been twelve years in preparation, and an idea of the importance of this splendid work may be gathered from the fact that upwards of twelve hundred and fifty thousand francs, or fifty thousand pounds, have been expended on its production, and it has obtained for MM. Hachette the Diplome d'Honneur at the Vienna Exhibition.

The English edition will contain the whole of the 132 steel etchings, and in addition some very exquisite woodcut ornaments.

The GOSPEL OF ST. MATTHEW will contain 41 Steel Etchings.
The GOSPEL OF ST. MARK „ 24 „
The GOSPEL OF ST. LUKE „ 40 „
The GOSPEL OF ST. JOHN „ 27 „
Size, large Imperial quarto.

It is intended to publish each Gospel separately, and at intervals of from six to twelve months: and in order to preserve uniformity, the price will in the first instance be fixed at £3 3s. each volume. This uniformity of price has been determined on the assumption that purchasers will take the whole of the four volumes as published; but, as it will be seen that the Gospels of St. Matthew and St. Luke contain more etchings and more letterpress than St. Mark and St. John, and are therefore proportionately more costly in production, it must be understood that at the expiration of three months from the first issue of each of these two volumes, the price (if purchased separately) will be raised to four guineas. This extra charge will, however, be allowed at any time to all bona fide purchasers of the four volumes.

The Gospel of St. John, appropriately bound in cloth extra, price £3 3s., will be the first volume issued, and will be ready for publication shortly.

Specimen pages of text and etchings may be seen on application to any bookseller in town and country, who will be happy to register the names of subscribers, either for each Gospel separately, or for the whole of the Gospels as published.

IMPORTANT ANNOUNCEMENT.

DR. SCHWEINFURTH'S TRAVELS AND DISCOVERIES IN CENTRAL AFRICA.

From 1868 to 1871.

Translated by ELLEN E. FREWER. With an Introduction by WINWOOD READE.

ESSRS. SAMPSON LOW & Co. have the pleasure of stating that they have completed arrangements with the celebrated African Traveller, Dr. GEORG SCHWEINFURTH, for the exclusive right to publish his new work, entitled—

THE HEART OF AFRICA.

OR, THREE YEARS' TRAVELS AND ADVENTURES IN THE UN-EXPLORED REGIONS OF THE CENTRE OF AFRICA.

This is unquestionably, in a scientific point of view, one of the most valuable contributions to a knowledge of the Natural History, Botany, Geography, and River System of Central Africa that has ever appeared: but its chief interest will consist in the personal adventures of the author amongst unknown tribes, and wanderings in lands hitherto unexplored. The Doctor carries his reader into a veritable wonderland, full of peculiar customs, and where his experiences have been of the most eventful nature. The district explored embraces a wide tract of country extending southward from the Meschera on the Bahr el Ghazal, and betwixt the 10th and 3rd degrees of north latitude.

The present work cannot fail to be of most unusual interest to general readers; inasmuch as it will include adventures in an unknown country amongst cannibals and pygmies, the discovery and exploration of twenty-two hitherto quite unknown rivers, the wonderful land of the Monbuttoo, his reception by King Munza, horrible cannibalism, fights with natives and struggles with wild animals, adventures on rivers, on mountains, and in jungles; and, in short, experiences of the most novel and startling kind that could be imagined in an unknown and savage country.

The work will form two volumes, demy 8vo., of upwards of 500 pages each, and will be illustrated by about 130 woodcuts from drawings made by the author—comprising figures of different races of men; animals, domestic and wild; remarkable fish and snakes; varieties of trees, plants, and fruits; landscapes; forest scenery; watered plains; episodes of the journey; cannibal feasts and dances; fording rivers; villages and huts; night encampments; meetings with chieftains; weapons of war, &c. &c.; with maps and plans.

It is proposed that the work shall be published in England and America (in English), and in the respective languages of Germany, France, Russia, Italy, &c., simultaneously, and arrangements are now in progress for this purpose; and the Publishers hope to have it ready for publication during the present Autumn.

New Works by the celebrated French Writer, JULES VERNE.

1.

THE FUR COUNTRY; OR, SEVENTY DEGREES NORTH LATITUDE.

By JULES VERNE. Translated by N. D'ANVERS.

A Story of remarkable Adventures in the Northern Regions of the Hudson's Bay Territory. Crown 8vo. with upwards of 80 very graphic full-page Illustrations. Cloth extra. Uniform in size and style with "Twenty Thousand Leagues under the Sea." Price 10s. 6d.   [*In October.*

2.

FROM THE EARTH TO THE MOON; AND A TRIP ROUND IT.

By JULES VERNE. Translated by L. P. MERCIER.

With numerous characteristic Illustrations. Crown 8vo. Uniform in size and price with the above. Cloth, gilt edges, 10s. 6d.   [*Ready.*

3.

AROUND THE WORLD IN EIGHTY DAYS.

By JULES VERNE.

Square crown 8vo. With numerous Illustrations. Uniform in size and style with "Meridiana," by the same author. Price 7s. 6d.   [*Nearly ready.*

One Vol., Demy 8vo., cloth, with numerous woodcuts and a map.

THE WILD NORTH LAND:

The Story of a Winter Journey with dogs across Northern North America.

BY CAPTAIN W. F. BUTLER,

Author of "The Great Lone Land."   [*In November.*

A WHALING CRUISE TO BAFFIN'S BAY AND THE GULF OF BOOTHIA.

With an Account of the Rescue, by his Ship, of the survivors of the Crew of the "Polaris."

BY CAPTAIN MARKHAM, R.N.

One Volume, demy 8vo., with Map and Illustrations, cloth extra.

New Ready, in One Volume, demy 8vo., with Maps and Illustrations, cloth extra, 16s.

THE THRESHOLD OF THE UNKNOWN REGION.

BY CLEMENTS R. MARKHAM, C.B., F.R.S.

Secretary of the Royal Geographical Society.   [*Now ready.*

A most beautiful Christmas Present.

WOMAN IN SACRED HISTORY.

BY MRS. HARRIET BEECHER STOWE.

Illustrated with 15 chromo-lithographs and about 200 pages of letterpress forming one of the most elegant and attractive Volumes ever published. Demy 4to., cloth extra, gilt edges, price 25s.   *(In November.*

NEW WORK BY THE REV. E. H. BICKERSTETH.

One Volume square 8vo., with Numerous very beautiful Engravings, uniform in Character with the Illustrated Edition of Heber's Hymns, &c., price 7s. 6d.

THE REEF, AND OTHER PARABLES.

By the Rev. E. H. BICKERSTETH, M. A., Author of "Yesterday, To-day, and for Ever," &c.   *(Nearly Ready.*

CARL WERNER'S NILE SKETCHES,

Painted from Nature during his Travels through Egypt. Facsimiles of Water-colour Paintings executed by Gustave W. Seitz, with Descriptive Text by Dr. E. A. Brehm and Dr. Dumichen. Third Series. Imperial folio, in Cardboard Wrapper, £3 10s.

Beautiful Work for Winter Evenings. Dedicated, by Permission, to His Royal Highness, Prince Leopold.

ILLUSTRATED GAMES OF PATIENCE.

By the Lady Adelaide Cadogan. Twenty-four Diagrams in Colours, with Descriptive Text. Foolscap 4to., cloth extra, gilt edges, 12s. 6d.

THE ROYAL PASTRY AND CONFECTIONERY BOOK

(Le livre de Patisserie). By Jules Gouffé, Chef de Cuisine of the Paris Jockey Club. Translated from the French and adapted to English use by Alphonse Gouffé, Head Pastrycook to Her Majesty the Queen. Illustrated with 10 large Plates printed in Colours, and 137 Engravings on Wood, after the Oil Paintings and Designs of E. Ronjat. Royal 8vo., cloth extra.   *(In the Press.*

Important New Work by Professor Guyot.

PHYSICAL GEOGRAPHY.

By Arnold Guyot, Author of "Earth and Man." In 1 Volume, large 4to., 128 pp., numerous coloured Diagrams, Maps and Woodcuts, price 10s. 6d., strong boards.

HISTORY OF THE AMERICAN AMBULANCE,

Established in Paris during the Siege of 1870-71. Together with the Details of its Method and its Work. By Thomas W. Evans, M. D., D. D. S., Ph. D., President of the American International Sanitary Committee, &c., Author of "La Commission Sanitaire des Etats Unis : son Origine, son Organisation et ses Resultats," &c. In 1 Volume, Imperial 8vo., with numerous Illustrations, cloth extra, price 35s.   *(Now Ready.*

Preparing for publication in one handsome small 4to., cloth gilt edges, price 15s.

PHYNNODDERREE, AND OTHER TALES:

Fairy Legends of the Isle of Man. By EDWARD MCALOE. To be profusely Illustrated with upwards of 120 Engravings on Wood.

THE POSTHUMOUS WORKS AND UNPUB-LISHED AUTOGRAPHS OF NAPOLEON III. IN EXILE.

Collected and arranged by COUNT DE LA CHAPELLE, Coadjutor in the last Works of the Emperor at Chiselhurst. 1 Volume demy 8vo., cloth extra, 14s.   [*Now Ready.*

RECOLLECTIONS OF THE EMPEROR NAPOLEON I.

During the First Three Years of his Captivity on the Island of St. Helena Including the time of his Residence at her father's house, "The Briars." By Mrs. ABELL (late Miss Elizabeth Balcombe). Third Edition. Revised throughout with additional matter by her daughter, Mrs. CHARLES JOHNSTONE. 1 Volume, demy 8vo. With Steel Portrait of Mrs. Abell, and Woodcut Illustrations. Cloth extra, gilt edges, 10s. 6d.   [*Now Ready.*

ENGLISH MATRONS AND THEIR PROFESSION;

With some Considerations as to its Various Branches, its National Value, and the Education it requires. By M. L. F., Writer of "My Life, and what shall I do with it," "Battle of the Two Philosophies," and "Strong and Free." Crown 8vo., cloth extra, 7s. 6d.   [*Now Ready.*

"All States among which the regulations regarding women are bad, enjoy scarcely the half of happiness."—ARISTOTLE.

SPECIAL NOTICE.—*The long-desired Map to Mr. King's Work has now been added, and also a Chapter of entirely new matter. (Dedicated to Professor Tyndal.)*

MOUNTAINEERING IN THE SIERRA NEVADA.

By CLARENCE KING. Crown 8vo. Fourth and Cheaper Edition. Cloth extra, with Map and Additional Chapter, 6s.   [*Nearly Ready.*

A CHRONICLE OF THE FERMORS; HORACE WALPOLE IN LOVE.

By M. F. MAHONY (Matthew Stradling), Author of "The Misadventures of Mr. Catlyn," "The Irish Bar-sinister," &c. In 2 Volumes, Demy 8vo. with Steel Portrait.   [*In the Press.*

MILITARY LIFE IN PRUSSIA.

First Series. The Soldier in Time of Peace. Translated (by permission of the Author) from the German of F. W. Hácklander. By F. E. R. and H. E. R. Crown 8vo., cloth extra, 9s.   [*Now Ready.*

University Local Examinations.
ST. MARK'S GOSPEL.

With Explanatory Notes. For the Use of Schools and Colleges. By GEORGE BOWKER, late Second Master of the Newport Grammar School, Isle of Wight. 1 Volume, foolscap, cloth. *[In Preparation.*

NEW NOVELS.

Victor Hugo's New Novel.
IN THE YEAR '93 (QUATRE-VINGT TREIZE).

Three Volumes, crown 8vo. *[In Preparation.*
This work, which will be published simultaneously in France, England, and America, is said to surpass in style and dramatic interest anything that Victor Hugo has yet produced.

New Work by the Author of "Lorna Doone."
ALICE LORRAINE;

A Tale of the South Downs. Three Volumes, crown 8vo. *[In Preparation.*

IN THE ISLE OF WIGHT.

Two Volumes, crown 8vo., cloth, 21s. *[Now Ready.*

BETTER THAN GOLD.

By Mrs. ARNOLD, Author of "His by Right," "John Hesketh's Charge," "Under Foot," &c. In 3 Volumes, crown 8vo., 31s. 6d. *[In the Press.*

New Work by Hain Friswell, Author of "The Gentle Life," &c.
OUR SQUARE CIRCLE.

Two Volumes, crown 8vo., cloth, 21s *[In the Press.*

New Work of Fiction by Georgiana M. Craik.
ONLY A BUTTERFLY.

One Volume, crown 8vo., cloth, 10s. 6d. *[Now Ready.*

ARGUS FAIRBAIRNE; OR, A WRONG NEVER RIGHTED.

By HENRY JACKSON, Author of "Hearth Ghosts," &c. Three Volumes, crown 8vo., cloth, 31s. 6d. *[In the Press.*

[New Volume of the John Halifax Series of Girls' Books.
MISS MOORE.

By GEORGIANA M. CRAIK. Small post 8vo., with Illustrations, gilt edges, 4s. *[Nearly Ready

Crown Buildings, 188, *Fleet Street*,
London, October, 1873.

A List of Books

PUBLISHING BY

SAMPSON LOW, MARSTON, LOW, & SEARLE.

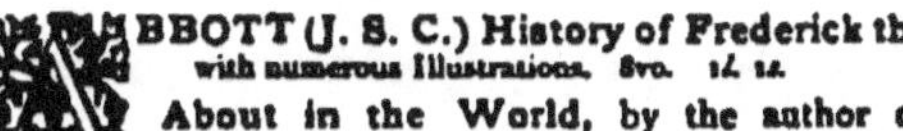

ALPHABETICAL LIST.

ABBOTT (J. S. C.) History of Frederick the Great, with numerous Illustrations. 8vo. 1*l.* 1*s.*

About in the World, by the author of "The Gentle Life." Crown 8vo. bevelled cloth, 4th edition. 6*s.*

Adamson (Rev. T. H.) The Gospel according to St. Matthew, expounded. 8vo. 12*s.*

Adventures of a Young Naturalist. By LUCIEN BIART, with 117 beautiful Illustrations on Wood. Edited and adapted by PARKER GILLMORE, author of "All Round the World," "Gun, Rod, and Saddle," &c. Post 8vo. cloth extra, gilt edges, new edition, 7*s.* 6*d.*
"The adventures are charmingly narrated."—*Athenæum*.

Adventures of a Brownie. See Craik, Mrs.

Adventures on the Great Hunting Grounds of the World, translated from the French of Victor Meunier, with engravings, 2nd edition. 5*s.*

"The book for all boys in whom the love of travel and adventure is strong. They will find here plenty to amuse them and much to instruct them besides."—*Times*.

Alcott, (Louisa M.) Aunt Jo's Scrap-Bag. Square 16mo, 3*s.* 6*d.*

——— **Little Men : Life at Plumfield with Jo's Boys.** By the author of "Little Women." Small post 8vo. cloth, gilt edges, 3*s.* 6*d.* Cheap edition, cloth, 2*s.* ; fancy boards, 1*s.* 6*d.*

——— **Little Women.** Complete in 1 vol. fcap. 3*s.* 6*d.* Cheap edition, 2 vols. cloth, 2*s.* ; boards, 1*s.* 6*d.* each.

——— **Old Fashioned Girl,** best edition, small post 8vo. cloth extra, gilt edges, 3*s.* 6*d.* ; Low's Copyright Series, 1*s.* 6*d.* ; cloth, 2*s.*

The *Guardian* says of "Little Women," that it is—"A bright, cheerful, healthy story—with a tinge of thoughtful gravity about it which reminds one of John Bunyan. The *Athenæum* says of "Old-Fashioned Girl"— "Let whoever wishes to read a bright, spirited, wholesome story, get the 'Old Fashioned Girl' at once."

Alcott (Louisa M.) Shawl Straps. Small post 8vo. Cloth
extra, gilt edges, 3*s*. 6*d*.

——— **Work, a Story of Experience.** 2 vols. cr. 8vo. 21*s*.

Allston (Captain). *See* **Ready, O Ready.**

Alexander (Sir James E.) Bush Fighting. Illustrated by
Remarkable Actions and Incidents of the Maori War. With a Map,
Plans, and Woodcuts. 1 vol. demy 8vo. pp. 328, cloth extra, 16*s*.

"This book tells the story of the late war in New Zealand, with its
many desperate encounters and exciting personal adventures, and tells
that story well."—*Naval and Military Gazette.*

" This is a valuable history of the Maori war."—*Standard.*

Alexander (W. D. S.) The Lonely Guiding Star. A
Legend of the Pyrenean Mountains and other Poems. Fcap. 8vo.
cloth. 3*s*.

Among the Arabs, a Narrative of Adventures in Algeria, by
G. Naphegyi, M. D., A. M. 7*s*. 6*d*.

Andersen (Hans Christian) The Story of My Life. 8vo.
10*s*. 6*d*.

——— **Fairy Tales,** with Illustrations in Colours by E. V. B.
Royal 4to. cloth. 1*l*. 5*s*.

Andrews (Dr.) Latin-English Lexicon. 13th edition.
Royal 8vo. pp. 1,670, cloth extra. Price 18*s*.

The superiority of this justly-famed Lexicon is retained over all others
by the fulness of its Quotations, the including in the Vocabulary Proper
Names, the distinguishing whether the Derivative is classical or otherwise, the exactness of the References to the Original Authors, and by the
price.

" The best Latin Dictionary, whether for the scholar or advanced
student."—*Spectator.*

" Every page bears the impress of industry and care."—*Athenæum.*

Anecdotes of the Queen and Royal Family, collected and
edited by J. G. Hodgins, with Illustrations. New edition, revised by
John Timbs. 3*s*.

Angell (J. K.) A Treatise on the Law of Highways. 8vo.
1*l*. 5*s*.

Arctic Regions (The). Illustrated. *See* **Bradford.**

——— **German Polar Expedition.** *See* **Koldeway.**

——— **Explorations.** *See* **Markham.**

Around the World. *See* **Prime.**

Art, Pictorial and Industrial, Vol. 1, 1*l.* 11*s.* 6*d.* Vols. 2 and 3, 18*s.* each.

Atmosphere (The). *See* Flammarion.

Aunt Jo's Scrap Bag. *See* Alcott.

Australian Tales, by the " Old Boomerang." Post 8vo. 5*s.*

ACK-LOG Studies. *See* Warner.

Baldwin (J. D.) Prehistoric Nations. 12mo. 4*s.* 6*d.*

———— Ancient America, in notes of American Archæology. Crown 8vo. 10*s.* 6*d.*

Bancroft's History of America. Library edition, vols. 1 to 9, 8vo. 5*l.* 8*s.*

———— History of America, Vol. X. (completing the Work.) 8vo. 12*s.*   [*In the press.*

Barber (E. C.) The Crack Shot. Post 8vo. 8*s.* 6*d.*

Barnes's (Rev. A.) Lectures on the Evidences of Christianity in the 19th Century. 12mo. 7*s.* 6*d.*

Barnum (P. T.) Struggles and Triumphs. Crown 8vo. Fancy boards. 2*s.* 6*d.*

Barrington (Hon. and Rev. L. J.) From Ur to Macpelah; the Story of Abraham. Crown 8vo., cloth, 5*s.*

THE BAYARD SERIES. Comprising Pleasure Books of Literature produced in the Choicest Style as Companionable Volumes at Home and Abroad.

Price 2s. 6d. each Volume, complete in itself, printed at the Chiswick Press, bound by Burn, flexible cloth extra, gilt leaves, with silk Headbands and Registers.

The Story of the Chevalier Bayard. By M. DE BERVILLE.

De Joinville's St. Louis, King of France.

The Essays of Abraham Cowley, including all his Prose Works.

Abdallah; or, the Four Leaves. By EDOUARD LABOULLAYE.

Table-Talk and Opinions of Napoleon Buonaparte.

Vathek: An Oriental Romance. By WILLIAM BECKFORD.

The King and the Commons: a Selection of Cavalier and Puritan Song. Edited by Prof. MORLEY.

Words of Wellington: Maxims and Opinions of the Great Duke.

Dr. Johnson's Rasselas, Prince of Abyssinia. With Notes.

Hazlitt's Round Table. With Biographical Introduction.

The Religio Medici, Hydriotaphia, and the Letter to a Friend. By Sir THOMAS BROWNE, Knt.

Ballad Poetry of the Affections. By ROBERT BUCHANAN.

Coleridge's Christabel, and other Imaginative Poems. With Preface by ALGERNON C. SWINBURNE.

Lord Chesterfield's Letters, Sentences and Maxims. With Introduction by the Editor, and Essay on Chesterfield by M. De St. Beuve, of the French Academy.

Essays in Mosaic. By THOS. BALLANTYNE.

My Uncle Toby; his Story and his Friends. Edited by P. FITZGERALD.

Reflections; or, Moral Sentences and Maxims of the Duke de la Rochefoucauld.

Socrates, Memoirs for English Readers from Xenophon's Memorabilia. By EDW. LEVIEN.

Prince Albert's Golden Precepts.

A suitable Case containing 12 volumes, price 31s. 6d. ; or the Case separate, price 3s. 6d.

EXTRACTS FROM LITERARY NOTICES.

"The present series—taking its name from the opening volume, which contained a translation of the Knight without Fear and without Reproach — will really, we think, fill a void in the shelves of all except the most complete English libraries. These little square-shaped volumes contain, in a very manageable and pretty form, a great many things not very easy of access elsewhere, and some things for the first time brought together." —*Pall Mall Gazette.* "We have here two more volumes of the series appropriately called the 'Bayard,' as they certainly are 'sans reproche.' Of convenient size, with clear typography and tasteful binding, we know no other little volumes which make such good gift-books for persons of mature age."—*Examiner.* "St. Louis and his companions, as described by Joinville, not only in their glistening armour, but in their every-day attire, are brought nearer to us, become intelligible to us, and teach us lessons of humanity which we can learn from men only, and not from saints and heroes. Here lies the real value of real history. It widens our minds and our hearts, and gives us that true knowledge of the world and of human nature in all its phases which but few can gain in the short span of their own life, and in the narrow sphere of their friends and enemies. We can hardly imagine a better book for boys to read or for men to ponder over."—*Times.*

Beecher (Henry Ward, D. D.) Life Thoughts. Complete in 1 vol. 12mo. 2s. 6d.

—— **Sermons Selected.** 12mo. 8s. 6d.

—— **Norwood, or Village Life in New England.** Crown 8vo. 6s.

—— **(Dr. Lyman) Life and Correspondence of.** 2 vols. post 8vo. 1l. 1s.

Bees and Beekeeping. By the Times' Beemaster. Illustrated. Crown 8vo. New Edition, with additions. 2s. 6d.

Bell (Rev. C. D.) Faith in Earnest. 18mo. 1s. 6d.

—— **Blanche Nevile.** Fcap. 8vo. 6s.

Bellows (A. J.) The Philosophy of Eating. Post 8vo. 7s. 6d.

—— **How not to be Sick, a Sequel to Philosophy of Eating.** Post 8vo. 7s. 6d.

Bickersteth's Hymnal Companion to Book of Common Prayer.

The following Editions are now ready:—

		s.	d.
No. 1. A Small-type Edition, medium 32mo. cloth limp		0	6
No. 1. B ditto roan limp, red edges ..		1	0
No. 1. C ditto morocco limp, gilt edges ..		2	0
No. 2. Second-size type, super-royal 32mo. cloth limp ..		1	0
No. 2. A ditto roan limp, red edges ..		2	0
No. 2. B ditto morocco limp, gilt edges ..		3	0
No. 3. Large-type Edition, crown 8vo. cloth, red edges ..		2	6
No. 3. A ditto roan limp, red edges ..		3	6
No. 3. B ditto morocco limp, gilt edges ..		5	6
No. 4. Large-type Edition, crown 8vo. with Introduction and Notes, cloth, red edges		3	6
No. 4. A ditto roan limp, red edges ..		4	6
No. 4. B ditto morocco, gilt edges ..		6	6
No. 5. Crown 8vo. with accompanying Tunes to every Hymn, New Edition		3	0
No. 5. A ditto with Chants		4	0
No. 5. B The Chants separately		1	6

No. 6. Penny Edition.

Fcap. 4to. Organists' edition. Cloth, 7s. 6d.

⁎ *A liberal allowance is made to Clergymen introducing the Hymnal.*

☞ THE BOOK OF COMMON PRAYER, bound with THE HYMNAL COMPANION. 32mo. cloth, 9d. And in various superior bindings.

Benedict (F. L.) Miss Dorothy's Charge. 3 vols. 31*s.* 6*d.*

Biart (L.) Adventures of a Young Naturalist. (See *Adventures.*)

Bickersteth (Rev. E. H., M.A.) The Master's Home-Call; Or, Brief Memorials of Alice Frances Bickersteth. 3rd Edition. 32mo. cloth gilt. 1*s.*

"They recall in a touching manner a character of which the religious beauty has a warmth and grace almost too tender to be definite."—*The Guardian.*

—— **The Shadow of the Rock. A Selection of Religious Poetry.** 18mo. Cloth extra. 2*s.* 6*d.*

Bigelow (John) France and Hereditary Monarchy. 8vo. 3*s.*

Bishop (J. L.) History of American Manufacture. 3 vols. 8vo. 2*l.* 5*s.*

—— **(J. P.) First Book of the Law.** 8vo. 1*l.* 1*s.*

Bits of Talk about Home Matters. By H. H. Fcap. 8vo. cloth gilt edges. 3*s.*

Black (Wm.) Uniform Editions:

—— **Kilmeny; a Novel.** Small Post 8vo. cloth. 6*s.*

—— **In Silk Attire.** 3rd and cheaper edition, small post 8vo. 6*s.*

"A work which deserves a hearty welcome for its skill and power in delineation of character."—*Saturday Review.*

"A very charming book."—*Pall Mall Gazette.*

"As a story it is all absorbing."—*Spectator.*

—— **A Daughter of Heth.** 11th and cheaper edition, crown 8vo., cloth extra. 6*s.* With Frontispiece by F. Walker, A.R.A.

"If humour, sweetness, and pathos, and a story told with simplicity and vigour, ought to insure success, 'A Daughter of Heth' is of the kind to deserve it."—*Saturday Review.*

"The special genius of the book is the conception of such a character as Coquette's."—*Spectator.*

"An inviting title, agreeable writing, humour, sweetness and a fresh natural style are combined."—*Pall Mall Gazette.*

"The 'Daughter of Heth' is a novel of real power and promise."—*Standard.*

Black (C. B.) New Continental Route Guides.

—— **Guide to the North of France,** including Normandy, Brittany, Touraine, Picardy, Champagne, Burgundy, Lorraine, Alsace, and the Valley of the Loire; Belgium and Holland; the Valley of the Rhine to Switzerland; and the South-West of Germany, to Italy by the Brenner Pass. Illustrated with numerous Maps and Plans. Crown 8vo., cloth limp. 6*s.* 6*d.*

—— **Guide to Normandy and Brittany,** their Celtic Monuments, Ancient Churches, and Pleasant Watering-Places. Illustrated with Maps and Plans. Crown 8vo., cloth limp, 2*s.* 6*d.*

Black (C. B.) New Continental Route Guides.

—— **Guide to the North-East of France,** including Picardy, Champagne, Burgundy, Lorraine, and Alsace ; Belgium and Holland : the Valley of the Rhine, to Switzerland ; and the South-West of Germany, to Italy, by the Brenner Pass, with Description of Vienna. Illustrated with Maps and Plans. Crown 8vo., cloth limp. 4s. 6d.

—— **Paris, and Excursions from Paris.** Illustrated with numerous Maps, Plans, and Views. Small post 8vo. cloth limp, price 2s. 6d.

—— **Guide to the South of France and to the North** of Italy : including the Pyrenees and their Watering-Places ; the Health Resorts on the Mediterranean from Perpignan to Genoa : and the towns of Turin, Milan, and Venice. Illustrated with Maps and Plans. Small post 8vo., cloth limp, 5s.

—— **Switzerland and the Italian Lakes.** Small post 8vo. price 2s. 6d.

———

Blackburn (H.) Art in the Mountains : the Story of the Passion Play, with upwards of Fifty Illustrations. 8vo. 12s.

—— **Artists and Arabs.** With numerous Illustrations. 8vo. 7s. 6d.

—— **Harz Mountains :** a Tour in the Toy Country. With numerous Illustrations. 12s.

—— **Normandy Picturesque.** Numerous Illustrations. 8vo. 16s.

—— **Travelling in Spain.** With numerous Illustrations. 8vo. 16s.

—— **Travelling in Spain.** Guide Book Edition 12mo. 2s. 6d.

—— **The Pyrenees.** Summer Life at French Watering-Places. 100 Illustrations by GUSTAVE DORÉ. Royal 8vo. 18s.

Blackmore (R. D.) Lorna Doone. New edition. Crown, 8vo. 6s.

"The reader at times holds his breath, so graphically yet so simply does John Ridd tell his tale . . . . 'Lorna Doone' is a work of real excellence, and as such we heartily commend it to the public."—*Saturday Review.*

—— **Cradock Nowell.** 2nd and cheaper edition. 6s.

—— **Clara Vaughan.** Revised edition. 6s.

—— **Georgics of Virgil.** Small 4to. 4s. 6d.

Blackwell (E.) Laws of Life. New edition. Fcp. 3s. 6d.

Boardman's Higher Christian Life. Fcp. 1s. 6d.

Bonwick (J.) Last of the Tasmanians. 8vo. 16s.

Bonwick (J.) Daily Life of the Tasmanians. 8vo. 12*s.* 6*d.*

—————— Curious Facts of Old Colonial Days. 12mo. cloth.
5*s.*

Book of Common Prayer with the Hymnal Companion.
32mo. cloth. 9*d.* *And in various bindings.

Books suitable for School Prizes and Presents. (Fuller
description of each book will be found in the alphabet.)

    Adventures of a Young Naturalist. 7*s.* 6*d.*
    —————— on Great Hunting Grounds. 5*s.*
    Allcott's Aunt Jo's Scrap-bag. 3*s.* 6*d.*
    —————— Old Fashioned Girl. 3*s.* 6*d.*
    —————— Little Women. 3*s.* 6*d.*
    —————— Little Men. 3*s.* 6*d.*
    —————— Shawl Straps. 3*s.* 6*d.*
    Anecdotes of the Queen. 3*s.*
    Atmosphere (The). By Flammarion. 30*s.*
    Bickersteth (Rev. E. H.) Shadow of the Rock. 2*s.* 6*d.*
    Butler's Great Lone Land. 7*s.* 6*d.*
    —————— Cradock Nowell. 6*s.*
    —————— Clara Vaughan. 6*s.*
    Bayard Series (See Bayard.)
    Blackmore's Lorna Doone. 6*s.*
    Changed Cross (The). 2*s.* 6*d.*
    Child's Play. 7*s.* 6*d.*
    Christ in Song. 5*s.*
    Craik (Mrs.) Adventures of a Brownie. 5*s.*
    —————— Little Sunshine's Holiday. 4*s.*
    Craik (Miss) The Cousin from India. 6*s.*
    Dana's Corals and Coral Islands. 21*s.*
    —————— Two Years before the Mast. 6*s.*
    Davies's Pilgrimage of the Tiber. 18*s.*
    De Witt (Mad.) An Only Sister. 4*s.*
    Erkmann-Chatrian's, The Forest House. 3*s.* 6*d.*
    Faith Gartney. 3*s.* 6*d.* cloth; boards, 2*s.* 6*d.*
    Favell Children (The). 4*s.*
    Favourite English Poems. 300 Illustration. 21*s.*
    Frane's Emily's Choice. 5*s.*
    —————— Marian. 5*s.*
    —————— Silken Cord. 5*s.*
    —————— Vermont Vale. 5*s.*
    —————— Minnie's Mission. 4*s.*

Books for School Prizes and Presents, *continued.*

Gayworthys (The). 3s. 6d.
Gentle Life, (Queen Edition). 10s. 6d.
Gentle Life Series. (*See* Alphabet).
Getting on in the World. 6s.
Glover's Light of the Word. 2s. 6d.
Hayes (Dr.) Cast Away in the Cold. 6s.
Healy (Miss) The Home Theatre. 3s. 6d.
Henderson's Latin Proverbs. 10s. 6d.
Hugo's Toilers of the Sea. 10s. 6d.
  „   „   „   6s.
Jack Hazard, by Trowbridge. 3s. 6d.
Kingston's Ben Burton. 3s. 6d.
Kennan's Tent Life. 6s.
King's Mountaineering in the Sierra Nevada. 6s.
Low's Edition of American Authors. 1s. 6d. and 2s. each. 83
  Vols. published. *See* Alphabet under Low.
Lyra Sacra Americana. 4s. 6d.
Macgregor (John) Rob Roy Books. (*See* Alphabet.)
Marigold Manor, by Miss Waring. 4s.
Maury's Physical Geography of the Sea 6s.
Parisian Family. 5s.
Phelps (Miss) The Silent Partner. 3s.
Picture Gallery British Art. 12s.
   —— Sacred Art. 12s.
Ready, O Ready. By Captain Allston, R.N. 3s. 6d.
Reynard the Fox. 100 Exquisite Illustrations. 7s. 6d.
Sea-Gull Rock. 79 Beautiful Woodcuts. 7s. 6d.
Stanley's How I Found Livingstone. 21s.
Stowe (Mrs.) Pink and White Tyranny. 3s. 6d.
   —— - Old Town Folks. Cloth extra 6s. and 2s. 6d.
   —— Minister's Wooing. 5s. ; boards, 1s. 6d.
   —— Pearl of Orr's Island. 5s.
   —— - My Wife and I. 6s.
Tauchnitz's German Authors. *See* Tauchnitz.
Tayler (C. B.) Sacred Records. 2s. 6d.
Titcomb's Letters to Young People. 1s. 6d. and 2s.
Twenty Years Ago. 4s.
Under the Blue Sky. 7s. 6d.
Verne's Meridiana. 7s. 6d.
   —— Twenty Thousand Leagues Under the Sea. 10s. 6d.
Whitney's (Mrs.) Books. *See* Alphabet.

Bowles (T. G.) The Defence of Paris, narrated as it was
  Seen. 8vo. 14s.

Boynton (Charles B., D.D.) Navy of the United States,
with Illustrations of the Ironclad Vessels. 8vo. 2 vols. *2l.*

*Under the Special Patronage of Her Most Gracious Majesty the Queen,
the Duke of Argyll, the Marquis of Lorn, &c.*

Bradford (Wm.) The Arctic Regions. Illustrated with
Photographs, taken on an Art Expedition to Greenland. With Descrip-
t ive Narrative by the Artist. In One Volume, royal broadside, 25 inches
by 20, beautifully bound in morocco extra, price Twenty-five Guineas.

Bremer (Fredrika) Life, Letters, and Posthumous Works.
Crown 8vo. 10s. 6d.

Brett (E.) Notes on Yachts. Fcp. 6s.

Bristed (C. A.) Five Years in an English University.
Fourth E lition, Revised and Amended by the Author. Post 8vo. 10s. 6d.

Broke (Admiral Sir B. V. P., Bart., K.C.B.) Biography
of 1l.

Brothers Rantzau. *See* **Erckmann Chatrian.**

Browning (Mrs. E. B.) The Rhyme of the Duchess May.
Demy 4to. Illustrated with Eight Photographs, after Drawings by
Charlotte M. B. Morrell. 21s.

Burritt (E.) The Black Country and its Green Border
Land: or, Expeditions and Explorations round Birmingham, Wolver-
hampton, &c. By Elihu Burritt. Second and cheaper edition. Post
8vo. 6s.

—————— **A Walk from London to Land's End.** With Illustrations. 8vo. 6s.

—————— **The Lectures and Speeches of Elihu Burritt.**
Fcp. 8vo. cloth, 6s.

Burroughs (John). *See* **Wake Robin.**

Bush (R. J.) Reindeer, Dogs, and Snow Shoes: a Journal
of Siberian Travel. 8vo. 12s. 6d.

Bush Fighting. *See* **Alexander (Sir J. E.)**

Bushnell's (Dr.) The Vicarious Sacrifice. Post 8vo. 7s. 6d.

—————— **Sermons on Living Subjects.** Crown 8vo. cloth.
7s. 6d.

—————— **Nature and the Supernatural.** Post 8vo. 3s. 6d.

—————— **Christian Nurture.** 3s. 6d.

—————— **Character of Jesus.** 6d.

—————— **The New Life.** Crown 8vo. 3s. 6d.

Butler (W. F.) The Great Lone Land ; an Account of the Red River Expedition, 1869-1870, and Subsequent Travels and Adventures in the Manitoba Country, and a Winter Journey across the Saskatchewan Valley to the Rocky Mountains. With Illustrations and Map. Fifth and Cheaper Edition. Crown 8vo. cloth extra. 7s. 6d. (The first 3 Editions were in 8vo. cloth. 16s.)

The *Times* says :—" He describes easily and forcibly. He has a sympathy with the beautiful as well as a sense of the ridiculous. But his prejudices and his egotism are merely the weaknesses of a frank, hearty nature, and we have a personal liking for him when we take leave of him at the end of his wanderings."

" The tone of this book is altogether delightful and refreshing."—*Spectator*.

" The impression left on the mind by his narrative is one of profound interest."—*Morning Post*.

" This is one of the freshest and most interesting books of travel that we have had the pleasure of reading for some time past."—*Examiner*.

" There is a delightful breeziness and vigour about Captain Butler's style of writing."—*Leeds Mercury*.

" His fascinating volume . . . . . not only exciting, but instructive reading."—*Pall Mall Gazette*.

" Captain Butler writes with rare spirit."—*Nonconformist*.

CALIFORNIA. *See* **Nordhoff.**

Carlisle (Thos.) The Unprofessional Vagabond. By THOMAS CARLISLE (Haroun Alraschid), with Sketches from the Life of JOHN CARLISLE. Fcap. 8vo. Fancy boards. 1s.

Changed Cross (The) and other Religious Poems. 2s. 6d.

Child's Play, with 16 coloured drawings by E. V. B. An entirely new edition, printed on thick paper, with tints, 7s. 6d.

Chefs-d'œuvre of Art and Master-pieces of Engraving, selected from the celebrated Collection of Prints and Drawings in the British Museum. Reproduced in Photography by STEPHEN THOMPSON. Imperial folio, Thirty-eight Photographs, cloth gilt. 4l. 14s. 6d.

China. *See* **Illustrations of.**

Choice Editions of Choice Books. New Editions. Illustrated by C. W. Cope, R.A., T. Creswick, R.A., Edward Duncan, Birket Foster, J. C. Horsley, A.R.A., George Hicks, R. Redgrave, R.A., C. Stonehouse, F. Taylor, George Thomas, H. J. Townshend, E. H. Wehnert, Harrison Weir, &c. Crown 8vo. cloth, 5s. each ; mor. 10s. 6d.

Bloomfield's Farmer's Boy.	Keat's Eve of St. Agnes.
Campbell's Pleasures of Hope.	Milton's l'Allegro.
Cundall's Elizabethan Poetry.	Rogers' Pleasures of Memory.
Coleridge's Ancient Mariner,	Shakespeare's Songs and Sonnets.
Goldsmith's Deserted Village	Tennyson's May Queen.
Goldsmith's Vicar of Wakefield.	Weir's Poetry of Nature.
Gray's Elegy in a Churchyard.	Wordsworth's Pastoral Poems.

Christ in Song. Hymns of Immanuel, selected from all Ages, with Notes. By PHILIP SCHAFF, D.D. Crown 8vo. toned paper, beautifully printed at the Chiswick Press. With Initial Letters and Ornaments and handsomely bound. New Edition. 5s.

Christabel. *See* **Bayard Series.**

Christmas Presents. *See* **Illustrated Books.**

Chronicles of Castle of Amelroy. 4to. With Photographic Illustrations. 2l. 2s.

Clara Vaughan. *See* **Blackmore.**

Coffin (G. C.) Our New Way Round the World. 8vo. 12s.

Commons Preservation (Prize Essays on), written in competition for Prizes offered by HENRY W. PEEK, Esq. 8vo. 14s.

Compton Friars, by the Author of Mary Powell. Cr. 8vo. cloth. 10s. 6d.

Courtship and a Campaign; a Story of the Milanese Volunteers of 1866, under Garibaldi. By M. DALIN. 2 vols. cr. 8vo. 21s.

Cradock Nowell. *See* **Blackmore.**

Craik (Mrs.) The Adventures of a Brownie, by the Author of "John Halifax, Gentleman." With numerous Illustrations by Miss PATERSON. Square cloth, extra gilt edges. 5s.
A Capital Book for a School Prize for Children from Seven to Fourteen.

—— **Little Sunshine's Holiday** (forming Vol. 1. of the John Halifax Series of Girls' Books). Small post 8vo. 4s.

—— **John Halifax Series.** *See* **Girls' Books.**

—— **Poems.** Crown, cloth, 5s.

—— **(Georgiana M.) The Cousin from India,** forming Vol. 2. of John Halifax Series. Small post 8vo. 4s.

—— **Without Kith or Kin.** 3 vols. crown 8vo., 31s. 6d.

—— **Hero Trevelyan.** 2 Vols. Post 8vo. 21s.

Craik's American Millwright and Miller. With numerous Illustrations. 8vo. 1l. 1s.

Cruise of "The Rosario. *See* **Markham (A. H.).**

Cummins (Maria S.) Haunted Hearts (Low's Copyright Series). 16mo. boards. 1s. 6d.; cloth, 2s.

Curtis's History of the Constitution of the United States. 2 vols. 8vo. 24s.

DALTON (J. C.) A Treatise on Physiology and Hygiene for Schools, Families, and Colleges, with numerous Illustrations. 7s. 6d.

Dana (R. H.) Two Years before the Mast and Twenty-four years After. New Edition, with Notes and Revisions. 12mo. 6s.

Dana (Jas. D.) Corals and Coral Islands. Numerous Illustrations, charts, &c. Royal 8vo. cloth extra. 21s.

> " This handsome book is of a kind unfortunately too rare. An eminent traveller and naturalist has here endeavoured to present a popular account of a subject in which he has been one of the foremost investigators. . . . Professed geologists and zoologists, as well as general readers, will find Professor Dana's book in every way worthy of their attention."—*The Athenæum*, Oct. 12, 1872.

> " That his work is likely to be more popular than most accounts of the corals and coral polypes that we have seen, we have no doubt whatever."—*Saturday Review*.

Darley (Felix O. C.) Sketches Abroad with Pen and Pencil, with 84 Illustrations on Wood. Small 4to. 7s. 6d.

Daughter (A) of Heth, by WM. BLACK. Eleventh and Cheaper edition. 1 vol. crown 8vo. 6s.

Davies (Wm.) The Pilgrimage of the Tiber, from its Mouth to its Source : with some account of its Tributaries. 8vo., with many very fine Woodcuts and a Map, cloth extra. 18s.

> " Et terram Hesperiam venies, ubi Lydius arva
> Inter opima virûm leni fluit agmine Tibris."
>
> VIRGIL, Æn. II., 781.

Devonshire Hamlets ; Hamlet 1603, Hamlet 1604. 1 Vol. 8vo. 7s. 6d.

De Witt (Madame Guizot). An Only Sister. Vol. V. of the " John Halifax" Series of Girls' Books. With Six Illustrations. Small post 8vo. cloth. 4s.

Dhow-Chasing. *See* Sulivan.

Draper (John W.) Human Physiology. Illustrated with more than 300 Woodcuts from Photographs, &c. Royal 8vo. cloth extra. 14s.

Dream Book (The) with 12 Drawings in facsimile by E. V. B. Med. 4to. 1l. 11s. 6d.

Duer's Marine Insurance. 2 vols. 3l. 3s.

Duplais and McKennie, Treatise on the Manufacture and Distillation of Alcoholic Liquors. With numerous Engravings. 8vo. 2l. 2s.

Duplessis (G.) Wonders of Engraving. With numerous Illustrations and Photographs. 8vo. 12s. 6d.

Dussauce (Professor H.) A New and Complete Treatise on the Art of Tanning. Royal 8vo. 1l. 1s.

—— General Treatise on the Manufacture of Vinegar. 8vo. 1l. 1s.

 NGLISH Catalogue of Books (The) Published during 1863 to 1871 inclusive, comprising also the Important American Publications.

This Volume, occupying over 450 Pages, shows the Titles of 32,000 New Books and New Editions issued during Nine Years, with the Size, Price, and Publisher's Name, the Lists of Learned Societies, Printing Clubs, and other Literary Associations, and the Books issued by them; as also the Publisher's Series and Collections—altogether forming an indispensable adjunct to the Bookseller's Establishment, as well as to every Learned and Literary Club and Association.   30s. half-bound.

. The previous Volume, 1835 to 1862, of which a very few remain on sale, price 2l. 5s.; as also the Index Volume, 1837 to 1857, price 1l. 6s.

—— Supplements, 1863, 1864, 1865, 3s. 6d. each; 1866, 1867 to 1872, 5s. each.

—— Writers, Chapters for Self-improvement in English Literature; by the author of "The Gentle Life." 6s.

Erckmann - Chatrian, Forest House and Catherine's Lovers. Crown 8vo. 3s. 6d.

—— The Brothers Rantzau: A Story of the Vosges. 2 vols. crown 8vo. cloth. 21s.

FAITH GARTNEY'S Girlhood, by the Author of "The Gayworthys." Fcap. with Coloured Frontispiece. 3s. 6d.

Favourite English Poems. New and Extended Edition, with 300 illustrations. Small 4to. 21s.

Favell (The) Children. Three Little Portraits. Crown 12mo. Four Illustrations. Cloth gilt. 4s.

"A very useful and clever story."—*John Bull*.

Few (A) Hints on Proving Wills. Enlarged Edition, sewed. 2s.

Fields (J. T.) Yesterdays with Authors. Crown 8vo. 10s. 6d.

Fleming's (Sandford) Expedition. *See* Ocean to Ocean.

Flammarion (C.) The Atmosphere. Translated from the French of CAMILLE FLAMMARION. Edited by JAMES GLAISHER, F.R.S., Superintendent of the Magnetical and Meteorological Department of the Royal Observatory at Greenwich. With 10 beautiful Chromo-Lithographs and 81 woodcuts. Royal 8vo. cloth extra, bevelled boards. 30s.

Franc (Maude Jeane) Emily's Choice, an Australian Tale. 1 vol. small post 8vo. With a Frontispiece by G. F. ANGAS. 5*s.*

—— Marian, or the Light of Some One's Home. Fcp. 3rd Edition, with Frontispiece. 5*s.*

—— Silken Cords and Iron Fetters. 5*s.*

—— Vermont Vale. Small post 4to., with Frontispiece. 5*s.*

—— Minnie's Mission. Small post 8vo., with Frontispiece. 4*s.*

Frey (H.) The Microscope and Microscopical Technology. 8vo. illustrated. 30*s.*

Friswell (J. H.) *See* Gentle Life Series.

—— One of Two. 3 vols. 1*l.* 11*s.* 6*d.*

GAYWORTHYS (The), a Story of New England Life. Small post 8vo. 3*s.* 6*d.*

Gems of Dutch Art. Twelve Photographs from finest Engravings in British Museum. Sup. royal 4to. cloth extra. 25*s.*

Gentle Life (Queen Edition). 2 vols. in 1. Small 4to. 10*s.* 6*d.*

THE GENTLE LIFE SERIES. Printed in Elzevir, on Toned Paper, handsomely bound, forming suitable Volumes for Presents. Price 6*s.* each; or in calf extra, price 10*s.* 6*d.*

I.

The Gentle Life. Essays in aid of the Formation of Character of Gentlemen and Gentlewomen. Tenth Edition.

" His notion of a gentleman is of the noblest and truest order. A little compendium of cheerful philosophy."—*Daily News.*
" Deserves to be printed in letters of gold, and circulated in every house."—*Chambers' Journal.*

II.

About in the World. Essays by the Author of "The Gentle Life."

" It is not easy to open it at any page without finding some handy idea."—*Morning Post.*

III.

Like unto Christ. A New Translation of the " De Imitatione Christi " usually ascribed to Thomas à Kempis. With a Vignette from an Original Drawing by Sir Thomas Lawrence. Second Edition.

" Evinces independent scholarship, and a profound feeling for the original."—*Nonconformist.*

" Could not be presented in a more exquisite form, for a more sightly volume was never seen."—*Illustrated London News.*

IV.

Familiar Words. An Index Verborum, or Quotation Handbook. Affording an immediate Reference to Phrases and Sentences that have become embedded in the English language. Second and enlarged Edition.

" The most extensive dictionary of quotation we have met with."—*Notes and Queries.*

" Will add to the author's credit with all honest workers."—*Examiner.*

V.

Essays by Montaigne. Edited, Compared, Revised, and Annotated by the Author of " The Gentle Life." With Vignette Portrait. Second Edition.

" We should be glad if any words of ours could help to bespeak a large circulation for this handsome attractive book ; and who can refuse his homage to the good-humoured industry of the editor."—*Illustrated Times.*

VI.

The Countess of Pembroke's Arcadia. Written by Sir PHILIP SIDNEY. Edited, with Notes, by the Author of " The Gentle Life." Dedicated, by permission, to the Earl of Derby. 7*s.* 6*d.*

" All the best things in the Arcadia are retained intact in Mr. Friswell's edition.—*Examiner.*

VII.

The Gentle Life. Second Series. Third Edition.

" There is not a single thought in the volume that does not contribute in some measure to the formation of a true gentleman."—*Daily News.*

VIII.

Varia: Readings from Rare Books. Reprinted, by permission, from the *Saturday Review, Spectator, &c.*

" The books discussed in this volume are no less valuable than they are rare, and the compiler is entitled to the gratitude of the public for having rendered their treasures available to the general reader."—*Observer.*

IX.

The Silent Hour: Essays, Original and Selected. By the Author of " The Gentle Life." Second Edition.

" All who possess the ' Gentle Life ' should own this volume."—*Standard.*

X.

Essays on English writers, for the Self-improvement of
Students in English Literature.

"The author has a distinct purpose and a proper and noble ambition to
win the young to the pure and noble study of our glorious English
literature. To all (both men and women) who have neglected to read
and study their native literature we would certainly suggest the volume
before us as a fitting introduction."—*Examiner.*

XI.

Other People's Windows. By J. HAIN FRISWELL. Second
Edition.

"The chapters are so lively in themselves, so mingled with shrewd
views of human nature, so full of illustrative anecdotes, that the reader
cannot fail to be amused."—*Morning Post.*

XII.

A Man's Thoughts. By J. HAIN FRISWELL.

German Primer; being an Introduction to First Steps in
German. By M. T. PREU. 2s. 6d.

Getting On in the World; or, Hints on Success in Life.
By WILLIAM MATHEWS, LL.D. Small post 8vo., cloth extra, bevelled
edges. 6s.

Girdlestone (C.) Christendom. 12mo. 3s.

———— **Family Prayers.** 12mo. 1s. 6d.

Glover (Rev. R.) The Light of the Word. Third Edition.
18mo. 2s. 6d.

Goethe's Faust. With Illustrations by Konewka. Small 4to.
Price 10s. 6d.

Gouffé: The Royal Cookery Book. By JULES GOUFFÉ,
Chef-de-Cuisine of the Paris Jockey Club; translated and adapted for
English use by ALPHONSE GOUFFÉ, head pastrycook to Her Majesty the
Queen. Illustrated with large plates, beautifully printed in colours, to-
gether with 161 woodcuts. 8vo. Cloth extra, gilt edges. 2l. 2s.

———— **Domestic Edition, half-bound.** 10s. 6d.

"By far the ablest and most complete work on cookery that has ever
been submitted to the gastronomical world."—*Pall Mall Gazette.*

———— **The Book of Preserves; or, Receipts for Preparing**
and Preserving Meat, Fish salt and smoked, Terrines, Gelatines, Vege-
tables, Fruits, Confitures, Syrups, Liqueurs de Famille, Petits Fours,
Bonbons, &c. &c. By JULES GOUFFÉ, Head Cook of the Paris Jockey
Club, and translated and adapted by his brother ALPHONSE GOUFFÉ,
Head Pastrycook to her Majesty the Queen, translator and editor of
"The Royal Cookery Book." 1 vol. royal 8vo., containing upwards of
500 Receipts and 34 Illustrations. 10s. 6d.

Girls' Books. A Series written, edited, or translated by the Author of "John Halifax." Small post 8vo., cloth extra, 4*s*. each.

    1. Little Sunshine's Holiday.
    2. The Cousin from India.
    3. Twenty Years Ago.
    4. Is it True.
    5. An Only Sister. By Madame GUIZOT DE WITT.

Gough (J. B.) The Autobiography and Reminiscences of John B. Gough. 8vo. Cloth, 10*s*. 6*d*.

Great Lone-Land. *See* Butler.

Grant (Rev. G. M.). *See* Ocean to Ocean.

Greenleaf's Law of Evidence. 3 vols. 84*s*.

Guizot's History of France. Translated by ROBERT BLACK. Royal 8vo. Numerous Illustrations. Vols. I. and II., cloth extra, each 24*s*.; in Parts, 2*s*. each (to be completed in about twenty parts).

Guyon (Mad.) Life. By Upham. Third Edition. Crown 8vo. 6*s*.

—— **Method of Prayer.** Foolscap. 1*s*.

HALL (E. H.) The Great West; Handbook for Emigrants and Settlers in America. With a large Map of routes, railways, and steam communication, complete to present time. Boards, 1*s*.

Harrington (J.) Pictures of Saint George's Chapel, Windsor. Photographs. 4to. 63*s*.

Harrington's Abbey and Palace of Westminster. Photographs. 3*l*. 3*s*.

Harrison (Agnes). *See* Martin's Vineyard.

Harper's Handbook for Travellers in Europe and the East. New Edition. Post 8vo. Morocco tuck, 1*l*. 1*s*.

Harz Mountains. *See* Blackburn.

Hawthorne (Mrs. N.) Notes in England and Italy. Crown 8vo. 10*s*. 6*d*.

Hayes (Dr.) Cast Away in the Cold; an Old Man's Story of a Young Man's Adventures. By Dr. I. ISAAC HAYES, Author of "The Open Polar Sea." With numerous Illustrations. Gilt edges, 6*s*.

—— **The Land of Desolation;** Personal Narrative of Adventures in Greenland. Numerous Illustrations. Demy 8vo., cloth extra. 14*s*.

Hazard (S.) Santo Domingo, Past and Present; With a
Glance at Hayti. With upwards of One Hundred and Fifty beautiful
Woodcuts and Maps, chiefly from Designs and Sketches by the Author.
Demy 8vo. cloth extra. 18s.

Extract from the notice in *Spectator*, March 22nd.—"This is a book
that, in view of the St. Domingo Loan and the New Samana Bay
Company, will prove peculiarly interesting to English readers."

—— **Cuba with Pen and Pencil. Over 300 Fine Wood-**
cut Engravings. New edition, 8vo. cloth extra. 15s.

"We recommend this book to the perusal of our readers."—
Spectator.

"Mr. Hazard has completely exhausted his subject."—*Pall Mall
Gazette*.

Hazlitt (William) The Round Table; the Best Essays of
WILLIAM HAZLITT, with Biographical Introduction (Bayard Series).
2s. 6d.

Healy (M.) Lakeville; or, Shadow and Substance. A
Novel. 3 vols. 1l. 11s. 6d.

—— **A Summer's Romance. Crown 8vo., cloth. 10s. 6d.**

—— **The Home Theatre. Small post 8vo. 3s. 6d.**

Henderson (A.) Latin Proverbs and Quotations; with
Translations and Parallel Passages, and a copious English Index. By
ALFRED HENDERSON. Fcap. 4to., 530 pp. 10s. 6d.

"A very handsome volume in its typographical externals, and a very
useful companion to those who, when a quotation is aptly made, like to
trace it to its source, to dwell on the minutiæ of its application, and to
find it illustrated with choice parallel passages from English and Latin
authors."—*Times*.

"A book well worth adding to one's library."—*Saturday Review*.

Hearth Ghosts. By the Author of 'Gilbert Rugge.' 3 Vols.
1l. 11s. 6d.

Heber's (Bishop) Illustrated Edition of Hymns. With
upwards of 100 Designs engraved in the first style of art under the
superintendence of J. D. Cooper. Small 4to. Handsomely bound,
7s. 6d

Higginson (T. W.) Atlantic Essays. Small post 8vo.
cloth. 6s.

Hitherto. By the Author of "The Gayworthys." New Edition.
cloth extra. 3s. 6d. Also in Low's American Series. Double Vol. 2s. 6d.

Hofmann (Carl) A Practical Treatise on the Manufac-
ture of Paper in all its Branches. Illustrated by One Hundred and
Ten Wood Engravings, and Five large Folding Plates. In One Volume,
4to, cloth; about 400 pages. 3l. 13s. 6d.

Hoge—Blind Bartimæus. Popular edition. 1s.

Holland (Dr.) Kathrina and Titcomb's Letters. See Low's
American Series.

Holmes (Oliver W.) The Guardian Angel; a Romance.
2 vols. 16*s.*

————— (Low's Copyright Series.) Boards, 1*s.* 6*d.* ; cloth, 2*s.*

————— Autocrat of the Breakfast Table. 12mo. 1*s.* ; Illustrated edition, 3*s.* 6*d.*

————— The Professor at the Breakfast Table. 3*s.* 6*d.*

————— Songs in Many Keys. Post 8vo. 7*s.* 6*d.*

————— Mechanism in Thought and Morals. 12mo. 1*s.* 6*d.*

Home Theatre (The), by MARY HEALY. Small post 8vo. 3*s.* 6*d.*

Homespun, or Twenty Five Years Ago in America, by THOMAS LACKLAND. Fcap. 8vo. 7*s.* 6*d.*

Hoppin (Jas. M.) Old Country, its Scenery, Art, and People. Post 8vo. 7*s.* 6*d.*

Howell (W. D.) Italian Journeys. 12mo. cloth. 8*s.* 6*d.*

Hugo's Toilers of the Sea. Crown 8vo, 6*s.*; fancy boards, 2*s.* ; cloth, 2*s.* 6*d.* ; Illustrated Edition, 10*s.* 6*d.*

Hunt (Leigh) and S. A. Lee, Elegant Sonnets, with Essay on Sonneteers. 2 vols. 8vo. 18*s.*

————— Day by the Fire. Fcap. 6*s.* 6*d.*

Huntington (J.D., D.D.) Christian Believing. Crown 8vo. 3*s.* 6*d.*

Hymnal Companion to Book of Common Prayer. *See* Bickersteth.

————CE, a Midsummer Night's Dream. Small Post 8vo. 3*s.* 6*d.*

————— Illustrations of China and its People. By J. THOMSON, F.R.G.S. Being Photographs from the Author's Negatives, printed in permanent Pigments by the Autotype Process, and Notes from Personal Observation.

**** The complete work will embrace 200 Photographs, with Letterpress Descriptions of the Places and People represented. In Four Volumes, imperial 4to., price 3*l.* 3*s.* each Volume. The First Volume, containing Fifty Photographs, is now ready.

Subscribers ordering the Four Volumes at once will be supplied for 10*l.* 10*s.*, half of which is to be paid on receipt of Vol. I., and balance on completion of the work. Non-subscribers' price is 3*l.* 3*s.* a Volume.

"In his succeeding volumes, he proposes to take us with him northward and westward ; and if the high promise held out in the present instalment of his book be fulfilled in them, they will together form, from every point of view, a most valuable and interesting work. The photographs are excellent ; . . . . artistically, they are all that can be desired. Accompanying each is a full, and what is somewhat unusual in books relating to China, an accurate description of the scene or objects represented."—*Athenæum.*

Illustrated Books, suitable for Christmas, Birthday, or
  Wedding Presents. (The full titles of which will be found
  in the Alphabet.)

Adventures of a Young Naturalist. 7*s.* 6*d.*
Alexander's Bush Fighting. 16*s.*
Anderson's Fairy Tales. 25*s.*
Arctic Regions. Illustrated. 25 guineas.
Art, Pictorial and Industrial. Vol. I. 31*s.* 6*d.*
Blackburn's Art in the Mountains. 12*s.*
——— Artists and Arabs. 7*s.* 6*d.*
——— Harz Mountains. 12*s.*
——— Normandy Picturesque. 16*s.*
——— Travelling in Spain. 16*s.*
——— The Pyrenees. 18*s.*
Bush's Reindeer, Dogs, &c. 12*s.* 6*d.*
Butler's Great Lone Land. 7*s.* 6*d.*
Chefs d'Œuvre of Art. 4*l.* 14*s.* 6*d.*
China. Illustrated. 4 vols. 3*l.* 3*s.* each vol.
Christian Lyrics.
Davies's Pilgrimage of the Tiber. 18*s.*
Dream Book, by E. V. B. 21*s.* 6*d.*
Duplessis' Wonders of Engraving. 12*s.* 6*d.*
Favourite English Poems. 21*s.*
Flammarion's The Atmosphere. 30*s.*
Fletcher and Kidder's Brazil. 18*s.*
Goethe's Faust, illustrations by P. KONEWKA. 10*s.* 6*d.*
Gouffe's Royal Cookery Book. Coloured plates. 42*s.*
——— Ditto. Popular edition. 10*s.* 6*d.*
——— Book of Preserves. 10*s.* 6*d.*
Hazard's Santa Domingo. 18*s.*
——— Cuba. 15*s.*
Heber (Bishop) Hymns. Illustrated edition. 7*s.* 6*d.*
Markham's Cruise of the Rosario. 16*s.*
Milton's Paradise Lost. (Martin's plates). 3*l.* 13*s.* 6*d.*
My Lady's Cabinet. 21*s.*
Ocean to Ocean. 10*s.* 6*d.*
Palliser (Mrs.) History of Lace. 21*s.*
——— Historic Devices, &c. 21*s.*
Peaks and Valleys of the Alps. 6*l.* 6*s.*
Pike's Sub-Tropical Rambles. 18*s.*
Red Cross Knight (The). 25*s.*
Sauzay's Wonders of Glass Making. 12*s.* 6*d.*
Schiller's Lay of the Bell. 14*s.*
St. George's Chapel, Windsor.
Sulivan's Dhow Chasing. 16*s.*
The Abbey and Palace of Westminster. 5*l.* 5*s.*
Viardot, Wonders of Sculpture. 12*s.* 6*d.*
——— Wonders of Italian Art. 12*s.* 6*d.*
——— Wonders of European Art. 12*s.* 6*d.*
Werner (Carl) Nile Sketches. 2 Series, each 3*l.* 10*s.*

Index to the Subjects of Books published in the United
  Kingdom during the last 20 years. 8vo. Half-morocco. 1*l.* 6*s.*

Innocent." By Mrs. OLIPHANT. 3 Vols. Crown 8vo. cloth.
  31*s.* 6*d.* [10s.]

In the Tropics.   Post 8vo.   6*s*.

In Silk Attire.   *See* Black, Wm.

Is it True?   Being Tales Curious and Wonderful.   Small post
8vo., cloth extra.   4*s*.

    (Forming vol. 4 of the " John Halifax " Series of Girls' Books.)

JACK HAZARD, a Story of Adventure by J. T.
Trowbridge.   Numerous illustrations, small post.   3*s*. 6*d*.

John Halifax Series of Girls' Books.   *See* Girls'
Books.

Johnson (R. B.) Very Far West Indeed.   A few rough
Experiences on the North-West Pacific Coast.   Cr. 8vo. cloth.   10*s*. 6*d*.
New Edition—the Fourth, fancy boards.   2*s*.

    " Variety and adventure abound in his book, which is written too
with never-flagging spirit."—*Athenæum*.

KAVANAGH'S Origin of Language.   2 vols. crown
8vo.   1*l*. 1*s*.

Kedge Anchor, or Young Sailor's Assistant, by
Wm. Brady.   8vo.   18*s*.

Kennan (G.) Tent Life in Siberia.   3rd edition.   6*s*.

    " We strongly recommend the work as one of the most entertaining
volumes of travel that has appeared of late years."—*Athenæum*.
    " We hold our breath as he details some hair-breadth escape, and
burst into fits of irresistible laughter over incidents full of humour. —
Spectator.

Kent (Chancellor) Commentaries on American Law.
11th edition.   4 vols.   8vo.   4*l*. 10*s*.

Kilmeny.   *See* Black (Wm.)

King (Clarence) Mountaineering in the Sierra Nevada.
crown 8vo.   Third and Cheaper Edition, cloth extra.   6*s*.
    The *Times* of Oct. 20th says :—" If we judge his descriptions by
the vivid impressions they leave, we feel inclined to give them very high
praise "
    " A fresh and vigorous record of varied kinds of adventure, combined
with vivid pictures of mountain scenery, and with glimpses of wild life
among Indians, Mexicans, and Californians, will commend itself to most
readers."—*The Athenæum*

**Kingston (W. H. G.) Ben Burton, or Born and Bred at
Sea.**   Fcap. with Illustrations.   3*s*. 6*d*.

Koldeway (Captain) The Second North-German Polar Expedition in the year 1869-1870 of the ships "Germania" and "Hansa," under Command of Captain Koldeway. Edited and Condensed by H. W. Bates, Esq., of the Royal Geographical Society. 1 vol. demy 8vo., numerous Woodcuts, Maps, and Chromo-Lithographs —*In the Press.*

AKEVILLE. *See* Healy.

Land of the White Elephant. *See* Vincent.

Lang (J. D.) The Coming Event. 8vo. 12s.

Lascelles (Arthur) The Coffee Grower's Guide. Post 8vo. 2s. 6d.

Lee (G. R.) Memoirs of the American Revolutionary War. 8vo. 16s.

Like unto Christ. A new translation of the "De Imitatione Christi," usually ascribed to Thomas à Kempis. Second Edition. 6s.

Little Men. See Alcott.

Little Preacher. 32mo. 1s.

Little Women. See Alcott.

Little Sunshine's Holiday. *See* Craik (Mrs.)

Livingstone (Dr.), How I Found. *See* Stanley.

Log of my Leisure Hours. By an Old Sailor. Cheaper Edition. Fancy boards. 2s.

Longfellow (H. W.) The Poets and Poetry of Europe. New Edition. 8vo. cloth. 1l. 1s.

Loomis (Elias). Recent Progress of Astronomy. Post 8vo. 7s. 6d.

———— Practical Astronomy. 8vo. 10s.

Low's Copyright and Cheap Editions of American Authors, comprising Popular Works, reprinted by arrangement with their Authors :—

1. Haunted Hearts. By the Author of "The Lamplighter."
2. The Guardian Angel. By "The Autocrat of the Breakfast Table."
3. The Minister's Wooing. By the Author of "Uncle Tom's Cabin.
4. Views Afoot. By BAYARD TAYLOR.
5. Kathrina, Her Life and Mine. By J. G. HOLLAND.
6. Hans Brinker: or, Life in Holland. By Mrs. DODGE.

Low's Cheap Copyright Editions, *continued—*

7. Men, Women, and Ghosts. By Miss PHELPS.
8. Society and Solitude. By RALPH WALDO EMERSON.
9. Hedged In. By ELIZABETH PHELPS.
10. An Old-Fashioned Girl. By LOUISA M. ALCOTT.
11. Faith Gartney.
12. Stowe's Old Town Folks. 2s. 6d.; cloth, 3s.
13. Lowell's Study Windows.
14. My Summer in a Garden. By CHARLES DUDLEY WARNER.
15. Pink and White Tyranny. By Mrs. STOWE.
16. We Girls. By Mrs. WHITNEY.
17. Little Men. By Miss ALCOTT.
18. Little Women. By Miss ALCOTT.
19. Little Women Wedded. (Forming the Sequel to "Little Women.")
20. Back-Log Studies. By CHARLES DUDLEY WARNER, Author of "My Summer in a Garden."

> "This is a delightful book."—*Atlantic Monthly.*

21. Timothy Titcomb's Letters to Young People, Single and Married.

**** Of this famous little work upwards of 50,000 have been sold in America alone at four times the present price, viz. 1s. 6d. flexible fancy boards; 2s. cloth extra.

22. Hitherto. By Mrs. T. D. WHITNEY. Double Volume, 2s. 6d. fancy flexible boards.

**** This Copyright work was first published in this country in 3 vols. at 31s. 6d.; afterwards in 1 vol. at 6s. It is now issued in the above popular Series.

23. Farm Ballads. by Will. Carleton, price ONE SHILLING.

The *Guardian* says of "Little Women," that it is "a bright, cheerful, healthy story—with a tinge of thoughtful gravity about it which reminds one of John Bunyan. Meg going to Vanity Fair is a chapter written with great cleverness and a pleasant humour."

The *Athenæum* says of "Old-Fashioned Girl": "Let whoever wishes to read a bright, spirited, wholesome story get the 'Old-Fashioned Girl' at once."

**** "We may be allowed to add, that Messrs. Low's is the 'Author's edition.' We do not commonly make these announcements, but every one is bound to defeat, as far as he can, the efforts of those enterprising persons who proclaim with much unction the sacred duty of *not* letting an American author get his proper share of profits."—*Spectator*, Jan. 4, 1873.

Each volume complete in itself, price 1s. 6d. enamelled flexible cover, 2s. cloth.

Low's Monthly Bulletin of American and Foreign Publications, forwarded regularly. Subscription 2s. 6d. per annum.

Low's Minion Series of Popular Books. 1s. each :—

The Gates Ajar. (The original English Edition.)
Who is He?
The Little Preacher.
The Boy Missionary.

Low (Sampson, Jun.) The Charities of London. For the the year 1872. 1*s.*

Ludlow (FitzHugh). The Heart of the Continent. 8vo. cloth. 14*s.*

Lunn (J. C.) Only Eve. 3 vols. 31*s.* 6*d.*

Lyne (A. A.) The Midshipman's Trip to Jerusalem. With illustration. Third Edition. Crown 8vo., cloth. 10*s.* 6*d.*

Lyra Sacra Americana. Gems of American Poetry, selected and arranged, with Notes and Biographical Sketches, by C. D. CLEVE-LAND, D. D., author of the " Milton Concordance." 18mo. 4*s.* 6*d.*

ACALPINE; or, On Scottish Ground. A Novel. 3 vols. crown 8vo. 31*s.* 6*d.*

Macgregor (John,) " Rob Roy " on the Baltic. Third Edition, small post 8vo. 2*s.* 6*d.*

——— A Thousand Miles in the " Rob Roy " Canoe. Eleventh Edition. Small post, 8vo. 2*s.* 6*d.*

—— — Description of the " Rob Roy " Canoe, with plans, &c. 1*s.*

——— The Voyage Alone in the Yawl " Rob Roy." Second Edition. Small post, 8vo. 5*s.*

March (A.) Anglo-Saxon Reader. 8vo. 7*s.* 6*d.*

——— Comparative Grammar of the Anglo-Saxon Language. 8vo. 12*s.*

Marcy, (R. B.) Thirty Years of Army Life. Royal 8vo. 12*s.*

——— Prairie and Overland Traveller. 2*s.* 6*d.*

Marigold Manor. By Miss WARING. With Introduction by Rev. A. SEWELL. With Illustrations. Small Post 8vo. 4*s.*

Markham (A. H.) The Cruise of the " Rosario " amongst the New Hebrides and Santa Cruz Islands, exposing the Recent Atrocities connected with the Kidnapping of Natives in the South Seas. By A. H. MARKHAM, Commander, R.N. 8vo. cloth extra, with Map and Illustrations. 16*s.*

" The crew of the ' Rosario ' were sent out from England in that wretched tub the ' Megæra.' Captain Markham's account of the cruise is pleasantly written."—*Standard.*

" We trust, therefore, that it may be generally read."—*Athenæum.*

Markham (C. R.) The Threshold of the Unknown Region.
Demy 8vo. with Maps and Illustrations. [*In the press.*
 ** The object of this Work is to give the public a correct knowledge
 of the whole line of frontier separating the known from the unknown
 region round the North Pole.

Marlitt (Miss) The Princess of the Moor. Tauchnitz Translations.

Marsh (George P.) Man and Nature. 8vo. 15*s.*

—— Origin and History of the English Language.
8vo. 16*s.*

—— Lectures on the English Language. 8vo. 15*s.*

Martin's Vineyard. By Agnes Harrison. Crown 8vo. cloth.
10*s. 6d.*

Matthews (Wm.) *See* Getting on in the World.

Maury (Commander) Physical Geography of the Sea and
its Meteorology. Being a Reconstruction and Enlargement of his former
Work; with illustrative Charts and Diagrams. New Edition. Crown
8vo. 6*s.*

Mayo (Dr.) *See* Never Again.

McMullen's History of Canada. 8vo. 16*s.*

Mercier (Rev. L.) Outlines of the Life of the Lord Jesus
Christ. 2 vols. crown 8vo. 15*s.*

Meridiana *See* Verne.

Milton's Complete Poetical Works; with Concordance by
W. D. CLEVELAND. New Edition. 8vo. 12*s.*; morocco 1*l.* 1*s.*

—— Paradise Lost, with the original Steel Engravings of
JOHN MARTIN. Printed on large paper, royal 4to. handsomely bound.
3*l.* 13*s. 6d.*

Miss Dorothy's Charge. By FRANK LEE BENEDICT, Author
of "My Cousin Elenor." 3 vols. crown 8vo. 31*s. 6d.*

Missionary Geography (The); a Manual of Missionary
Operations in all parts of the World, with Map and Illustrations. Fcap.
3*s. 6d.*

Monk of Monk's Own. 3 vols. 31*s. 6d.*

Montaigne's Essays. *See* Gentle Life Series.

Morgan's Macaronic Poetry. 16mo. 12*s.*

Mother Goose's Melodies for Children. Square 8vo., cloth
extra. 7*s. 6d.*

Mountain (Bishop) Life of. By his Son. 8vo. 10*s. 6d.*

My Summer in a Garden. See Warner.

My Cousin Maurice. A Novel. 3 vols. Cloth, 31*s. 6d.*

My Lady's Cabinet. Charmingly Decorated with Lovely
Drawings and Exquisite Miniatures. Contains Seventy-five Pictures set
in Frames, and arranged on Twenty-four Panels, thus representing the
Walls of a richly adorned Boudoir. Each page or panel interleaved with
Letterpress sufficient to explain the Subjects of the Drawings, and give
the Names of the Artists. Printed on royal 4to., and very handsomely
bound in cloth. 1*l.* 1*s.*

"The fittest ornament for a Lady's Cabinet which this season has produced."—*Athenæum.*

"Forms an excellent pretty book for the drawing-room table."—*Pall
Mall Gazette.*

"A very pretty idea, carried out with much taste and elegance."—
Daily News.

My Wife and I. *See* Mrs. Stowe.

NEVER Again: a Novel. By Dr. MAYO, Author of
"Kaloolah." New and Cheaper Edition, in One Vol., small
post 8vo. 6*s.* Cheapest edition, fancy boards, 2*s.*

"Puts its author at once into the very first rank of
novelists."—*The Athenæum.*

New Testament. The Authorized English Version; with the
various Readings from the most celebrated Manuscripts, including the
Sinaitic, the Vatican, and the Alexandrian MSS., in English. With
Notes by the Editor, Dr. TISCHENDORF. The whole revised and carefully collected for the Thousandth Volume of Baron Tauchnitz's Collection. Cloth flexible, gilt edges, 2*s.* 6*d.*; cheaper style, 2*s.*; or sewed,
1*s.* 6*d.*

Nordhoff (C.) California : for Health, Pleasure, and Residence. A Book for Travellers and Settlers. Numerous Illustrations,
8vo., cloth extra. 12*s.* 6*d.*

Nothing to Wear, and Two Millions. By WILLIAM
ALLEN BUTLER. 1*s.*

Nystrom's Mechanics Pocket Book. 10*s.* 6*d.*

OCEAN to Ocean. Sandford Fleming's Expedition
through Canada in 1872. Being a Diary kept during a
Journey from the Atlantic to the Pacific with the Expedition
of the Engineer-in-Chief of the Canadian Pacific and Inter-
colonial Railways. By the Rev. GEORGE M. GRANT, of
Halifax, N.S., Secretary to the Expedition. With Sixty Illustrations.
Demy 8vo., cloth extra, pp. 372. 10*s.* 6*d.*

Old Fashioned Girl. See Alcott.

Oliphant (Mrs.) Innocent. 3 vols. Crown 8vo. cloth.
31*s.* 6*d.*

Only Eve. By Mrs. J. CALBRAITH LUNN. Three Vols.
post 8vo. cloth. 31*s.* 6*d.*

Other Girls (The). *See* Whitney (Mrs.)

Our American Cousins at Home. By VERA, Author of
"Under the Red Cross." Illustrated with Pen and Ink Sketches, by
the Author, and several fine Photographs. Crown 8vo, cloth. 9s.

Our Little Ones in Heaven. Edited by Rev. H. ROBBINS.
With Frontispiece after Sir JOSHUA REYNOLDS. Second Edition.
Fcap. 3s. 6d.

PALLISER (Mrs.) A History of Lace, from the
Earliest Period. A New and Revised Edition, with upwards
of 100 Illustrations and coloured Designs.   1 vol. 8vo. 1l. 1s.
"One of the most readable books of the season ; permanently
valuable, always interesting, often amusing, and not inferior in all the
essentials of a gift book."—*Times.*

——— **Historic Devices, Badges, and War Cries.** 8vo.
1l. 1s.

Paper Manufacture. *See* Hofmann.

Parsons (T.) A Treatise on the Law of Marine Insurance
and General Average. By Hon. THEOPHILUS PARSONS. 2 vols. 8vo.
3l. 3s.

Parisian Family. From the French of Madame GUIZOT DE
WITT ; by Author of "John Halifax." Fcap. 5s.
"The feeling of the story is so good, the characters are so clearly
marked, there is such freshness and truth to nature in the simple incidents recorded, that we have been allured on from page to page without
the least wish to avail ourselves of a privilege permitted sometimes to the
reviewer, and to skip a portion of the narrative."—*Pall Mall Gazette.*

Peaks and Valleys of the Alps. From Water-Colour Drawings by ELIJAH WALTON. Chromo-lithographed by J. H. LOWES, with
Descriptive Text by the Rev. T. G. BONNEY, M.A., F.G.S. Folio,
half-morocco, with 21 large Plates. Original subscription, 8 guineas. A
very limited edition only now issued. Price 6 guineas.

Phelps (Miss) Gates Ajar. 32mo. 6d. ; 4d.

——— **Men, Women, and Ghosts.** 12mo. Sewed, 1s. 6d.
cloth, 2s.

——— **Hedged In.** 12mo. Sewed, 1s. 6d. ; cloth, 2s.

——— **Silent Partner.** 5s.

Phillips (L.) Dictionary of Biographical Reference. 8vo.
1l. 11s. 6d.

Phillips' Law of Insurance. 2 vols. 3l. 3s.

Picture Gallery of British Art (The). Twenty beautiful and
Permanent Photographs after the most celebrated English Painters.
With Descriptive Letterpress. One Volume, demy 4to. cloth extra,
gilt edges. 12s.

Picture Gallery of Sacred Art (The). Containing Twenty very fine Examples in Permanent Photography after the Old Masters. With Descriptive Letterpress. Demy 4to. cloth extra, gilt edges. 12*s.*

Pike (N.) Sub-Tropical Rambles in the Land of the Aphanapteryx. In 1 vol. demy 8vo. 18*s.* Profusely Illustrated from the Author's own Sketches, also with Maps and valuable Meteorological Charts.

"Rarely have we met with a book of travels more enjoyable, and few have been written by a sharper or closer observer. To recapitulate a tithe of the heads of the information he provides would exhaust the limits of the longest paragraph, and we must content ourselves with saying that he has left very little indeed to be gleaned by his successors in the task of bringing home to the English mind what a wealth of beauty and novelty there is to be found on the island."—*The Standard.*

Pilgrimage of the Tiber. *See* **Davies (Wm.).**

Plutarch's Lives. An Entirely New and Library Edition. Edited by A. H. CLOUGH, Esq. 5 vols. 8vo. 3*l.* 3*s.*

"'Plutarch's Lives' will yet be read by thousands, and in the version of Mr. Clough."—*Quarterly Review.*

"Mr. Clough's work is worthy of all praise, and we hope that it will tend to revive the study of Plutarch."—*Times.*

——— **Morals.** Uniform with Clough's Edition of "Lives of Plutarch." Edited by Professor GOODWIN. 5 vols. 8vo. 3*l.* 3*s.*

Poe (E. A.) The Works of. 4 vols. 2*l.* 2*s.*

Poems of the Inner Life. A New Edition, Revised, with many additional Poems, inserted by permission of the Authors. Small post 8vo., cloth. 5*s.*

"These books (Palgrave's and Trench's) are quite beyond the range of the ordinary compiler, and praise similar in character, if not in degree, may be awarded to the careful Editor of the little volume before us."—*Spectator.*

Polar Expedition. *See* **Koldeway.**

Poor (H. V.) Manual of the Railroads of the United States for 1873-4; Showing their Mileage, Stocks, Bonds, Cost, Earnings, Expenses, and Organisations, with a Sketch of their Rise, &c. 1 vol. 8vo. 24*s.*

Portraits of Celebrated Women. By C. A. ST. BEUVE. 12mo. 6*s.* 6*d.*

Preces Veterum. Collegit et edidit Joannes F. France. Crown 8vo., cloth, red edges. 5*s.*

Preu (M. T.) German Primer. Square cloth. 2*s.* 6*d.*

Prime (I.) Fifteen Years of Prayer. Small post 8vo., cloth. 3*s.* 6*d.*

——— **(E. D. G.) Around the World.** Sketches of Travel through Many Lands and over Many Seas. 8vo., Illustrated. 14*s.*

Publishers' Circular (The), and General Record of British and Foreign Literature; giving a transcript of the title-page of every work published in Great Britain, and every work of interest published abroad, with lists of all the publishing houses.

Published regularly on the 1st and 15th of every Month, and forwarded post free to all parts of the world on payment of 6s. per annum.

Queer Things of the Service. Crown 8vo., fancy boards. 2s. 6d.

 **ASSELAS, Prince of Abyssinia.** By Dr. JOHNSON. With Introduction by the Rev. WILLIAM WEST, Vicar of Nairn. (Bayard Series). 2s. 6d.

Ready, O Ready! or These Forty Years: A book for Young Fellows. By Captain ALLSTON, R.N. Small post 8vo., cloth extra. 3s. 6d.

Recamier (Madame) Memoirs and Correspondence of. Translated from the French, and Edited by J. M. LUYSTER. With Portrait. Crown 8vo. 7s. 6d.

Red Cross Knight (The). *See* Spenser.

Reid (W.) After the War. Crown 8vo. 10s. 6d.

Reindeer, Dogs, &c. *See* Bush.

Reminiscences of America in 1869, by Two Englishmen. Crown 8vo. 7s. 6d.

Reynard the Fox. The Prose Translation by the late THOMAS ROSCOE. With about 100 exquisite Illustrations on Wood, after designs by A. J. ELWES. Imperial 16mo. cloth extra, 7s. 6d.

"Will yield to none either in the interest of its text or excellence of its engravings."—*Standard*.

"A capital Christmas book."—*Globe*.

"The designs are an ornament of a delightful text."—*Times*, Dec. 24.

Rhyme of the Duchess May. *See* Browning.

Richardson (A. S.) Stories from Old English Poetry. Small post 8vo., cloth. 5s.

Rochefoucauld's Reflections. Flexible cloth extra. 2s. 6d. (Bayard Series.)

Rogers (S.) Pleasures of Memory. *See* "Choice Editions of Choice Books." 5s.

Romance (The) of American History. By Prof. De Vere. Crown 8vo. cloth. 6s.

 **ANDEAU (J.)** *See* Sea-Gull Rock.

SANTO DOMINGO, Past and Present. *See* Hazard.

Sauzay (A.) Marvels of Glass Making. Numerous Illustrations. Demy 8vo. 12s. 6d.

Schiller's Lay of the Bell, translated by Lord Lytton. With 42 illustrations after Retsch. Oblong 4to. 14*s.*

School Books. *See* Classified.

School Prizes. *See* Books.

Sea-Gull Rock. By Jules Sandeau, of the French Academy. Translated by ROBERT BLACK, M.A. With Seventy-nine very beautiful Woodcuts. Royal 16mo., cloth extra, gilt edges. 7*s.* 6*d.*

"A story more fascinating, more replete with the most rollicking fun, the most harrowing scenes of suspense, distress, and hair-breadth escapes from danger, was seldom before written, published, or read."—*Athenæum.*

"It deserves to please the new nation of boys to whom it is presented."—*Times.*

"The very best French story for children we have ever seen."—*Standard.*

"A delightful treat."—*Illustrated London News.*

"Admirable, full of life, pathos, and fun. . . . It is a striking and attractive book."—*Guardian.*

"This story deserves to be a great favourite with English boys as well as with French."—*Saturday Review.*

"Can be recommended alike for the graphic illustrations and admirable subject-matter."—*John Bull.*

"Is quite a gem of its kind. It is beautifully and profusely illustrated."—*Graphic.*

"A finely illustrated and beautifully adorned volume."—*Daily News.*

Seaman (Ezra C.) Essays on the Progress of Nations in civilization, productive history, wealth, and population; illustrated by statistics. Post 8vo. 10*s.* 6*d.*

Sedgwick, (J.) Treatise on the Measure of Damages. 8vo. 1*l.* 18*s.*

Shadow of the Rock. *See* Bickersteth.

Shakespeare's Songs and Sonnets, selected by J. HOWARD STAUNTON; with 36 exquisite drawings by JOHN GILBERT. See "Choice Series." 5*s.*

Shawl Straps. *See* Alcott.

Sheridan's Troopers on the Borders. Post 8vo. 7*s.* 6*d.*

Sidney (Sir Philip) The Countess of Pembroke's Arcadia, edited, with notes, by the author of "Gentle Life," 7*s.* 6*d.* Large paper edition. 12*s.*

Silent Hour (The), Essays original and selected, by the author of "The Gentle Life." Second edition. 6*s.*

Silent Partner. *See* Phelps.

Silliman (Benjamin) Life of, by G. P. FISHER. 2 vols. crown 8vo. 1*l.* 4*s.*

Simson (W.) A History of the Gipsies, with specimens of the Gipsy Language. 10*s.* 6*d.*

Smiley (S. F.) Who is He? 32mo. 1*s.*

Smith and Hamilton's French Dictionary. 2 vols. Cloth, 21*s.*; half roan, 22*s.*

Snow Flakes, and what they told the Children, beautifully printed in colours. Cloth extra, bevelled boards. 5*s.*

Socrates. Memoirs, from Xenophon's Memorabilia. By E. Levien, Flexible cloth. 2*s.* 6*d.* Bayard Series.

Spayth (Henry) The American Draught-Player. 2nd edition. 12mo. 12*s.* 6*d.*

Spenser's Red Cross Knight, illustrated with 12 original drawings in facsimile. 4to. 1*l.* 5*s.*

Spofford (Harriet P.) The Thief in the Night. Crown 8vo., cloth. 5*s.*

Spray from the Water of Elisenbrunnen. By Godfrey Maynard. Small Post 8vo. Fancy Boards. 2*s.* 6*d.*

St. Cecilia, a modern tale of Real Life. 3 vols. post 8vo. 31*s.* 6*d.*

St. George's Chapel, Windsor, or 18 Photographs with descriptive Letterpress, by John Harrington. Imp. 4to. 63*s.*

Stanley (H. M.) How I Found Livingstone. Including Travels, Adventures, and Discoveries in Central Africa. Illustrations, Maps, &c. 8vo. cloth. 21*s.*

Steele (Thos.) Under the Palms. A Volume of Verse. By Thomas Steele, translator of "An Eastern Love Story." Fcap. 8vo. Cloth, 5*s.*

Stewart (D.) Outlines of Moral Philosophy, by Dr. McCosh. New edition. 12mo. 3*s.* 6*d.*

Stone (J. B.) A Tour with Cook Through Spain; being a Series of Descriptive Letters of Ancient Cities and Scenery of Spain, and of Life, Manners, and Customs of Spaniards. As Seen and Enjoyed in a Summer Holiday. Illustrated by Photographs produced by the Autotype Process. Crown 8vo. cloth. 6*s.*

Stories of the Great Prairies, from the Novels of J. F. Cooper. With numerous illustrations. 5*s.*

Stories of the Woods, from J. F. Cooper. 5*s.*

———— ———— **Sea,** from J. F. Cooper. 5*s.*

Story without an End, from the German of Carové, by the late Mrs. Sarah T. Austin, crown 4to. with 15 exquisite drawings by E. V. B., printed in colours in facsimile of the original water colours, and numerous other Illustrations. New edition. 7*s.* 6*d.*

———— square, with illustrations by Harvey. 2*s.* 6*d.*

———— **of the Great March,** a Diary of General Sherman's Campaign through Georgia and the Carolinas. Numerous illustrations. 12mo. cloth, 7*s.* 6*d.*

Stowe (Mrs. Beecher). Dred. Tauchnitz edition. 12mo. 3*s.* 6*d.*

—— Geography, with 60 illustrations. Square cloth, 4*s.* 6*d.*

—— House and Home Papers. 12mo. boards, 1*s.* ; cloth extra, 2*s.* 6*d.*

—— Little Foxes. Cheap edition, 1*s.* ; library edition, 4*s.* 6*d.*

—— Men of our Times, with portrait. 8vo. 12*s.* 6*d.*

—— Minister's Wooing. 5*s.* ; copyright series, 1*s.* 6*d.* ; cloth, 2*s.*

—— Old Town Folk. 6*s.* Cheap Edition, 2*s.* 6*d.*

"This story must make its way, as it is easy to predict it will, by its intrinsic merits."—*Times.*

"A novel of great power and beauty, and something more than a mere novel—we mean that it is worth thoughtful people's reading. . . It is a finished literary work, and will well repay the reading."—*Literary Churchman.*

—— Old Town Fireside Stories. Cloth extra. 3*s.* 6*d.*

—— My Wife and I; or, Harry Henderson's History. Small post 8vo, cloth extra. 6*s.*

"She has made a very pleasant book."—*Guardian.*

"From the first page to the last the book is vigorous, racy, and enjoyable."—*Daily Telegraph.*

—— Pink and White Tyranny. Small post 8vo. 3*s.* 6*d.* Cheap Edition, 1*s.* 6*d.* and 2*s.*

—— Queer Little People. 1*s.* ; cloth, 2*s.*

—— Religious Poems ; with illustrations. 3*s.* 6*d.*

—— Chimney Corner. 1*s.* ; cloth, 1*s.* 6*d.*

—— The Pearl of Orr's Island. Crown 8vo. 5*s.*

—— Little Pussey Willow. Fcap. 2*s.*

—— (Professor Calvin E.) The Origin and History of the Books of the New Testament, Canonical and Apocryphal. 8vo. 8*s.* 6*d.*

STORY'S (JUSTICE) WORKS:

Commentaries on the Law of Agency, as a Branch of Commercial and Maritime Jurisprudence. 6th Edition. 8vo. 1*l*. 11*s*. 6*d*.

Commentaries on the Law of Bailments. 7th Edition. 8vo. 1*l*. 11*s*. 6*d*.

Commentaries on the Law of Bills of Exchange, Foreign and Inland, as administered in England and America. 4th Edition. 8vo. 1*l*. 11*s*. 6*d*.

Commentaries on the Conflict of Laws, Foreign and Domestic, in regard to Contracts, Rights, and Remedies, and especially in regard to Marriages, Divorces, Wills, Successions, and Judgments. 6th Edition. 8vo. 1*l*. 15*s*.

Commentaries on the Constitution of the United States; with a Preliminary Review of the Constitutional History of the Colonies and States before the adoption of the Constitution. 3rd Edition. 2 vols. 8vo. 3*l*. 3*s*.

Commentaries on the Law of Partnership as a branch of Commercial and Maritima Jurisprudence. 6th Edition, by E. H. Bennett. 8vo. 1*l*. 11*s*. 6*d*.

Commentaries on the Law of Promissory Notes, and Guarantees of Notes and Cheques on Banks and Bankers. 6th Edition: by E. H. Bennett. 8vo. 1*l*. 11*s*. 6*d*.

Commentaries on Equity Pleadings and the Incidents relating thereto, according to the Practice of the Courts of Equity of England and America. 7th Edition. 8vo. 1*l*. 11*s*. 6*d*.

Commentaries on Equity Jurisprudence as administered in England and America. 9th Edition. 3*l*. 3*s*.

Treatise on the Law of Contracts. By William W. Story. 4th Edition, 2 vols. 8vo. 3*l*. 3*s*.

Treatise on the Law of Sales of Personal Property. 3rd Edition, edited by Hon. J. C. Perkins. 8vo. 1*l*. 11*s*. 6*d*.

Sub-Tropical Rambles. *See* Pike (N.)

Suburban Sketches, by the Author of "Venetian Life." Post 8vo. 6*s*.

Sullivan (G. C.) Dhow Chasing in Zanzibar Waters and on the Eastern Coast of Africa; a Narrative of Five Years' Experiences in the suppression of the Slave Trade. With Illustrations from Photographs and Sketches taken on the spot by the Author. Demy 8vo, cloth extra. 16*s*. Second Edition.

Summer in Leslie Goldthwaite's Life, by the Author of "The Gayworthys," Illustrations. Fcap. 8vo. 3*s*. 6*d*.

Swiss Family Robinson, 12mo. 3*s*. 6*d*.

 **AUCHNITZ'S English Editions of German Authors.** Each volume cloth flexible, *1s.*; or sewed, *1s. 6d.* The following are now ready :—

On the Heights. By B. AUERBACH. 3 vols.

In the Year '13. By FRITZ REUTER. 1 vol.

Faust. By GOETHE. 1 vol.

Undine, and other Tales. By FOUQUÉ. 1 vol.

L'Arrabiata. By PAUL HEYSE. 1 vol.

The Princess, and other Tales. By HEINRICH ZSCHOKKE. 1 vol.

Lessing's Nathan the Wise.

Hacklander's Behind the Counter, translated by MARY HOWITT.

Three Tales. By W. HAUFF.

Joachim v. Kamern; Diary of a Poor Young Lady. By M. NATHUSIUS.

Poems by Ferdinand Freiligrath. Edited by his daughter.

Gabriel. From the German of PAUL HEYSE. By ARTHUR MILMAN.

The Dead Lake, and other Tales. By P. HEYSE.

Through Night to Light. By GUTZKOW.

Flower, Fruit, and Thorn Pieces. By JEAN PAUL RICHTER.

The Princess of the Moor. By Miss MARLITT.

An Egyptian Princess. By G. EBERS. 2 vols.

Ekkehard. By J. V. SCHEFFEL.

Tauchnitz (B.) German and English Dictionary, Paper, *1s.* : cloth, *1s. 6d.*; roan, *2s.*

———— **French and English.** Paper *1s. 6d.*; cloth, *2s.*; roan, *2s. 6d.*

———— **Italian and English.** Paper, *1s. 6d.*; cloth, *2s.*; roan, *2s. 6d.*

———— **Spanish and English.** Paper, *1s. 6d.*; cloth, *2s.*; roan, *2s. 6d.*

—— **New Testament.** Cloth, *2s.*; gilt, *2s. 6d. See* New Testament.

Tayler (C. B.) Sacred Records, &c., in Verse. Fcap. 8vo, cloth extra, *2s. 6d.*

"Devotional feeling and sentiment are the pleasing characteristics of the Rector of Otley's charming and elegant little volume of poems. . . . Fluency, fervour, and ready command of rhyme—criticism must willingly accord to the Rev. C. B. Tayler . . . attractive and lovable little volume of verse."—*Morning Post.*

Taylor (Bayard) The Byeways of Europe; Visits by Unfrequented Routes to Remarkable Places. By BAYARD TAYLOR, author of "Views Afoot." 2 vols. post 8vo. 16*s*.

———— **Story of Kennett.** 2 vols. 16*s*.

———— **Hannah Thurston.** 3 vols. 1*l*. 4*s*.

———— **Travels in Greece and Russia.** Post 8vo. 7*s*. 6*d*.

———— **Northern Europe.** Post 8vo. Cloth, 8*s*. 6*d*.

———— **Egypt and Central Africa.**

———— **Beauty and the Beast.** Crown 8vo. 10*s*. 6*d*.

———— **A Summer in Colorado.** Post 8vo. 7*s*. 6*d*.

———— **Joseph and his Friend.** Post 8vo. 10*s*. 6*d*.

———— **Views Afoot.** Enamelled boards, 1*s*. 6*d*. ; cloth, 2*s*. *See* Low's Copyright Edition.

Tennyson's May Queen; choicely Illustrated from designs by the Hon. Mrs. BOYLE. Crown 8vo. *See* Choice Series. 5*s*.

Thomson (J.) *See* Illustrations of China.

Thomson (Stephen). *See* Chefs-d'Œuvre of Art.

Thomson (W. M.) The Land and the Book. With 300 Illustrations. 2 vols. 1*l*. 1*s*.

Threshold of the Unknown Region. *See* Markham.

Timothy Titcomb's Letters to Young People, Single and Married. (Low's American Series). Vol. xxi. 1*s*. 6*d*. boards ; 2*s*. cloth.

Tischendorf (Dr.) The New Testament. *See* New Testament.

Tolhausen (A.) The Technological Dictionary in the French, English, and German Languages. Containing the Technical Terms used in the Arts, Manufactures, and Industrial Affairs generally. Revised and Augmented by M. Louis Tolhausen, French Consul at Leipzig. This Work will be completed in Three Parts.
The First Part, containing French-German-English, crown 8vo. 2 vols. sewed, 8*s*. ; 1 vol. half roan, 9*s*.
The Second Part, containing English-German-French, crown 8vo. 2 vols. sewed, 8*s*. ; 1 vol. bound, 9*s*.
A Third Part, containing German-English-French, is also in preparation.

*** The First Half of Part I. sewed. 4*s*.

Townsend (John) A Treatise on the Wrongs called Slander and Libel, and on the remedy, by civil action, for these wrongs. 8vo. 1*l*. 10*s*.

Tuckermann (C. K.) The Greeks of To-day. Crown 8vo.
cloth. 7*s*. 6*d*.

Twenty Thousand Leagues Under the Sea. *See* Verne.

Twenty Years Ago. (Forming Volume 3 of the John Halifax
Series of Girls' Books). Small post 8vo. 4*s*.

Twining (Miss) Illustrations of the Natural Orders of
Plants, with Groups and Descriptions. By ELIZABETH TWINING.
Reduced from the folio edition, splendidly illustrated in colours from
nature. 2 vols. Royal 8vo. 5*l*. 5*s*.

Unprofessional Vagabond. *See* Carlisle (T.)

VANDENHOFF'S (George), Clerical Assistant.
Fcap. 3*s*. 6*d*.
———— Ladies' Reader (The). Fcap. 5*s*.

Varia; Rare Readings from Scarce Books, by the author of
" The Gentle Life." Reprinted by permission from the " Saturday Review," " Spectator," &c. 6*s*.

Vaux (Calvert). Villas and Cottages, a new edition, with
300 designs. 8vo. 15*s*.

Verne (Jules), Meridiana: Adventures of Three Englishmen and Three Russians in South Africa. Translated from the French.
With numerous Illustrations. Royal 16mo. cloth extra, gilt edges.
7*s*. 6*d*.
"This capital translation of M. Verne's last wild and amusing story is,
like all those by the same author, delightfully extravagant, and full of
entertaining improbabilities . . . The illustrations are not the least
amusing part of M. Verne's book, and certainly the reader of ' Meridiana' will not fail to have many a hearty laugh over it."—*Morning Post.*
"There is real merit here in both the narrative and the woodcuts."—
North British Daily Mail.
"Eminently readable."—*Daily News.*
"One of the most interesting books of the season. . . . Ably translated "—*Graphic.*
"Jules Verne, in ' Meridiana,' makes the account of the scientific pro-
ceedings as interesting as the hunting and exploring adventures, which is
saying a good deal."—*Athenæum.*

———— Twenty Thousand Leagues Under the Sea. Translated and Edited by the Rev. L. P. MERCIER, M.A., with 113 very
Graphic Woodcuts. Large Post 8vo. cloth extra, gilt edges. 10*s*. 6*d*.
Uniform with the First Edition of " The Adventures of a Young Naturalist."
"Boys will be delighted with this wild story, through which scientific
truth and most frantic fiction walk cheek by jowl . . . . It is an ex-

cellent boys' book. We devoutly wish we were a boy to enjoy it."—*Times*, Dec. 24.

" Full of the most astounding submarine adventures ever printed."—*Morning Post*.

" Illustrated with more than a hundred engravings that make the hair stand on end, and published at a low price. If this book, which is translated from the French, does not ' go,' boys are no longer boys. . . Grave men will be equally borne along in the grasp of the accomplished author."—*Standard*.

Very Far West Indeed. *See* Johnson.

Viardot (L.) Wonders of Italian Art, numerous photographic and other illustrations. Demy 8vo. 12s. 6d.

—— **Wonders of Painting,** numerous photographs and other illustrations. Demy 8vo. 12s. 6d.

—— **Wonders of Sculpture.** Numerous Illustrations. Demy 8vo. 12s. 6d.

Vincent (F.) The Land of the White Elephant : Sights and Scenes in South-Eastern Asia. A Personal Narrative of Travel and Adventure in Farther India, embracing the countries of Burmah, Siam, Cambodia, and Cochin China, 1871-2. With Maps, Plans, and numerous Illustrations. 8vo. cloth extra. [*In the press.*

AKE ROBIN ; a Book about Birds, by JOHN BURROUGHS. Crown 8vo. 5s.

Warner (C. D.) My Summer in a Garden. Boards, 1s. 6d. ; cloth, 2s. (Low's Copyright Series.)

—— **Back-log Studies.** Boards 1s. 6d. ; cloth 2s. (Low's Copyright Series.)

We Girls. *See* Whitney.

Webster (Daniel) Life of, by GEO. T. CURTIS. 2 vols. 8vo. Cloth. 36s.

Werner (Carl), Nile Sketches, Painted from Nature during his travels through Egypt. Facsimiles of Water-colour Paintings executed by GUSTAV W. SEITZ ; with Descriptive Text by Dr. E. A. BREHM and Dr. DUMICHEN. Imperial folio, in Cardboard Wrapper. 3l. 10s.

CONTENTS OF THE SECOND SERIES :—Banks of the Nile near Achmins—Coffee-house at Cairo—Money broker in Esneb—Tombs of Kalifs of Cairo—Assoan—The Temples of Luxor.

*** PART I., published last year, may still be had, price £3 10s.

Westminster Abbey and Palace. 40 Photographic Views with Letterpress, dedicated to Dean Stanley. 4to. Morocco extra, £5 5s.

Wheaton (Henry) Elements of International Law. New edition. [*In the press.*

When George the Third was King. 2 vols., post 8vo. 21s.

Where is the City? 12mo. cloth. 6s.

White (J.) Sketches from America. 8vo. 12s.

White (R. G.) Memoirs of the Life of William Shake-speare. Post 8vo. Cloth. 10s. 6d.

Whitney (Mrs. A. D. T.), The Gayworthys. Small post 8vo. 3s. 6d.

———— **Faith Gartney.** Small post 8vo. 3s. 6d. And in Low's Cheap Series, 1s. 6d. and 2s.

———— **Hitherto.** Small post 8vo. 3s. 6d. and 2s. 6d.

———— **Summer in Leslie Goldthwaite's Life.** Small post 8vo. 3s. 6d.

———— **The Other Girls.** Small post 8vo., cloth extra. 3s. 6d.

———— **We Girls.** Small post 8vo. 3s. 6d. Cheap Edition, 1s. 6d. and 2s.

Whyte (J. W. H.) A Land Journey from Asia to Europe. Crown 8vo. 12s.

Wills, A Few Hints on Proving, without Professional Assistance. By a PROBATE COURT OFFICIAL. Fourth Edition, revised and considerably enlarged, with Forms of Wills, Residuary Accounts, &c. Fcap. 8vo, cloth limp. 1s.

Woman's (A) Faith. A Novel. By the Author of "Ethel." 3 vols. Post 8vo. 31s. 6d.

Wonders of Sculpture. *See* Viardot.

Worcester's (Dr.), New and Greatly Enlarged Dictionary of the English Language. Adapted for Library or College Reference, comprising 40,000 Words more than Johnson's Dictionary. 4to. cloth, 1,834 pp. Price 31s. 6d. well bound; ditto, half mor. 2l. 2s.

"The volumes before us show a vast amount of diligence; but with Webster it is diligence in combination with fancifulness,—with Worcester in combination with good sense and judgment. Worcester's is the soberer and safer book, and may be pronounced the best existing English Lexicon."—*Athenæum.*

Words of Wellington, Maxims and Opinions, Sentences
and Reflections of the Great Duke, gathered from his Despatches,
Letters, and Speeches (Bayard Series).   2s. 6d.

Work: a Story of Experience.   By LOUISA M. ALCOTT.
In 2 vols.   Crown 8vo.   21s. cloth.

Young (L.) Acts of Gallantry; giving a detail of every act
for which the Silver Medal of the Royal Humane Society has been
granted during the last Forty-one years.   Crown 8vo., cloth.   7s. 6d.

THE INEXHAUSTIBLE MAGIC INKSTAND

*Is Patented in Great Britain and her Colonies, France, the United States,
and other Countries.   It is manufactured to produce Black, Coral
Red, Violet, Sky Blue, Sea Green, Pansy, and Copying
Black Inks, in stands from Four Shillings upwards.*

Producing Ink for every-day use for more than a Hundred Years.
Various Models in Porcelain, Crystal, Wood, Bronze, &c. are in
preparation.

NOTICE.—This little apparatus contains a chemical product unknown in
the arts. The composition, which possesses remarkable colouring properties,
is soluble in cold water; but, by a peculiar arrangement in the interior, the
water dissolving the product can only become, as it were, saturated with it,
but without diluting the material or converting it into pulp or syrup.

The material acting like a soluble salt, the solution having attained a certain degree of density, it remains stable, without precipitate, and the liquid,
always limpid, constitutes an Ink of a doubly superior character, rivalling in
all respects the best modern Inks.

MESSRS. SAMPSON LOW & CO. *and* MESSRS. HACHETTE &
CO. *are the Proprietors and Patentees.*

CHISWICK PRESS:—PRINTED BY WHITTINGHAM AND WILKINS,
TOOKS COURT, CHANCERY LANE.

www.ingramcontent.com/pod-product-compliance
Lightning Source LLC
Chambersburg PA
CBHW020236110726
47898CB00004B/1289